THE UNQUIET

J. D. ROBB

MARY BLAYNEY

PATRICIA GAFFNEY

RUTH RYAN LANGAN

MARY KAY MCCOMAS

JOVE BOOKS, NEW YORK

THE BERKLEY PUBLISHING GROUP
Published by the Penguin Group
Penguin Group (USA) Inc.
375 Hudson Street, New York, New York 10014, USA
Penguin Group (Canada), 90 Eglinton Avenue East, Suite 700, Toronto, Ontario M4P 2Y3, Canada
(a division of Pearson Penguin Canada Inc.)
Penguin Books Ltd., 80 Strand, London WC2R 0RL, England
Penguin Group Ireland, 25 St. Stephen's Green, Dublin 2, Ireland (a division of Penguin Books Ltd.)
Penguin Group (Australia), 250 Camberwell Road, Camberwell, Victoria 3124, Australia
(a division of Pearson Australia Group Pty. Ltd.)
Penguin Books India Pvt. Ltd., 11 Community Centre, Panchsheel Park, New Delhi—110 017, India
Penguin Group (NZ), 67 Apollo Drive, Rosedale, Auckland 0632, New Zealand
(a division of Pearson New Zealand Ltd.)
Penguin Books (South Africa) (Pty.) Ltd., 24 Sturdee Avenue, Rosebank, Johannesburg 2196,
South Africa

Penguin Books Ltd., Registered Offices: 80 Strand, London WC2R 0RL, England

This is a work of fiction. Names, characters, places, and incidents either are the product of the authors' imaginations or are used fictitiously, and any resemblance to actual persons, living or dead, business establishments, events, or locales is entirely coincidental. The publisher does not have control over and does not have any responsibility for author or third-party websites or their content.

THE UNQUIET

A Jove Book / published by arrangement with the authors

ISBN: 978-1-61793-099-7

JOVE®
Jove Books are published by The Berkley Publishing Group,
a division of Penguin Group (USA) Inc.,
375 Hudson Street, New York, New York 10014.
JOVE® is a registered trademark of Penguin Group (USA) Inc.
The "J" design is a trademark of Penguin Group (USA) Inc.

PRINTED IN THE UNITED STATES OF AMERICA

CONTENTS

CHAOS IN DEATH

J. D. ROBB

Who knows what evil lurks in the hearts of men?

THE SHADOW

Good and evil we know in the field of this world grow up together almost inseparably.

JOHN MILTON

ONE

He found life in death. And delight in the whirlwind of fear and fright. To hunt, to steal the light, the life, the blood, the soul. Well, he'd been born for it.

It made him laugh to dance around the madness of his creating, cape swirling—and wasn't *that* a wonderful touch—legs kicking in a joyful jig.

Even the sound of his own laughter, deep and rich and free, thrilled him, made him laugh all the harder.

He was *alive*.

"And you're not!"

He hopped, skipped, leaped over the three bodies he'd arranged on the floor. Tilting his head, he grinned at his handiwork. He'd laid them out so they sat—well, slumped, but that was dead for you—in a line against the wall.

Pitiful specimens, really, this trio of junkies who'd barely had the wit or the will to put up a fight. But God knew a man had to start somewhere. Still, their fear was his now, and their tears, their cries and pleas—all his.

It tasted so delicious.

He needed more, of course, so many more. But he'd made a most excellent start. No more playing by the rules, no *sir*! No more Mr. Good Guy.

Boring guy.

He patted his own chest. "I feel like a whole new man."

Chuckling, he stowed the bloody scalpel, the vials, all the lovely specimens in his kit. And inspiration struck.

Clichéd? he asked himself, his head tipping from side to side, his gleaming red eyes bulging with glee and madness as he scanned the room, the bodies, the walls. Maybe, maybe, but irresistible!

After dipping a gloved finger into a pool of congealing blood, he composed his message on the dingy wall. He had to dip back into the well—ha-ha-ha—several times, but the time was well worth it.

To whom it may concern:

Please take out the trash. Don't forget to recycle properly!

Oh, his belly hurt from laughing. He pressed a hand to it, nearly snagging one of the long, pointed nails that stabbed through the glove. Then found himself hesitating before signing his name. He knew his name. Of course, of course he did. For a moment his glee teetered toward fury, his laughter toward guttural grunts.

Then all righted again. He did another quick jig, dipped his finger again.

Thank you for your attention to this matter.

Dr. Chaos.

Perfect. Absently, he sucked the blood and grime from his finger and read the message over twice.

Time to go, he decided. Things to do. And he was absolutely *famished*.

He picked up his kit, lifted an arm in salute.

"Adieu, mes amis!"

On a last cackle of laughter, he turned, swirling the cape—he just loved doing that—as he skipped to the back room and climbed out the window.

He couldn't remember ever having more fun.

And couldn't wait to do it all again.

Lieutenant Eve Dallas studied the scene. Cops saw it all, but there was always something new, some fresh brutality even in the dying summer of 2060 to stretch the boundaries of *all*.

The room stank of blood—so much blood—and death, of fresh puke and piss. Blood soaked into one of the board-thin mattresses shoved into a corner. One of the three victims had died there, she thought. The middle one, she concluded, the black male, age as yet undetermined, with multiple stab wounds and a missing left ear.

Beside Eve, her partner breathed slowly in and out through her teeth.

"If you're going to hurl, Peabody, do it outside."

"I'm not going to hurl." But it came out as a plea rather than a statement.

Eve shifted her gaze, studied Peabody. The short, jaunty, flippy tail she'd pulled her dark hair into looked distinctly out of place now that her skin held a faint green cast. Peabody's dark eyes, slightly unfocused, held their line of sight a few inches above the bodies.

"I just need a minute for everything to settle."

"What was this place?" Eve asked.

"It used to be retail space." Peabody still held her PPC, and her hand was steady enough. "Apartments above, three levels. Slated for rehab." Peabody shut her eyes for a moment.

"Find out who owns it, how long it's been shut down. Take it outside. We need the data," Eve said before Peabody could object. "Get the data."

With a nod, Peabody slipped out the door to where the uniforms responding to the nine-one-one had cordoned off the sidewalk.

With her hands and feet already sealed, her recorder engaged, Eve stepped around and over the debris of shattered bottles, scattered clothes, trash, a broken chair to the bodies.

Her golden brown eyes weren't unfocused, but cop flat. "Three victims, two male, one female, carefully arranged to sit, backs against the front wall. Black male, center, multiple stab wounds, torso, shoulders, arms, legs, neck, and face. Left ear removed. Caucasian female on the left appears to have been strangled. Mixed-race male, right of center, bludgeoned. Left eye removed."

Hell of a party, she thought, and let out a breath that fluttered the bangs on her short cap of brown hair.

"Three mattresses, some bedding, clothes, mini friggie, battery lamp, two chairs, two tables. It appears all three vics flopped here. Money scattered around, what shows looks to be about a grand. So robbery's out. First on scene ascertained forced window, rear of building, street level. Probable point of entry."

She took the female first, hunkered down on her long legs, opened her field kit. "Female also suffered blows to the face, knees. Hard blow to the knees," she murmured. "Pipe, bat, board—take her down—a couple punches. Manual strangulation."

She ran the victim's prints.

"Female is identified as Jennifer Darnell, age twenty-four. Current address listed on West Sixteenth. Got a sheet, including juvie. Primarily illegals busts."

Peabody came back in. "The Whitwood Group bought the property about seven months ago," she said. "From what I can tell, the building was condemned a little over a year ago. Permits for rehab pending."

"Okay. So the killer or killers took his ear, his eye. Isn't there a saying—what is it? Hear no evil, see no evil . . ." Carefully, Eve opened Jennifer Darnell's mouth. "Yeah, speak no evil. He cut out her tongue."

"Jesus."

"Work see-no guy, Peabody. I need ID, TOD." Eve fit on microgoggles, engaged their light to peer into the victim's mouth. "Clean cut, neat and tidy. She was either already dead or unconscious when he took her tongue, and he had a good, steady hand."

Struggling to find her own good, steady hand, Peabody opened her kit. "Taking the body parts, those particular body parts, do you think ritual?"

"Possibly." She looked up at the message on the wall. "Mostly, I think he likes to joke. Real funny guy. He did what he wanted, took what he wanted, now he's telling us to clean up the mess. Dr. Chaos."

Eve looked around the room. "That's what this is. The middle guy? The killer took him out where he lay. Uses a knife, or a scalpel. But he doesn't use it on the others, except for the removal. He switches to bludgeoning for the other male."

"Coby Vix, age twenty-six," Peabody told her. "There had to be two killers, maybe three. One for each vic?"

"Maybe. It's a lot of work for one man. But only one takes credit?"

As Eve had, Peabody studied the bloody message. "Dr. Chaos. It could be the name of a group."

Eve considered it while she used the gauges. "Yeah, it could. TOD on Darnell, two hundred thirty-eight."

"If there was only one, why didn't she run like hell when he's stabbing the bejesus out of that guy or beating the crap out of Vix?"

"Took her out, blows to the knees. Shattered kneecaps. But yeah, it could be more than one. Three distinct methods of killing."

"Vix, TOD two hundred twenty."

"So, he took some time with Darnell. Enough for rape." Eve lifted the hem of the short nightshirt. "No bruising, bleeding, tearing I can see, but the ME will determine sexual assault." Eve lifted the cheap, thin chain around Darnell's bruised neck. "She's wearing a ninety-day chip from Get Straight."

"Vix has sixty." Peabody held up the chip.

With a nod, Eve rose and moved to the middle victim. "Hear-no has thirty. Wilson Bickford," she said when she'd run his prints. "Age twenty-two. That same precision, surgical removal on the ear. Dr. Chaos may just be a doctor, or at least have medical training. Hmm, TOD two hundred thirty. Didn't die first."

She sat back on her heels, tried to see it.

"He's the biggest of the three. The killer went at him first," she continued. "I bet your ass he did."

"Hey, bet your own ass."

"Defensive wounds, hands, arms. Bickford put up a fight. Take it a couple ways. Say three killers, one for each vic. Teamwork. One stabs, one beats, one strangles. But this doesn't look like teamwork," Eve said, scanning the room again. "It looks like . . ." She gestured to the message on the wall.

"Chaos."

"Yeah. Could be the team just went to town on the place. But I'm only seeing one type of bloody footprint, and it's too much to swallow they all wore the same size and type of shoe."

"Missed that," Peabody muttered.

"Maybe there's more, and I've missed them. Or maybe the others were more careful."

"But you don't think so."

"I think that's an interesting gap of time between TODs. I think the same hand did the removals, an experienced hand, steady. We've got serious overkill on the two males, and manual strangulation—which is personal and intimate—on the female. The destruction of the scene is over the top, and that reads rage. But the message is jokey, which reads control and intellect. It could be more than one. One with a cool head, one just batshit crazy.

"Let's get them bagged, tagged, and transported. I want to talk to the nine-one-one caller."

———

Katrina Chu hunched in the back of the black-and-white, her face white as death, her eyes puffy from weeping. One of the uniforms had gotten her some water. Her throat clicked on every swallow. But to Eve's relief, it looked like Katrina had cried herself out. Her puffy, pale green eyes stayed dry and focused on Eve.

"I need you to tell me what happened," Eve began.

"Jen didn't show up for work. She volunteers on the break-fast shift at Get Straight. The one off Canal. And she and Coby and Wil, they go to the meeting after."

"You worked with her?"

"I'm her sponsor. I work at the free clinic on Canal."

"Louise Dimatto's clinic?"

"Yes. Do you know Dr. Dimatto?"

"Yeah."

The connection seemed to steady her. "I'm an aide there. I'm studying to be a nurse. Jen came into Get Straight a couple months ago, and I offered to be her sponsor. We hit it off. She was really working it, you know? Really trying hard. She got Coby to come in. They wanted to turn their lives around."

"I have her living on West Sixteenth."

"They couldn't pay the rent. They started squatting here a couple weeks ago. Maybe three, I guess. Nobody was using the place, and she said Dr. Rosenthall said it would be okay, for a few weeks."

"Dr. Rosenthall?"

"He and Dr. Dimatto donate time to Get Straight. He and Arianna basically fund the organization."

"Arianna."

"Whitwood. They're engaged. Arianna and Dr. Rosenthall. She's a therapist. She donates her time, too. Jen, she wanted to get clean, stay clean. She never missed the morning meeting. And she started working at Slice—a pizza joint—about two months ago. She'd help serve breakfast, take in the meeting, then study for an hour or two—Arianna hooked her up with an online business course—then go to Slice if she had the lunch shift, go into the Center—the Whitwood Center—if she had the dinner shift. But she didn't show up, not to serve breakfast, not for the meeting. She didn't answer her 'link. Neither did Coby or Wil. I got worried."

A tear leaked through after all. "I thought maybe they'd taken a slide. It happens. I didn't want to think it. I really trusted she'd tag me if she got in a situation. But I did think it, so I came by on my way to work, to check on her. I knocked. I couldn't see in the window. It's boarded and grilled, but Jen gave me a key, so I opened it and . . . I saw."

"Do you know anybody who'd want to hurt her, or Coby or Wil?"

"No." Pressing her lips together, she shook her head. "I know some people think once a junkie, but they were trying. They were clean, and trying to stay that way."

"What about people they associated with when they were using?"

"I don't know. Jen never told me about any trouble, not this kind. She was happy. I went by Slice last night for takeout, and we talked awhile. She was happy. Coby got a job there delivering, and Wil was working as a stock boy at the twenty-four/seven a couple blocks away. They were going to pool their money and rent a place. Last night she told me they had nearly two thousand in the rent kitty so they were going to start to look for one.

"She was happy."

TWO

"Run Rosenthall and Whitwood," Eve told Peabody. "And get what you can on the Canal Street Get Straight."

"Already on it. And the sweepers are on their way."

"Good." Eve walked back into the building. "It's going to take them a while to sort through this mess." She poked through a bit. "Credits, cash, even loose change. I'm not finding any 'links."

"They probably had them—who doesn't?—so the killer probably took them."

"Takes the 'links but leaves the scratch. He, or they, didn't care about the money. Just the kill. And if he took the 'links, he either had contact with them or thought they talked about him to each other, or someone else, via 'link."

"It's sad," Peabody murmured. "They were young, and trying to reboot their lives. They had a good chance of making it, too. The floor's clean."

"Suddenly I question your cleanliness standards."

"I mean if you overlook the blood and the mess. It's not dusty or dirty. They kept the floor clean. And see, somebody repaired and painted this chair. They weren't very good at it," Peabody added as she picked up one of the broken legs. "But they tried. And when I checked out the bathroom, I guess it's an employee's restroom deal. Anyway, it was clean. The killers must not have used it. But the vics, they kept it clean."

"Lieutenant?" One of the uniforms stepped in. "We found this in the recycler out back."

He held up the clear protective coat, covered with blood, like the ones she'd seen countless doctors wearing. "Just one?"

"So far, sir."

"Keep checking. Anything pop from the canvass?"

"Not yet."

"Keep on that, too. Bag that for the sweepers. They're on their way. Rosenthall, Peabody."

"Dr. Justin Rosenthall, thirty-eight. He specializes in chemical addictions—and was given a grant by the Whitwood Group for same—cause, rehabilitation. He works primarily out of the Whitwood Center, a facility for the study of addiction, with a health center and visitor's lodging attached. No criminal."

"Let's go see if the doctor's in."

"He's very studly," Peabody added and continued to work her handheld as they walked to the car. "Has numerous awards for service and innovations in his field. Donates time to the Canal Street Clinic, Get Straight, and others."

Peabody slid into the car as Eve took the wheel. "I got lots of pops on gossip and society pages. He and Arianna are quite the item. She's a looker. And really, really rich. Not Roarke rich," Peabody said, referring to Eve's husband, "but she's up there. Or the Whitwood Group—headed by her parents—is. She's thirty-four, a therapist, again specializing in addictions. From the fluff pieces I'm skimming, it looks like they met four years ago, and were engaged last fall. The wedding's set for next month, billed as the wedding of the year. And . . . oh, she had a brother. Chase, died at the age of nineteen. OD'd. She was sixteen. The Whitwood Center opened three years later.

"Oh, listen to this. Rosenthall had a sister. She made it to twenty-two before she OD'd. He was on track to becoming a topflight cardiac surgeon. Switched his focus after his sister's death."

"A surgeon. Gave that up," Eve commented, "to work with junkies. Like his sister, like his fiancée's brother. Day in and day out, seeing them, listening to them, treating them, hearing bullshit out of them. Something could snap."

"Cynic alert. Honest, Dallas, from what I'm reading here, the guy sounds like a saint. A studly saint. Saint Studly of Rosenthall."

"Do you know why the saints are all dead?"

"Why?"

"Because dead's the only way you can pull it off. Living's messy, and everyone living has some dirty little secret. That's why we have jobs."

"A dirty little secret that has a renowned and studly doctor slaughtering three recovering addicts?"

"Somebody did it. He's got the connection, he's got the skill, and according to our source, he's the one who gave them the green light to squat there. If he's so saintly, why didn't he float them a couple months' rent?"

"That's a good question."

"It's one I'm going to ask him."

Old, time-faded brick housed the Whitwood Center. No flash, Eve noted, no gloss—at least not on the exterior—so the building sat comfortably in the old Meatpacking District.

With Peabody, she walked in the front entrance. The lobby area was large and quietly furnished. Comfortable chairs, simple art, some plants gave off the atmosphere of a living area rather than a waiting one despite the reception counter manned by two people.

The man, early thirties, continued to work on his comp while the woman, a few years younger with a pretty face and earnestly welcoming eyes, smiled in their direction.

"Good morning. How can we help you today?"

Eve approached the counter, laid her badge on it. "We need to speak with Dr. Rosenthall."

"I see." The woman didn't so much as blink at the badge. "Is the doctor expecting you?"

"I couldn't say."

"His offices are on the second floor, east. One of his interns or his assistant should be able to help you."

"Okay."

"Stairs to the left, elevators to the right."

As Eve angled left, the woman continued. "You'll want to take the right corridor, go over the garden breezeway, then take the first turn to the left."

"Thanks."

"It's nice work," Peabody said as they started up. "The work they've done on the old building. Kept its character. It's comfortable, and it doesn't shout, 'We're really rich philanthropists.'"

On the second floor they walked by several doors, all discreetly shut, with their purposes or a doctor's name on a plaque.

They passed people in lab coats, in street wear, in sharp suits, and in tattered pants. Eve noted the security cameras, and the card slots and palm plates on some of the doors. They passed a nurse's station and the waiting area across from it.

Then they came to the garden breezeway. Below, through treated glass, a central fountain gurgled in a fantasy of flowering plants, shrubs, trees in riotous bloom. White stone benches offered seating, bricked paths wound in an invitation to stroll.

"That says, 'We're really rich philanthropists,'" Eve commented.

"But in a really pretty way."

They made the left into a small blue and cream reception area. The woman behind the counter tapped her earpiece, turned away from the smart screen where, it looked to Eve, she'd been working on updating a complex schedule.

"Can I help you?"

"Lieutenant Dallas and Detective Peabody." Eve held up her badge. "We need to speak with Dr. Rosenthall."

"Is there a problem?"

"There almost always is."

The woman didn't look pleased by the answer, and reminded Eve of Dr. Mira's admin. The dragon at the gates of the NYPSD's shrink and top profiler.

"Dr. Rosenthall's in his lab this morning."

"Where's his lab?"

"I really must insist you tell me your business before I disturb the doctor."

"I really must insist you take us to his lab." Eve tapped her badge. "And this has a lot more insistence than you because it can arrest you for interfering with a police investigation."

"I'll check with the doctor." The words sounded as sour as the woman's face looked. She tapped her earpiece again. "Yes, Pach, would you tell Dr. Rosenthall two police officers are here and insist on speaking with him. Yes. No, they won't say. Thank you." She waited a moment, staring holes through Eve. Then scowled. "Very well."

After another tap, she spoke to Eve. "The doctor's lab assistant will come out and take you back. The doctor will see you."

She aimed her nose in the air before turning back to her screen.

Moments later a side door opened. The man who came out had deep brown skin and large, heavy-lidded eyes nearly as black as his crown of curly hair. He wore a standard white lab coat over jeans and a red T-shirt that asked, "My petri dish or yours?"

"Officers?"

"Lieutenant Dallas and Detective Peabody."

"Oh. Um . . ." He flashed a very white smile. "If you'll come this way?"

Through the door was a maze, a rabbit warren of rooms off angled corridors. The lab assistant negotiated them on flapping gel sandals. He paused at double steel doors, swiped his card, spoke his name. "Pachai Gupta."

The security blinked green in acceptance, and the doors slid open into a large lab. Eve felt a weird juxtaposition as her friend Mavis's voice wailed out about love on the wild side over the pristine red and white room. Strange equations and symbols held frozen on one of the wall screens while something bubbled blue in a heated beaker. A woman with short, sleek red hair hunched over a microscope while her foot tapped to Mavis's grinding beat. Another lab coat diligently worked two comps at a long white counter. He sported a short stub of a ponytail and ragged skids.

In the center of it, amid the coils of tubing, the sparkling electronics, the busy screens, and the forest of test tubes, beakers, and specimen dishes, stood Justin Rosenthall.

He wore a lab coat like other men wore a tux, perfectly fitted and somehow elegant. His gilded mane of hair gleamed under the bright lights. Vid-star handsome, poetically pale, he removed a beaker from its heater with tongs and set it in a bath of water. Steam hissed and curled.

Through the thin curtain of it, Eve saw his eyes, tawny as a lion's, fix intently on some sort of gauge.

"What's he working on?" she asked their guide.

"An antidote."

"To what?"

"To evil." At her raised eyebrows, Pachai flushed, shrugged.

Eve heard a low beep. Justin lifted the beaker again, slid it into a container, sealed it, set another gauge.

Only then did he step back, look over.

"Sorry." There was an absent charm in his smile, in his movements as he crossed to them. "The timing's crucial. You're the police?"

"Lieutenant Dallas, Detective Peabody, NYPSD."

"Dallas. Of course, you're Roarke's wife." His smile warmed as he extended a hand. "It's nice to finally meet you. How is Roarke? I haven't seen him in . . . it's probably been a year. More."

"He's good. This isn't a social call, Dr. Rosenthall."

"Justin. No, of course not. Sorry. How can I help you?"

"You know Jennifer Darnell, Coby Vix, Wilson Bickford."

"Yes." His smile faded. "Are they in trouble? I can assure you they've been working very hard against their addictions. It's a hard road, and there will be stumbles, but—"

"They were murdered early this morning."

Behind her, Pachai let out a strangled gasp as Justin just stared at her. "What? Sorry, what?"

"They were murdered between two and two-forty this morning in the building where they were squatting."

"Dead? Murdered? *All?*"

"How?" Pachai took Eve's arm, then quickly released it. His eyes were liquid onyx swimming under inky lashes. They only shimmered more intensely when Justin laid a hand on his shoulder.

"Pach, let's sit down."

"No. No. I'm sorry, but how can they be murdered? I saw them only yesterday."

"When?"

"Pach," Justin repeated, gently. "Music off," he ordered. The redhead called out a protest when Mavis stopped wailing.

"Not now, Marti." Justin rubbed his temple. "There's no mistake?"

"No. When did you see them last?" she asked Pachai.

His lips trembled, and tears continued to swarm those heavy-lidded eyes. "Before Jen and Coby went to work, after Wil got off. We had coffee. We have coffee almost every day."

"You were friends?"

"Yes. We—I—I don't understand."

"No, neither do I," Justin said. "What happened?"

The lab rat with the stubby ponytail had turned and, like the redhead, watched.

"Early this morning Wilson Bickford was stabbed to death, Coby Vix was bludgeoned to death, and Jennifer Darnell was strangled."

Pachai began to weep, and the harsh sobs bore him down to the floor, where he covered his face with his hands.

Justin turned ashen. At her station the redhead sat very still, staring at Eve as if she'd spoken in an ancient foreign language. The other man slumped back in his chair, shuddered, then closed his eyes, lowered his head.

No one spoke.

THREE

———➤———

In the silence, Eve gave Peabody a signal, and responding, Peabody moved to Pachai. "I'm sorry for your loss," she began in the comfort voice she used so well. "Let me help you. Let me help you up. Why don't we go over here, sit down?"

"How could—was it—I'm sorry," Justin said. "I just can't think. They were attacked? In the building on West Twelfth?"

"Yes."

"But why, for God's sake? None of them belonged to a gang, none of them had any valuables to speak of. Was this just some random killings?"

"Do you know anyone who'd wish them—any one of them—harm?"

"No. No, I don't. They were turning their lives around, and the three of them had formed a strong bond. Their own small support group."

"They were addicts."

"In recovery," Justin said quickly.

"Was there anyone who they—again any one of them—used to associate with prior to their recovery who might have resented the fact that they were getting clean, staying clean?"

"I don't know, but if so, they didn't mention it to me. If there was someone, something, one of them might have told Arianna.

Arianna Whitwood. She was the therapist of record for all three of them."

"Your fiancée."

"Yes." He looked away, pressed his fingers to his eyes. "My God, they were so young, so hopeful."

"You gave them permission to squat in that property."

"Yes. They couldn't make the rent on Jen's apartment. She'd fallen behind before she'd made the commitment to recovery. Pachai told me they were sleeping on the street. I thought . . . it would be a roof over their heads until they found a place."

"You formed an attachment to them?"

"To Jen, then through her to Coby and Wil. She was so determined, and you could see the light coming back into her. You could see her finding her quiet. It was gratifying. Even inspiring."

"I guess I'm curious why you didn't float them the rent."

"I wish I had." Mouth tight, he glanced over to where Peabody murmured to Pachai. "We have a policy not to lend money to anyone in the program, but to try to find another way to help, to guide them to help themselves. I never imagined . . . The three of them together should have been safe. God knows, each one of them had experience on the street, handling themselves."

"I have to ask where you were between one and four this morning."

"Yes. I . . . Well, here. I was here."

"That's a lot of midnight oil to burn."

"What I'm working on, it's—I believe—at its tipping point. I worked until after two, then bunked on the sofa in my office."

"Did you see or speak with anyone during that time?"

"No. I sent Ken and Pachai home about eleven, I think it was. You can ask them, or check the log-outs. Marti left earlier. I spoke with Arianna . . . I'm not sure, I'd have to check the 'link log. Maybe ten or ten thirty before I sent the boys home."

"What are you working on?"

"A serum to counteract deep and chronic addiction and substance abuse. It will treat the craving on both a physical and psychological level, quiet the violence of that need during withdrawal, and after."

"There are medications for that already."

"Medications that basically substitute one chemical for another. I'm attempting to work with natural ingredients that will trigger the chemistry in the brain and the body to return to the levels prior to the addiction. A rebalancing, we'll say."

He rubbed at his temple again, the same two fingers on the same spot in the same circular motion. "Is there anything I—we—can do for them now? Contacting family? I can't remember the details of that, but Arianna will have it. With the burial, memorial? Anything?"

"We'll be notifying next of kin. I'll need to talk to Ms. Whitwood, and as soon as possible. First I'd like to speak with your other assistants."

"Interns," he corrected automatically. "Marti Frank and Ken Dickerson are here on intern scholarships. Sorry, it hardly matters. I want to tell Ari in person, face-to-face, not over the 'link. We lose patients, Lieutenant. To their addiction, to the violence it often generates, or the physical abuse it causes. But this? This comes very, very hard."

"Is she in the Center now?"

"Yes, she should be in session now. I'll go up, tell her."

"If you'd tell her I want to speak with her before we leave, I'd appreciate it."

"Yes. I'm sorry to meet you this way. I'm just . . . sorry."

Eve let him go, and decided to take the redhead first.

"You got the picture," Eve began.

"Yeah. It's a really ugly picture."

"Were you close to the victims?"

"I hate that word. Victim." She folded her hands together on her lap as if she wanted to keep them still. "It's overused."

"It is in my line of work."

"Yeah, I guess. Not especially close. I liked them. Jen in particular. She was just so damn likable."

"You work in the lab. Do you get friendly with a lot of people in the program?"

"There's interaction. It's part of it. There's a communal eatery on-site, so a lot of times staff's eating with patients and recoverings. When work allows, we're encouraged to attend sessions or lectures. It's more than lab work, especially for

Justin. It's our whole life, and understanding who and what we're working for. You're going to find out," she added. "I know how it works. My brother was a junkie, favored Jazz laced with Zeus. He favored it a lot right up until he OD'd. He made my life, my mother's, my father's, hell. I hate the junk, and it took a long time before I stopped hating the junkie."

She glanced over her shoulder. "With Ken it was his father. Came into it late, you could say. Started with prescriptions after a car accident, escalated until he'd destroyed his marriage, did time for smacking his wife and Ken around, ended up on the street where he stabbed somebody to death for twelve dollars and a wrist unit. He died in prison when somebody returned the favor."

Eve connected the dots. "And Pachai?"

"Childhood friend. They were tight, like brothers. The friend played around with recreationals, liked them too much until he was flying on Ups and Bounce, crashing on Chill. Then he was just one more OD when Pachai found him dead—two days dead. Justin wants people invested who work for him, people who know all the sides, all the layers, and have a reason to be here."

"He wants it personal."

"Yeah, and it is." She looked over at Pachai, then down at her folded hands. "This happening to Jen and the others, people who had a real shot at redemption, who really put it all into kicking it? That's personal, too. For all of us."

"Understood. If you know how it works, you know I have to ask. Where were you between one and four this morning?"

"In bed." Her gaze tracked up, met Eve's. "Alone and asleep. I had a date, but it didn't go anywhere. I got home just after midnight. I've got a roommate, but she had a date and it did go somewhere. She didn't get home until six this morning."

She gave Eve a narrow look. "Anyway, from what you said, how they were killed? The three of us would've had to go batshit together, break in to that place, and kill them like a pack."

"That's a thought, isn't it? I appreciate the time. If you think of anything, contact me or my partner."

Eve moved on to the last.

"Ken Dickerson," he said. "Did they maybe get attacked on the street?" He watched Eve with horror and hope. His face, pale and thin, showed signs of fatigue. "Maybe they ran," he continued, in a voice that hitched in a battle against tears. "And the people who attacked them went at them when they got to the building."

"No."

"It just doesn't seem real," he murmured, rubbing at his damp, tired eyes. "I feel like I'm going to wake up and none of this happened."

"How well did you know the victims?"

"I . . . God. I don't know. To talk to. Not like Pach, but we hung out a couple times. My uncle manages a Slice, and I helped Jen, then Coby, get jobs there. I mean, I asked my uncle if he could give them a try. He's good about giving people a chance."

"Did you ever go to the place they were staying?"

"Once. The restaurant's close to where I live, so I go in a lot. I walked back with Jen and Coby one night. My uncle gave them some food. And we hung out." He smiled a little. "It was nice."

"Did they own 'links?"

He blinked in puzzlement. "Sure. Everybody has at least one 'link."

"Do you know anyone who'd want to hurt them?"

"I don't see why anyone would. They were harmless. They didn't have anything, didn't hurt anybody. Jen was studying so she could do secretarial work. She wanted to work in an office. That's not much to ask."

No, Eve thought. It wasn't much to ask.

When Justin came back in, he looked drained. "If you could give Arianna a few minutes, she'll meet you in the Meditation Garden."

"All right."

"Is there anything more we can do?"

"Not at this time."

"Will you keep me—us—informed?"

"I can do that. If anything occurs to you, anything at all, let me know." She signaled Peabody, who put her hand on Pachai's shoulder before rising.

"Arianna Whitwood, down in the gardens," Eve told her. "Did you get anything?"

"He was in love with Darnell," Peabody said as they headed down again. "He didn't hesitate to tell me, or that he thought maybe she felt something back. No alibi, but he gives off this gentle, kind of sweet vibe. I can't see him slaughtering three people."

"On the other hand, he and everyone in that lab knew all three vics, and where they were squatting. At least two of them—and I'd add Rosenthall as a third—had been there, knew the setup. That weighs. There are going to be others who knew them and the setup from Get Straight, and Slice. This wasn't random."

"No. Random doesn't fit."

"Because?"

"Oh boy, a quiz. Deliberate break-in through the back, and the other killers—because I can't see it being one guy—got into the front, attacked them in a frenzied but systematic manner. Wrecked the place, but as far as we know took nothing but their 'links—and at least one of them had the protective gear, so no blood on his—or their—clothes. It's most probable they brought the weapons—a knife, scalpel, and some sort of bludgeoning tool—with them. Prepared, premeditated, and target specific.

"Did I pass?"

"Not bad." They passed through an atrium on the main level and into the burgeoning gardens. "Not bad at all," Eve said with a look around.

"Totally mag. Peaceful. Kind of Zen. Look, butterflies." A smile broke over Peabody's face. "Butterflies just make you happy."

"They've got that buggy body and those creepy little antennas. People don't think about that because they get distracted by the wings. I always wonder if they have teeth. They must have tiny, sharp little teeth."

"You're not spoiling my happy."

Eve took the path marked Meditation Garden, angled through blossoms and butterflies. She saw Arianna on one of the stone benches, the diamond on her left hand on fire in the streams of light. She wore a leaf-green suit with a foam of lace and high, razor-thin heels of the same color that showcased long legs. Her hair, a rich, nutty brown, was wound up in some complicated twist that left her exceptional face unframed. Everything about her said classic and class, and reminded Eve of Mira.

At their approach, Arianna turned her head. Her eyes, a color caught somewhere between green and brown, sparked with anger.

She rose.

"Lieutenant Dallas. I'd hoped to meet you, but not like this. Detective Peabody. Can we sit?" She did so, folded her hands again. "I wanted to talk to you here. I'd hoped to find some quiet here. But not yet."

"You were the therapist for all three victims," Eve began.

"Yes. They would have made it. I believe that. On a professional and personal level, I believe Coby and Wil would have made it. I know Jen would have. She'd come so far in such a short time. She'd found the quiet."

"Dr. Rosenthall used that term. *The quiet.*"

"Yes, I guess I picked it up from him." Arianna laid a hand on her heart. "Addiction is never quiet. It's violent or sly or seductive. Often all three. But Jen found her quiet and her strength, and was helping Coby and Wil find theirs."

"Other addicts, not making such progress, might resent them for theirs."

"That's true. They would have told me if anyone was pressuring them, threatening them. Jen was addicted to heroin, preferred it in the mix they call Chill on the street. She often bartered her body for hits. Her mother was the same, her father was her mother's dealer—she thinks."

"She did some time in the system," Eve put in. "Juvie, group homes, foster homes."

"Yes. She had a troubled, difficult childhood. Jen ran off when she was sixteen, and continued that troubled, difficult life up until nearly four months ago when she woke up after a binge. She'd lost three days, and came back to herself covered in cuts, bruises, filth, her own vomit in some basement flop with no recollection of how she'd gotten there. She got out, began to walk. She thought of the next score, thought of just ending her life, and she came to Get Straight. Instead of walking on, trying for the next score, or ending her life, she went in."

"This wasn't her first try at rehab."

"No." Arianna turned her head to meet Eve's eyes. "She'd had three court-assigned rehabilitations, and none of them took. This time, she chose. She walked in on her own. She was ready to be helped, and they helped her. Justin and I were there that day. She often said that was the beginning for her. When we met."

Arianna looked away again as her voice roughened.

"Withdrawal is hard and painful, but she never gave up. She brought Coby in. We encourage recoverings to sever ties with people who are part of their addiction, but she wouldn't listen. She saved Coby, simply because she wouldn't give up on him either, and then Wil. They loved her, and their love for her and each other proved stronger than the addiction. That's a kind of miracle. And now . . ."

"Did they tell you about anyone who concerned them, who gave them any grief, put any pressure on them to use again?"

"No. None of them had any family, no one they were close to or had contact with, not for a long time. They formed friendships, associations at the Center, and at Get Straight. They were still in the honeymoon stage, so happy to be where they were, so happy to have each other."

"Were they intimate?"

"No, not sexually. Jen and Coby had been, if you can call it intimacy, when they were both using. What they'd formed now was a family, so they lived that way. For Jen, sex had been that bartering tool, or something to do with another addict. She'd become desensitized about sex. I think she was beginning to feel normal and natural urges. She was attracted to Pach—Pachai Gupta—and he to her. But neither of them moved on it."

"How can you be sure?"

"She would have told me. Honesty had become a vital tool for her in recovery, and she trusted me. They'd made a vow—Jen, Coby, and Will—to abstain for six months, to focus on themselves as individuals. Coby joked about it. He was funny, sharp. He'd used that charm and wit to survive on the streets. Now he used it to keep himself and his friends steady. Wil went the more spiritual route. He'd lived with his great-grandmother until she died, and she'd taken him to church. He'd started to go back. Jen and Coby went with him a few times, but more for friendship than interest."

"What church?"

"Ah . . . Chelsea Baptist."

"Where else did they go routinely, do routinely?"

"They liked to hang out at the Twelfth Street Diner, drink coffee, and talk. They all put in time at Get Straight, attending meetings, taking on chores—cleaning, organizing donations— that's part of the program. They attended group there, too, as well as here. They'd see a vid now and then, but primarily they worked—saved their money toward finding a place to live— concentrated on the program, studied. Or Jen did. She was taking a business class."

"You gave them permission to live in the building?"

"Yes. Justin asked me, and we thought it would give them a breather, allow them to live on their own, save, stay close to the Center. The stipulation was they had to keep the place, and themselves, clean. They did."

"You visited them there?"

"Either Justin or I would drop by once a week. Spot-check," she said with the first hint of a smile. "We trusted them. But you can't trust the addiction."

"Arianna!"

The sharp call sliced through the quiet garden. A man, tall, his dark hair cropped close to a tanned face, hurried toward them. His eyes, a green as sharp as his voice, were all for Arianna. Ignoring Eve and Peabody, he grabbed her hands, got to his knees.

"I heard what happened. What can I do for you?"

"Eton." Tears shimmered in her eyes. Eve saw her bear down against them. "I was going to tell you myself, but I needed to speak with the police. Lieutenant Dallas, Detective Peabody, my associate, Eton Billingsly."

"The police." He shot Eve a disgusted look. "At a time like this?"

"Murder usually brings the cops."

"It's hardly necessary to interrogate Arianna at all, and particularly before she's had time to process."

"Okay. Let's interrogate you. Where were you between one and four a.m. this morning?"

He blustered. Eve couldn't think of another word for the sounds he made or the look on his face as he sprang to his feet. "I'm not answering any of your insulting questions, and neither is Arianna."

"Oh yeah, you are," Eve corrected, "here or at Cop Central. Your choice."

"Eton." Arianna rose. "Stop now. You're upset. The police are trying to find out who hurt Jen and the boys, and why."

"They'll hardly find out here, with you." He took her hands again. "Justin should never have allowed it."

"Justin doesn't *allow* anything." Gently, but deliberately, Arianna drew her hands away.

"You're right, of course. But it's natural to want to shield you from this kind of ordeal. I know how much you'd invested in these recoverings."

"I haven't heard an answer yet, Mr. Billingsly."

"*Dr.* Billingsly," he snapped at Eve. "And at that time of the morning, I was home in bed."

"Alone?"

"Yes."

"What was your relationship with the victims?"

Perhaps due to the fact that his face went red, Arianna answered for him. "Eton is one of our psychologists. He specializes in hypnotherapy. The process can help them through withdrawal, give them focus, and can often help them bring the root of their addiction to the surface."

"So, did you do the 'you're getting sleepy' with the victims?" Eve asked him.

"Yes."

"And?"

"As Arianna can tell you, they were making excellent, even exceptional, progress."

"When's the last time you had contact with them—each of them?"

"I'd have to check my book. I can hardly remember off the top of my head."

"Do that. Did you ever visit the building where they were living?"

His lips thinned. "No. Why would I? Instead of wasting time here, you should be out on the street, looking for the maniacs who did this. It's obviously the result of violent addicts, people they associated with before they began the program."

"Nothing's obvious at this point. You've been very helpful," she said to Arianna.

"Can you let us know when . . . Justin and I would like to arrange a memorial. We'd like to arrange for their remains."

"Arianna," Billingsly began.

"Eton, please. It's little enough."

"I'm required to inform the next of kin," Eve told her. "I'll be in touch once I have. You have transcripts of your sessions with them. They could help me. Doctor-patient privilege doesn't apply when the patients are dead."

"I'll have them sent to you this afternoon. I'll show you the way out."

"We've got it, thanks."

As they walked away, Eve glanced back. Eton had her hands again, his head bent toward hers as he talked rapidly.

"Asshole," was Peabody's opinion.

"Big, flaming asshole with a big, flaming temper. Looks like he keeps in good shape. Bet he puts in plenty of gym time. And he wants Arianna Whitwood for his own."

"Oh yeah, and she doesn't want him for hers."

"That's a pisser for him. I bet she gave the vics a lot more of her time, attention, and affection than she gives Billingsly, which is another pisser for him."

"Killing the hell out of them doesn't change that. Would be a pretty murky motive."

"Maybe, but I really hate him already. Plus, hypnotherapy. Who knows what he's up to with that?"

"Why didn't you ask for his transcripts?"

"Because he wouldn't give them up, not without a warrant, which you're going to put in the works while we head over to Get Straight."

"Oooh, that's going to be another pisser for Billingsly."

"I can only hope it's not the last."

FOUR

———◆———

They got little more from Get Straight but confirmation of everything they'd heard before, and more grief. Even as they stepped out into the air holding the first faint hint of fall, Eve's com signaled. She recognized the first on scene on her screen.

"Officer Slovic."

"Sir, we dug up a wit claims she saw someone near the rear of the crime scene, and observed him stuffing something in the recycler where we found the bloody protective gear."

"That's a break. How good a look?"

"She claims a good, solid one. There's a streetlight, and she states she saw him clearly, and he was dancing."

"Sorry?"

"That's her statement, Lieutenant." Eve heard the shrug in his voice. "Her description's pretty strange, but she's sticking to it, and doesn't strike me as a whack job. Her apartment's got a good view of the area, and she was up walking her kid—kid's teething. She's a short-order cook on parental leave. We got her on the canvass."

"What did she see?"

He cleared his throat. "A monster. Possibly a demon."

"Officer Slovic, are you actually wasting my time on this?"

"Sir, I wouldn't, but she gave details, she had the time down, and she admits it sounds crazy."

"Give me the details."

"Male, medium build—she thinks—dark hair, wild and stringy." He made the throat-clearing sound again. "Greenish skin, red, bulging eyes, contorted features, and prominent teeth, wearing a black cape and carrying a black satchel."

"And this green, red-eyed monster was dancing in the streetlight."

"And laughing, sir, in what the wit describes as a wild, guttural laugh. I believe her, Lieutenant, I mean about what she saw. It could be the subject was wearing a mask or a disguise."

"Yeah." Eve heaved out a sigh. "Will she work with an artist?"

"She's anxious to."

"Contact Detective Yancy at Central, and get her to him."

"Yes, sir."

She shoved the com into her pocket. "A green, red-eyed, cape-wearing monster."

"Or possibly demon," Peabody put in and earned a sneer. "I'm not saying I believe in monsters and demons, but somebody hyped up on Zeus, say, convinced he is one, gets in the gear to top it off. Since the wit only saw one man, and the evidence leans toward one man—he'd have to be hyped on something. Zeus not only makes you crazy, but it deadens you to pain, pumps the adrenaline."

"Maybe. We'll see it through." She checked the time. "I want you to go by Slice, talk to the boss, the coworkers, and do the same at the twenty-four/seven. You can round it off with the diner they used as a hang spot. Maybe they had some trouble last night, or somebody followed them home. I'm going to swing by the morgue, see what Morris can give us. We'll hook up back at Central."

"I'd sure as hell rather go to a pizza joint than the morgue. Want me to bring you a slice?"

"No . . . maybe. Yeah."

Eve slid behind the wheel and headed for the morgue.

Zeus was a good fit, she thought, but not a perfect one. It fit the violence, the frenzy of it. But not the calculation. Still, a blend . . . and some enterprising soul was always coming up with a new and improved in the illegals game.

Flying on Zeus, a man could hack, beat, choke—and laugh his ass off while doing it. But he couldn't plan—costume, satchel with weapons and protective gear, gloved or sealed hands. She didn't expect the sweepers to gift wrap the killer's prints for her.

He'd broken in through the back window, Eve thought, bringing the scene back into her head. Need a tool for that, in the satchel. Climb in, nice and quiet—something else that didn't fit the Zeus, not pure Zeus. Bathroom, back room all neat and tidy, so the killer had moved straight into the front of the shop and the vics.

Target specific, premeditated, planned. She was sure of it. Motive was a murky area.

She considered, rejected, fiddled with various theories through downtown traffic, then let them simmer as she walked into the white tunnel of the morgue.

Morris wore a gray suit and a strong red tie. The choice cheered her a little. His wardrobe rarely varied from black since the murder of his lover. The band twined through his braid of dark hair matched the tie.

His long, clever eyes met hers over the open body of Jennifer Darnell. Through the speakers, a sax wailed out a jazzy riff.

"I see you got me a triple-header."

"The monster did it."

"Not difficult to believe, given the condition of these young people. There's internal abuse, self-inflicted from years of illegals ingestion, poor diet. They lived hard for their short time. I found signs of recovery and reversal. If they'd lived and kept clean, they should have done well enough."

"Were they keeping clean?"

"Knowing you'd ask, I ran and rushed the tox screen first, and they were. Their last meal, which I assume they shared about midnight, was pizza, a diet cola for the girl, straight cola for the boys."

"Sexual activity, consensual or forced?"

"No. Victim one—in order of TOD—suffered multiple broken bones and ribs, some of them postmortem. COD would be a fractured skull. He'd literally had his brains bashed in. By a bat or pipe, some three inches in diameter, and extreme force. I found some paint flakes in the wounds. I've sent them to the lab."

"Head blow first?" Eve speculated.

"From my reconstruction, which is still preliminary, yes. A blow here." Morris tapped the side of his hand diagonally over his right temple. "It would have knocked him out cold. It's unlikely he felt the rest."

"Small favor."

"Victim two, multiple stab wounds inflicted with a jagged-edged blade, some four inches in length. Not a hunting or carving knife. More likely an inexpensive meat knife. The tip broke on bone, and that's at the lab as well. He was stabbed first center of the chest, two strikes, and once in the abdomen. Again, from my prelim, the rest of the wounds came several minutes later."

"Incapacitate both males."

"And her. As in your notes, she was struck with the same bat as killed her friend, across the knees, shattering her knee-caps. The ear, eye, and tongue were removed postmortem, and with a smooth, sharp blade—a scalpel would be my opinion. And it was done with precision. Do you know how many are responsible for this?"

"One."

Morris's eyebrows shot up. "One? You never fail to intrigue." He looked over the bodies again. "The damage here, the strength, the sheer energy it took to beat the first vic was considerable. On the second, the stab wounds are very deep, very forceful, and there are eighty-five holes in that unfortunate boy. That also takes strength and energy. Considerable endurance."

"And when he'd finished there, he still had enough to manually strangle—correct?"

"Yes," Morris confirmed, "he used his own hands."

"To manually strangle the third, which also takes strength. And still after that, he had it in him to break chairs, tables, basically wreak havoc. He ended it, according to the wit we're working with, by dancing down the sidewalk."

"Then he has a powerful constitution, probably chemically enhanced. He enjoyed this." Morris laid a gentle hand on Jennifer

Darnell's head. "I'm not Mira, so that's simply a dead doctor's take. But you and I see, every day, what one human being is capable of doing to another. This one enjoyed himself."

"Yeah, and when they have that much fun, they want to do it again."

She headed to Central. She needed to review her notes, write an initial report—harass the sweepers and the lab for theirs—start her murder board and book. And she wanted a look at the wit, or at least Yancy's sketch.

Somewhere in there she wanted to carve out some time to do a good, solid run on Eton Asshole Billingsly.

She smelled cookies the minute she stepped into the bull-pen, caught the scatter of crumbs on Jenkinson's shirt, watched Baxter stuff the remains of one in his mouth before he offered her a big smile.

"Nadine's in your office, LT."

"Pathetic. Pathetic that a bunch of cops, fat-assing at their desks instead of out taking down bad guys, can be bribed with cookies."

Jenkinson shot up a hand. "We got one, Dallas. Reineke's walking him down to lockup. I'm doing the fives."

"With cookie crumbs on your shirt."

He brushed at them hastily as she turned away to stride to her office. Where Nadine Furst, reporter extraordinaire, lounged in her visitor's chair, nibbling on a cookie and working on her PPC.

Saying nothing, Eve lifted the lid of the bakery box on her desk, took out a fat chocolate chip. "What do you want?"

"A man of amazing sexual prowess, great sensitivity, stupendous abs, and the face of an angel. Toss in a wicked sense of humor and stupendous wealth, who adores the very ground I walk on. Oh wait, you already have him."

Eve bit into the cookie.

"Second choice?"

Nadine fluffed back her streaky blond hair, smiled her feline smile with her cat's eyes glinting. "I heard you caught a messy one."

"That's right. I don't have anything to give you. I haven't put it together yet."

"Three victims, beaten, stabbed, and strangled, recovering addicts with a connection to the Whitwood Group—killed, in fact, on property owned by same. The Whitwoods are always a strong story."

"The victims are the story."

"I know." Nadine's smile faded. "They were young, trying to turn things around. Are you looking at gang and/or illegals-related murders?"

"I'm looking at everything, everyone."

"Including the Whitwoods, and the very dreamy Justin Rosenthall."

"Including." Nadine, Eve calculated, was always a good source. "What do you know about Eton Billingsly?"

"He's a dick."

"I got that much."

"Is he a suspect?"

"Nadine, it's too early."

"Well, I hope he is, because he's, as I said, a dick. Comes from money. Not quite on the Whitwood level, but he's got a fat portfolio. He also seriously courted the lovely Arianna, who fell head over skirt for Rosenthall—who is not a dick. I don't know much about him, but I can find out."

"I'm working on it." Eve took another bite of cookie. Damn fine cookie. "What else do you want?"

"You're just back from closing a big one in Dallas. Isaac McQueen—the second time you took him down. It's a hot story, Dallas. Him coming after you, abducting one of his former victims. I want you to come on *Now* and talk about it."

Eve set the cookie aside. Damn fine or not, her appetite dried up. "I'm not going to do that."

Before she could say anything else, Nadine held up a hand. "And I'm not going to press you. I had to ask."

"It's not like you to give up so easy."

Nadine recrossed her legs. "A couple of years ago when you and I hooked up over the DeBlass case, I did a little research. I like to know who I'm working with."

Eve said nothing.

"It's not easy getting much background on you, but I know you were found in Dallas when you were a child, and you'd been . . . hurt. The reporter wants an interview, Dallas, but the friend won't push. Friendship's stronger than a story."

"Okay." And it was.

"When you get something on this new case, maybe you can give me a heads-up."

"Maybe I could. You should contact Bree and Melinda Jones," Eve said as Nadine rose. "You should go to Dallas, where it happened, talk to them there."

"I intended to contact them." Nadine angled her head. "An on-location special? That's not bad. Some of it in the apartment where he kept Melinda Jones and the girl, some in the hotel suite where he came after you. No, that's not half-bad. I've got to go."

At the door, Nadine paused, glanced back. "Dallas, anytime you want to talk to the friend, about any of it, the reporter will step back."

"I appreciate it."

Alone, Eve turned to her 'link and contacted another friend. She was shuffled directly to Dr. Louise Dimatto's v-mail, left a message asking for a meeting.

Rising, she programmed coffee, then began to set up her board. She'd work better with the visuals.

When she finished, she started her report.

"That's particularly gruesome," Roarke said from her doorway.

Nadine had been right, Eve thought, in her summary of him. Oh, she'd left a few things out, but all in all. He did have the face of an angel, a fallen one, with the wings well-singed, but that only made him more compelling. That and those wildly blue eyes, the silky black hair. He wore one of his sharp business suits, but there was no asshole vibe here as with Billingsly.

This was power, success, sex, and danger all rolled into one streamlined package with Ireland gilding his voice.

Still.

"What are you doing here?" she demanded.

"I had business nearby, and took a chance I'd see my wife. And here she is. This is new," he said, looking at her board again.

"Caught it this morning. Oh, Justin Rosenthall and Arianna Whitwood say hi."

"Is that so?" He shifted his gaze back to her. "What would they have to do with this?"

"That's a question. How well do you know them?"

"Not that well." He ran a hand absently over Eve's shoulder as he moved closer to the board. "Surface, socially, charitable foundation events sort of knowing. He's intense without being preachy, and she's dedicated without being tiresome. And they both put their time and effort into their particular cause."

"Eton Billingsly."

"Git," Roarke said, using his childhood slang in insult.

"Maybe you can elaborate on that later, but right now I have to—" She broke off, answered her 'link.

"Dallas."

"I've got the sketch, Lieutenant," Yancy told her. "I think you're going to want to see it."

"On my way."

She clicked off, rose.

"Why not have it sent to your comp?"

"Because he's going to want to explain it to me." She thought of the description. "You can tag along."

"Why not, since it's unlikely I can talk you into a late lunch or early dinner." He flipped open the bakery box, helped himself to a cookie. "This will have to do. I haven't had time to monitor the police reports," he added as they walked. "Tell me about the case."

She did as they used the glides to get to Yancy's level.

"A strong Whitwood-Rosenthall connection," he commented. "As I said, I don't know them well, but I can't see them involved in that. Unfortunately, I can't see Billingsly involved either. Certainly he wouldn't stoop to getting his hands dirty."

"People who work with addicts, day in, day out, sometimes end up using themselves. Maybe one, or more than one of them, gets in too deep. Newly recoverings can be like converts. Fervent. One of them finds out, threatens to spill it. Reputation's ruined, the Center blackened, blah, blah.

"Whoever did it had some medical training," she added. "Morris confirms the amputations weren't the work of an amateur."

"Any number of people at the Center and Get Straight would have medical training."

"Yeah, and I'm going to look at all of them."

She moved through Yancy's division, straight to the glass cube where she saw him and a woman in her early thirties with a baby on her lap.

Yancy gave Eve a nod.

"Cynthia, this is Lieutenant Dallas. LT, Cynthia Kopel— and Lilian."

"Thanks for coming in Ms. Kopel."

"I'm happy to. I only wish I'd contacted the police last night, when I saw him. But I just thought it was some crazy. I didn't know about those people until Officer Slovic knocked on the door today."

As she spoke, the baby sucked heroically on one of the plugs parents used to keep babies from screaming—as far as Eve knew.

"We appreciate your cooperation and information. Can I see the sketch?"

Yancy exchanged a look with the witness, and Cynthia sighed. "It's what I saw. I know how it looks, but it's what I saw."

Eve held out a hand for the printout. And when Yancy gave it to her, looked at the face of a monster.

FIVE

———◄►———

The crooked jaw accented a twisted mouth with teeth long, sharp, and prominent. A thin nose hooked over it. The eyes bulged and gleamed red against skin of pale, sickly green. Hair fell in oily twists over a wide forehead, over ears with a defined point, nearly to the shoulders of a swirled black cape.

"I know how it looks," Cynthia repeated, bouncing the baby on her knee either out of nerves or habit. "I know I sound like a nutcase, but I'm not. I got a good look because he was dancing around in the streetlight, like it was a spotlight on a stage. Just weird. Well, I thought—after it scared the hell out of me for a second—just some weird guy. But then when the police came and said those three people had been murdered right across the street . . ."

"Maybe he dressed up for it," Eve considered. "Theatrics."

"I know he was creepy. And that laugh." Cynthia shuddered. "It was this maniacal laugh, but low and deep—and kind of raw. Like he had something stuck in his throat. After he stuffed something in the recycler, he bent over, his hands on his knees, laughing and laughing. I started to go wake up Reed—Lilian's daddy—but then he—this guy—left. He went up the street—spinning around so the cape he was wearing twirled."

She let out a sigh. "You see all kinds of strange stuff and

people in the city, and half the time you barely notice or get a kick out of it, you know? But this was . . . Well, it made the hairs on the back of my neck stand up."

"When you see something like this in the middle of the night outside your window, it would spook you," Eve commented.

The tension in Cynthia's face eased. "I didn't think anyone would believe me. I felt stupid, but then those three people, I had to report it once I knew. However he looked, how could he be laughing and dancing around after killing them? He is a monster." She drew the baby closer. "On the inside, he's exactly how he looked. Evil."

"I know how it looks, too," Yancy said after he'd walked Cynthia out. "But she was solid, Dallas."

"Yeah, I got that. I don't think we'll be issuing a BOLO on this face at this time, but she saw what she saw. The attitude fits—the laughing, dancing around, the theatrics. There was definite glee in the killings. So he dresses up for it, adds some punch." She frowned over the sketch. "He strangled Darnell face-to-face. Is this what he wanted her to see? Adds more fear, but it's not as personal if she's seeing this mask, this disguise, and not him."

"Are you certain she knew him?" Roarke asked.

"Oh yeah. They knew each other. He knew all of them. Ear, eyes, tongue. What did they hear, see? What was he afraid they'd say? So . . . send me the file copy," she said to Yancy. "We'll start checking costume shops, theaters."

"If it's makeup," Yancy told her, "he's a pro *and* an expert. If it's a mask of some kind, it's damn good, so it'd cost large."

"Yeah. And that should help. Nice job, Yancy."

"Here to serve. Strangest sketch I've ever done, and I've done some strange."

"Have you considered a combination?" Roarke asked as they walked back. "That he has some sort of deformity and played it up. The jaw—if your witness has it right—it looks severely dislocated."

"I'm going to be working that angle, but nobody I've inter- viewed so far has any kind of facial deformity. You can't hide something like that. If it's a medical condition . . . I'm waiting for Louise to tag me back. Maybe she'd have some ideas on that. Or Mira. I need to walk this through with Mira."

When they stepped back into the bullpen, Peabody hailed her. "Not much to add from Slice or the twenty-four/seven or the diner. I'm writing it up. Hey, Roarke. Lucky I brought back a personal pie. Maybe Dallas will share with you."

Eve picked up the takeout, passed it to Roarke. "Maybe she will. Did you see anybody like this?" She offered Peabody the sketch.

"Whoa. Seriously?"

"Yancy thinks the wit's solid, and as I talked to her myself, I agree."

"Part demon, part monster, part human. He's like a mutant."

"He's like somebody in costume," Eve corrected. "Start running down this look. Theaters, costume outlets. See if you can find anything that fits." She started to dig out money for the pizza.

"You got the last one," Peabody told her.

"I probably did. And let's see if we can find anyone connected to the center or Get Straight who's involved in theater or theatrical makeup. Costume parties," she added. "Places like the Center have fund-raisers like that, right? Where they make people dress up like idiots, then squeeze them for donations."

"I doubt they think of it in quite those terms," Roarke considered. "But, yes."

"We'll look at that. If you get anything close to a hit," she told Peabody, "let me know."

She went back in her office with Roarke. "Go ahead," she said, gesturing at the take-out box. "I want to try to get a meet with Mira."

She sat and began chipping away at the scales of the dragon at Mira's gates. "Ten minutes," Eve insisted. "I've got three DBs."

"And Dr. Mira has a full schedule today."

"Ten minutes," Eve said again. "For this." She angled so her 'link captured the murder board.

"In thirty minutes," the admin told her. "Don't be late."

"I won't."

Sampling the pizza, Roarke wandered over to her board. "You know, you could contact Mira directly."

"Yeah, but it's not right. Channels are channels for a reason, even when they're annoying."

"I suppose. You've discounted this being done by someone from their past? An addict, a dealer."

"Not discounted." She tried the pizza herself. "But the probability's low any of them knew someone back then who had the skill to surgically remove body parts. I think he was on something when he did—the frenzy, the strength and endurance, then laughing and dancing. So even flying he had skill, a steady hand. Add to it, Darnell's been out of that for nearly four months and wouldn't be tough to track down. If she'd known something that threatened someone with this skill, wouldn't he have dealt with her before? For four months she's been immersed in the Center and the program. It's somebody attached to that."

"I can't fault your logic. I rarely can."

Her 'link signaled. "Dallas."

"Dallas, I was in surgery." Louise, still in scrubs, mask dangling, came on screen. "I just heard. I can't quite believe it."

"You knew them."

"Yes. I'm actually Jen Darnell's physician of record. I do her monthly exams. Did," she corrected. "I'd see her often when I did a rotation at either the Center or Get Straight. And Coby, too, in the last few months. I met Wil recently. He hasn't been in the program as long."

"How well do you know Rosenthall and Arianna Whitwood?"

"Very well. They were in Haiti helping to set up a new clinic when Charles and I got married or they'd have been at the wedding."

"Eton Billingsly."

Louise's pretty face pruned. "He's an excellent therapist and a complete jerk."

"I need to talk to you about this."

"I've got another surgery scheduled. It's minor, but they're already prepping the patient."

"Have her and Charles meet us for drinks," Roarke suggested and got a blank look from Eve.

"Here." He simply nudged her aside. "Hello, Louise."

"Roarke. I didn't realize you were there."

"Why don't you and Charles meet us for drinks after work? You and Eve can discuss what needs to be discussed."

"Yes, I think that would work."

While Roarke set it up, Eve turned back to her board. She liked Louise and Charles, but wasn't sure how she felt about her interview with a source turning into a social hour.

What the hell.

"Find somewhere to meet up near the crime scene," Eve said, and gave Roarke the address. "I want to go back over it."

"There." Roarke turned away from the 'link when he'd finished. "Now you can talk to Louise, revisit your crime scene, and have a little time with friends. Interlude on West Eleventh, between Sixth and Seventh. At five, or as close as you can make it."

He skimmed a fingertip down the dent in her chin. "It's efficient."

"I guess it is."

"I've got a meeting shortly, so I'll see you there." Leaning down, he brushed his lips over hers. "Take care of my cop," he told her, then left.

It should have weirded her out, Eve mused, sharing pizza and good-bye kisses, making dates for drinks in her office. It did, she admitted, but not as much as expected. Her gaze landed on the bakery box, narrowed.

She said, "Hmmm," and, picking it up, walked out. She ignored the noses that came up sniffing as she passed through the bullpen, and caught a glide to Mira's office.

The admin, busy on her comp, glanced up with a stern frown. "You're early."

"Then I'm not late." Eve set the box on the desk. "Thanks for clearing time for me."

Stern turned suspicious as the woman lifted the lid of the box a fraction, then more as she peered in. "Cookies? You brought me cookies?"

"They're good. I had one. Is she free now?"

Still eyeing Eve, she tapped her earpiece. "Lieutenant Dallas is here. Of course. You can go right in."

"Thanks."

"Are these a thank-you or a bribe?" the admin asked as Eve moved to the door.

"They're chocolate chip." Pleased with herself, Eve stepped into the calm of Mira's office.

Mira smiled from behind her desk. Maybe it was a shrink thing, Eve considered, thinking of Arianna. The warm looks, the pretty, feminine suits, perfect blend of color and jewelry.

"I know you don't have much time."

"Enough, I hope. Have a seat." As Eve took one of Mira's blue scoop chairs, Mira came around the desk, took the one facing. "I looked over the data, the crime-scene photos. My first question is, how sure are you there's only one killer?"

"Very. We have a wit who saw him at the rear of the building, where he broke in. She worked with Detective Yancy." Eve took out the sketch, offered it.

"Well." In her placid way, Mira studied the sketch. "Now I have to ask, how good is your witness?"

"Again, I have to say very. I figure he geared himself up for it, added the drama. The wit says he danced in the streetlight, laughed his ugly ass off. My sense of the scene is frenzied glee. He had to be on something because killing three people that dead takes endurance."

"I agree." Mira tucked a lock of sable-colored hair behind her ear as she continued to study the sketch. "Theatrical, confident, organized. He knew where to break in, came prepared, and was able to kill, with extreme violence, three people, alone, and in a relatively short amount of time. Endurance, yes, and rage."

She shifted, met Eve's eyes with her own quiet blue ones. "I agree with your assessment that he has some sort of medical training. The amputations were skillfully done. I believe he'll keep these trophies, these symbols. His victims are no longer able to see, hear, or speak of him."

"But they had, prior to their deaths."

"Almost certainly. They knew each other. Dancing, laughing, so yes, he enjoyed himself. He can celebrate—and in the light, perhaps hoping he'd be seen. Spotlighting after his success.

"He envied their friendship," Mira continued. "Their bond, and their happiness. He won't make friends easily, won't feel that bond. He most likely lives alone, feels underappreciated at his work. He's skilled. The elaborate disguise tells me he wants to be noticed, and doesn't feel he is, not enough. Nothing is enough. He wants what others have—friends, family, community—and at the same time feels superior to them. He's better than they are. 'Take out the trash,' he wrote, in their blood. That's what he made them. And it amused him. He's a series of contradictions, Eve. Two people—perhaps more—in one. You have a violent sociopath under the influence of a strong illegal. He's both controlled and out of control, canny and reckless. He has a god complex battling with low self-esteem, a bitter envy, and has found satisfaction and personal delight in killing."

"He'll do it again."

"As soon as he can."

"This face. Under the makeup or the mask, whatever it is, could he have a deformity? The jaw's extreme."

"Yes, I see that, but a deformity such as this? He'd be in constant pain. It would be all but impossible for him to eat. His speech would be garbled. As someone with medical training, and connections, he would certainly have had this repaired."

"A recent injury, accident?"

"Possibly," Mira considered. "But again, I can't think of any reason it wouldn't be treated. If, for some reason, he refused to have it treated and is dosing himself with painkillers and other drugs, it might explain the frenzy, the duality in his profile. But why would anyone endure the pain of this, the social stigma? And it contradicts, again, his confidence, his need to be seen as superior."

"It must be faked. Peabody's running down costume shops, theaters." Eve paused a moment, changed angles. "Do you know Justin Rosenthall and Arianna Whitwood?"

"Yes. Arianna's an excellent therapist. A bright, compassionate woman. She and her parents have done a great deal, not only in research and application on addictions and rehabilitation, but they built their Center with the purpose of treating the whole person. Physically, emotionally, mentally, spiritually. They turned a personal tragedy into a great gift."

"And Rosenthall?"

"Very skilled, remarkably gifted. More intense than Arianna, I'd say. It seems to me—though I don't see or socialize with them often—she's softened that intensity. Before Arianna, he was much more of a loner, and rarely stepped away from his work. Not unlike someone else," Mira said with a smile. "With her, he remains skilled, gifted, dedicated to his work, but he's happier. And not capable of murdering three people like this."

"Everyone's capable," Eve stated.

"Yes, you're right. All of us are capable under certain circumstances of extreme and violent behavior. We control it, channel it—in some cases medicate it. Justin's a doctor, dedicated to healing, a scientist and man of reason. The person who did this rejects reason and humanity. He's given himself a monster's face. Humanity means little to him."

"Okay. How about Eton Billingsly?"

"A skilled therapist, and an enormous pain in the ass."

Eve had to grin. "I don't think I've ever heard you call anybody a pain in the ass."

"I don't like him so it's hard to be objective. He's a pompous snob who sees himself as perfect. He's rude, annoying, and full of himself."

"A god complex?"

Mira's eyebrows rose. "Yes, I'd say. You wonder if he's capable. I don't know him well enough. He's skilled—he has an MD, and would have done some time with a scalpel before he focused on his specialty."

"Hypno-voodoo."

Mira let out a quick, exasperated laugh. "I know you're suspicious of the technique, but it's valid, and can be very effective. Billingsly certainly wants to be noticed and rewarded and praised. But . . ." She studied the sketch again. "It's very difficult for me to envision a man like him deliberately making himself hideous. He's also vain."

"Something to think about, though. I appreciate the time."

"I'm happy to give it. Tell me how you are."

"I'm fine."

"You haven't been back long. How's your arm?"

Eve started to dismiss it, then settled on the truth. "A little sore in the morning, and by the end of the day. Mostly good, though."

"That's to be expected with that kind of injury. Nightmares?"

"No. Maybe just being back in New York's enough. At least right now. Isaac McQueen's back in a cage where he belongs. That doesn't suck. I'm not thinking about my mother, what happened there," she said before Mira could ask. "Not yet. It's done, and right now I'm okay with it."

"When and if it's not, you'll talk to me?"

"I know I can. That's a pretty big start, right?"

"Yes, it is."

Eve got up, started for the door. "Is she like you?" she asked. "Arianna Whitwood?"

"Like me?"

"That's the sense I got from her. She made me think of you. Not just because she's an attractive female shrink. It was . . . I don't know, a sense. If she is like you, then she's got no part in this. And thinking that, I hope to hell Justin Rosenthall doesn't, because you believe she loves him. I hope he's clear."

"So do I."

"I'll let you know," Eve said, and left.

SIX

Eve glanced over at Peabody as she walked back into the bull-pen, got a shake of the head.

So no luck, yet, on masks or makeup. She went into her office, got coffee, then sat at her desk, put her boots up, and studied the board.

Everybody liked Rosenthall; nobody liked Billingsly. Instinct dictated a push on Billingsly—and she intended to listen. But she'd give a little push on the good doctor as well.

Arianna Whitwood. Beautiful, rich, smart, dedicated, caring. The good daughter, and again, the good doctor.

Didn't that make an interesting triangle? Billingsly wanted her—and didn't bother to (ha-ha) disguise it. Rosenthall had her.

And what did that have to do with the three vics?

They were Arianna's. Her patients, her investment, her success—at least so far. Rosenthall's, too.

Maybe Arianna had given them too much time, attention, made too big an investment. A man could resent that. She sometimes wondered why Roarke didn't resent all the time, the attention, the investment she put into the job.

But there weren't a lot of Roarkes in the world.

Maybe the three vics—or any one of them—overheard Arianna and the good doctor going at it over her work, that time and attention again. Hey, bitch, what about *me*? Shouldn't I be the center of your world? Maybe he'd lost his temper. Couldn't have the gossip mills grinding that one.

And no, just not enough for that kind of slaughter.

Maybe the vics, or one of them, overheard the two doctors-in-love arguing because Rosenthall was sampling product. Experimenting. That's what you did in a lab. You experimented. Maybe he'd developed a problem of his own during those experiments. Now that, combined with being found out, could lead to bloody, vicious murder. Could be Arianna didn't know. Can't have her find out he's become what he's supposed to cure.

That could play.

Or, onto Billingsly. He pushed himself on his beautiful associate, and again one or all of them saw the incident. Possible.

Or the annoying doctor fooled around with a patient, maybe—hmm—maybe tried a move on Darnell. Rejected, humiliated, worried she'd tell Arianna. He'd lose any chance with the woman he wanted, and his license to practice.

That could play, too.

But none of it played very well. Maybe she just needed to fine-tune a little.

For now, she read over Peabody's notes on her interviews at Slice and the twenty-four/seven, the diner hangout. Nothing buzzing there, Eve thought, but continued as Peabody had started or completed a number of deeper runs on the players in those arenas.

Rising, Eve got another cup of coffee, then started deeper runs of her own on Rosenthall, Billingsly, Arianna, Marti Frank, Ken Dickerson, and Pachai Gupta.

Gupta came from some wealth, and an upper-class social strata, and she considered the fact that his parents, also doctors, had worked with Rosenthall years before.

Now Gupta had the plum position of the renowned doctor's lab assistant on a major project. Couldn't something like that make a career?

How would Gupta's upper-class parents feel about him pining for a recovering addict? Possibly he wanted to keep that on the down low, and possibly Darnell wanted to go public.

Possibly.

Both Marti Frank and Ken Dickerson came from the ordinary, and in Dickerson's case the rough, with his dead addict of an abusive father. Both had excelled in school, she noted. Frank top of her class in college—on a full scholarship. Dickerson third—accelerated path. He'd graduated high school at sixteen, college—again on scholarships—at nineteen, and straight into medical school.

And they were both still on scholarships, she noted, in the intern program at the Center.

She brought the lab setup back into her head. Working together on the project, she mused, but they'd seemed very separate, hadn't they? With Rosenthall center. Neither Dickerson nor Frank had gone to Gupta when he'd broken down.

So not friends—not especially.

Competitors? Didn't you have to have a competitive streak to come in first in your class, or in the top tier with acceleration?

And was it interesting, she wondered, or frustrating to learn that all six of them had sufficient medical training to have performed the amputations?

She'd eliminate the females, except one of them might have acted in collusion. Dead low on the list, she decided, but it felt too soon to eliminate.

All of them knew the vics' location. None of them had alibis for the time in question. All of them knew and/or interacted with the vics. All of them had access to drugs and could easily put their hands on the protective gear.

She picked her way through the data on each suspect, added to her notes, her board. When the sweepers' initial report came through, she pounced. More paint flakes, some black fibers from the window casing, some hairs—no roots. All sent to the lab.

None of the victims' 'links had been found on scene. So he'd taken them. Taken the 'links, she mused, but not the money. Fibers on the windowsill, footprints in blood. So he'd only sealed his hands, or worn gloves.

And walking through the blood, that was just stupid. Amateur hour. If they found the shoes, they had him.

First kill, she thought. She'd make book this had been his debut.

Time to circle back.

She walked out to Peabody. "I'm going back to the scene."

"Okay. I'm not getting anywhere anyway."

"No, you keep at it. I'm going to talk to Louise after, then work from home."

"I'm serious about getting nowhere." Peabody huffed out a breath, shoved at her hair. "I've talked to the top costume shops—and some costume and theatrical makeup designers in the city. What I get is, sure the skin color's no problem; hair, no big; nose, teeth, you bet. But the eyes? Every one of them tells me if they used apparatus like that—to make them bulge out, or appear to, and turn that red—it would hamper vision. Same with the jaw."

"It was dark, even with the streetlight. Middle of the night. Maybe the wit exaggerated some."

"Maybe. A couple of the people I talked to were all juiced up about it, trying to figure out how to make it work. I've got them promising to experiment, see what they can do. But nobody's got anything like this. Not in any sort of mask, or doable with makeup and prosthetics. Nothing that would allow the person wearing it to see clearly, speak, or laugh the way the wit described."

"Keep at it anyway, because it is doable, as it was done."

"What if he's some kind of freak?"

"Peabody."

"I didn't say demon or monster. Like a circus freak, you know? A contortionist or a freak show type. He looks like this—or something like this and he just pumped it up."

"Circus. That's an angle. I'll work that at home. Not bad, Peabody."

"You'd kick my ass if I said monster."

"Keep that in mind if you become tempted," Eve warned, then headed out.

She thought of makeup, freaks, altered appearances as she drove—and had a brainstorm. "Contact Mavis Freestone, pocket 'link."

Contact initiated.

"Hey, Dallas!" Mavis's pretty, happy face filled the dash screen. "Say hi to Dallas, Bellorama."

Instantly, the baby's chubby, grinning face replaced her mother's. "Das!" she cried with absolute joy, and pressed her wet lips to the screen of the pocket 'link.

"Yeah, hi, kid. Kiss, kiss."

"Slooch!"

"Right. Smooch."

"Make the sound, Dallas," Mavis said offscreen.

Eve rolled her eyes, but complied with a kissing sound. Bella squealed with yet more delight.

"Playtime." There was some shifting, giggling, then Mavis came back on behind the film of Bella's slobber. "Why didn't you tell me you were going to Dallas?" Mavis demanded.

"I didn't have time. It was—"

"We're going to chit some serious chat about this."

"Okay." With Mavis, it would be okay. "But later. I need you to—can you wipe your screen off? You look like you've been licked by a Saint Bernard."

"Oh, sorry. So what's the up?" Mavis asked as she whipped out a cloth and polished the screen.

"I'm going to send you a sketch, and I need you to get in touch with Trina, show it to her."

"Why don't you just send it to her?"

"Because I'm busy."

Mavis angled her head. Her hair, a curling mass of gold-streaked red today, bounced. "Coward."

"I'm a busy coward. I don't want her giving me grief because I didn't rub some shit on my face, or in my hair. Or listen to her tell me I need my hair cut or whatever. I've got something hot, and she might be able to help."

"Give me the goods. So I finished my gig on the vid," she said as Eve ordered the sketch accessed and sent.

"What vid?"

"Nadine's vid—your vid. *The Icove Agenda*. It's mag to the nth they wanted me to play myself. And the chick playing you? Man, they made her a ringer. I got wigged when I— Holy shit on a flaming stick!"

"Shit," Bella echoed happily in the background.

"Oh hell—hello," Mavis muttered. "I swore in front of the baby. But holy you know what, this is too totally scary. I'm scheduling my nightmare right now."

"Sorry. I need to know what it takes to make somebody look like this."

"A pact with Satan?"

"With makeup and prosthetics, and that stuff. Trina knows that crap."

"I'll be passing it on—and getting it off my 'link just in case it has the power to materialize."

"Come on. Other angle. You did some carny work."

"Back in the day, sure. Always plenty of marks at a carny."

"Ever see anything like this? Freak show–wise."

"I saw plenty of mega weird, but nothing like this. You wouldn't ask unless it—he—whatever—killed somebody. He looks like he's born to kill. Jes—jeepers," she corrected. "I got bumps of the goose all over. I'll tag Trina now, so I don't have to wig alone."

"Thanks. Let me know."

Eve pulled over at the curb in front of the crime scene.

She unsealed the door, used her master. And stood inside, left the lights off. Not as dark as it would've been, she thought. But there was a streetlight, enough for some backwash.

Still, he'd had to know which mattress each vic slept on. He'd moved with purpose, with a plan despite the ferocity.

She moved straight through to the back, opened the window, climbed out.

And yeah, the building across the street had a good view of the window, the sidewalk, the recycler. Eve imagined the killer dancing and spinning in the spot of the streetlight, laughing.

Spinning and dancing up the street, Cynthia had said. So he didn't care about being seen. A vehicle nearby? Or a hole to crawl into. His own place?

If he'd taken a cab, the subway, a bus? Even in New York somebody would've reported it. All of the lab rats lived within blocks. Both of the doctors and Arianna had vehicles.

Eve turned back to the window. He jimmies it, she thought—quiet now. No dancing and laughing, not yet. Climbs in.

She followed the steps, easing in, sliding down to her feet—left fibers behind. Opens the satchel for the protective coat.

Some boxes in here, she noted, and tidy piles of old materials—but he doesn't bump into them. He's been here before. And he walks right into the front.

As she did, the door started to open.

She had her weapon out, trained. Then hissed when Roarke stepped in.

"Damn it."

"I'm the one with a stunner aimed at me. I get to say, 'Damn it.'"

She shoved it back in the holster. "You're not supposed to pick the lock on a crime scene."

"How else would I get in? Your vehicle's outside, and the seal's broken. I knocked like a good civilian, but you didn't answer."

"I was out the back window."

"Naturally." He stood where he was, looking around. "What an unholy mess. The crime-scene records never have quite the same impact."

Since he was here, she'd use him.

"He jimmied the window, rear, quietly stepped around the stuff back there—in the dark or near dark. Not much would come through the window—it's grilled—from the streetlight. But he doesn't wake them."

"He'd been in here, and back there, before."

"Yeah. Knew just how to navigate, and knew where each one slept. Leads with the bat." She swung. "Cracks Vix across the side of the head where he lay. He's the lucky one. I doubt he ever woke up. Changes to the knife." She mimed switching hands. "Puts it into Bickford's chest—two blows, and another in the gut. Fast. Bickford might've made some sound, tried to call out, but his lung's punctured. Now it's time for Darnell."

"She'd have woken, don't you think?"

"Bash, slice, movement. I think she woke up before he'd finished with Bickford. Got up, either tried to run or tried to fight. He uses the bat, breaks her kneecaps. Maybe she screamed—nobody heard—or maybe she just passed out or went into shock. But he went back to Vix, beat him into jelly. Blood's flying everywhere, bones snapping, shattering. He put the protective gear on in the back room, but blood's on his face. It feels warm, tastes hot. He loves it. He wants more, so he goes back to Bickford with the knife and stabs and hacks. Over eighty times."

Eve shifted. "She tried to drag herself away. See, the blood's smeared on the floor there from her knees, from her trying to pull herself away. But she's in terrible pain, in shock, in hysterics. He's laughing now because this is so much fun. Just better than he'd ever imagined. And now it's her turn."

She could see it, all but smell the blood.

"He says her name. I bet he said her name, and his. He wanted her to know him. It's face-to-face, it's his hands on her throat so he can feel her pulse going wild, then slowing, slowing, slowing while her eyes bulge and her body beats itself against the floor. While that pulse stops, and her eyes fix, and her body goes limp."

"Christ Jesus, Eve."

"That's how it happened." Inside she was as cold as the images fixed in her head. "That's close, anyway. He's not done. It's too funny and thrilling. He doesn't use the knife. He takes a scalpel out of his satchel because he takes pride in the work. Now he makes a point. An ear, an eye, her tongue. They're a trio, aren't they, like the monkeys. Hear no, see no, speak no."

"Evil," Roarke finished. "Because he is. What you've just described is evil."

"Maybe, maybe even to him. But he likes it. Likes the taste of evil, the smell of it. He just can't get enough, so he breaks the place up, what little they had. Destroys it. He stages them against the wall. Then he uses their blood to leave us a message."

Roarke studied the wall. "It took time to do that. His letters so carefully formed. Not dashed off, but clearly printed. He gave it some thought."

"He's so clever, a real joker. Dr. Chaos. I bet he slapped his knees over it."

She paused a minute. "Arianna said something. How they'd found their quiet. Especially Darnell. That addiction steals the quiet. That's what he brought back. The unquiet. The chaos. So that's the name he picked."

She walked away, into the back. "He takes off the protective gear. Turns it inside out to keep the blood off his clothes, and he climbs back out, shuts the window. He laughs, and he dances, just so full of the fun of it he can't contain it. He stuffs the gear in the recycler, properly disposing of it like he tells us to do with the bodies. A little clue, so we'll be sure to find it.

And that has him doubled over with laughter. Then he dances away, high on the unquiet. Dr. Chaos had the time of his life."

"Did you learn any more from this re-creation?"

"Maybe. Yeah."

"Then you can tell me about it over the drink I find I want very much right now."

SEVEN

Eve looked around the bar as they went in. Quiet and cozy, with a neighborhood feel, she observed. A couple of guys sat at the bar, deep in their brews and conversation. She bet they were regulars, bet the seats of the stools all but carried the imprint of their asses.

The bartender, bright, young, female, joined in with them, idly swiping the bar with a rag as she laughed at something they said. A couple sat at a table—had a first-date, drink-after-work-to-see-how-it-goes look about them. Another four had a booth, scarfing down bar chips while they held one of those quick, coded conversations of intimate friends.

Roarke took a booth, smiled at her over the table. "Satisfied?"

"About what?"

"That you won't have to arrest anyone in here."

She smiled back. "You never know."

She opted for a beer when the waitress came over, and Roarke held up two fingers. "Now, as we're a bit early, tell me what you learned back there."

"It was the girl. It was Jen. She was the primary motive. He wanted her to see what he did, how he killed the others, took away what mattered most to her in the cruelest way. She was the easiest kill of the three, but he saved her for last because she was the most important. Then he killed her with his hands, so she could see his face and he could see hers. The others didn't matter as much, except for their connection to her. He wanted her, and she said no—or worse, didn't *see* him as a man."

"He didn't rape her. I looked at your board."

"It had gone past sex or rape as power and control, and he got off on the killing. But taking the body parts—they'd seen or heard something he couldn't afford them to talk about. Whatever it was, it was recent."

She waited until the waitress served the beers. "See that group over there." She lifted her chin toward the booth of four. "Two guys, two girls. But they're not couples."

"Aren't they?" Roarke said, enjoying her.

"Look at the body language. They're tight, but it's not sexual. Pals. And they never run out of conversation. Blah, blah, blah. They talk all the time, hang all the time. When they're not together, they tag each other. He took their 'links because he got that, he knew they connected that way when they weren't together, and had to conclude they'd talked about whatever they'd seen or heard via 'link."

"All right."

"He worked alone. He doesn't connect, he doesn't have that closeness with anyone. So that bumps the two female suspects down the list for me. It wasn't Arianna Whitwood or Marti Frank. They may know something, may not know they know it, but this one had to have all the fun for himself. He's smug, and a show-off, which is why I like Billingsly just on principle."

"Arianna said no to him," Roarke pointed out.

"But he still believes he can get her. She's also on his level. How humiliating would it be for a man like that to want an addict, a squatter, a *nothing*, and be rejected by her?"

"That's a great deal for a second look at the crime scene."

"But not enough. Here's Louise and Charles."

Roarke stood, greeting Louise with a kiss, Charles with a handshake.

As Charles, former licensed companion turned sex therapist, slid in beside his wife, he grinned at Eve. "How's it going, Lieutenant Sugar?"

"I've got three bodies and a short list of suspects. It could be worse. Sorry," she said to Louise. "Insensitive."

"No. We both deal with death all too often, but at least I come into it when there's still a chance."

"You look tired," Roarke commented.

"Long day. Good day," she added, "as I didn't deal with death."

Both she and Charles ordered a glass of the house white.

"What can I tell you about your short list of suspects?"

Eve drew out the sketch, laid it on the table. Puzzled, Louise leaned closer. "We've still got a month till Halloween."

"This is who the witness saw outside the crime scene."

"It's a hell of a disguise," Charles commented. "Why would anyone want to dress up, be that noticeable when doing murder?"

"Maybe it added to the thrill. We're not having any luck on replicating the disguise, and Mira says it's unlikely he could tolerate the jaw—broken or dislocated that way."

"Now you have two doctors telling you that. This is extreme." Louise tapped a finger, tipped in pearly pale pink, on the sketch. "There would be airway blockage, difficulty breathing, speaking, eating. There should be considerable swelling, but I don't see any in this sketch. The pain would be enormous. And the eyes certainly aren't natural. Not just the color. Hyperthyroidism can cause the eyes to bulge, but I've never seen anything that severe. And the skin? I'd diagnose multiple organ failure at worst, anemia at best. He had to fake all this."

"Hey, I saw that guy." The waitress paused as she served the wine.

"When?" Eve demanded. "Where?"

"Last night. Well, this morning. You don't forget a face like that," she added with a laugh.

"Exactly what time? Exactly where?" Eve drew out her badge, laid it next to the sketch.

"Oh. I guess he wasn't just a weirdo. I had the late shift last night, so I didn't leave until after two. I live on Jane, right off Greenwich Street. I did some yoga when I got home. It relaxes me. I don't know exactly, but it was probably about three fifteen, three thirty or thereabouts, when I finished. I heard this weird laughing, and went to the window. I had it open, and I saw this dude here sort of skipping down the sidewalk across the street. You see all kinds, you know, so I didn't think anything of it. I saw him jump up, swing on the pole of the streetlight, waving this black bag. I just thought, weirdo, shut the window, and went to bed."

"Which way was he going?"

"East, toward Eighth, it looked like. What'd he do?"

"Enough so if you see him again, contact the police." She hitched up a hip, dug out a card. "Contact me."

"Sure. Wow, a lieutenant. Homicide. Wow. He killed somebody?"

"Yeah. I'd like your name and address."

"Sure. Sure." Once she'd given it, the waitress hurried away.

"You scared the hell out of her," Charles said.

"She'd be smart not to walk home alone, and to keep her windows closed." She put the sketch away, sipped at her beer. "Do you know any of Rosenthall's lab people?" she asked Louise.

"No."

"Okay, we'll set them aside for now. Did Rosenthall ever move on you?"

"No! He was with Arianna when we met, then I was with Charles not long after. He's in love with Ari, and added to that, his work doesn't give him a lot of time for moving on other women."

"It doesn't take that much time. She's the one backing his research and work—or the Group is. If she cut him loose, it'd be a big loss."

"She's in love with him, and they're bonded over the work," Louise began. "If something went wrong between them, it would be a blow for both of them, personally and professionally."

"But scientists are easier to find than backers like the Whitwood Group. If his work's important to him."

"Essential, I'd say."

"Then he'd do a lot to protect it."

"Not this, Dallas. Never this. Not Justin."

"I'm going on the theory the three victims knew something about the killer. Something he killed to protect. Has Justin ever sampled product?"

"Absolutely not."

Okay, Eve thought, as long as Louise spoke in absolutes they wouldn't get anywhere on Rosenthall.

"How about Billingsly?"

"I can't say. I'd certainly doubt it, but I don't know him well." Louise smiled a little over her wine. "That's a deliberate choice."

"He put moves on you."

"He puts them on every female he finds attractive or believes can enhance his career. But Ari's the gold ring."

"How'd he react when you brushed him off?"

"Like it was my loss. He has a temper, but I've never seen anything to indicate he's capable of murder or real violence. He's rude and demanding, but from what I've heard, very good in therapy."

"And if Arianna cut him off—from the Center?"

"He has money of his own, and should have a lot of contacts. But it would be humiliating, and he wouldn't take it well. That's just opinion, Dallas. I have as little to do with him as possible."

"Okay, thanks."

"Not much help."

"You confirmed and elaborated on Mira's opinion on the killer's face. You gave me a few more details on two of my suspects, and meeting you here gave me another wit who tells me the killer went up to Jane before heading toward Eighth. That's pretty good over one drink."

When they left, Roarke took her hand as she walked. "You did very well, managing nearly a half an hour on non-work-related topics after your interview with Louise."

"I can talk about other stuff."

"You can, yes, but I know it's not easy when you're steeped in a case."

"The bar waitress was a stroke of luck. Heading toward Eighth. If it's either of the doctors, he's probably got a vehicle near there. If it's Dickerson, he goes one crosstown block to home. Gupta, north on Eighth for a block and a half to home. Nobody at Slice or Get Straight lives in that direction—and they don't fit anyway, but it's another negative on that group.

"Where's your car?" she asked when they reached the crime scene.

"I had it picked up so I could drive home with my adoring wife."

"Good. You drive." She took out her notebook, added the new information, new thoughts on the way home.

Roarke left her to it until she began to mutter.

"Is anybody really that good, the way everybody describes Rosenthall?"

"Some people have fewer shadows than others, fewer dark places. Others have more."

"And illegals speak to those dark places, make more noise so they spread. Everyone on this list connects to illegals. Lost someone to them, works with them, lives with them. The killer's a user—has to be. I don't have enough on any of them to require a drug test. Yet. But if I asked each of them, and they're clean, why wouldn't they cooperate?"

"General principles," he said as he drove through the gates of home. "But certainly worth a shot."

"I'll give it one tomorrow. Plus a scientist should be able to create an elaborate disguise."

She chewed on it as they walked inside where Summerset and the cat waited in the foyer.

"A monumental day," Summerset announced. "Home together, in a timely fashion, and unbloodied. Applause."

"If he actually applauded, the bones in his skeletal hands would break and crumble to dust."

Roarke just shook his head as Eve started upstairs. "The two of you really have to stop this love affair. I'm a jealous man. We'll get dinner in the lieutenant's office," Roarke added to Summerset.

"I'm shocked beyond speech."

"If only," Eve muttered.

"But before." Roarke took her hand again, turned her toward the bedroom. "Let's deal with that arm."

"It's okay."

"You're starting to favor it."

"It's just a little sore."

"Which means it's time for some of the physical therapy and treatment. Don't be such a baby."

She jabbed him with a finger. "You just want to get my shirt off."

"Always a bonus. Peel it off, Lieutenant." To make her smile, he leered. "And take your time."

So okay, it twinged a little when she took off her jacket, her weapon harness. Get it over with, she thought, and began the stretching exercises, working her range of motion as Roarke ditched his jacket and tie.

Her shoulder gave a couple of clicks as she stretched, punched out.

"It's coming along."

"So I see. Try to avoid actually punching someone for a few more days," he suggested as he got the topical cream from a drawer. He rolled up his sleeves as he crossed to her, then started to unhook her trousers.

"I knew it. All you think about is getting in my pants."

"With every breath I take. But for now, I just want a look at that hip. It was the worst of the cuts. Nearly healed," he murmured, tracing a fingertip along the edges where McQueen's knife had sliced. "Mira does good work."

"We've both had worse."

His eyes lifted to hers, held, and said a great deal. So she leaned into him a little, touched her lips to his.

"I'm okay."

"Nearly. Lose the tank and sit down. I'll finish you up."

She did as he asked, thinking he needed the tending as much as, maybe more than, she. Then his hands—he had magic hands—smoothed the cream over the ache, and she closed her eyes.

"Feels good. Really good."

"Mira credits your constitution, and your hard head, for the healing process. A couple more days, you'll likely be good as new. Tell me if I hurt you."

"You're not."

They hadn't made love since she'd been hurt—and she realized she should have figured why he'd been so careful with her, hadn't touched her that way, had avoiding being touched by her.

"You're not," she said again and, opening her eyes, turned to him. "You won't." And took his hand, laid it on her breast. "Feels good," she repeated. "Really good."

"I only want to give you time to heal. In every way."

"I have it on good authority I have an excellent constitution. Let's test it out." Going with the instinct that told her they didn't just need the physical intimacy, but the fun that could go along with it, she tossed her leg over his lap, straddled him. "Get it up, pal."

Smoothing those magic hands down her sides, he smiled. "You're very demanding."

"You ain't seen nothing yet." She took his mouth, gave it a nice little bite as she ground against him. "There you are," she murmured.

"Well, you've left me no choice."

"A cock's always ready to crow."

He laughed, wrapped his arms around her. "Crowing's not what mine's ready for."

"Show me." She went to work on his trousers.

Amused, aroused, he watched her. "In a bit of a hurry, are we?"

"I've got to use you and get back to work, so no dawdling." Then she laid her hands on either side of his face. "Okay, maybe a little dawdling," she said and brought her lips to his again.

"I'm okay." She unbuttoned his shirt so she could press against him. Skin to skin, heart to heart. "I want you to touch me. I want you to be with me. I want you."

He could drown in her, he thought, every minute of every day he could lose himself in what she was, what she gave him, what she took. Now, with her warm and eager against him, he could drown himself, lose himself, and set his worry for her aside.

She didn't want him to be careful, but he would take care, of her injuries at least. He gave her the controls, took his pleasure from the rise of her passion, from the sprint of her heartbeat under his lips.

When she took him in, she laid her hands on his face again. Her eyes looked deep into his. "You're holding back. Don't. Don't hold back.

So he gripped her hips, careful to avoid the healing wound. And drove her as she drove him. Over the edge of that drowning pool.

With her brow resting on his, she fought to get her breath back. If anything twinged or ached, she didn't feel it. All she felt was peace.

"Did you really have business downtown today?"

"You're my business."

She lifted her head, looked at him again. "You have to stop worrying."

"That's never going to happen. But I will stop hovering, which I've been doing a bit of. I love you beyond the telling of it, Eve, and what you went through—"

"We. We went through it."

"All right, that's true enough. What we went through doesn't heal as quickly as a cut or a bruise."

"Working on it, though. Okay?"

"Yes." He pressed his lips to her healing shoulder. "Yes."

"Okay. Well, now that I'm done with you, I'm going back to work."

He sat where he was a moment as she got up, pulled the tank back on. "I feel so used. I find I like it."

She rolled her injured shoulder, nodded in satisfaction. "Always more where that came from, ace."

EIGHT

In her office she set up a second murder board while the cat sat on her sleep chair and watched her. Through the adjoining door she heard Roarke talking on the 'link. Probably dealing with business he'd postponed during the hovering mode.

Better now, she decided. Both of them were better now. Not just the sex, but the understanding that came with it—or out of it. And the normalcy that went hand in hand.

"Nothing normal about that," she said as she studied the sketch. "Not a damn thing normal there."

She circled around to her desk, noticed that her message light was activated. She called up the message, and actually jolted when Trina's voice spiked into the room.

"Got the ugly bastard and the question. Could do the skin, hair, ears, nose, teeth, no prob. Could do the red eyes, but not so they look like red balloons coming out of the sockets. Couldn't do the jaw, not that crooked. The answer is I couldn't make anybody look like that, and I'm the best. You've got yourself a freakazoid, Dallas.

"You need a treatment—hair, face, body. The works. Mavis says she and Leonardo and Bella can come to your place for a visit on Saturday afternoon. I'll be with them, and bring my gear."

"Why," Roarke wondered, "do you look more horrified by that than by the face on your board?"

"She's coming. We have to stop her."

"Don't look at me. You could use a treatment."

"Hey." Though she was anything but vain, the careless comment gave her another jolt. "Insulting my hair, face, and body won't get you banged again anytime soon."

"You know very well I adore your hair, face, and body. You could use a massage, a relaxation treatment, and some downtime with good friends. In fact, so could I. I believe I'll contact Trina and have her bring another operative. I'll have a massage along with you."

"Traitor." She stomped to the kitchen for coffee, stomped back. "I'm not thinking about it. It's not Saturday yet. Anything could happen."

She wiped a hand through the air. "So. Everybody says it can't be done. Not costuming, not physically. But it has to be one or the other. If it's physical, maybe it's long-term. Something he's learned to live with. Peabody's circus freak angle. And if that's it, I eliminate everybody on my list."

She scowled at her board. "Pisser."

"Maybe one of your suspects hired the killings."

"I'm going to run probabilities on that, but it rips up the theory—and it's *more* than a theory—that the killer knew the vics. That it was personal."

"Maybe he just takes pleasure in his work."

"Crap. Crap. Crap. Somebody's wrong. Either the medical experts or the cosmetic/costume experts. I like it better if the cosmetics are wrong, but I've got to work it both ways. I've got to go back to the beginning."

"You can go back with me over a meal."

It usually helped to do just that, talk it through with him, bounce theories and angles off him. But this time, she felt she only circled without getting any closer to the center.

"I don't believe anyone looks like that," she said. "And if I decided to believe somebody did, I can't believe he'd stay off the grid. I ran that sketch through every program we've got and didn't get a single hit."

"Maybe it's more recent."

"The hypo-whatever, the multiple organ failure—and why

isn't he dead, if so—and whatever trauma would cause the lower part of his jaw to be so dislocated it's nearly under his right ear? I don't think so. If he was a hire, how did anybody know about him—because he'd have popped if he was a pro, even semipro. If he killed them for himself, why doesn't anyone else know about him? Unless . . . maybe he's a patient at the Center. Maybe he's a kind of experiment they're keeping on the down low."

"As in botched?" Roarke twirled some seafood linguine on his fork. "As in mad science?"

"Mad, bad. Maybe. It's something to poke at. Maybe the vics knew him from before, and found out he was there, confronted the mad-bad scientist, or threatened to tell people on the outside."

"You don't like that very much."

"Not as much as one of them slapping gunk on their face, pumping themselves full of a Zeus cocktail, and whaling away, but it's another route to take."

She took it, working angles, running probabilities, reformulating, juggling through the pieces. When Roarke finally tugged her out of her chair hours later, she was more than ready to give it up for the night.

Clear her head, she decided. Let it simmer for a few hours.

―――――――

Shortly after midnight, Eton Billingsly coded himself into Justin Rosenthall's lab using a cloned key card and a recording he'd made of Justin's voice.

He thought himself very clever.

It was time—past it—to prove to Arianna she was wasting her time and resources on Justin. The man was obsessed with this serum, and far too secretive about it in the last weeks.

Because he was getting nowhere, Billingsly concluded. The financial resources Justin wasted had become intolerable, particularly since they could and *should* be redirected to his own department. Once Arianna saw the truth, she'd rethink the relationship, and this wedding business.

He went directly to the main comp station, noted Justin had locked it down for the night.

But no problem, or very little of one. He'd worked with

Justin long enough to know the man kept such things simple, so his assistant and interns could access data when needed.

Justin called it teamwork. Billingsly called it naivete. One day one of those underlings would steal data and take credit for whatever advance Justin managed to stumble onto.

But in this case, it simply made the job easier.

He tried various names as passwords, working patiently. At one point he thought he heard a sound, froze, turned to look around. Then shook his head at his own foolishness.

He continued until, inspired, he tried *Ari102260*. The date they'd chosen to be married. Sentimental fool, Billingsly thought as access was granted.

Quickly now, he scanned through file names.

UNQUIET. Justin's term for the core of addiction.

Before he could call it up, something crashed behind him. "What the devil—?"

He whirled, then froze.

"Some might call me that," the voice ground out, like rocks beneath a boot heel. "But I prefer Chaos. Dr. Chaos." The creature issued a deep, cape-swishing bow. "At your service."

"What kind of sick joke is this?"

"My kind. Sticking your nose where it doesn't belong, aren't you, Billingsly? Well, we'll just have to take care of that."

"I have every right to . . ." But he backed up as he spoke, with his heart hammering in his dry throat. "I'm contacting Security."

"Wanna bet?"

As Billingsly began to run, the creature let out a delighted laugh. Strength, speed, excitement poured through him as he leaped. Billingsly went down under him, screaming.

Chaos used the knife. But before the knife, he used his teeth.

And continued long after the screaming stopped.

———

The signal of her communicator pulled Eve out of a dream where she chased her killer while he danced down an empty street juggling an ear, an eye, and a tongue.

"Gross," she mumbled, then called for the lights at ten percent before she answered. "Dallas."

Dispatch, Dallas, Lieutenant Eve. Report to the Whitwood Center. See building security and officer on the door for access to Laboratory Six.

"Justin Rosenthall's area."

Affirmative. Possible homicide.

"Acknowledged. Inform Peabody, Detective Delia. Request that she meet me on scene as soon as possible. Has the victim been ID'd?"

Victim identification is not confirmed.

"I'm on my way. Dallas out."

She shoved at her hair, saw Roarke was already up, getting dressed. "Shit. Shit. You don't have to come. That's hovering, isn't it?"

"In this case it's sheer curiosity. The likelihood is it's your man, and since I'm awake now in any case, I'd like to see for myself."

It was quicker not to argue. Besides, he had an eye as good as most cops she knew. And drove faster and better.

"Inside job, what did I tell you?" She watched buildings whiz by on the way downtown. "It's one thing to break into the place on Twelfth, but it takes a lot more to get through the security they have at the Center."

At his noncommittal sound, she gave Roarke a narrowed stare. "For most people. Rosenthall's lab. He works late a lot. Shit, shit, *shit*."

She was out of the car the instant Roarke parked, flashing her badge at the NYPSD uniform and the building security officer.

"Lieutenant. Security Officer Tweed will take you to the scene. My current orders are to remain on the door."

"Has Detective Peabody arrived?"

"No, sir."

"Send her in when she gets here. She knows the way. Tweed?"

"This way."

"I know the way, too. Who found the body?"

"I did. I was doing a standard cam sweep, and I saw . . . a figure."

"Green, deformed face, red eyes, wearing a cape?"

"I wouldn't have believed it if I hadn't seen it myself."

"And you've got him on disc."

"Yeah. He was heading down from the second level, east, moving fast in a kind of—boogie. Part of me was spooked, I admit. The other part figured somebody was playing a joke. But we have to check out any unauthorized activity. By the time I got to that sector—along with the other guard I'd alerted—he was gone. I went up, saw the lights were on in Dr. Rosenthall's lab, so I keyed in, and I saw . . . The place is wrecked, Lieutenant, and there's a body. It's male, but I couldn't tell who it was. The face, it's, well, wrecked, too. And there's blood everywhere."

"Okay." She nodded to the uniform outside the lab doors. "Key me in, Tweed, then I'm going to want those discs. The originals."

"I'll take care of it."

"And stand by," she told him.

Wrecked was a mild word for it, Eve thought as she scanned the area. Smashed comps lay on the floor on a sea of broken beakers, dishes, specimen bowls. The body lay faceup—what was left of the face. Blood stained the hacked and ripped clothes, spread over the floor, left its obscene abstract art on the sides of a counter.

And on the top, in blood, his message.

Memo to: Lt. Dallas.

Nobody liked him anyway.

You're welcome!

Sincerely, Dr. Chaos.

"It's Billingsly."

"How can you be sure?"

"That's the suit he had on this morning." She took a can of

Seal-It out of her kit, used it, tossed it to Roarke. "This takes him off the suspect list."

"I doubt he'd feel grateful."

"What was he doing in here? He doesn't strike me as the type who'd come by for a late-night visit with Rosenthall, and this isn't his area. He's another floor up, in the other wing."

"He might have been lured here."

"Yeah, maybe. But it's late, way after hours. Why is he in the building, and where's Rosenthall? I need to know who keyed in before Security."

"Would you like me to see to that area?"

"Yeah, that would save time."

"His nose is gone."

"It sure is. What does that mean? Smell no evil? No, that's just stupid. To me it says nosy. You're nosy, Billingsly; now you're dead."

She turned as Peabody came in.

"Wow. Another day, another slaughter." Peabody eased out a breath. "McNab's with me. I had him start on Security. I thought maybe Roarke would be here, so we'd have two e-men on it."

"Then I'll go hook up with Ian."

"What do you see?" Eve asked Peabody when they were alone.

"I see Billingsly's off the suspect list."

Despite the circumstances, Eve smiled a little. "And?"

"He's been stabbed a whole bunch. It might even be more than Bickford, but it's hard to tell. He's missing his nose."

"What does that say to you?"

"It's another quiz. This time I want a grade. It says to me Billingsly won't be sniffing around anymore. Maybe around Arianna, maybe around something else—something lab related. The note's addressed directly to you this time, so he knows it's our case—and that Billingsly wasn't a popular guy around here."

"I'd say A minus."

"A minus?" Both insult and sulk piped through Peabody's voice. "I want A plus."

"For an A plus you'd need to observe, identify, and relate the teeth marks in the vic's face and throat."

"Teeth . . . oh jeez." Observing and identifying them now, Peabody swallowed hard. "He *ate* him."

"Just here and there. He's accelerating," Eve concluded. "This time blood wasn't enough. He wanted a taste of flesh." She scanned again, noted the open door on an empty cabinet. "Did the killer walk in on the vic, or the other way around?"

"If this is extra credit, I want a review of my earlier grade. Let me think." To help herself do that, Peabody looked away from the body. "I can't think why Billingsly would be here. He and Rosenthall aren't pals, and this isn't his area—not only sector-wise, but professionally. Maybe if Rosenthall asked him to come in—but I don't buy it. He's not going to do his competitor any favors. He'd come if Arianna asked him, but that puts her in this, and it just doesn't fit well for me."

Pausing, she made herself look at the body again. "If he came here—which, okay, obviously, he did—it was to get something on Justin, or screw with something, or poke around looking . . . Poke his nose in!"

Eve took the cloned key card and recorder out of Billingsly's pocket. Hit Play.

"Justin Rosenthall."

"Billingsly tried a little B&E," Peabody commented.

"That's an A plus."

"Yay!"

"Billingsly keys in using the dummy card and the recorder. He's poking around. The killer is already here—looking for something, doing something, waiting for something. Billingsly sees him, and that's the end of Billingsly. The killer chews on him, stabs him, amputates his nose, wrecks the lab, takes time to leave the message, then boogies out. They've got him on disc, so we'll be able to track his movements."

"That's a break."

"For us, not for Billingsly." Eve opened her field kit again, crouched by the body. "Let's verify ID, get TOD."

"If there are bite marks, they should get some saliva, and the impressions, too," Peabody began.

"We got better." Eve lifted Billingsly's lifeless hand. "We got skin under the nails. Billingsly got some flesh, too."

NINE

————▶————

Eve put on microgoggles for a better look before she bagged the hand. "Tinted green flesh, so that's our guy. We'll get DNA."

"And see if one of our main suspects shows some recent scratches."

Eve looked up as Roarke came back in. "McNab's working with Security," he told her. "Everyone in the lab logged out, Rosenthall being the last at eleven twenty-six. The log shows Rosenthall swiping in again at twelve oh-seven, but the discs show Billingsly swiping in at that time, clearly entering alone."

Eve held up an evidence bag. "Billingsly had a clone swipe and a recording of Rosenthall's voice."

"Nosy becomes very apt. No one else entered the lab after the last log-out at eleven twenty-six except Billingsly. No one exited until your Dr. Chaos at one fifteen."

"Well, he didn't just materialize."

"TOD," Peabody announced before Roarke could comment, "twelve fifty."

"That's a lot of time between when Billingsly entered and TOD. It didn't take that long to kill him. Contact the sweepers, and the ME," Eve ordered, then, avoiding blood and debris, did another long study of the room, walked over to the break room area.

"Peabody! Get us a warrant for these lockers. Six, digital locks." Looking up, she studied the open ceiling vent. "There's his access. It's big enough for a man to get through."

"Low tech," Roarke commented. "But classic."

"I need the ventilation layout. But for now . . . boost me up."

Obliging, Roarke hooked his fingers together. With her foot in the hammock of his hands, Eve bounced up, gripped the edge of the open vent. "Yeah, the grille's in here. Maybe he initially planned to go back out this way." She took a penlight out of her pocket, shined it in the skinny ventilation tunnel. "Tight squeeze. I see some scuff marks. So he logs out, comes back in somewhere else. Through the health center area, maybe the visitor's lodging, pretty much anywhere. Scoots and crawls along. Pops out, then—"

"Are you going to solve the case while I'm holding you off the floor?" Roarke wondered.

"Hmm? Sorry." She jumped down. "Pops out," she continued. "Maybe gets into his gear here. Lockers, bathroom. Sweepers could find traces of the makeup. Would he be stupid enough to leave something in a locker?"

"Shall I open them?"

"When we get a warrant."

"Stickler," he said and made her smile.

"I could claim they're part of the crime scene, which they are, so the PA could probably hold that line. But a defense attorney would make noises, so a warrant keeps it clean."

She set her hands on her hips, turned a slow circle. "Was he meeting Billingsly here? In it together, there's a disagreement, death ensues. I don't like it. This guy works alone. Billingsly got nosy, then got dead. The killer wasn't expecting company. He came in for the serum, and he got it. Billingsly's a bonus round."

"Why didn't he go out the way he came in?"

"Too hyped up from the kill to care," she concluded. "By then, leaving where he'd be caught on disc—if he thought of it—just added some fun. Look at me!"

Peabody came to the doorway. "I tagged Cher Reo," she said, speaking of the APA. "She was about to call me a very bad name, but I showed her the body."

"Good thinking," Eve told her.

"She's all over the warrant."

"Okay. When the morgue gets here, I want the skin sent to the lab asap. I want that DNA the same way. I need something for a bribe. Something really good," she told Roarke. "For Dickhead."

Chief Lab Tech Dick Berenski wouldn't drag himself to work in the middle of the night for less than a first-class bribe.

"Two tickets, skybox, first game of the World Series, with locker-room passes."

"Excellent, but we're still in play-offs."

"Wherever it is—transpo included."

"Nice. I'll start with one, let him squeeze me for the second ticket—which he will. I'll tag him on the way to Security. I want to see those discs. Peabody, wait for the morgue and the sweepers. I want that skin hand-carried to the lab. And I want to know as soon as the warrant comes through."

In Security, Eve studied the screen, the movement, the face. She ordered magnification, ordered freeze, replay.

"Gotta be a new strain of Zeus, or something like it. Along with some serious prosthetics. Nothing's quite right about him. It's almost as if his whole body's disjointed."

She magnified again to study the hands. Gloved, she noted, with long, sharp nails slicing through the tips. Then went back to the face.

"He couldn't have taken those bites out of the vic wearing that gear. So he didn't put it on until after the kill. Or he can manipulate it, because the bites had puncture marks like those pointed incisors he's got. What is his deal?"

"Totally freak show," was McNab's opinion.

Eve glanced at the e-man, and Peabody's cohab. He wore his long blond hair in a tail secured with silver rings that matched the half dozen hanging from his earlobe. His skinny frame vibrated with color from the many pocketed baggies in Day-Glo orange that picked up the zigs in his shirt.

The zags were nuclear blue.

"You're wearing that getup and talking freak show."

He grinned. "Easy to find these pants in the dark."

"It'd be easy to spot them on Mars in the night sky with the naked eye."

"They blind the bad guys," he claimed, still grinning. "Anyway, Dallas, it looks real. This guy, I mean. He looks real."

"Nothing about this guy looks real," she corrected. "I want you to take this in to EDD for a full anal."

She looked down at her com when it signaled. "Warrant's in. Let's open those lockers."

———

"You're not going to like this," Roarke said as they walked back. "But I agree with McNab."

"Yeah, I figure those pants could blind somebody if they stared at them too long."

"Something I try to avoid. I also have to agree with him that your killer doesn't look as if he's wearing a disguise."

"Because it's a combination. Disguise and some kind of powerful drug."

"How does he blink?"

That put a hitch in her stride. "What?"

"If his eyes aren't real, if he's using devices for the size, the shape, how does he blink? He looked directly at the security camera at several points, and his eyelids closed and opened. He smiled, if you can call it that. His jaw shifted, his mouth turned up. And we both saw him contort his body in impossible ways, and move at considerable speed."

He did have a damn good eye, she thought.

"If he's a scientist—and he damn well is—he's figured out how to devise something, and he's taking something that boosts his adrenaline. Monsters exist," she added. "But they're flesh and blood. They're human, just like the rest of us. It's what's inside them that's twisted. This guy isn't some Frankenstein monster."

"Actually, I was thinking of another classic. Mr. Hyde."

"You've got to lay off those old vids," she commented, and led the way to the lab.

"If you can believe a scientist can create devices and substances to disguise himself this way, why isn't it possible for that scientist to create something that causes him to *be* this way?"

"Because," she said as they approached the door, "appearing and being are different things." She paused outside the door. "Maybe—*maybe*—there's been something going on in this lab that's whacked. Something botched. And we're going to salvage Rosenthall's records and find out. But for now, we've got a killer on a spree, and none of my suspects pop out as a fucked-up science experiment."

"Maybe the more human face is the real disguise."

With that thought planted in her head, she walked into the lab.

Police business moved forward, with sweepers and the dead crew already at work. With Roarke she headed straight back to the lockers.

She thought of the destruction of the lab and the open, unbroken door of the serum lockup.

"No point in busting them open since you're here."

"None at all," Roarke agreed.

It didn't take him long. As he moved down the line of lockers uncoding the locks, she called Peabody in for the search.

And hit pay dirt in Pachai Gupta's.

Eve took out the silver pipe.

"Weighted it for extra punch. And he didn't even clean it thoroughly," Eve noted. "There's still some blood, some matter. It shows some nicks and dents where it hit bone."

"He loved her—Darnell." Peabody shook her head. "It was all over him, Dallas. Love and grief, all over him."

"He wouldn't be the first to destroy what he loved. But this is so damn stupid, so careless. Steal the serum by unlocking the cabinet rather than busting it up. Then just leave one of the murder weapons in your work locker?"

"A frame-up? It makes more sense to me," Peabody said. "I know I did the interview, and I hate thinking I missed anything, but a frame-up makes more sense."

"He's got this in the locker, but doesn't use it. Kills Billingsly, and unless he's really stupid, knows we'll search the lockers, knows we'll question the fact the serum cabinet was opened with its lock code. He's unstable, and the drug makes him more so, but he's organized. Takes care not to be seen coming in—but does murder, then shows himself."

"Because he wanted us here," Peabody concluded. "Following the bread crumbs to Gupta. No, not crumbs. Big, chunky hunks of bread."

"Reads that way. Seal it up, get the weapon taken to the lab for processing. And let's have all our players picked up, brought in."

She walked out with Roarke. "A frame-up, if that's what it is, that's human. So's screwing up and leaving evidence where it can be found, if that's what it is. Either way, with the weapon, the DNA, we'll lock it down."

"I have every faith. I'm going into the office."

"Now? It's . . ." She checked the time as they stepped outside. "It's shy of five a.m."

"Should I point out you've been working since shortly after two? I'll get my own jump on the day, and as I'm curious enough, I may come down to Central later, watch you lock it down."

"If you need the car, I could— Guess you don't," she added when a dark limo glided smoothly to the curb. "I'm going to hit the lab first, give Dickhead a push. A DNA match will save the innocent bystanders from a round in the box. Thanks for the bribe."

"Never a problem." He touched her cheek. "Take care, will you? This one gives me a very uneasy feeling."

"Too many old horror vids, and an Irish nature. I think I can handle some murderous scientist."

"Try not to punch him. You'll set the healing on that arm back."

She watched him drive away, then went back in to talk to the head sweeper and get Peabody for the trip to the lab.

———

Dick Berenski's ink black hair was slicked back over his egg-shaped head. Rather than his usual lab coat, he wore a multi-colored floral shirt that would have made even McNab wince.

"What the hell are you wearing?"

"Clothes. It's five-fucking-a.m. I'm not officially on yet. And I want a bottle of single malt scotch for the game."

"We already agreed to terms."

"That was before." He shot her a sour look, and since the last time she'd seen him he'd been scarily sweet—and in love—she assumed there was trouble in paradise.

"Before what?"

"Before I got here and found Harpo pulling an all-nighter."

"Why is that my problem?"

"She's on your hair—first murder—and you're not going to like it." He played his spider fingers over his comp. "She'll come out here."

"What about my skin?"

"She goes first. And I want that scotch."

"Fine, fine, if you give me something I can use."

"Oh, I'll give you something."

Harpo, all spiky red hair and tired eyes, walked out from her section into Berenski's. "Yo," she said to Eve and Peabody, then dropped onto a stool. "You tell her?" she asked Berenski.

"I said you'd do it."

"Yeah, yeah, okay. So," she said, swiveling to Eve. "On one hand this is totally iced. On the other, it's majorly fucked."

"What is?"

"The hair. I'm the goddess of hair and fiber, and if I can't ID it, nobody can. And I can't."

"What do you mean?"

"Sorry, I've been at this all night. I'm a little wired on Boost." She gestured with the jumbo tube in her hand before she took a gulp.

"Have you tried the new black cherry flavor?" Peabody asked her.

"Yeah, but it's got an aftertaste. I'm pretty well hooked on the Lemon Zest. It's got a nice zing."

"I like Blue Lagoon. There's something about drinking blue that feels energizing."

"Excuse me," Eve said, brutally polite. "This talk of flavors and favorites is fascinating, but maybe we could take a moment to discuss—oh, I don't know—evidence?"

"Sure," Harpo said as Peabody cleared her throat. "I got hair from your crime scene. ID'd some from each of your vics, no prob. Got some not theirs, but no roots. So no DNA for you on that, but I started a standard anal. You want to eliminate animal—like a rat, or a stray cat, whatever. And I could—I figured anyway—give you some basics. Synthetic, human, if it was treated, color, and like that. But I can't, 'cause it's not."

"Not what, Harpo?"

"It's not synthetic. That's solid. But it's not exactly human and not exactly animal. It's sort of both."

"It can't be both."

"That's right." Harpo pointed a finger tipped with a metallic purple nail. "But it is." She glanced at Berenski for permission, then used one of the comps to call up her file. "What you have here," she said, tapping that bright nail to the image, "is human hair, and this"—she split the screen with a second image—"is ape."

"If you say so."

"Science says. See, on the human hair the cuticle scales overlap smoothly. On the ape hair, they're rough—they, like, protrude. Get it?"

"Okay, yeah. So?"

"So this—" Harpo added another image. "Okay, this is from your crime scene. It clearly shows characteristics of both—rough and smooth—on one strand. What you got here, Dallas, is mutant hair. It's like somebody mated a human with an ape, and here's the hair of the result."

"Give me a break, Harpo."

"Science doesn't lie. It screws up sometimes, but it doesn't lie. I ran this through everything I've got and did the same with the other strands the sweepers sent me. Same result. About two this morning, I gave up and tagged my old man—"

"Your—"

"My father's head of forensics at Quantico. Look, Dallas, it's not like I go running to Daddy whenever I hit a snag. In fact, this is the first time ever because it's way out of orbit, and he's the best there is—anywhere."

"Okay, Harpo, okay. What was his take?"

"He's stumped, just like me. This sort of mutation shouldn't be possible. But I've got hair—five samples—that says it is."

"So, you're telling me I'm looking for an ape-man? Seriously?"

"I don't know what the hell you're looking for, is what I'm telling you. Come on, Dickie, give her yours so she stops looking at me like they let me out of the ward too early."

Berenski folded his arms. "Harpo got what she got, and I got what I got. You got green skin."

"I know that, goddamn it."

"I mean green. Not makeup, not tinted. It's green down

through the subcutaneous tissue. Your vic got some blood along with the flesh, and that's not right either."

"Green blood?" Eve asked, ready to be annoyed all over again.

"It's red enough, but it's not human. Not all the way. I get what Harpo got on the hair. A combination of human and ape. DNA's like nothing I've seen before, and I've seen it all. It is what it is," he snapped out before Eve could protest. "You've got some mutant freak running around killing people. I want some fucking coffee."

He shoved up, stomped away.

"His girlfriend dumped him a couple days ago," Harpo said. "He hasn't said it, but we figure. He's been hell to be around since. But he's right. It is what it is. My old man, he'd like to consult on this if you give him the nod."

Eve squeezed the bridge of her nose. "I'm going to get DNA from the suspects. When I do, can you match it to this?"

"Dickie's got DNA from the skin and blood the vic scraped off. He can match it if you get him the killer's. You get hair, I can match it. But it shouldn't be a problem to find some half-ape guy with green skin. Right?"

"Jesus," was all Eve could think of.

Wisely Peabody kept her thoughts to herself. She managed to be wise until they'd gotten back in the car.

"You know Harpo's solid. And Dickhead's a dickhead, but he's one of the best there is. If they both come up with the same results, and really, when you look at the killer, he's just not . . ."

"Human? Bullshit. Bullshit. And one more bullshit. They're doing some sort of weird experiments in Rosenthall's lab. Something unauthorized and twisted."

"That's what I'm saying. They created a monster—a killer ape-man monster. And now it's broken out and wreaking havoc on the city. And—"

"Don't make me slap you. It's so damn girlie."

"Not when you're on the receiving end."

"Experiments," Eve continued. "The serum. It screws up the DNA, causes severe anemia. Louise said that could cause a green cast to the skin."

"All the way down?"

"Obviously."

"But the face, Dallas."

She wanted to believe it was prosthetics, a device, some sort of elaborate mask. But . . . "I don't know, but we're going to grill Rosenthall like a trout until he clears this up. Mr. Hyde," she muttered. "Maybe that's not so far off."

"Mr. Hyde?" Peabody scooted up and over in her seat. "Oh, oh, Rosenthall created the evil Dr. Jekyll. No wait, Dr. Jekyll's the good part. Hyde's the evil one. But they're the same person. Rosenthall's Mr. Hyde!"

"D minus, and only because you got the names right. Why would Rosenthall kill Jennifer Darnell—in that manner? That personal, intimate manner? The killer wanted her, and couldn't have her."

"Back to Pachai."

"Think about it. You said he loved her—and wit statements indicate she was interested. Now maybe he moved, she decided she wasn't interested after all. But who's the odd man out in this? Who got Darnell and her friend the jobs at Slice? Gets her and her friend work, but she's more interested in Gupta. And golly, where do we find one of the murder weapons? In Gupta's locker—with blood and brain matter still on it."

"Ken Dickerson. It is a frame-up."

"Gupta's Rosenthall's assistant. Dickerson's still an intern. Gupta's caught the eye of Darnell, even though Dickerson went to his uncle and got her work—then did her another favor and got work for Vix. Gupta comes from a family of doctors, scientists, and had a leg up since his father knows Rosenthall. Dickerson had to work his way through, push for scholarships. And Gupta's still ahead of him."

"Why not kill Pachai?"

"One of the first three vics got wind of something Dickerson was up to, so they had to go. What better way to destroy Gupta than by killing the girl he loved and pinning it on him? Whatever he's on makes him feel superior, but that was already in there. It makes him feel powerful, free. It makes him happy, and more, he's found out killing makes him even happier. He destroyed the lab, took the serum. He doesn't want anyone else to have what he's got. It's all his."

"It plays, but it doesn't explain the mutations."

"So Rosenthall better," she said as she pulled into the garage at Central. "We'll take him first."

TEN

————————➤————————

As Eve headed down to Homicide, Arianna sprang up from a bench in the corridor and rushed toward her. "Lieutenant Dallas, please, can you tell me what's happening? The police came to my home this morning. They said Eton's been murdered."

"That's correct."

"God. But when? How?"

"Shortly before one this morning, in Dr. Rosenthall's lab."

"In Justin's lab? But I don't . . ."

She closed her eyes a moment. "How can this be happening? They said we needed to come here—Justin and I. They took him somewhere else, wouldn't let me stay with him. They just said I had to wait. It's been more than an hour."

"I'm sorry it's taken so long. I'm going to be talking to Dr. Rosenthall shortly."

"But what happened? My God, this is a nightmare. Eton murdered, and in Justin's lab."

"Do you know why Dr. Billingsly would have been in Dr. Rosenthall's lab at that time of night?"

"No. No. He shouldn't have been. He's not involved in Justin's work. The killer must have been after Justin. After Justin." Arianna rubbed a hand between her breasts back and forth. "He was going to work late, stay in his office again last night, but I asked him not to. I asked him to come home with me, stay with me. I wanted him with me, and I was upset enough that he gave in."

"You left the Center together?"

"Yes, about eleven thirty, I think. I had a fund-raiser, and called Justin from the car when I left."

"Did anyone stay in the lab?"

"I don't know. Justin met me out front. We were together all night. I swear it. You can't believe Justin had anything to do with this. I know people talk about Eton being jealous of him."

"Was he?"

"Yes, but Justin isn't bothered by it. We—God, it seems cruel now—we'd joke about it sometimes. Can I see him now? Do we need a lawyer?"

"He's not under arrest, but I need to ask him a few questions. If he wants a lawyer present he can have one. Peabody, why don't you take Ms. Whitwood to the lounge? She can wait there while we talk to Dr. Rosenthall. It shouldn't be long."

As long as it takes, Eve thought as she headed toward the first interview room.

Justin straightened in his chair when Eve entered.

"So it's true," he said, "about Billingsly. He's dead."

"Yes. Record on, Dallas, Lieutenant Eve, in Interview with Dr. Justin Rosenthall on the matters of Darnell, Vix, and Bickford, case number H-45893, and Eton Billingsly, case number H-43898. I have to record this. Procedure."

"I understand."

"I'm also going to read you your rights." As she did, Justin said nothing. "Do you understand your rights and obligations?"

"Yes. You think I killed them?"

She let the question hang a moment. He looked worn-out, she noted, as Arianna had.

"All the victims were connected to you and the Center. Billingsly was murdered in your lab."

"In *my* lab?"

"Yes. There are questions that have to be asked, but first, I'd like a sample of your DNA."

"My—all right, but it's on file."

"Just consider it a spot check." She took out a swab.

When it was done, she went to the door, passed it off to the waiting uniform.

She sat at the table across from Justin. "What was Billingsly doing in your lab?"

"I have no idea. He shouldn't have been there. He shouldn't have been able to get in without my authorization. How did he?"

"He cloned your swipe card and had a recording of your voice."

Justin simply stared at her. "He went that far? He disliked me—that's not news—but I can't believe he'd go as far as breaking into the lab. And for what?"

"Would he have business with your assistant or interns?"

"No, none I can think of. And he knew none of us were there. I saw him before I left, and he commented on the fact that I was actually going home."

"You didn't get along."

"Not well." Justin braced his elbows on the table, pushed his hands over his face, back into his hair. "That's no secret, as he made it very clear he didn't think I was good enough for Ari—and he was."

"That must have pissed you off."

"Some," he admitted. "But frankly, I didn't give Billingsly much thought. Arianna loves me; we're about to be married. And my work occupies the rest of my thoughts at this stage."

"What is this stage?"

"We're about to begin the next round of testing."

"Meaning?" Eve said as Peabody entered. "Peabody, Detective Delia, entering Interview. Go on, Doctor."

"We've injected a test group of lab rats with specific addictive substances over a course of time."

"You've made addicts out of rats?"

"Yes. We observe and monitor, chart, record. Now we'll inject them with the serum, run them through tests. Once we—"

"You don't test on human subjects."

"No. That's months off, maybe years. This isn't a quick process. We can't risk testing an unproven substance on a human being."

"It must be tempting to push it some, to kick up the pace."

"You don't go into research to rush."

"Do your assistants ever get antsy?"

"I'm sorry?"

"Maybe your assistants want to take it up a notch, show off some, impress you."

"They're young. Sure, there's some frustration, impatience—competition from time to time. But we have a very strict protocol, a timetable, procedures that must be followed not only for success but for safety."

"Who has access to the serum?"

"It's locked in the lab, in an environmentally controlled case. No one but myself and Pachai have access. You don't think Billingsly tried to—"

"The case was open," Eve told him. "And empty."

"Empty?" Looking stricken, Rosenthall rubbed at his temple. "The serum's gone? God. *God!* We're so close. A competing lab? Espionage? Would Billingsly have done that?"

"Your two interns can't access the serum?"

"No. Well, that's not completely accurate. Ken's worked late with me several nights, and I gave him the code. I change it every three days. I'd have changed it this morning, in fact. We can re-create the serum. But the time lost . . ." He shook his head. "But I don't understand what this has to do with the murders, with Jen and the boys. I can't believe they'd be involved in some plot to steal or sell the work."

"That's okay. I understand. Interview end. If you'd just wait here a minute. Peabody?"

"You're cutting him loose?" Peabody asked when they stepped out.

"I want you to take him to the lounge, ask him and Arianna to wait. I might need him to talk to Dickerson, interpret some of the science stuff when we get to it. Then do a round with Gupta. He may have something to add here, and he knows you now."

"Okay. You're taking Dickerson alone?"

"I'll start on him. When you think you've got all you can get from Gupta, take him to the lounge, then come in to Interview."

"Check."

"And bring Dickerson a drink."

Peabody sighed. "Because I'm good cop."

"So far." Eve walked down to the next interview room, entered.

"Dallas, Lieutenant Eve," she began and completed the documentation. "Hey, Ken, you look a little wrung out."

"I've been waiting a long time. Like two hours."

A little sweaty, Eve observed. Hollow-eyed and very pale. "These things take time." She read him his rights, watched those hollow eyes widen.

"I'm a suspect? Why are you saying all that?"

"For your protection, Ken. Just procedure. You know about procedure. Do you understand your rights, your obligations?"

"Yes, but I don't understand why—"

"Four people are dead, Ken, and you knew all of them."

"I'm not the only one who—"

"We're talking to the others. So what did you think of Billingsly?" she continued, conversationally. "An asshole, right?"

"I don't really have an opinion. I didn't know him, really."

"Take my word. Asshole. Anybody who tries to horn in on another man's woman, especially when she's not interested, is an asshole."

She smiled when she said it, watched his eyes skitter away. "I nearly forgot." She took out a swab. "I need some spit. DNA check."

"I—I don't have to do that."

"Seriously? It's just some spit, Ken."

"I don't have to do that unless you have a warrant. That's my right."

"Suit yourself." She shrugged. "Now, about assholes."

"Should I get a lawyer?"

"Do you want one? Fine with me. It'll take more time. Probably a couple more hours." She started to rise.

"It's okay, for now. I just want to get out of here."

"Can't blame you. Like I said, you look wrung out. Up late?"

"I didn't sleep well. It's hard, with what happened."

"I bet. You liked Jen."

"Everybody liked Jen."

"But you really liked her. You got her a job."

"It was no big deal."

"Come on, take some credit. An addict with barely a month's recovery under her belt before you asked your uncle to give her a break. Then you do her another solid and help her addict friend get a job. She owed you."

"I was just trying to help."

"Did she pay you back?"

"I don't know what you mean."

"I don't think she did, not when she had her eye on Pachai—and he had his on her. That must've stung."

He scratched at his arms as if something crawled along his skin. "She was just a friend."

"Because that's the way she wanted it. And Pachai, what did he do for her? He didn't get her and her addict friend jobs. His uncle didn't give her food to take home. He comes from money, though. Isn't that always the way? Gets to be Rosenthall's head guy—over you. You worked harder, I bet. Put in more hours. You're smarter—I can tell. You've got ideas, don't you, Ken? Ideas about the serum."

She leaned forward. No visible scratches, she thought. But he'd left his hair down, over the back of his neck.

"I bet you put in lots of your own time on that project. Off the books, so to speak. Busting your ass. Rosenthall's so conservative, such a stickler for protocol, procedure. But you've got balls. You're willing to take some risks. Did Jen find out you were taking one?"

He kept scratching, swallowing, looking anywhere but at Eve. "I don't know what you're talking about."

"She came in the lab a lot, didn't she? Making excuses to drop in so she could see Pachai. Flirted with him right in front of you. Did she come by when you were working alone one night? Off the books. Did you let her in?"

"We're not allowed to work in the lab off hours unless Dr. Rosenthall's there."

"Rules." Eve waved them away. "Real innovation says screw the rules. Real progress is risky, takes gambles. And Rosenthall's poking along with his yes-man Gupta getting all the attention—and the girl. It's not right. But you can show them you're better, smarter. Did she catch you at it, or did you tell her? Had to brag about it. But she still didn't want you. In fact, she threatened to tell on you if you didn't stop. To tell Rosenthall you were experimenting with his work, testing it, and not on rats."

He began to shiver now, as if cold even while the sweat dribbled down his temples. "You're making all this up."

"Am I? Scientists keep records. We're going to get a search warrant for your apartment, and we're going to find yours. We're going to find the pipe you used to beat Coby Vix to death with. Then—"

"You can't find the pipe at my place because . . ."

"Why is that, Ken?"

"I'm not talking anymore."

"Suit yourself." Eve sat back, watched him sweat a few moments until Peabody came in with a tube of ginger ale.

"Peabody, Detective Delia, entering Interview. He could use that. Have a drink, Ken, take a little time to think. The way I look at it, things just got out of hand, out of your control. You had a really bad reaction to the serum."

"I'm not saying anything else." But he took the tube, cracked it, guzzled.

And when she came back in, Eve thought, she'd take the tube—and have his DNA.

"Think about it," Eve suggested. "Interview pause. Dallas, Lieutenant Eve, and Peabody, Detective Delia, exiting the room."

"He looks sweaty, shaky," Peabody began outside the door. "He looks like—"

"An addict jonesing for a fix. He's scared, too. He's either going to crack or lawyer up—that could go either way. Let's get a search warrant for his apartment. We've got enough for that. He's got logs and records. That stupid cape, the gloves, the shoes, maybe the knife and scalpel."

"Maybe we should have Rosenthall observe the next round. Like you said, if he gets into the science, Rosenthall could tell us what it means."

"Good idea. Go get him, take him to an observation room. I'm going to give Dickerson another couple minutes."

She could use a drink herself, Eve thought, and gave Vending a hard eye. The machines didn't always cooperate with her.

"Let me do that." Roarke plugged in credits, ordered her a tube of Pepsi.

"Thanks. Come to watch the show?"

"It's usually worth the price of admission."

"I've got Dickerson sweating in the box. Literally. I think he's been taking the serum—or a version of it. And I think he dosed himself real good two nights in a row. It's got him strung out. I'm about to go in for the second round. Peabody's bringing Rosenthall into Observation, in case we need an interpreter for the science."

"I'll go find them."

He gave her a tap on the chin, then strolled off—as at home in the cop shop as she was, she thought.

She cracked the tube, took a long drink, then walked back to the interview room. When she stepped in, Dickerson was standing in the far corner, facing the wall. His shoulders shook.

"Dallas, Lieutenant Eve, reentering Interview. Jesus, Ken, man up."

"That's Dr. Chaos to you."

She arched her eyebrows at the rough sound of his voice. "Now we're getting somewhere. Have a seat, Doc, and we'll—"

He turned. She'd thought little could genuinely surprise her at this stage of her life and career, but she froze in shock.

His face rippled in front of her eyes. Sickly green, it twisted itself until the jaw locked at a grotesque angle. His teeth sharpened; his eyes protruded and bulged in their sockets, and began to gleam red.

"And I'm not a man."

She heard the snap and crack of migrating bones as his spine seemed to warp. "I'm a god."

She pulled her weapon. "What you are is under arrest."

He leaped at her. She got a stream off, was sure she struck midbody, but he was so *fast*. She had a fraction of a second to prepare, and used the force of his body ramming hers to go down, kick up, and send him flying over her and into the wall.

He careened off, bloodied, and nimble as a spider. This time when she fired, he jerked. Then he smiled.

"Oooh, it tickles! I'm so much stronger now."

"So I see. But not pretty. You're smart." He would attack again, she thought. There was too much animal in him not to. "You're in the middle of Cop Central. Even if you get through me, you won't get out. You'll die here."

"I can't die. But you can. You're an insect to me. All of you. Weak and breakable."

"He's still in you. The weak and breakable Dickerson."

"Not for much longer. He cried over the girl, but he enjoyed killing Billingsly. He'll enjoy killing you. We're going to carve out your heart, and eat it."

She fired again, kept firing. It slowed him, caused him to stumble, but he came on.

The door burst open. Roarke rushed in, steps ahead of Peabody and a swarm of cops. Chaos whirled, snarled—jittered from the stun streams.

"Go down, you fuck!" Eve shouted.

"Allow me." Face cold and fierce, Roarke rammed his fists into the twisted face. Right, left, right again.

Blood streaming, body spasming, Chaos went down.

"Jesus Christ, Jesus Christ, Jesus Christ." Eve muttered the oaths—prayers—as she snapped on restraints. "I want leg irons," she called out. "Now. Peabody, keep your weapon on him."

"Believe me," her partner responded.

"I want him shackled, in a cage, before he comes to. Isolation. Let's move!"

"Are you hurt?" Roarke gripped her hand as she rose.

"No. I've got to get him contained. I'll be back. And hey, thanks for the assist," she added as she moved aside to let some of the men lift Chaos.

Roarke watched her go, then glanced down at his raw knuckles. "Ah, well."

EPILOGUE

Eve found him waiting in her office, settled in her ratty visitor's chair with his PPC. He set it aside when she came in, and with one look at her face, went to the AutoChef, programmed coffee for both of them.

"He's dying." Eve dropped down at her desk. "Multiple organ failure—Louise had that one. And he's got a brain tumor for good measure. They're not going to be able to save him."

"I'm trying to be sorry, as you seem to be."

"He was an idiot—Dickerson. Jealous, ambitious, reckless. But he wasn't a murderer. Or not until he started taking the serum. His version of it. He'd improved it, so he thought. He was going to impress the girl, his boss, the whole fucking world. Now he's dying because he unleashed something in himself that perverted what he was, what he wanted. Something he couldn't control."

Roarke sat on the corner of her desk, facing her. "He would have killed you."

"Yeah. What he became was as addicted to killing as Dickerson was to the serum. As the people Rosenthall's trying to help are to the illegals. Rosenthall's with him now—pretty much crushed. Dickerson's barely able to talk, but we got all we need to close the cases."

"It's never just about closed cases for you."

"Four people slaughtered. And now we'll have five bodies. Dickerson was dead the first time he took the serum. He just didn't know it. He asked Darnell to come into the lab. He was so proud, had to show off. Had to hope she'd see how special he was, and want him the way he wanted her. Instead, she disapproved, told him he had to go to Rosenthall, had to stop."

"She would have recognized the addiction," Roarke concluded.

"Yeah, I'd say. She was black-and-white on it. If he didn't tell his boss, she would, because he was making himself sick, she said."

"And that only made him take more."

"He promised he'd do what she said, then increased the dose. To prove to her he was better than Pachai, better even than Rosenthall."

"And Chaos was born."

"I guess that's true enough. He says he thought the murders were a dream, a hallucination."

"You don't believe that."

"No," she confirmed. "I don't. He knew what he'd done. He just couldn't face it on one side, couldn't give it up on the other. Dickerson told us Billingsly was trying to hack into Rosenthall's computer when he got to the lab."

"Jealousy again."

"The green-skinned monster."

Roarke started to correct her, then shrugged. "Well, in this case."

"And this case is closed." She finished off her coffee, set it and the sadness aside. "I need to write it up, and I promised Nadine I'd give her a head start. I don't know why."

"Friendship, and because you know she'll be fair and accurate. I'll leave you to it then, find myself a spot to finish a bit of business. Tag me when you're done. We missed breakfast altogether. I'll take you to lunch—whenever."

"I can grab something. You don't have to wait around."

"Eve." He touched the shaggy tips of her hair. "I'd just stepped into Observation when he turned around. I saw what he was, or what he was becoming. We never quite see everything there is, do we? What I did see was the delight—the

murderous delight on his face. I didn't know if I'd get there,
get to you, in time."

"I'd stunned the shit out of him," she began. "And yeah, he
might've gotten a piece of me anyway. You finished him off
real nice."

"Well then, you'd loosened the lid. I'll wait for you." He
leaned forward, touched his lips to hers. "Always."

"Sap."

"Guilty. And when we get home tonight, we'll take care of
that arm."

"I know what *that* means."

He laughed, kissed her again. "You've had it cradled since
you sat down."

She glanced down, saw he was right. "I guess it took a knock
in there." She released it, took his hand to examine his knuckles. "You, too."

"Then we'll take care of each other."

"Sounds good."

And it did, she thought, when he'd left her to find his quiet
spot. Before the work, she rose, walked to her skinny window.
She looked out at New York—safe, for the moment, from one
of the monsters who hunted.

And stood awhile, holding vigil for the dying.

HER GREATEST TREASURE

MARY BLAYNEY

For Mary Kay, Nora, Pat, and Ruth

PROLOGUE

For nine months the nightmare plagued her, not coming every night but ruining her sleep when it did. The dream left her in tears and reminded her, quite needlessly, that Alexei would never come home again.

Without Alexei beside her, Lydia lived a quiet life. The quiet was a comfort, relieving, if only a little, the heartache of losing him.

A loving, passionate man, Alexei Chernov had a selfish streak that even his mother could not deny. Alexei's charm delighted men and women both. But his obsession with secrecy bothered Lydia the most. Secrets, endless secrets. Even in the nightmare, he still kept a secret.

He came to her, in his last moments.

The sea, an angry monster, churned around him, turning the ship into random pieces of wood and canvas. Alexei's eyes welled with tears of despair as he fought against the torn sails that smothered him, the ropes binding his legs, dragging him down, down, down.

Lydia felt the unquiet of his soul, the grief that seized his heart. "Wish!" he called to her. Not "Help me!" or "Save me!" but "Wish! Wish! Wish!" The word repeated over and over until the sea filled his mouth and all she could hear was the death rattle of water filling his lungs. She woke with the image of life fading from his eyes.

The dream came at first light, so Lydia rose to face the day. While she waited for the maid to come start the fire and lace her stays, Lydia sat at the window, saying the morning prayers that gave her some measure of comfort. Always for Alexei first. Then for his dear mother. And finally a plea for understanding of Alexei's message: *Wish.*

She could imagine a hundred things Alexei would wish for. That he had taken a different ship at the very least. But the more she thought about his plea, the more convinced she became that "Wish" was a message for her. One she would have to decipher, like all the rest of his secrets, hers now to keep or expose.

She held on to the chain and the coin he had given her, his last gift. "Wear this for me. It will be your greatest treasure." he'd said as he put it around her neck. Now she would wear it always, not because Alexei had given it to her, but as a reminder that her most valued possession could not be worn or its worth measured in pounds or pence.

ONE

Lydia Chernov put on her cloak and gathered her things so she could hurry out to the hackney as soon as it drew to a halt in front of her shop door. Chernov Drapers might be on the best street of shops in Birmingham, but at dusk and beyond, one could not be too careful.

Carriage wheels rattled across the stones and slowed to a stop at her door. Lydia pulled her cloak tight around her, doing her best to control the hum of excitement that made her heart beat faster. Tonight's meeting could change everything.

Lydia glanced to the left and right as she locked the shop door behind her. The fog hung just above the rooftops, turning to rain as it came closer to earth, inviting shadows or worse.

With her umbrella and bags in hand, Lydia hurried to the conveyance. After calling the direction to Mr. Leopold, she settled back and calmed herself. She felt safe in the hackney, and in fifteen minutes she would be seated with Irina and her husband, sipping tea and discussing business.

Mentally running through her list of items—umbrella, satchel with periodicals, trim kit, and reticule—Lydia turned her mind to business and rehearsed her speech, hoping to sound both businesslike and optimistic. Yes, Irina Allerton was Alexei's sister, but Mr. Allerton was a mill owner first and last, and family would mean nothing if he thought the offer unsound.

The fact that a woman now ran Chernov Drapers was offset by the recipe for purple dye, definitely the Chernov's greatest asset. That Grandmama would allow Mr. Allerton the use of it in exchange for his exclusive business would, Lydia had no doubt, tip the balance entirely in her favor.

The purple the Chernovs produced was perfection. This purple was the truest color of royalty, of wealth. The color every woman who aspired to be fashionable wanted. The fabrics colored from royal to lavender were expensive to make and even more dear to purchase. Allowing Allerton the use of the dye recipe would expand its availability and make them both wealthy.

Of course, Mr. Allerton was already wealthy, and she was not much more than modestly successful. True wealth for her was years away. But she would allow the exaggeration. Of all people, Mr. Allerton understood the usefulness of hyperbole.

Fully prepared, Lydia sat back and closed her eyes.

Wish.

The word whispered through the carriage and she grabbed at the coin on a chain around her neck, shock if not fear making her sit bolt upright.

Wish.

There it came again. It was not a spoken word, certainly not Alexei or his ghost. It was the sound of the wheels on the wet road. She listened for it again, but the only sound she heard now was the light patter of rain. Her heartbeat slowed and she drew a steadying breath, but did not close her eyes again.

When the hackney rocked over some loose stones, Lydia realized that Mr. Leopold was moving the horses more quickly than usual. As she raised her umbrella to knock on the roof, the conveyance skidded to a halt. Before she could lean out and question Mr. Leopold, the street-side door swung open.

Cold, wet air was not the only intrusion. A man jumped aboard. At the same moment, the hackney began moving again.

I should never have come out without a maid, was Lydia's first thought. *Or a pistol.*

She had faced bigger threats than one strange man in her

conveyance, but still her brain conjured a dozen horrors. The ghastly images of her own body broken, bleeding, or worse made her stomach churn, but she pushed beyond terror to action. Thank God her fear did not paralyze her. She touched her necklace again, as if it could comfort her, and spoke with as strong a voice as she could muster.

"Who are you? What on earth are you doing?" Terror hid behind her indignation. Holding tight to her umbrella, she made ready to use it as a weapon.

"Mr. Leopold!" she called. "Do you have your pistol?" She had no idea if he carried one or not but hoped the question would give the intruder second thoughts.

The man, a very large man, laughed and settled on the opposite seat, his feet raised and propped against one door, leaning his body against the other so she could not reach either handle. "Leopold is counting his bribe money and heading for the nearest whorehouse. My man is driving." The intruder smiled with smug complaisance, still blocking the doors with his shoulders and feet.

"What do you want?" If he wanted money or her supplies, she would willingly abandon them to him.

"The Russian wants what you have."

"What does that mean? I don't know any Russians."

"But you do. Alexei Chernov."

Her heart rose to her throat. "Mr. Chernov is dead."

The man shrugged, and the careless gesture frightened Lydia more than his words.

Lydia caught her breath. This was not a random abduction. This man wanted her. Or something of Alexei's. Alexei had died, yes, but even with him dead, a line of those who wanted something from him would wind around the block. She'd had enough proof of that this last year. "What is it you want?" she asked again.

"Your most valued possession."

Her necklace? She forced herself not to touch the chain around her neck, hoping it was not visible. No, not her necklace. It only had value to her and Alexei.

He wanted the recipe for the purple dye. The recipe belonged to Grandmama, a family heirloom, really.

Despite her growing anxiety, Lydia's mind worked as fast

as the machine at the new cotton mill. She would not take this horrible man back to the shop to search for the recipe, not with Grandmama and the maid upstairs.

"Yes, I can see you know what I want. Hand it over or I will take it from you, wherever you hide it."

The man took out a large knife and pretended he needed to clean his fingernails.

His crude threat upset her, but her whole body chilled at the sight of the nasty blade. Lydia choked back the scream that clogged her throat, all pretense of calm gone in an instant.

Holding her umbrella by the tip, she used the curled handle to hit him where the inseams met. The man bent double, cursing, and Lydia grabbed the moment to fling open the door and leap from the hackney, dragging her bags with her.

Stumbling on the wet cobblestones, Lydia twisted her ankle and cursed a little herself. Ignoring the pain and without the slightest idea of where she should go, she ran toward the noise coming from the one lighted building glimmering through the fog.

When she was within a few yards of safety, a man stepped out of the shadows.

She barreled into him, the feel of the fine wool of his greatcoat announcing his wealth to her as surely as a ring would have to a jeweler.

No gentleman should be walking these mean streets. With no time to ask and fearing that he might be part of the threat, Lydia raised the satchel holding the periodicals with strength born of desperation and clunked him on the head before his words registered.

"Do you need help, miss?" He then made a sound between an *oof* and *ow*.

Lydia stopped short. "Oh, I'm so sorry."

"What in the world did you hit me with?" He stepped back and looked about for his hat but showed no sign of abandoning her. Finding his hat, he brushed it off, acting very much the gentleman, seemingly unaware of the scoundrel from the hackney hurtling down the street toward them. "I offer help, miss, not harm."

The clothes of a gentleman and the voice of one as well, Lydia thought, her panic easing a bit.

With his hat firmly on his head, the man from the shadows waited until she nodded her understanding, then stood between her and her abductor, easing her anxiety enough so she could breathe again. In an instant the gentleman raised his walking stick as if it was a weapon to be respected. "Begone, you villainous thug. Leave this woman alone."

Even though dread still had a hold, Lydia almost laughed. Her rescuer's words could have come straight out of a Minerva Press novel.

The thug hesitated only slightly. "Leave us be. She's my wife and trying to run off with her lover."

"I am not his wife!" Lydia hoped she did not have to say that for the gentleman to recognize it for the truth. Her abductor was a disgusting example of a man, and she pitied the woman who might be married to him.

"Your wife? No, she is not. A lady would never even be seen with a pig like you."

The ruffian lurched forward without a moment's pause, knife at the ready. Her rescuer stepped toward him, disarming him so quickly that Lydia could not see how he did it. As the knife skittered across the cobblestones, her rescuer punched the man in his ample stomach and then in his jaw. The pig fell to the ground with a graceless *thump*.

With his foot on the man's chest, the gentleman drew a fine sword from the sheath of his walking stick and held it to the villain's throat.

"I would kill you and relieve the world of one more venomous pig, but it would most likely upset the lady."

The gentleman stepped back, his sword still at the ready, while the man struggled up from the street. He moved out of range of the sword and then seemed to regain his courage.

"You'll pay for this!" The vitriol in his voice made payment sound life-threatening.

"Ah, but first you will have to find me." He raised his sword toward his head in a sort of salute.

"I will, and after I take care of you, I'll make that bitch Mrs. Chernov pay as well."

The gentleman leaned closer and nicked the fat of the pig's arm with the sword. "If you so much as come near her again, I will beat you to a pulp before a cheering throng and leave you for the dogs. I know my way around Birmingham and can find the likes of you, Nesbitt, without a moment's trouble."

Though he looked surprised at the mention of his name, the man called Nesbitt ignored the blood dribbling down his shirt-sleeve and stood his ground. Lydia herself prepared to run.

"Begone!" her rescuer shouted again, causing both Lydia and Nesbitt to jump.

"I'll find you. I'll bring a mob and make you pay! Both of you!" Nesbitt said as he backed away.

"Empty threat, Nesbitt. Even your driver won't help you." He nodded toward the hackney, where the driver waited, still seated, watching the action not fifty feet away.

"Damn you both to hell!" Nesbitt called out as he stumbled backward and away from them. The hackney rumbled away with the same air of defeat as its passenger.

Lydia's rescuer wiped his sword and sheathed it in one easy move, then turned to her and bowed. "For you, the rain has stopped." He gestured to the generous heavens. "I beg your pardon for his offensive language, Mrs. Chernov, and for the violence."

"Who are you, and what are you doing here?" It was the first of at least five questions to which she wanted answers.

"Help when you needed it."

"Obviously." She straightened and stood as tall as she could. "But I would have made good my escape."

"I'm sure you would, but these streets are not safe for any lady out alone, especially at night."

As if he were the innocent he pretended. Exactly what was he doing here? She forbore to ask. "How did you know that man's name?"

"The man is tall with a girth to match and much too ready to use his knife. They call him Nesbitt the Butcher. Not many like that in Birmingham. It was an educated guess."

"Nesbitt the Butcher?" The name made Lydia feel weak in the knees.

The gentleman took her by the arm. "Now, now, you have bested the villain. A heroine does not faint, but calls for champagne."

"Perhaps in your world, sir." Lydia laughed. Profound relief and genuine amusement mixed. "Who *are* you?"

"A gentleman come to your aid. Names are not necessary."

"Then you have the advantage of me."

He smiled and his face went from dangerous to delightful. "You don't believe that any more than I do. Ladies always have the advantage."

Lydia hefted her sample bag and used the voice that always cowed her servants. "If you are flirting, sir, you have picked a miserable time and place."

"If I am a flirt, then you are an original, Mrs. Chernov."

His smile grew to a grin, at her expense she was sure.

"From your name, to your vicious weapon disguised as a bag and your presence in this neighborhood at this hour, you are very much an original. You can call me Chase."

Before she could decide how to answer, he continued, with a slight bow. "Tell me where you are bound, madame, and I will see you there safely."

No! she almost shouted. The last thing she needed was to show up at the Allertons' with a man to whom she was not married. Irina and her husband were too much pretenders to society to tolerate anything less than proper.

"I can guess if you won't tell me," Mr. Chase teased. "You are off to see a customer, a lady, someone you call on in the evening because you would also like to see her husband."

Lydia almost dropped her satchel. How could he know that?

"We are within a short walk of one of the better neighborhoods in Birmingham, which I assume is your direction, but I do think that a carriage would be far more comfortable."

As if by magic, a covered conveyance rolled to a halt behind him.

"Thank you." Lydia summoned all the dignity she could. One of them had to. "I will not be keeping my appointment. I will go directly back to my shop. I do not need or want an escort."

"You are not worried that Nesbitt will be lying in wait?"

Oh dear, the thought had not even occurred to her. "Are you trying to frighten me?" He was succeeding.

"Not at all, merely trying to keep you safe." He smiled, but it definitely did not reassure her. It was the kind of smile that invited her to a private party, one that would be more fun than anything she could imagine.

"I *will* see you safely home," he said without apology.

So Mr. Chase had some of the bully in his makeup, too. "If you wish to see to my safety, then ride atop with the driver. I have my reputation to consider."

"No one is about tonight, madame. Your reputation is as safe as you want it to be."

Mr. Chase opened the carriage door, offering his hand to help her inside as she called the direction to the driver.

She wore gloves. He did not. He squeezed her hand a little, and the heat of his fingers traveled and warmed parts of her that had been stone cold for much too long.

Lydia missed the carriage step and almost fell. Mr. Chase caught her by the waist, steadied her, and made to lift her into the conveyance.

Shaking her head, she moved into the carriage and out of his grasp. She did not want him any closer.

"Good-bye, sir."

"Not quite yet, Mrs. Chernov."

She ignored him and knocked on the roof for the hackney to move on. Mr. Chase stepped up and into the hackney and took a seat beside her. She ignored the feel of him close, the scent he favored, which was something as fresh as mint but much more alluring.

No one knew better than she did that station and place in life meant nothing when it came to one body responding to another. It did not matter that she was a shopkeeper and he was quite obviously a gentleman, though also something of a rogue or even a rake.

She did not need the complication of a man like Mr. Chase in her life or, God help her, in her bed. In a few moments she would say good-bye and mean it.

TWO

----◆----

Lydia would not give in to the confusion roiling through her. Holding the edge of the window so tightly her fingers grew numb, she ignored the man beside her and watched for any sign of her attacker.

Mr. Chase spoke the truth. Despite her rescuer's threats, Nesbitt would not give up that easily. He might well try again now, when she was shaken and, beneath her bravado, terrified.

"The streets are empty. Except for that man over there and the doxy in the doorway. Do you see her?" Mr. Chase leaned closer to point out the window.

"Do be quiet," Lydia snapped.

"As you wish," Chase answered and fell silent.

Which made him no easier to ignore. How could she have forgotten how this felt—this attraction that made no sense at all? She knew little more than his name.

"Mrs. Chernov, do you have any idea why Nesbitt would have singled you out? How would he know that you would be out this evening? Was it common knowledge?"

Perhaps conversation *was* the best way to pass the time. "No, I did not announce it to my customers, but I did not keep it a secret either. Mr. Allerton is married to my husband's sister, but for all that, I planned to discuss business."

"And why is your husband not with you? On a buying trip perhaps?"

"Mr. Chernov died a year ago." Should she have lied to discourage him? That would be foolish. Alexei's death was common knowledge.

"I'm so sorry, Mrs. Chernov. What a devastating loss." He watched her as he spoke; she could feel his eyes on her. Lydia nodded. *Devastating? Yes, in so many ways.* But she would not discuss it with a stranger.

"I must have something he wants, but I cannot puzzle out what it could be." She shook her head thoughtfully. "When I asked what he wanted, he said, 'Your most valued possession.'"

"And what is that?"

Lydia touched the necklace. "What I value most is a gift from Mr. Chernov, and it has no monetary worth." That was vague enough to leave him guessing. For all of a second she debated telling Mr. Chase about the purple dye recipe, but a gentleman of his station would never understand its value.

Lydia turned to face him, which proved unwise. He was very close in the narrow hackney. He was so near she could see the fine lines around his eyes, the bold shape of his brow, the fullness of his mouth. She cleared her throat and tried to recall her train of thought.

"Are any of your husband's associates suspect?"

How gently he phrased that question. "Without a doubt. I have spent the last year clearing my life of Alexei's morass of business dealings." *Not all of them legal.*

"Aha, and were they all above the law?"

She stared at him, suspecting him of reading her mind. "Are you implying that I am dishonest?"

"Not you, Mrs. Chernov, but perhaps your husband put profit before honesty. That could certainly come back to haunt you after his death."

Lydia thought of her dreams and the one word: *Wish.* Haunting indeed. "Alexei's life was a muddle of science and business and gaming."

"Gaming?" Mr. Chase straightened as if she had just spoken a magic word.

"Yes, he played cards and roulette but never to excess." She paused and then added with too much honesty, "Or at least, never to excess that I knew of."

As the conveyance slowed, Mr. Chase patted her hand, a rather fatherly gesture for a flirt but it brought some comfort.

"For the moment, we need only keep you safe for the rest of the night. In the morning I will have some answers."

"You will? This is not your problem, Mr. Chase." Though, in truth, Lydia had no idea how she would investigate Nesbitt. The Butcher.

When the carriage stopped, Lydia made to open the door, but Mr. Chase stayed her with his hand. "This is the most dangerous moment. From here to your door. Wait."

Fear, which had been like a banked fire, burst alive again. Mr. Chase climbed out, looked up and down the street, walked over to the alley between her shop and Mr. Florencio's bakery shop next door. A minute later he came back whistling and opened the hackney door.

"How can you whistle when you should be afraid for your life?" As grateful as she was for his concern, she could not control her annoyance.

"Hardly afraid for our lives, Mrs. Chernov. The man is a bully but not a murderer."

"But you called him Nesbitt the Butcher."

"That's how he earns his living. He slaughters animals with the occasional foray into something less than legal. But not murder. Never that I have heard."

"And why would a gentleman like you have heard?"

"I may be a gentleman but I do make occasional visits into the less savory parts of Birmingham." He bowed to her and offered her his hand to help her down from the conveyance. "Not that I ever actually do anything illegal."

With a sigh, Lydia marveled at her ability to be attracted to men who felt the law was a convenience to be disregarded when one wished. Ignoring him as best she could, Lydia asked the driver to wait while she wrote a note. He nodded with a gap-toothed smile.

She unlocked the shop door, stepped in, lit a candle, and composed a hasty note to the Allertons. She came back onto the street to hand it to the driver, along with payment and a generous tip.

All the while, Mr. Chase watched her so intently that Lydia patted her neckline to be sure her shawl was in place, the chain still fast around her neck.

As the hackney moved away, without Mr. Chase, Lydia noted, he continued to scan the area with her at his back. Nothing filled the street but the ground fog, and Lydia finally relaxed enough to draw a deep breath.

He turned to face her as she stepped back into the shop. "Mrs. Chernov, what will you do if Nesbitt tries again?"

"If Nesbitt does come back I will deal with him. Bullies do not intimidate me."

"Even bullies with a knife?"

"Stop trying to frighten me," she said sharply, to hide her anxiety. "I have a pistol and I know how to use it. Nesbitt will find that out for himself if he causes any more trouble." She would not look away from him.

"Yes, I see that you mean for me to understand the same warning." He stepped back and bowed. "I will have someone watching the shop tonight. I assume you live upstairs."

She pursed her lips and nodded.

"He will be wearing a white scarf around his neck so you will know he is my man. He is not afraid of bullies either."

"That is entirely unnecessary, Mr. Chase."

"Even so, I will not leave a task half-done. Consider it my duty as your knight rescuer."

Frowning, she inclined her head. "If you cannot be dissuaded, I thank you. Now, good-bye, sir." Lydia tried for a firm and final farewell. Of course, that had not worked the first time. She began to close the door, but he stopped it with a hand on the frame.

"You asked before if I was flirting. If you have to ask, then it has been much too long since anyone told you how beautiful you are." His voice was low and inviting, his eyes so filled with good humor that she wanted to grab him and turn away at the same time.

Lydia opted to turn away, closing the door quickly, not caring if the abrupt move pinched his fingers.

After double-checking the locks with hands that were not quite steady, she walked into the back room, closing the door behind her. Only with that barrier between them did she finally let her guard down and lean her forehead against the door.

Without his smile as a distraction, a dozen questions assailed her. What would have happened if Mr. Chase had not been there? What did Nesbitt want? Would he try again? What did they think she valued most? Why? Why? Why?

Lydia steadied herself with routine, unpacking her valise and putting everything where it belonged. She stopped the familiar moves as a new thought struck. It made her feel quite ill. What if Mr. Chase was part of the plan? What if he was the one who wanted her "most valued possession"?

Warming to the subject, Lydia recalled that he had *told* her that he was familiar with things illegal. Of course, that kind of statement would arouse suspicion, and if he was guilty, he would never want to do that.

And he was so clearly English and not Russian, and Nesbitt had said, "The *Russian* wants what you have."

Her head ached. It was too much to think about tonight. Especially when she knew what was waiting upstairs. She hurried through the last of her routine, and as she hung the valise on its hook, a voice echoed down the stairs.

"Lydia, is that you?" Natalia's heavy accent made the words sound foreign.

"Yes, and if it was not, Grandmama, what would you do?" Lydia called up. She wanted to avoid explanations until she had sorted some out for herself.

"I would send Delphie down the back stairs for Mr. Florencio, then pretend I am old and frail, and when the thief came after me, I would beat him with a stick and then stab him with my knitting needles."

Pretend she was old and frail? Not to mention blind. Lydia laughed a little. "Babushka, I am happy to know that you are so well prepared."

"There, that's better than the upset I heard before. Come up and tell me why you have come home so distraught. What went wrong?"

The woman was a mind reader. But then, Lydia realized, she was back much earlier than she had told Grandmama to expect her.

"Do you need Delphie to come help you?"

"No, no, Grandmama. I'm perfectly fine. I'm coming up. I'm coming."

Lydia went upstairs, kissed Natalia Chernov on both cheeks as was their custom, and then locked the door of the flat behind her.

"Why are you locking the door up here? I have never heard you do that before." Natalia's concern was now suspicion.

"Give me your arm," Lydia said, resigned to telling the truth. "Let me help you back to your room and I will tell you."

The old woman leaned on her, more heavily than usual, and Lydia hoped that she was not taking a turn for the worse. Her coughing spasms had eased, but flesh still hung on her frame. No matter how many delicacies Lydia urged her to eat, Natalia Chernov did not seem to be gaining her weight back since her last cold.

Natalia insisted on taking the chair where she spent most of her waking hours. The carefully ordered knitting and fabric samples were within reach, and the old lady lifted a piece of fine purple cotton and began stroking it with her fingers.

The maid waited, as she always did, until told exactly what to do. "Bring us the vodka and two glasses, Delphie."

The maid's eyes widened but she left the room promptly and came back in a flash with two glasses and the decanter.

"Delphie, go to bed. I'll wake you when I need to undress."

"No, Lydia. She will only listen at the door."

Delphie smiled at the old lady and sat on the stool at the foot of her chair.

"Then you will keep this to yourself," Lydia commanded the maid with as hard a look as she could summon. "You will tell no one tomorrow or the day after that. Never."

Delphie stopped smiling and nodded several times, her eyes showing some fear.

"Tell us what happened," Grandmama invited, as if this were a fairy tale.

Drawing a deep breath, she made one valiant effort to steady her voice. "A man accosted me tonight right after I left to see Irina and Mr. Allerton."

Grandmama nodded and Delphie gasped.

"He told me . . ." She reached out and took the old lady's hand. "That he wanted my 'most valued possession.'"

"The recipe." The old lady nodded again, certain she was right.

"Do you think so?" It was not what had come to her mind first, but the recipe for the purple dye was truly their most valuable possession.

Natalia pulled her hand away and waved for Delphie to pass her the vodka. She downed it in one toss of the glass and handed it back to the maid.

Lydia sighed. "I have no idea what game he was playing."

"You escaped." It was a statement. "Lydia, you should have waited to hear what *he* considered so valuable."

Lydia shook her head. "Yes, I suppose so, but, Grandmama, that is asking too much. He frightened me. We have been so safe here, so conventional and content this last year." She raised the old lady's hand and kissed it. "What could Alexei's enemies want from us now?"

"Not enemies, Lydia. Not enemies. Alexei had no enemies. Just friends who were as devious as he was. Some more. Some less."

Lydia looked down at her own hands, smoothing the skin, rubbing the spot where a wedding ring should be.

Now the old lady found her hand, patted it, and kept holding. "He cared for you. He loved you."

How many times had Alexei's grandmother assured her of that?

"I do believe it was your English reserve that fascinated him. Such a contrast to his capricious ways. He loved the way you spoke Russian, and we both know the way he spoke French was seduction in itself."

She let go of Lydia's hand and sat back in her chair, feeling for her lap robe. "Most of all, he trusted you in a way that he never, ever trusted anyone else. That is a kind of love no one else ever knew from him."

Lydia nodded, tears too close for her to speak. Maybe it was true. Maybe he had seduced her because he loved her, but in the end he had used her just as he used everyone else.

"Who could know that Alexei's luck would run out?" Natalia echoed Lydia's own thoughts. "That his ship would sink and he would sink with it." She was silent a moment and then rallied. "Tell me how you escaped."

Lydia recounted the scene, and Natalia's eyes lit with excitement. She was so entertained by the tale that Lydia added every detail she could recall.

Natalia grinned despite her bad teeth. "There is something so intriguing about a man who carries a sword stick. The hint of danger beneath the civility, I think."

"Sword or not," Lydia said as she finished, "I think I could have made good an escape on my own."

"I think it was a timely appearance," Natalia insisted. "But what was a gentleman doing on the streets in that part of the city?"

"I have no idea and do not wish to know." She bit her lip on the lie.

"What did you tell Irina and her husband?"

"That the weather made a night visit ill-advised."

"Irina is Alexei's sister, Lydia. And my granddaughter," she added. "She will see through that and be here when you open tomorrow to insist on the whole true story."

"Yes, Grandmama, I expect so." What Natalia said was too true, and now Lydia knew she would have to concoct some version of the truth for Irina. But that was hardly her biggest concern.

"Why would someone try to steal the recipe, Grandmama? It would be easy enough to name the thief once he began to use the color."

"Perhaps he hoped to ruin you. Your reputation could be considered of great value. You are a single woman with your own business, a successful one. In fact, now that your mourning is over, more men than a bully like Nesbitt would be interested in you if you would give them encouragement."

Lydia stood up. This was going down a familiar path, and she answered as she always did. "I am not interested in sharing anything with a man, Grandmama." Lydia did her best to ignore the image of Mr. Chase.

"You are too young to sleep alone forever. Tell me what this man who rescued you was wearing."

"Grandmama, it was dark, I could not see him."

"What did it feel like?"

"A tightly woven, very fine wool. Perfect for a wet night. His greatcoat was made of a heavier wool."

Natalia nodded. "He wore it well?"

Lydia rolled her eyes at the unsubtle question.

"Do not roll your eyes, girl. I am shut up with my imagination all day and little to fuel it. Have pity on me."

Lydia smiled and hoped Natalia could sense her affectionate amusement as easily as she could sense her exasperation. "He was tall and had broad shoulders."

"Not fat, like the Regent?"

Lydia thought of the feel of him as he pressed her protectively behind him, sat next to her, held her hand. "No, not at all."

"So will he call to see if you are all right?"

"If he does, I promise I will introduce you." Lydia kissed Natalia good night and left her with Delphie to see her to bed.

Once she was in the parlor, Lydia went directly to the window that looked onto the street. Yes, there was a man under the lamppost, arms folded, a white scarf tied loosely around his neck over his bulky coat. Her guardian. No matter what Mr. Chase's motive was, for now she felt more secure.

Lydia took her glass of vodka and drank it in one revolting swallow, hoping it would help her sleep. Dreamlessly.

THREE

"I met a woman named Mrs. Chernov this evening," Chase announced as the night porter showed him into Tibold's card room. "Do any of you know anything about her?"

The three men looked up from their cards.

"Do you have a timepiece, Chase? We've been waiting almost an hour." Tibold did not wait for an answer and returned his attention to his cards.

Chase had never met a man who complained more than Tibold.

"There's that shop near the Bull Ring." Bellwood looked back at his cards. "Could this Mrs. Chernov be married to the owner?"

"Chernov Drapers." Griffin straightened. "Yes, I know it. My mother and sister love the place."

Chase took a seat and waited for them to finish the hand they were playing. The pile of coins was modest, but the evening was young.

"Thank you, my man," Tibold said as he pulled the coins to his side of the table. "I think Bellwood could have won that hand."

Bellwood swore as Griffin began to shuffle the cards.

"So what do you know about Mrs. Chernov, Bellwood?"

"Not a thing other than she is a beauty and a widow."

"I learned that much for myself."

"In which case, she might be interested in some consolation," Griffin suggested, as he finished dealing the cards. He looked at the others. "Care to wager how long before he beds her?"

"Do you see that scar near my eyebrow, Griff?" Chase picked up his cards but did not look at them.

All three glanced at him and then at the scar and waited.

"That convinced me never to bet on anything so personal, and to discourage it in others."

Bellwood nodded. Tibold snickered.

"And what does that mean?" Chase asked, turning his head slowly to stare at Tibold.

"Only that one hardly expects such niceties from a man with your reputation for betting on everything and anything."

"Yes, I do see your point." Chase relaxed. "If I hadn't made that foolish wager with Cummings, I would not be stuck in this benighted place for three months."

"Only two months to go, Chase," the always-cheerful Griffin reminded him.

"Thank you, Griff."

"Benighted? You don't like Birmingham?" Bellwood asked.

"I've found a number of things that hold my interest, but all who play here talk more than they gamble."

"You're the one who came late and interrupted us," Tibold griped.

The four settled into several hands, with Tibold still winning steadily. Chase called for higher stakes, which he well knew always made Tibold nervous, and the next round went to Bellwood.

"So how did you meet Mrs. Chernov?" Bellwood asked, proving that copious amounts of wine might slow his brain but did not keep it from working.

Chase weighed his answer and opted for the truth. "She ran into my arms escaping from some bully trying to abduct her."

Tibold and Bellwood put down their cards. Griffin looked up with a quizzical expression.

"Hey, hey, details, my lord," Tibold urged.

"What was she doing out alone at night? Or was she not alone?"

He ignored Bellwood's questions and tried one of his own. "Do any of you know a man named Nesbitt?"

"A gentleman named Nesbitt?" Tibold asked.

"Yes, I know him. Nesbitt the Butcher. He's most definitely not a gentleman." Griffin looked at Chase for confirmation. When Chase nodded, Griffin went on. "He's a bully who can be had for the right price. He runs an operation selling stolen items. He's moving down in the underworld if he's taken on abduction."

It was what Chase suspected, but before he could pursue the subject, Tibold spoke as he stacked the counters. "Are we going to play cards or spend the rest of the night embroiled in one of Chase's affairs?"

"I just met the woman, and it is not an affair," Chase clarified, well aware of Mrs. Chernov's good reputation. "I was very much the gentleman helping a lady in distress."

"A lovely lady," Tibold reminded him.

"Are you implying I would have ignored her need if she had been old or ugly?"

"Not at all, I'm sure," Bellwood intervened.

Chase poured him another glass of wine and repressed his annoyance. Tibold was an idiot who drank and gambled too much. His opinion hardly mattered. "You're starting to lose, Tibold. A break is just what you need. I'll wager ten pounds that you can't sit there for five minutes without speaking while I determine if Mrs. Chernov needs a champion."

Tibold pressed his fingers to his lips and sat back, arms folded. The wager was accepted.

"So what do you know about this reprobate, Griff, and where can I find him?"

"No more than what I just said," Griffin answered. "I ran into him last year when I was looking for that idiot servant of my mother's. The one she hired from the poorhouse who showed her thanks by stealing Mother's cameo and then trying to sell it. I convinced Nesbitt to return it to the rightful owner without an exchange of funds."

"Where did you meet Nesbitt?"

"Some coffeehouse on neutral ground, though I expect he had as many men lurking about as I did."

"Can you take me there? Tonight?"

"Good God, no. I'm hardly at my best at the moment. Maybe tomorrow when my head is clear. The thing is, Chase, it was a year ago."

"You're getting to be an old man, Griffin," Tibold said.

"You've lost the bet," Bellwood shot back.

Tibold swore.

"It's wisdom, you nodcock," Griffin went on as Tibold slid a chunk of his winnings toward Chase. "Only a complete fool would go traipsing about at this hour in a neighborhood he does not know looking for a thug who likes violence."

"Tomorrow's good enough." Chase poured his winnings into a leather bag and stuffed it in his pocket. "Gentlemen, it's been a pleasure, but a lovely lady awaits me and I dare not offend her."

"You haven't been here an hour!" Tibold groused.

"Yes, and why would I stay longer when there is a beauty warming the bed and waiting for my attention?"

With a hand to his head in salute, Chase left the group before Tibold could start complaining again.

He didn't have to wait long for Griffin to join him. Even his well-sprung carriage rocked as Griff hefted himself into the seat. Neither spoke until they were well on their way.

"Your secret word codes fascinate me, my lord. I don't see why you cannot just say, 'Griff, come with me.'" Griffin laughed, a chortle that always made Chase smile. "No, you give me a code that is so very self-serving. Not that I doubt you could have a lady waiting."

"I have to preserve my reputation, Griff. It would hardly do me credit if I could not find an interested lady here as easily as I could in London."

"But why play the rake at all?"

"It's a distraction that serves my purpose."

Griff nodded.

Which was another of his assets. Griffin knew when to leave a subject alone.

"So what did you find, Chase? This one's different from your usual adventure. What can I do to help?"

"Yes, just when I thought even adventures could grow boring, I am truly called on to help someone."

"A woman. A lady?"

"Very much so, which is its own puzzle, as she is a shop-keeper. All I know is that she was particularly singled out for her 'most valued possession.'" Chase told the story and ended with, "I don't know what she may be hiding, but I do know she needs help."

"Shall I nose around and see what more I can find out about Nesbitt, or do you want me to take the last of the night watch?"

"Nesbitt. I'll take the watch."

Griffin looked suspicious.

"I cannot lie and say I would object to knowing her better, but I will not take advantage while she is upset."

"That's much too noble, Chase."

"You're right." Chase reconsidered his wording. "I will not take any steps that might ruin her reputation."

"Yes, that's a little more loosely worded."

The carriage stopped where Griffin lived with his aging mother and spinster sister. "I will set out first thing in the morning, in disguise. I have not learned to box at Jackson's as you have. Of course, I could simply bowl the man over and sit on him." He laughed.

Chase did, too. "I can see the caricature. By Cruikshank, perhaps. With the caption 'Gentleman proves that might makes right.'"

Griffin shook his head despite his amused smile. "All in all, I think I will exercise some restraint, spare my family embarrassment, and pose as a workingman."

"As you will, Griff."

Griffin waited until the steps were lowered and then made his way out of the conveyance, the whole rocking as he exited.

Chase waited until his one true friend in Birmingham let himself into the night-dark house, then knocked for the coachman to proceed.

He could never decide whether to feel sorry for the man or not. Trapped in Birmingham by family responsibilities was one way to look at it. But Griffin never complained, even spoke fondly of his mother and his sister. Chase supposed that family was not always an unwelcome presence. Though he was sure *unwelcome* was the only way to describe his presence among his mother, the duke, and siblings.

As directed, the coachman stopped near the Bull Ring—and wasn't that a strange name for a shopping arcade? Chase made his way on foot to the next street and Chernov Drapers. Manning was waiting under the streetlamp.

"Nothing amiss, my lord. I spent some time in the back to be sure the sounds I heard were only the night cart on its rounds and not someone who wanted more than leavings of the chamber pots."

Manning looked more like the boxer he had been than the competent tutor he now was. His size was impressive, but it was his expression that made it clear his tolerance for trouble was minimal at best. The boys in his charge toed the line, there was no doubt about that.

"Off you go, then, Manning. I'll take over until full light. Have two of the boys find me in a couple of hours, after their breakfast. They can watch the place during the day. Nesbitt has a shop to run himself so I don't expect any more trouble from him until dark, and by then I will have had some time to talk to him." He rubbed his hands over his knuckles, hoping that Nesbitt was ready for some rough education. "Oh, and have the boys bring my writing case. The one I use when I travel."

"Very good, my lord." With a salute of sorts, Manning handed Chase the white scarf and hurried off down the street.

The sky was beginning to lighten. The old moon gave its bare light and the first of the dairymaids began their morning rounds. They were as interested in flirting with him as they were in selling milk and cream.

Nothing was going to happen, Chase was sure of that. Clearly Nesbitt was taking orders from someone and would not make a move again without further instructions. Chase considered whether one would prefer a hireling with a more independent spirit, one willing to think on his own to finish the job.

It's what he would have done. But then, no one had ever praised him for following directions well. Even Gentleman Jackson had commented on that, and if there was one place where you wanted to learn fast, it was in a boxing ring.

Chase's time would be better spent sleeping. He yawned. But he'd told Mrs. Chernov that someone would be on guard all night.

Chase wrapped the white silk scarf around his neck and kept to his task, watching and waiting.

He smiled, thinking about their odd meeting. Even stranger was his reaction to the woman as she ran into him. Even though he was sure she was running from danger, the bash on the head being proof positive, his body, his mind, even his heart had reacted instantly, not to the danger but to the feel of her in his arms.

He would have helped her no matter what, but in that instant he wanted to protect her, something entirely different from helping a lady in distress.

Before he had seen her face, her clear, direct gaze, her red lips, firm chin, he'd felt a connection with her that was about more than lust. Intimate and lasting, he felt it now as he looked up at the window of her flat and imagined her in bed asleep.

FOUR

Lydia slept better than she had expected, but still there was an ache or two from her unaccustomed run of the night before. She rose and stretched. Delphie had started the fire and the room was overly warm, as it was wont to be. This morning the heat was welcome.

With some curiosity, Lydia went to the window to see what kind of day it promised. And to see if her guard was still on duty. Indeed, there he was. But it was a different man from the one she had seen the night before. This one was taller and not as big, though one would never call him small. While she watched, she saw him raise his hand, holding a walking stick, to cover a yawn, and realized it was Mr. Chase himself.

Delphie bumped through the door from downstairs with the morning tray. Tea in a glass for Grandmama, coffee and one of Mr. Florencio's rolls for Lydia.

"Delphie, take my roll and coffee to the gentleman outside, the one wearing a white scarf."

"Missus?" Which was as close as Delphie ever came to saying, "Are you mad?"

"It's the gentleman who rescued me last night," Lydia explained. "He has been on guard and deserves some reward."

"Oh yes, missus. Yes." Delphie plunked down the heavy

tray, wrapped up the bun, and with the cup and saucer in the other hand, hurried down and out the front door of the shop.

It was not at all an elegant presentation, but after a moment of uncertainty, the gentleman accepted both with a bow that Lydia knew would fluster Delphie more than his good looks.

Mr. Chase looked up at her window and raised the cup in salute. For her part, Lydia ignored the gesture but broke all known records for dressing quickly. Delphie returned to do her stays and ties, eager to report her encounter.

"He bowed to me." Delphie's awe was clear in her tone. The maid put her mind to Lydia's stays and when she was finished, added one more thought.

"He's handsome, too," Delphie pronounced. "Even handsomer than Mr. C."

Which is what she had always called Alexei, as if Chernov were as complicated a name as she'd ever heard. Never mind the places in England that were near impossible to pronounce without a guide.

The maid shook her head and lifted the smaller tray that held Grandmama's tea, opening the door to her bedroom and disappearing inside.

Lydia started downstairs with more than her usual speed, then stopped abruptly, remembered suspicion suddenly complicating her gratitude. How could she have forgotten the possibility that Mr. Chase was the true scoundrel, the one who was after something of hers? That his rescue of her might be part of a greater plan?

By the light of day it did seem rather contrived. And he could not have known she would escape at the precise spot where he was. Unless it was close to the place where he had told Nesbitt to bring her. And why would he pummel Nesbitt? That was easy: For allowing her to escape.

She mulled it over and then decided she was using more imagination than sense. Indeed, the sensible part of her could come up with its own reasons to avoid Mr. Chase, every single one of those reasons circling around her proven attraction to charming rogues.

Instead of hurrying out to the front of the shop, Lydia worked in the back. There were bolts of fabric to rewrap and tidy, though that was usually Ida's job, and the endless paperwork of both paying and sending bills. When she made her third error in addition, Lydia decided that she had best confront this bête noire and send him on his way once and for all.

The front of the shop was lit only by natural light coming through the windows and the glass in the door, so she could see without being seen. Either Mr. Chase had magically shrunk in size or he had handed his post over to a boy.

The child was wearing the white scarf, though, so Lydia assumed that he was the Chase-appointed day guard, as if a child that size could be any real protection.

At the moment he was playing some sort of punching game with another boy that was bound to end up with one in tears or enraged. Lydia shrugged. This, at least, was not her problem.

She turned to go back to the work room when she spied a slip of paper pushed under the door. The seal was tight, so she had to unbolt and open the door a little to free the message.

Dear Mrs. Chernov,

Good morning. Two reliable boys are on duty today. If there is a problem, one will run for help while the other assists you. Later, before dark, I hope to return with information on Nesbitt, who he is working for and what that miscreant hopes to gain.

Your servant,
Chase

Two boys? Were they his boys? Was he married? That possibility had not occurred to her before. Certainly a gentleman would not have his sons stand guard. No matter if he was married or not, a gentleman like Mr. Chase did not have marriage in mind when he flirted with a shopkeeper.

Lydia mumbled a string of unkind words in Russian, not sure if she was more angry with herself or the mysterious Mr. Chase. Even if he was her knight in shining armor and not in collusion with Mr. Nesbitt, there was a far more compelling reason to dismiss his attentions. A woman's reputation was a fragile thing. She had learned that in a hard school.

Besides, she didn't need some man's help. Had she not managed well on her own this last year? She could find out who Nesbitt was working for as easily as Mr. Chase could. She could take Ida's brother with her. Arnold was strong enough to handle the heavy bolts of fabric like they were kindling. Surely he would be all the threat she needed if she could find Nesbitt's butcher shop.

Three hours later, Ida came to the door of the back room.

"Mrs. Chernov, there are two boys loitering across the street. Should I have Arnold come round and scare them away?"

"No!" Lydia calmed her voice. She should never have told Ida about the near abduction. Now she would see danger everywhere. "I know who asked them to wait there, and they are doing his bidding." Vague as this was, Ida nodded and went back to work.

A minute later she was back. "Oowee. Mrs. Chernov, come tell me if you know this man. Or if he is bedeviling those boys."

Lydia came out into the shop and caught sight of Mr. Chase as he crossed the street with the two boys.

"Yes, yes, that's their . . ." Lydia was at a loss as to how to describe Mr. Chase's relationship to the boys. She cleared her throat and tried again. "That's the man who came to my aid last night. I believe the boys work for him and he asked them to watch out in case Nesbitt came back again."

"Very strange," Ida mused, her eyes still glued to the three across the street. "He dresses well." Ida would notice that, just as Lydia herself had. "And he carries a cane. Just like that gentleman who accompanies Miss Pascal."

"Mr. Unrow was born a gentleman, but that is his only claim to the honor." Unrow might have the money to buy Miss Pascal whatever she wanted, but Lydia had no doubt that he had bought Miss Pascal as well.

Ah well, her work was not to judge but to sell whatever she had that they might want to buy. "That's enough gawking. Back to work, Ida." Lydia left the window and went behind the counter, wishing a customer would come in so she really would stop thinking about the man outside.

"Yes, Mrs. Chernov, but I can see even from here that he has the devil in his smile."

Lydia raised her eyes to heaven. Since Ida had found religion among the Presbyterians, it didn't take much for her to see the devil in anyone. But then, what was the difference between her choice of *rogue* and Ida's *devil*?

"You be careful if he decides to come in here." Ida's face reddened at the very idea.

Before Lydia could respond, a carriage pulled up in front of the shop. An outrider jumped down and opened the door just as the carriage came to a complete stop. The steps were lowered and not a minute later Irina Chernov Allerton filled the shop with her scent and her presence.

"Lydia! What happened last night? Why did you cancel your appointment?" As she spoke she gave Lydia a kiss on both cheeks and tossed her cloak to Ida, who let it fall on the counter.

"Take that and hang it on a hook so it does not wrinkle," Irina ordered.

Ida did as she was told, but Lydia could hear her grumble as she went into the back.

"I'm so sorry I had to cancel our appointment, Irina. Was Mr. Allerton upset?"

"Well, of course he was. He said that no man would have had any hesitation about venturing out. But I told him you were just being polite, that something terrible must have happened. But now I wonder, as you seem quite all right."

"I am now." Lydia glanced out the window but the carriage blocked her view of where Mr. Chase had been standing. "Irina, you will not credit it, but someone tried to abduct me last night, or at least he wanted something from me and was willing to abduct me if I would not give it to him."

"Oh, dear mother of God, what a hideous experience!" Though Irina said the right words, Lydia could see the gleam of excitement in her eyes. Why was it not nearly as endearing as it had been in Grandmama's? "Who was it and what did he want?"

"It was a man who was working for someone else. A Russian, he said."

At that Irina straightened, looking alarmed.

"One of Alexei's cronies, I suspect."

Irina nodded slowly. "Yes, that's possible."

"He said he wanted my most valued possession." Lydia touched the coin at her throat.

"What do you think he meant?" Irina asked, looking more suspicious than confused.

"Why, the recipe for the purple dye, of course."

"Oh yes, and he did not know it actually belongs to Grandmama because it must be kept in the family."

"Yes, but since I am known as Mrs. Chernov, do you not see that he thought it belonged to me?"

"Yes, of course." Irina was silent a moment, which was so rare that Lydia wondered what had upset her. "How were you able to escape?"

Lydia gave her a much-abbreviated version of her rescue, leaving out the fact that Mr Chase and his fellows even now stood on guard. She did not even consider mentioning how attractive he was.

"Fascinating, Lydia." Irina seemed content with the story, or at least she had no further questions.

Snapping her fingers at Ida, which meant she wanted her cloak, Irina gathered her reticule. "I will go say hello to Grandmama while I am here."

"Please do not, Irina. In the time it takes for you to hand your cloak to Delphie, you and Grandmama will be shouting at each other. I promise you that I will arrange for another meeting with Mr. Allerton to discuss our business collaboration. He will have the use of the dye recipe. Even Grandmama agrees to that since you will be the one to inherit it eventually."

"That's what you said last week when you made the appointment that you canceled." Irina could not hide her petulance.

"What happened last night was beyond all imagining and I must be excused. I know Mr. Allerton has gone to Manchester, but I promise that as soon as he returns, I will reschedule the meeting. Please trust me in this."

"All right." Irina's agreement was suspect. Trust did not come easily to any of the Chernovs. Grandmama was right about that.

With the same flurry in which she'd arrived, Irina left the shop and the carriage sped away.

"What I want to know, missus, is how come you are not the

one to inherit the recipe, since you are Mr. Chernov's widow? Is it some devilish Russian law?"

Before Lydia could think of an explanation or even a reprimand for such familiarity, the delicate ting of the shop bell distracted both of them. Mr. Chase entered, leaving the boys still on guard outside.

"Go work in the back, Ida."

"I'll have some tea," Ida said with a sniff.

"Good morning, Mr. Chase," Lydia began, and hoped the man could not hear the nerves in her voice. His smile astounded her. It filled his cheeks with dimples, and the lines around his eyes mirrored the grin. His blue, blue eyes went straight to her heart and brought color to her cheeks.

"Good morning, Mrs. Chernov." He bowed as though he knew she was a lady disguised as a shopkeeper.

How could he know? No one knew. She busied herself tidying the counter. He knew nothing. The smile was all part of his game. She did not curtsy in return, but he did not seem offended by the insult.

"How are you this morning?" He took only one step closer, but now she could see the turquoise flecks in his dark blue eyes. *Stop staring,* she commanded herself. *You are a grown woman.*

"I'm very well." She searched for something less intimate to discuss. "Thank you for the guard last night. I am sure his presence was the only reason that I slept at all." As if how she slept was less intimate than her health. But she suspected that Mr. Chase could make a conversation about the weather too intimate a subject for a lady to discuss.

"If you have a moment, I can tell you what I found out about Nesbitt the Butcher."

A *thunk* from the back told her that Ida was close enough to hear. That only strengthened her determination to keep this discussion about business. "Please, yes. Tuesdays are always quiet. Most of my customers know that Wednesday is the day for new fabrics. I used to try to entice them to come into the shop by holding back some of the bolts. But that created a sense of competition that is not what I had in mind at all." She stopped herself and, touching the chain at her neck and the coin, she closed her eyes and drew a breath.

In a calmer voice, she began again. "My apologies. I am

chattering because I am not sure I do want to hear who Nesbitt works for and why."

Mr. Chase took her hand and warmed it between his. "I wish I could give you all the answers you need, even if you are not sure you want them, but I am not such a good investigator as that."

Lydia pulled her hand from his. The kind of warmth his touch conveyed affected far more than her hand. He let it go without comment and continued.

"A friend of mine took on the task of locating Nesbitt. It should not have proved difficult and indeed it was not difficult to find his shop, since all involved in related trades are in the same area."

"Not a place a gentleman would visit?" she asked, as if that was the reason Mr. Chase had not gone himself.

"Not at all. My friend is very adept at blending in. A skill that I have no talent for. I am too tall."

Lydia pressed her lips together to keep from laughing. As if his height was the only reason people noticed him. What nonsense. His arresting looks and a certain charisma attracted attention the way a woman's too revealing décolletage drew a man's eyes.

He had actually reddened a little, so perhaps he was reading her mind again.

Lydia felt heartened at his discomfort, relieved to be one of two distracted by whatever floated in the air between them. Mr. Chase cleared his throat and went on.

"Nesbitt has not been in his shop for two days and did not come in this morning either."

"But how can he stay in business if he is so unreliable?" She shook her head, that being the least important of the dozen questions that came to mind. "I beg your pardon, Mr. Chase, but as a shopkeeper I am appalled that anyone would be so irresponsible. It is very bad for business."

"Yes, but we have established that Nesbitt has other sources of income. And he is also fortunate to have an apprentice who is five times the butcher Nesbitt is."

"Then, in fact, we are no better off now than we were before your friend found the shop."

FIVE

———▸———

"We," Chase thought. She had said, *"We."* What was her Christian name? Thank the great and good she was a widow. Chase had thought her pretty last night by the scant light of gas lamps. If he had seen her in full light for the first time, he would have realized *pretty* did not do her justice. He thought a moment. Hers was a quiet beauty of which he was becoming more and more aware. Yes, *quiet beauty* was entirely accurate.

He cleared his throat again. "We have made progress. Fortunately for us, his apprentice enjoys talking. With the apprentice's help, my friend learned Nesbitt's direction and the places where he usually spends his day when he is not in his shop. The boy even agreed to send word when Nesbitt returns if we are not able to find him sooner."

Mrs. Chernov nodded and her body lost some of the tension he had feared was due merely to his presence. Chase decided that *we* was fast becoming his favorite word.

"In any case, until we are able to find Nesbitt and are sure he has been convinced to find other interests, I will have my men and boys remain on watch to assure myself of your safety."

She closed her eyes and he realized that the allure radiating from her eyes was the key part of her loveliness. He had not been able to see her golden blond hair last night or the lovely face framed by eyes of such amazing green that, when she closed them as she just had, his world dimmed a bit. He suspected that the rest of her, now covered in a gown of the most perfect shade of lavender, was every bit as alluring as her eyes. *Face it, Chase,* he said to himself. *You are well on your way to playing the fool.*

She opened her eyes and his world brightened.

"I wish I could say it was not necessary, Mr. Chase, but if I did not worry for myself, I have Grandmama to think of and the servants."

"Yes, you do, and I'm relieved that you are being sensible."

"Oh, Mr. Chase, if there is one thing I have learned how to be, it is sensible. Or perhaps *prudent* is the better word."

He wanted the story, the whole miserable story, of how she learned that prudence was the better impulse.

She straightened and her eyes took on a stern cast. "Before we pursue this incident any further, Mr. Chase, I must know something."

He nodded, willing to tell her his deepest secret if it meant her eyes would brighten again.

"Those boys who were on guard this morning—who are they and how are they related to you?"

"Not by blood but by friendship, for I have not yet married," he answered promptly.

"A little less cryptic an explanation, if you please." Her expression was as severe as an annoyed governess's. One did not need to be married to have children. Was that what she thought? he wondered.

"They are being tutored by a man who is educated and understands their needs. He is willing to allow them an adventure when the need arises."

"How odd. Where are their parents?" Mrs. Chernov said, raising a hand to her cheek.

"I have no idea." And that was the complete truth, but he thought he'd best leave before he was compelled to lie. "For now I bid you good day." He took her hand and bowed over it, wanting to press a kiss to the wrist or her palm but staying himself. *His* prudence, a virtue he rarely practiced, was going to be tested.

He paused at the door because he could not resist one last question. "Mrs. Chernov, what is your Christian name?"

She shook her head a little and pointed to the bolts of cloth behind her, an array of shades of purple that were the perfect backdrop to her golden beauty. An image of her, naked and wrapped in purple silk, distracted him quite thoroughly for a moment.

"My Christian name?" She paused and he wondered if she would refuse outright to tell him or if she was distracted by images of him naked as well. He could hope so.

"Well, Mr. Chase," she said with a smile, not coy but teasing, "I do work with purple cloth."

It meant nothing to him at first. "Could *you* be a little less cryptic?" he asked, smiling as he used her own phrase. Then it came to him. "Lydia!" he announced as he turned more fully toward her.

"Very good, sir." She laughed and touched the chain at her neck. "You know the Bible."

"Not all that well, I'm afraid. But I had a . . ." He stopped before he used the word *tutor*. "Um, teacher who insisted on starting each day's lesson with readings from the New Testament."

He closed the door that he had opened only a crack. "And what else do you share with St. Paul's Lydia? It's from one of his letters, is it not?"

"No, from Acts: 'a certain woman named Lydia, a seller of purple.' It's unclear whether she sold the dye or the fabric, but for my purposes it's fabric."

"But the important thing about Lydia is that she was a successful woman of faith and generosity. A lovely name, Mrs. Chernov. You wear it well."

"Thank you, Mr. Chase. I will see you tomorrow."

It was a dismissal as surely as if she had opened the door for him, but he had left her smiling.

He admired so much about her besides her amazing beauty. She was brave, independent, and sensible, with a few less appealing attributes mixed in: cautious, skeptical, and prickly.

All of those qualities, the good and the less than perfect, would put him at a disadvantage when he told her his true name. How odd that the "advantage" of birth and wealth would not work in his favor at all.

Then she would have to decide if she wanted any more to do with him. And he wanted to be part of her life. As much as he wanted her physically, he wanted to know where she came from, why she lived here, what she hoped for the future. But he was afraid that once she knew who he was, the image of Lydia Chernov swathed in purple cloth might be as close as he would ever come to making love with her.

———————

"Lydia, dearest, you must stop worrying. It has been days now and there has been no sign of trouble." Grandmama struggled up from her seat and moved to the table, feeling her way to her place. "Come eat your dinner and tell me when you have re-scheduled your meeting with Mr. Allerton."

Lydia sat down and stared at the usually appetizing fish in a clear sauce. The filet was a modest serving at her request, but still she could not bring herself to do more than take one small bite. She made sure to clink the silver on the edge of the plate so that Grandmama would think she was eating.

"Mr. Allerton will be away for another week. Irina has been in once since Tuesday and is all impatience when there is nothing I can do about his travels."

"Yes, Irina wants everything now, if not sooner, and you are left to pacify her as best you can. Wise you are to discourage her from calling on me, or I fear I would be reduced to poking my own granddaughter with my stick to make her leave." Grandmama took a dainty bite of her fish before she went on. "Now, that gentleman who keeps calling. The one who rescued you. Please do send him up to visit."

Lydia all but shuddered at the thought of Mr. Chase and Grandmama with their heads together. If Grandmama considered him worthy, Lydia would not have one secret left. Grandmama would tell him everything. God forbid, she prayed.

"I would not embarrass you, I promise, my dear one. I only want to meet the man who gives all appearances of appreciating what a treasure you are."

And so it went. By the time Delphie had cleared away their supper and came to help Grandmama to bed, Lydia had a headache from Grandmama's pressure, kindly meant, but pressure nonetheless. Taking a seat by the window, she thought about sending a cup of tea to the man standing on guard, but then she saw him take a drink from a bottle.

It was another drizzly, fog-bound night and she certainly did not begrudge him his bottle, but she found herself praying that he did not drink himself into oblivion.

Leaning back, she closed her eyes and wondered when Mr. Chase would decide that Nesbitt was done with her. They had only known each other for a short while, but already she knew she would miss Mr. Chase's visits, the way he invited himself to take tea in the back room, how easily he coaxed her to tell him about the business, and the way he told stories about his boys and his own inclination to gamble.

"No more than is wise," he'd insisted, telling her how he came to be in Birmingham for two more months.

"Of course, little did I know that this hiatus would be such a blessing in disguise. How else would I have met you?"

Was it a bad sign that his flirting no longer embarrassed her? She drifted off to sleep in the chair, wondering if he would stop at flirting and if she should introduce him to Grandmama. No one understood people better than she did.

Lydia was more asleep than awake when the sound came to her.

Wish.

It sounded like a slipper dragged across the floor, but she knew that Grandmama was abed and Delphie asleep on the pallet beside her.

Wish.

Lydia stiffened but kept her eyes closed. Could Alexei's unquiet soul be haunting her, or was this her brain playing tricks? Finally she opened her eyes and looked around the night-darkened room. There were no apparitions, no signs of anything out of the ordinary. Her imagination, she decided. Indeed, if she was brutally honest with herself, she would have to admit that it was her own heart that was unquiet.

Lydia closed her eyes, thinking she should go to her room and make ready for bed, but she fell asleep before she gathered the energy to move.

SIX

Fog quieted everything and the damp air chilled him to the bone. Chase huddled in his greatcoat and wished he'd worn warmer gloves. Just as he was about to check his timepiece, he heard something other than the creak of old wood and brick buildings, more than the scratching of cats and rodents.

Footsteps.

Heavy footsteps.

Chase had learned over the last few nights that during his short stretch of guard duty, this street was virtually untraveled until first light. He had yet to see one man abroad, so the sound he heard now told him there was trouble on the way.

It came from the mews behind the building that housed Chernov Drapers. With his walking stick at the ready, he moved as quietly as possible down the alley between the bakery and the fabric shop. He leaned around the corner cautiously. And saw no one. Sheathing his half-released sword, he stepped more fully into the mews and went to test the door that was the back entrance to Mrs. Chernov's flat.

"You're mine now, you prissy fool!" Nesbitt bellowed.

Since Nesbitt was kind enough to announce his presence, Chase had time to see the heavy cudgel aimed for his head. He raised his left arm to stop the blow and released his sword from its cover.

Chase heard the crack before he felt the break in his arm. In that split second before the pain overwhelmed him, he raised his sword stick and ran it through Nesbitt's arm. The man jumped back. You would think the fool would have learned the first time how dangerous the sword stick could be.

With his own wounded arm pressed against his chest, Chase dropped his sword and, using his good arm, landed one sound punch on Nesbitt's jaw. The man collapsed to the ground like a woman in a dead faint.

Just as the altercation ended, the door of the baker's shop opened, as did Mrs. Chernov's door.

"What goes on here?" a man shouted.

"It's all right, Mr. Florencio." Lydia hurried to Chase.

Even through the haze of pain, Chase noticed that though her hair was tousled, she was still fully dressed, even with shoes on. Had she just risen or never slept?

Looking over her shoulder, she continued her explanation to the baker. "This gentleman has been guarding my place of late from just such an intruder as the man on the ground."

"Ah, Mrs. Chernov. I thought that now with Mr. Chernov no longer among us, your life might be quieter."

"Yes, well, it has been for most of this last year, and I hope it will be again soon."

"You do not need my help?"

"No, thank you, sir. You are kind to offer it. But I think Mr. Chase can handle this miscreant. Indeed, it appears he already has."

With a cautious nod, Mr. Florencio closed the door.

"Are you hurt, Mr, Chase?" Her voice was anxious. "It's so dark. Come inside and let me see."

Chase shook his head, even though he could feel where the bone was broken.

Holding his arm against his chest and doing his best to ignore the throbbing pain, Chase stepped away from her and nudged Nesbitt with his boot. The man groaned but did not open his eyes.

"Mr. Chase, please leave him unconscious. Your needs come first, and we must send someone for the magistrate."

"No, Mrs. Chernov, go inside if you do not have the stomach for this. I want answers and I want them now." He looked at her over his shoulder and read shock in her eyes. "I promise you that after this conversation, Nesbitt will not bother you again."

"That is what I'm afraid of," she said, clutching the chain at her neck.

"Yes, I am angry enough to run him through, but I have learned control, I assure you." As he spoke he gathered up his sword stick.

"Thank you." She let go of her necklace and stepped back but did not go inside.

So be it, Chase thought. He nudged Nesbitt harder this time, and when the man opened bleary eyes, Chase swung his sword dramatically and stopped it just before it sliced Nesbitt's throat.

"I want to know two things, Nesbitt, and I want the answers now. Do you understand?"

Nesbitt didn't answer, and Chase pressed sword to skin so that a thin trickle of blood appeared.

"Yes, yes, move that sword away from my throat and I'll tell you whatever you want."

Chase could have sworn he saw tears in Nesbitt's eyes, but they drew no mercy from him. Chase's arm hurt like hell, as if he needed a reminder of the kind of trouble this man could cause.

He moved his sword and Nesbitt drew a breath, but when Chase let the point rest over Nesbitt's heart, the sneak thief tensed again.

"Tell me who hired you and what they want."

"I don't know. I swear on the Bible I don't know the man's name. He was wearing a hood when we met. All I know is he had a foreign accent."

"What kind of accent?"

"A Russian accent. I think that's what it was because that woman's name is Chernov and that's a Russian name, isn't it?"

If Lydia had not been standing nearby he would have used language that would surely impress Nesbitt. Dealing with a stupid thief had its advantages. But drawing out accurate information was not one of them. "So you actually aren't sure what kind of foreign accent it was?"

"No, but there aren't that many foreigners in Birmingham."

Chase tried to imagine stopping everyone who spoke with an accent and questioning them. "And what did this person with an accent want?"

"He told me to tell the woman that he wanted what she valued most. A necklace."

"What?"

Chase had to agree with Mrs. Chernov's single word. That made no sense. All of this for a necklace?

"He said it was her greatest treasure, and she would know what he meant, and he would have it from her by any means necessary."

Chase glanced back at Lydia. She was holding the chain she seemed to wear all the time. She shook her head, looking intent and determined. "I have only one necklace and it has no value beyond sentiment."

"You may or may not be telling the truth, Nesbitt." Chase pressed the sword to his cheek and drew blood. "I am tempted to brand you here and now."

Lydia gasped and Chase nodded. "But since it would upset Mrs. Chernov, I will allow you this. Listen to me. You make the circuit to your work, your home, and your favorite coffee-house. You go nowhere else. I will know with whom you meet or if you go anywhere other than those three places. Do you understand?"

"Yes," Nesbitt whispered, finally cowed.

"If you violate this order, I will find you and brand you a thief in a way that will announce itself to the world forever. Do you believe me?"

Nesbitt nodded and whispered, "Yes."

"If anyone else comes after Mrs. Chernov's most treasured necklace or hurts anyone I care about, I will destroy your shop and you. I have more resources in more places than you can imagine, and I will use every one of them to find and kill you. And I promise you, the magistrate will bless me for it."

Nesbitt gulped and said, "Aye."

Chase removed his sword and waited until the beaten man struggled to his feet. Nesbitt began to back down the alley, apparently afraid that Chase would save himself the trouble of hunting him down and end it now. When Nesbitt was beyond the reach of Chase's sword, he turned, hurried out of the alley and out of sight.

The pain in Chase's arm sang out then, and he almost dropped his sword as a wave of light-headedness overtook him.

"Mr. Chase, you are hurt!"

Chase shook his head, unable to speak for the moment. He scooped up his walking stick and sheathed his sword on the second try and then remembered that he had not cleaned the blade.

Lydia was beside him now. She reached out to touch his arm but then stopped.

"You hurt your arm?"

"Broken." He gasped as his vision began to darken.

"Do not faint," Lydia commanded. "I cannot carry you. Come inside and I will give you some vodka and send for a bonesetter."

Chase groaned at the thought of anyone handling his arm, but her urgent tone reached him and his need to collapse faded just a little. Lydia took his good arm and much of his weight. They moved through the outside door. He paid no attention to the route she followed but an eternity later he was sitting on what felt like a very soft chair—or was it a bed?

"I will be back in a minute with some vodka."

Chase leaned his head against the wall and closed his eyes. At least it was his left arm. He would not be completely helpless.

"Mr. Chase?"

He opened his eyes a little to find Lydia seated beside him, a small glass in her hand.

"This is vile but as good a medicine as I have right now. Shall I help you with the glass?"

He shook his head, took the small glass, and downed the vodka in one gulp. It burned, but the taste was not vile, just different. Very Russian, he decided, and laughed a little.

"There is nothing funny about this situation."

He turned to her. She was pale—or was it just the weak candlelight that made her look so lost? She was clutching her chain, which left him in no doubt of her upset.

"I will be all right." *Eventually,* he added to himself.

"How badly is it broken?"

"It did not break the skin."

"Thank God, Mr. Chase. I suppose it could be worse." She stared at the sleeve of his coat. Lydia looked as ill as he felt, her hand now tightly gripping the charm at the end of her necklace. When she looked up at him, her eyes were filled with tears.

"As gallant as your defense was, I so wish you had not broken your arm." She spoke with such urgency that he found himself forgetting the pain as he tried to think of a way to comfort her.

"I cannot think of a more worthy reason to risk life and limb." He closed the small space between them and pressed his mouth to hers. It was hardly a kiss at first, but the feel of her lips, soft and willing, the warmth of her breasts pressed against his chest, fired his blood so that he wanted more than sweetness. Even as the feeling raced through him, truly less than a thought, he felt her mouth open to his, her response given willingly with, he hoped, the same welcome impulse that had him pulling her into his arms. A light enveloped them, so bright he saw it through his closed eyes, followed by a warmth that surrounded them until the heat made Chase draw back to see if she felt the same.

Lydia's dazed expression changed in a blink to one of concern. "Your arm, sir, your arm. It must be paining you awfully to have me pressed so close."

"The pain is gone." He wasn't lying or trivializing the injury. His arm could not have been broken, not if it felt so pain free now.

They both looked down at his arm. He was no longer cradling it protectively against his chest. His hand rested casually on his thigh.

"You are pretending," she said without much conviction.

"I am not. You saw me almost pass out from the pain. You had to help me in here."

"Perhaps you dislocated your shoulder. Yes, that must be it."

"And kissing you caused it to pop back into place? I have seen it done before, and one screams with the pain of it. Our kiss exceeded all my expectations, though I will say that it ended too soon, but even that fine a kiss could not distract me so much I would not feel my shoulder right itself."

Chase could see Lydia's cheeks grow pink, and she did not

look at him as she spoke. "Could the vodka have deadened the pain enough that you did not feel it?"

"Whatever the reason, the pain is virtually gone."

He took the scissors sitting on the table closest and cut the coat from wrist to elbow.

Lydia gasped.

"One coat is easily replaced."

"But it is such fine fabric, Mr. Chase. What a waste."

"Of course you would think the fabric not worth my curiosity." As he spoke he pulled back his shirtsleeve. "My apologies for being so impulsive."

His arm was bruised a vicious dark purple. He touched the spot and grimaced. "I will have a fine bruise but nothing that will even slow me down. I suppose it was not broken."

Lydia stood up and Chase did as well. She folded her hands at her waist and might as well have shouted, *Do not come any closer!*

With the slightest encouragement he would have taken her on this cot and been sure that she enjoyed it as much as he did. But he was a patient man with a prize worth waiting for. He wanted more than the luscious body before him. A lifetime of experience had taught him that lovemaking was best shared with body, spirit, and mind.

Chase bowed, to assure her that he could take a hint, but was not willing to lie. "I would never wish to give offense, Mrs. Chernov, but I find I cannot apologize for that kiss, as forward as it was."

"Then I will be honest as well," she said, her stern mouth softening, even if she did not actually smile. Curtsying, she went on, "You had best leave, Mr. Chase."

Aha, so she was tempted more than she wanted to admit. He tried not to grin and moved promptly to the back door. "I am going to check on Nesbitt."

"Do not go alone!"

"I will not, if only to make sure you do not worry. I want to know if he's doing exactly as I ordered and I would very much want him to see that my arm is not at all injured."

"Pride goeth before a fall, Mr. Chase."

"Well, in this case the fall came before the pride, so I should be all right, don't you think?"

She shook her head at his joke but smiled a little. Soon he could have her laughing, he was sure of it. It would be something to which he would look forward. "I will continue with the guards for a night or two."

"Oh please, I hate to think of men and boys denied their sleep because of me."

"They have plenty of time to sleep during the day. They think it an adventure, especially the boys."

"I've thought more than once that you are a bit of a bully yourself, Mr. Chase."

"I prefer to think of myself as thorough, though perhaps just a bit stubborn." Not wanting to see her smile disappear, he bowed again. "Good night, Mrs. Chernov. Whether it was the kiss or the vodka or some other magic, I thank you for your ministrations this evening."

He opened the door and stepped out into the early-morning light, waiting to hear her lock the door from the inside.

———

Lydia leaned her head against the locked door. It was ridiculous, but she was more upset by the kiss than by Nesbitt's attempt at breaking into the shop. Not the kiss so much as the temptation, the longing, the desperate need to give more and take as much as he wanted to give. Not even with Alexei had she felt so wanton. She stood without thought and then realized the difference between Alexei and Mr. Chase.

Alexei had seduced her, hardly giving her time to think before he swept her up into his world of love and family. Alexei had made it impossible to refuse.

Mr. Chase charmed her. He flirted but he never once pressed her for more than she was ready to give. Mr. Chase understood that "no" was not an insult. She played with the coin around her neck and wondered if he would always be that understanding.

The sound of footsteps made Lydia straighten. Delphie was up and about her business. The last thing Lydia wanted was for the maid to have hysterics over the attempted robbery.

Lydia flung herself on the cot and turned to face the wall, feigning sleep. When she was first alone she had often fallen asleep here, fully dressed, until she realized that no matter when she climbed the stairs and went to her own bed, Alexei would not be there.

Delphie came into the back room humming, unlocked the door, and slipped out to collect the breakfast rolls from Mr. Florencio. She didn't even notice that Lydia was in the room.

Taking advantage of her absence, Lydia hurried up the stairs and into her bedchamber. Even though Delphie had been in to start the fire, the curtains were still drawn around her bed. Lydia climbed into the big empty bed and for the first time in more than a year thought about sharing it with someone besides Alexei.

The moment before she slipped into the world of dreams she heard the word *wish* whisper through the room, beneath the curtains, and settle on the pillow beside her. This time the word brought with it an air of completion, of satisfaction, of farewell. Lydia smiled and touched the coin as she fell asleep.

SEVEN

"I tell you, Griff, I would have bet fifty quid that my arm was broken. God, it was all I could do to stay conscious." Chase was flexing his fist and shaking his arm as the two of them headed from Griffin's house toward the street where Nesbitt lived and worked.

"I'm no expert on bones, Chase, but I could ask my mother's physician for an explanation."

"I spoke to Lord Mayhew at the club this morning. He's as good a man of science as any physician. He said that I had to be mistaken about the break. I was in pain from the blow and merely thought I had broken my arm."

"That makes as much sense as any other explanation."

"It makes me sound like a girl. I've been boxing for years and can take a hit as well as any man." There was no point in insisting, but the puzzle of it plagued him. "Never mind, Griff. Tell me what Nesbitt has been up to while I caught up on my sleep."

"He was home until noon and then went to his shop, where he took a strap to his apprentice, and then left for the coffee-house next door. He growled at everyone who approached him and was sitting in the corner when the boys came along to take up watch."

"Good, very good. It sounds like he took my threat as seriously as I meant it." Chase knocked on the roof, and the carriage slowed to a stop. "We walk from here."

"Chase," Griffin began as he hefted himself up and out of the carriage, "exactly why are we going there now? I thought you were satisfied with my report."

Twirling his walking stick with his only-bruised arm, Chase explained, "Very much so, Griff. No insult intended, but I want Nesbitt to see that I suffered no injury. I want him to see that you are one of the resources I warned him about last night. I want him to think that every stranger he sees is one of my resources." He paused and Griffin nodded, laughing at the game.

"And I want to relieve him of his apprentice. The boy has learned all he can from Nesbitt."

"I say, Chase, that's a noble move, but he may not give him up easily. From my observations, I think the boy's the only reason he stays in business."

"I will offer him another apprentice. Ronald, I think."

"Yes, Ronald shows some talent there." Griffin thought a minute, then laughed with pleasure. "Nesbitt will not dare abuse him, since he knows Ronald is one of your, ahem, resources."

"Exactly, and near enough his size to give Nesbitt pause before beating him."

All in all, it went even better than Chase had hoped. Nesbitt was willing to hand over his apprentice and accept a new one, especially when Chase told him there would be no fee to change hands, that he'd made arrangements with the guild himself.

The only aspect that Nesbitt found hard to believe was that Chase had not broken his arm. "Virtue rewarded," Chase suggested, and Nesbitt all but spit his ale across the table.

"You, virtuous?" Nesbitt shook his head. "No more than I am, only better dressed."

Chase prayed that wasn't true, but left Nesbitt thinking what he liked. He had convinced more than one former adversary to join his ranks, but he doubted Nesbitt would ever be so inclined.

Just as he was congratulating himself on a more than successful outing, Griffin burst his bubble of complacency.

"My mother and sister plan to visit Mrs. Chernov today."

"Why?"

"Because she has shades of purple cloth like no other. And possibly they are intrigued because I may have mentioned that you had helped her out of a predicament." Griffin had the grace to look sheepish at his uncharacteristic storytelling.

"For all that is good, Griff! That's the last thing I need."

It was Griffin's turn to ask, "Why?"

"Because she thinks I'm simply Mr. Chase. She has no idea that I'm related to the Duke of Bournemouth."

Griffin nodded but looked puzzled. "I don't see how that's an insult."

"Because you are not a lady shopkeeper." He rubbed his brow and wondered what Lydia Chernov would make of the information. "Speaking to a Mr. Chase, perhaps even taking tea with him, would be risqué enough, but to do the same with Lord Chase would invite all sorts of unwelcome speculation."

"Huh. I know the niceties of behavior, but she is only a shopkeeper, Chase. Do the same rules apply?"

"Yes, for her they do. I am not at all sure she is 'only a shopkeeper.' She has at least as many secrets as I do." He thought for a long moment before he spoke again. "Griff, what would you say is your most valued possession?"

"That's easy. My mother and my sister." Then he frowned. "But then they would be offended if I called them such."

"So, some *thing* you treasure above all else."

"The timepiece my father left me." He patted his pocket. "I carry it with me all the time even though it has not worked for a year. I do keep meaning to have it repaired."

"Yes, you carry it with you all the time. Mrs. Chernov wears a necklace her husband gave her but she says it has no value." But how did she know that for sure? "I think I must have a look at it. In any case, we need to determine what is her greatest treasure. I do not think our villain will abandon his plot."

"But if she has no idea, how can you know?"

"If"—Chase emphasized the word and glared at Griff—"if Mrs. Chernov will talk to me now, I think a fresh discussion of the subject will help."

———

"Good evening, my lord." Lydia hoped *his lordship* could hear the frost in her voice and it turned him to ice.

"Good evening, Mrs. Chernov, and I see you have found out one of my secrets."

"One of them, my lord?"

"I would never have thought those two words could ring with such condemnation. It was an innocent error I thought wiser to leave alone."

So you could seduce me and I would think there was a future, Lydia thought. *Just like Alexei.* "I have learned from experience that there are very few innocent omissions, my lord."

"Then I will tell you the truth about my name," Lord Chase said, his voice hardening.

Where had the irritation come from? Lydia wondered. She reached for the coin around her neck.

"I do not mean to frighten you." He came around the counter and took her hand. He bowed over it. "You are as much a lady as any woman I have ever met. I suspect that your origins are one of your secrets, but everything about you is as wellborn as my aunts and sisters. My reasons for not announcing my courtesy title have everything to do with me."

It would have been churlish to pull her hand away. She could not doubt his sincerity and wondered how he had managed to see what so few others had ever noticed.

She softened. "Come into the back room. There is some tea and cakes."

"Thank you, Mrs. Chernov." He followed her through the door.

"Ida, close up for me today. Lord Chase and I are going to have tea and talk. You may go home as soon as you have drawn the curtains."

Ida nodded, and Lydia could almost hear her trying to discern what devilment she and Lord Chase were up to.

"To call this 'the back room' hardly does it justice." His eyes scanned the room, the shelves. "It's like a treasure cave complete with a magic carpet on the floor.

She nodded. "Alexei felt one should be comfortable wherever one spent the most time." *You should see our bed,* she thought, but wisely kept that to herself. "And there is no doubt that both of us spent as much time in here as we did in the flat upstairs. Sometimes we even took dinner here."

Lydia sat at the table where the teapot and cakes waited.

The cot was on the other side of the room, pressed against the wall, in front of shelves of great bolts of purple, lilac, and lavender cloth.

They did not speak while she poured their tea. When she offered him the cakes, she broke the silence, which seemed to her to be growing awkward. "I count myself lucky on those days when Mr. Florencio does not sell all his orange cream cakes. They are my favorite, and he sends them over so they do not go to waste."

"Then I will take this lemon bar, or is that your other favorite?" He smiled, and she felt her heart speed up.

"Have one of each, my lord."

"Ah yes," he said, as if just recalling why they were seated in such a private place. "My name is Chase Weldon Cyrus Bourne. My mother is the Duchess of Bournemouth." He cleared his throat and went on. "The duke recognizes me as his third son, but I am no blood relation to him."

Chase paused. Lydia was almost sure he was waiting to see her shock, if she would send him on his way without hearing another word. What she wanted to do was to cover her ears. She didn't want to hear this. It was too intimate, too personal a thing to share with a casual acquaintance.

She only nodded, unwilling to send him away when he would surely misinterpret her reason. At her nod, he relaxed and relief began to overtake his embarrassment.

"I do not know who my father is. My mother will not discuss it. My situation is not common knowledge, so you must know how highly I value your opinion that I would tell you this. I trust you will respect my privacy."

"Yes, Lord Chase." Lydia leaned toward him. "I do, and once again I promise you my complete discretion." She picked up her teacup but did not think she could swallow even a sip.

"Thank you." He took a long sip of his tea. "My family prefers to see as little of me as possible. I accept the allowance that the duke sends quarterly and make the required appearances with the family during the Season when we can appear to be *en famille* but do not actually have to speak to one another.

"For all intents and purposes I fill my time the way many gentlemen do: gambling, dancing, boxing, going to the theater, and buying anything that appeals to me. In truth, I spend my time finding and caring for children—boys actually—who are bastard sons not as fortunate as I am."

"You mean you consider it your life's calling?" She paused a moment then went on. "The boys who were guarding me. They are your foundlings." The last was a statement. Her surprise was so genuine that the words burst from her without thought. "I beg your pardon, my lord. But you must admit that is an unusual calling for a gentleman. Not for a monk, perhaps," she added.

"I am hardly a monk."

His wry smile made her shiver, and not out of fear. She pressed her lips together to keep from smiling back. "Most English gentlemen are barely aware of those in need."

"I decided long ago that the ton is not as blind to these troubles as I thought. Rather, they are overwhelmed by the magnitude of the problem and have no idea where to start. They think in grand terms and leave it to the government. Some like Mr. Wilberforce succeed, but most bills fail."

"Wilberforce might have put an end to the slave trade, but it took him years and years."

"Yes, a lifetime, I expect."

So he saw it as a life's work. "But you have help from among your friends?"

"I would say that one out of three wants to be included. Here in Birmingham, Mrs. Griffin's son has been a boon companion."

"Yes, all three Griffins are thoughtful people. I can see how he would be won over." She touched her necklace as another thought came to her. "Now I see why you came to my rescue. You make a habit of it."

"No." He spoke more slowly. "Not so much rescuing as helping people find themselves. In your case, Mrs. Chernov, you had already rescued yourself."

"I made that claim myself, my lord, but now I suspect that without your help there would not have been nearly as tidy an ending."

"We are not at the end yet, Mrs. Chernov. We still do not know who wants your necklace and why."

He stood up and began to pace the room. "Do you know which necklace the thief wants?"

"My lord?" She touched the chain at her neck. "As I told you the other night, this is the only necklace I own. Alexei sold everything when we made our escape from Russia ahead of Napoleon's troops."

"And why did he not sell that one?"

"Well, I am not sure he had come into possession of it at the time. He only gave it to me just before he left on what proved to be his final trip. He told me to wear it always, that it would be my greatest treasure and he would explain its value when he returned. He was lost at sea and never did come back."

"He used those words?" He stopped pacing and cocked his head. "Mr. Chernov used the same words that Nesbitt said his contact used?"

"Yes."

"Then it must be someone who knew him, someone he told of its value." They both spoke almost the same words at the same time.

The silence settled around them. It was the like-mindedness of their thought that distracted her.

"May I see the necklace, Lydia?"

It was the first time he had used her Christian name. Bemused by the significance of that, Lydia pulled the chain out and would have taken it off, over her head, but Lord Chase came close to her and took the coin in his hand. She felt everything about him when he stood this close: his breath, his scent, his undeniable manliness.

He looked up. The expression in his eyes changed and challenged Lydia to tell the truth. A truth that had nothing to do with her necklace or Nesbitt's stupidity.

"Why are you looking at me like that?" she asked.

"I want you to admit that you know as well as I do that we were brought together by fate, drawn together by this adventure. I want you to tell me you see that we are destined for so much more."

"Chase, yes, I feel the attraction, but I hardly know you. The purely physical is not enough."

"It would be if you trusted me." He held the coin as he spoke. "Lydia, I wish you would believe me when I say that you are unique among all the women I have ever met and that you will look beyond my empty name and see me for who I truly am and for what we can be together."

The coin flashed golden, but Chase barely noticed as he kissed her. "Bright and vibrant," he whispered against her lips. "Everything about you is enchanting."

Just one kiss, she thought. In the mere second it took to make that decision, a dozen thoughts pirouetted through her mind. Her attraction to him felt fast, but it felt right. Not like Alexei. Not selfish. Not secretive. For her this was not a choice colored by desperation. Could it be no more than lust? Or might it be love? There was only one way she would find out.

EIGHT

———▶———

She didn't so much surrender to his kiss as welcome it. The blending of their mouths felt so much like finding her other half that tears trickled down her cheek. She wanted to give all of herself to him, take all he had to offer and never let go.

They kissed and whispered and played the sweetest games until they bumped up against the edge of the cot. It startled both of them, and they had another choice to make. Chase framed her face with his hands, using his thumbs to wipe away the tears.

"I can't imagine ever walking away from you, not being with you in every way a man and a woman can be."

She lowered her head and a frisson of fear whispered through him to her. "I cannot imagine sending you away."

He relaxed. "But first?" It was a question he did not have to finish.

"Oh yes, there is a *but*," she said, sure she was echoing his frustration as well. "My prudence insists that we first solve the mystery of the necklace so that we are not—um—distracted."

With a slow nod, Chase stepped away from her, straightening his clothes and drawing deep breaths. Lydia did the same, hoping that no one interrupted them now, when they were both so disheveled.

How hideous to be caught this way when nothing had happened. She laughed a little as she finished smoothing her hair, and he turned to look at her, a question in his eyes.

"I was thinking how awful it would be to be found looking as though we have made love when we have not."

Chase came to her again, tipped her chin up with a finger, and kissed her lightly and very quickly. "We have made love, Lydia. Not as completely as we will, but as surely as you wear that necklace."

Lydia looked down, not embarrassed but a little shy at what she saw in his eyes. "But, Chase, we have known each other only a little more than a week."

"A very intense week."

"That I cannot argue, my lord." She kissed him on both cheeks and then laid her forehead against his. "We have seen in each other more than most who have known each other much longer." She leaned back and broke out of his hold. *And there is too much you still do not know about me.* The thought made her stomach ache and her hands shake. She could not look at him.

"We know the most important thing, that we are willing to risk everything for what we think is important, life and love and the people we value."

She looked up quickly. "How do you know that about me?"

"You talk about Mr. Chernov's mother with great affection. You do your best to keep Mrs. Allerton from irritating her."

She nodded, relieved his judgment was based only on such superficial observations.

"If you will pour," he said, "I think even lukewarm tea would be just the thing to settle my nerves."

Nerves? The man did not know the meaning of the word. Then it occurred to her that *nerves* was a euphemism for sexual need. *That* she could understand. He might be a bastard by birth, but he was the finest gentleman she had ever met.

She poured him more tea and offered him a cake. He shook his head and the two sat in silence for a minute as they had before. She watched as he pursed his lips and narrowed his eyes, staring at the coin hanging from its chain. At least she thought that's what he was staring at.

"Your coin was obviously made for foreign trade, with the

great seal of England on one side and odd writing on the other. For India, I would guess, but if I make that guess based on the odd writing then I sound distinctly like Nesbitt with his guess at a Russian accent."

"Hardly. You speak much better English."

He raised his head and smiled at her teasing, then grew serious as before. "Mr. Chernov gave you the coin but you have no idea how he came to own it?"

"No idea at all." *He could have stolen it for all I know.* She had learned early on not to question Alexei's largesse.

"Perhaps, Lydia, the lady you call Grandmama knows something about it. Have you ever asked her?"

"No." She had not wanted to know the truth if said truth was a story of theft and trickery. But what difference did it make now that Alexei was dead?

"Do you have any objection to asking her now?"

"Not really, though I think it best to wait until morning. She fades early in the evening." Lydia looked away from him as she spoke the lie. She needed time to think when she was not distracted by his presence.

———

Mrs. Griffin and her daughter left the dining room. The footman poured some brandy and Griff let out a laugh that startled Chase.

"What is bothering you, my lord? You are as restless as a ten-year-old, or mayhap a twenty-year-old thinking of what he would rather be doing than having dinner with an old lady and her two aging children."

"I enjoy your mother, and your sister has a wicked sense of humor."

"Always so much more amusing when it is not aimed at me," Griff said sourly. "I suspect it is why she never married. No man could ever match her repartee."

"There are worse things than being on the shelf, Griff, and your sister seems to realize that."

"Yes, we are too contented, the three of us. I'm not sure that's always good." Griff stood up and went behind the screen to use the chamber pot.

Had he ever been content? Chase wondered. He thought

about it as he savored the newly imported French brandy, which had been unavailable during the war—one of the inconveniences he had borne without complaint, or not much complaint, while his countrymen fought the French.

He'd enjoyed being away at school. He'd enjoyed the London Season, but the only contentment he could recall was that moment sitting in the back room of Chernov Drapers, enjoying tea and superb cream cakes with Lydia.

But while he might have been content, his Lydia had secrets she had not yet shared. He hoped when she trusted him enough she would lay them before him and realize that, whatever they were, they were all in a past that might influence the present but was not part of their future.

He turned to Griff, who had just sat down again and was breathing in the brandy. "What have you been able to find out about Alexei Chernov?"

"The man was a chameleon," Griff began. "He was loved or hated," Griffin went on, "depending on who you talk to. One thing they all agree on is that he always had an eye on the main chance, on a way to make money quick and easy."

"Legally?"

"If one does not put too fine a point on it. For example, he would not hesitate to cut yardage from a bolt or substitute a bolt of lesser quality if he thought the buyer would be taken in. Almost always it worked. Not too many as quick as he was."

Chase sipped the brandy. What he really wanted to do was knock it back and call for more. "How deep was his wife into this chicanery?"

"Everyone, to a man, says that Mrs. Chernov has spent the last year trying to right his wrongs. Money's been tight for the family since he drowned, not because a woman is running the business, but because she is trying too hard to clear the Chernov name."

"How did you find out all of this?"

"My mother. She knows everyone in town, including Chernov's sister, who's married to Allerton, the biggest mill owner in Birmingham. Mrs. Allerton's the one who gave my mother that last bit about how hard Mrs. Chernov is working to make the Chernov name respectable again. Mrs. Allerton wants nothing more than to rise in society."

"Then how do you know she was telling the truth about Mrs. Chernov's efforts?" It was easier to think objectively when he wasn't drowning in Lydia's eyes, in that floral scent she favored, in the way she held on to her necklace when she was moved or afraid.

"I talked to a few of the merchants involved myself. They said Mrs. Chernov has been honest, even too honest. One of them said he took her aside and explained a few home truths about the way a merchant makes money. He said she thanked him for his insight but that she would do business so she did not need brandy to sleep at night."

Chase smiled into his glass. That sounded like the woman he loved. He almost choked on the sip that accompanied that thought, then put it out of his mind as Griff went on.

"According to Mrs. Allerton, Mrs. Chernov and Mr. Allerton are about to sign an agreement. She is going to give him the purple dye recipe that Alexei Chernov would never share with anyone."

He straightened. "Why in the world would she do that? It's arguably the most valuable item she owns." *Except, possibly, for the mysterious coin.*

"Mrs. Allerton told my mother that the contract would guarantee that the recipe stayed in the family."

The whole thing gave him a headache. Or maybe it was the brandy he had done without for so long. Wasn't Lydia family enough? "Thank you, Griffin. And do thank your mother. I have no idea how she is able to convince people to confide in her, but I am glad she does."

"She adds something to their tea," Griff said with a straight face and then chuckled at Chase's shocked expression.

"No, no. She is one of those people who listen, and people do always want to talk about themselves. She once had a woman confess to an affair with Prinny."

"Yes, well, those stories abound."

"Not here in Birmingham. Mother was shocked and still will not tell me who it was."

They talked on about scandals of Seasons past, and by the time he was in his carriage headed back to his town house, Chase wished he had not consumed quite so much brandy.

Griffin had just told him that Lydia Chernov was too honest.

How interesting. He was almost positive she had been less than honest with him. Gambling, years of serious gambling, had taught him what to look for. For all her honesty in business, Chase was sure that there was something in her personal life she was hiding from him. When would she trust him enough to tell him?

NINE

"Chase, I'm not sure meeting Grandmama is a good idea. Let me talk to her alone." Lydia began to reach for the coin around her neck and then stayed her hand, dropping it back to her waist.

"Lydia, take me upstairs. I expect she is as curious about me as I am about her."

"Yes," Lydia said with an anxious sigh. "She has been nagging me endlessly."

"Are you afraid she will not like me or she will like me too well, before you've decided what you think?"

"I don't know. Both, I suppose."

"That's what your hesitation is about? You do not want to be pressured into a decision?" He took her face in his hands and kissed her, letting his hands slide to her neck and then her shoulders as he pulled her to him. When they broke apart, each gasping for breath, he smiled. "I think you have decided. Or else I have misjudged you and you're not nearly as virtuous as I believe."

Lydia's face drained of color. Didn't she know he was teasing? Or was she the sort that did not take teasing well? Chase began to walk toward the stairs. "Take me up to her, my dear. I cannot stand a moment more of the suspense."

With an annoyed huff, she punched his arm lightly and went ahead of him. So as not to crowd her, he left a few steps between them, which gave him a delightful view of her swaying hips.

The flat that Lydia called home was small and tidy, just as he expected. One table was piled with fabric samples in no apparent order, but that was the only sign of disarray in the main room. There were two—no, three—doors off the main room, and one of the doors was ajar. No sooner had Lydia closed the door behind them than someone called out to her.

"Lydia!" The voice was strong but tinged with age and impatience. "Who do you have with you?"

"A friend, Babushka. When you are ready for a caller, have Delphie bring you out."

Chase could hear the woman berating the serving girl. Lydia turned to him and shrugged her apology. Going over to a cabinet, she pulled out a bottle, vodka he assumed, and three glasses. Vodka before sunset? Is that how Russians dealt with difficult conversations?

"We are at the table, Grandmama," Lydia said as a very old, very frail woman came out of the bedroom, using a cane to feel in front of her rather than for support.

"A friend? You said this man is a friend. Is this the gentleman that you have been seeing?"

"This is Lord Chase. He is related to the Duke of Bournemouth. He is the gentleman who rescued me from the abduction."

"Exactly, and he has been here almost every day since. It's about time you brought him to see me."

"Yes, Grandmama," Lydia said.

"Do not use that long-suffering tone with me, Lydia. Someone must look out for your best interests if your own family will not. Where is my vodka?"

"Right here, dearest." Lydia led her to a chair and helped her make a comfortable seat.

A few minutes passed in conventional conversation. When the topics of weather, fashion, and the health of the king had been dispensed with, Lydia filled the silence with the first pressing question. "Grandmama, before he left on his last trip, Alexei gave me a coin that he asked me to wear and regard as my greatest treasure."

Grandmama straightened her already straight spine and spoke in Russian, paused, and then reverted to English. "Alexei gave you the coin. Thank God! I thought he drowned with it."

"You know about the coin?" Lydia touched the necklace and hurried on as if after all this time a few more minutes mattered. "Grandmama, why would he call it my greatest treasure?"

And who else would know, and why would they try to steal it? Chase thought.

"Because it is a magic coin." Lydia's Grandmama sat forward, her rheumy eyes still managing to convey her excitement.

"Magic?" Lydia asked as though the old lady had misspoken.

"Yes, the coin grants a wish, one wish, to whoever is holding it at the time." She turned her head as if looking from one to the other. Following the sound of their voices, Chase surmised.

"How do you know it grants the wish?" Chase asked. The story was preposterous. Maybe the old woman just craved attention.

"How else would you explain how Lydia came into our lives and we were able to escape Russia only a little ahead of Napoleon's invasion?"

"You *wished* for it, Grandmama?"

"Yes, this is exactly what I said: 'I wish that my family and I could escape the tragedy that is about to befall our country.' Not one week later, Alexei brought you home to us and announced that your father would give us the papers we needed to ensure our safe travel. What was that if not magic?"

"But Alexei and I had known each other for months before I met you that evening."

The old lady waved that away. "He had no idea your father worked at the British embassy when he met you at the shop. You know as well as I do that you were the means by which we escaped."

"Not to put too fine a point on it, Grandmama, but it was my father who gave you the papers."

"Yes, that was the beginning, but you were the one who dealt with all those hideous border guards when Alexei had to stay behind. You were the one who suggested that Irina dress as a boy to save her virtue. You were the one who faced death or worse that night we were trapped in that German village. You were the one who found passage for us, and you were the one who knew that Birmingham was the best place for us to settle once Alexei had joined us."

Lydia closed her eyes, looking for all the world as if she wanted to be invisible. Finally she gave up the pretense. "Anyone would have done that for the people they loved, Grandmama."

"No, they would not. You know that for the truth, my lord, do you not? You know how special our Lydia is."

"Yes, I do, and you are right. I have never met anyone quite like Lydia." It was not magic, but the short story of their escape further proved how loyal Lydia was.

"Exactly so," Grandmama said and went on. "I gave the coin to Alexei right after we arrived in England. I have no idea what he wished for, but he must have wished for something before he gave the coin to you. What I don't understand is why he didn't tell you it was magic."

"I can guess that Alexei thought he had years and years and years to influence what I wished for."

"Or he thought that there was nothing magic about the coin." Chase did not want to sound like a practical Englishman, but that made the most sense to him.

"Then why would he tell me it was my most treasured possession?" Lydia asked.

No one said anything for a minute, but Chase had a feeling the two women were communicating all the same. On Alexei's failings or what he might have wished for? Or how to prove to him that the coin was magic?

Chase straightened so quickly that the two women were startled. He was an instant convert to the power of the magic coin. "You used your wish, Lydia!"

"I did?"

"Yes, yes, the second time I confronted Nesbitt. He broke my arm. I know he did. And I remember you holding on to your necklace, as you do when you are upset, and then wishing—you used the word *wish*—that I had not broken my arm."

"Was there a bright light and a sense of heat?" Grandmama asked.

Chase and Lydia looked at each other and nodded. Chase thought it was the kiss that had generated that sensation. Was it the coin?

"Yes, Grandmama, there was. We were distracted at the moment but, yes, there was both light and heat."

"Distracted?" she queried, slowly raising her eyebrows. "Indeed."

Lydia glanced at Chase, who was looking at the ceiling.

"Well, now we know why someone wants the necklace." Chase spoke into the silence.

To Lydia's relief, Grandmama allowed the change of subject.

"But we do not know who wants it," Lydia said. And then added, "Do we?"

"According to Nesbitt, someone with an accent."

"I have no idea who Nesbitt is." Grandmama's annoyance at being left out was obvious. "But I suspect the villain is Irina."

"Irina!" Lydia stood up. "But how did she know anything about it? Did you tell her?" Lydia answered her own questions. "Of course not." She walked around the room, wishing she understood people better. "Alexei must have told her about it. Nesbitt referred to it as the necklace that is my 'greatest treasure,' which is exactly how Alexei described it."

Lydia stopped her pacing and looked at Chase. "But why would she not just ask me for it? Surely there is magic enough to share."

Grandmama answered without pause. "Because Irina is a selfish witch who cannot imagine anyone as generous as you are. It is not enough for her to inherit the purple dye when I go to God. If there is more money to be had, she wants it. Money is the reason she married Mr. Allerton. Not affection for anything but the riches he could shower on her. But I am telling you, Lydia, this coin has no value outside of its magic. You can be sure that Alexei investigated that thoroughly."

"Yes, Grandmama, he would," Lydia said, as if this was a story with which she was all too familiar. She nodded her head, her resolve clearly firm. "I am going to call on Irina right now and see if we can come to some agreement."

The old lady raised her hands in disgust. "You would give everything away if I did not restrain you."

Lydia leaned down to kiss her on both cheeks. "Yes, Babushka, you are completely right. I am lucky to have you help me be sensible. But in this I am firm. I will go to her and give her the coin." Then another thought occurred to her and she turned to Chase. "Unless, my lord, you would like to make a wish first."

"Thank you, Lydia, but I already have."

"You did?"

"Like you, it was an accident, but it was what I would have wished for if I had known the coin was magic." When she still looked blank, he added, "Last night I wished you would appreciate me for the man I am despite the title."

Oh yes, she thought, she did recall that. "I am so sorry you wasted your wish. I think I already appreciated you as fully as possible." Indeed, he had already won her heart.

"Oh, lovely," the old lady said as she clapped her hands together in pleasure.

The two words convinced Chase that he had won Grandmama's approval. Lydia might have been hesitant to introduce them, but he now saw that it was an essential step to gaining her trust.

With another kiss of farewell, Lydia gathered her bonnet and gloves, inviting Chase to accompany her to see Mrs. Allerton. As if she had a choice.

His carriage waited outside the shop, and she allowed him to help her inside and then gave the direction to the driver.

They settled back and Lydia stared out the window. He watched her profile. There was a loneliness about her that made him sad for her. "Are you thinking about your husband?"

"I was thinking that it was time to tell you the truth."

"Thank you, Lydia. I must admit that the conversation with Mrs. Chernov roused as many questions as it answered."

"What is the first that comes to mind?" She faced him with a slight smile, as if the first question he would ask was a test.

"Your father helped the Chernovs leave Russia. Where is he now?"

"He died three weeks before we left St. Petersburg. I had no plans to leave with the Chernovs, but when Papa died there was no reason for me to stay, no means of support, no family to turn to. With Napoleon so near, the embassy was in chaos, so when Alexei suggested I accompany them as his wife, I accepted."

He listened to the way she phrased that last sentence and wondered, but went in another direction instead. "Your father worked for the embassy?"

"Yes, he did. I spent most of my life in St. Petersburg." She closed her eyes and he watched defeat overtake her. "My grandfather was an earl. My father was young and easily influenced when my mother convinced him to run away with her to Gretna Green. My grandfather disowned him, but when Grandfather died, the new earl, my father's brother, found a place for my father with the embassy in Russia. If he promised never to come back to England."

Lydia is the legitimate relation of an earl and, in fact, better born than I am. "So your family does not even know that you exist?"

"I do not know or care."

They were about to turn off the road when Lydia grabbed his stick and knocked on the roof. The carriage rolled to a stop.

Lydia spoke in a rush. "I am not finished."

"All right," he said, wise enough to wait while she put together her thoughts.

"After he died, Alexei used to come to me in my dreams and at other times when I was almost asleep and say one word. 'Wish.' I never understood what he meant. And now of course I do." She looked at him, fear in her eyes. "Do you think I am going mad?"

"Absolutely not. Now, if you told me that Alexei was sitting beside us, then I might speak differently. But we can no more control the dreams that come to us when we are asleep or half-waking than we can control who will hold a winning hand."

Lydia laid her head on his shoulder, and he knew she was either very upset or very reassured. He knocked on the roof, and the carriage began moving again.

"One last thing, Lord Chase."

"I already know," he said, taking her hand in a gesture he hoped she read as comfort. "You did not inherit the recipe for the purple dye because you were never married to Alexei Chernov."

Tears filled her eyes, and she looked down at his gloved hand over hers, the slightest nod confirming his statement.

They had reached their destination, and before Lydia could say anything else, the damned servant had the door opened and the stairs lowered.

Lydia brushed the tears off her cheeks. "If we hope to have the truth from Irina, I think it is best if I talk to her alone."

"All right," he said grudgingly. "I will wait here, but you must send a footman for me if there is any trouble."

"I am going to give her exactly what she wants. What kind of trouble could there be?"

———

It took forever for the servants to find Mrs. Allerton, and then the footman led Lydia to the garden where a small tributary of the river flowed under a too-picturesque bridge that Mr. Allerton had added recently. The water was running fast after the last week of incessant rain, and was brown, muddy, and wholly unappealing.

Irina was sitting on a bench built into the center of the railing overlooking the stream, lost in thought. She stood when Lydia's footsteps sounded on the wooden bridge.

"How are you, Irina?" Lydia asked cautiously. It was unlike Irina to be less than formal, to receive her outside without the offer of tea.

"I am well. It is such a lovely day that I thought we could both use some fresh air."

Lydia nodded and they sat. Now that she was here, Lydia was not at all sure how to start. She did not want to accuse Irina of wrongdoing. There was enough tension in the family without adding Nesbitt to the picture, especially since there was no real proof that Irina had been the one to hire him.

Hadn't Nesbitt said it was a man? Yes, but perhaps it was a woman disguised as a man. Irina had traveled from Russia dressed as a boy. It was an affectation she had perfected.

Whether Irina had been part of the subterfuge didn't matter. The coin with its one magic wish was hers now.

Lydia pulled the chain out from underneath her chemise and let the coin lie on her dress. "Alexei gave me this just before he left on his last trip."

Irina jumped up from her seat and looked at Lydia with poisonous eyes. "It does not belong to you, you imposter. You are not Alexei's wife. You are no more than his kept woman who has taken all she could from the Chernovs, even now when Alexei is dead."

Lydia stood up, too, wishing she had let Chase accompany her. "Irina, please. Just listen to me a moment."

Irina grabbed the necklace and jerked as hard as she could; the necklace was fragile and gold, so it broke without much pressure. Still, Lydia cried out and tried to grab it back.

"Alexei told me it would be the family's most treasured possession." She examined the coin, confusion replacing triumph. "It doesn't look very valuable to me. What kind of coin is it?"

"It's a magic coin, Irina. Listen to me. You are allowed one wish on it. Just one."

"You are the worst liar in the world. Do you think I am going to make my wish and hand it back to you? It has some value, I'm sure of it."

Chase came running around the side of the house, his stick in hand, the sword still sheathed, but his hand at the ready.

"Please, Irina," Lydia begged as Chase joined them on the bridge. "Give it back to me if you don't believe what I am saying. The coin's worth is in its magic. Other than that it is only a trading coin. Alexei investigated it completely. You know he would not have left me with anything of such value when he could have used it to build the business."

Irina's agitation lessened as she considered what Lydia said. Finally she held up the coin, a sneer twisting her pretty face. "Here is what I wish for, that you and your idiot lover find exactly what you deserve."

"Now give it back to Mrs. Chernov," Chase said with that cold edge to his voice that always made Lydia shiver.

"Or what? You will run me through with your sword stick?"

Lydia glanced at Chase, not because she was afraid that he might do just that, but at the admission, however unintentional, that Irina had spoken to Nesbitt—for how else could she know about the sword stick?

Irina shrieked then and threw the glowing coin away from her. "The damn coin burned my fingers!"

The coin flashed in the afternoon sun, and the three of them watched it as it arced into the air, splashed into the water, and was swept away by the current.

Silence, complete silence settled around them. Chase was convinced. He wondered if Irina was.

"A magic coin. You charlatans. What did you treat it with so that it would burn my hand?"

She would never be convinced, Lydia realized and, really, it didn't matter anymore.

"Leave right now, both of you, or I will send the servants to oust you." Irina left them and ran toward the house while both Chase and Lydia stared at the stream, the coin nowhere to be seen. Chase offered Lydia his arm.

They walked back around the house to where the carriage waited. They sat very close this time.

"I wonder what will happen to the coin," Lydia speculated. "Do you think it's lost forever?"

"I'm not sure it matters. Even if it is found, who will think to wish on it without some guidance?"

"What a waste of good fortune."

"We have all we need, though." Chase took her hand and kissed it. "I love you, Lydia."

"But my past—" she began.

He spoke over her protests. "Has made you the wonderful woman you are. Your family failed you, Alexei failed you, but somehow that has only strengthened your generous heart. Of course I love you. Never, ever doubt that."

"All right," she agreed, smiling at him.

"And I will marry you," he said pointedly, then added, "when you are ready."

"Oh, Chase," she whispered, her lips close to his. "It would make the secret wish of my heart come true." *Marriage, children, and a life with someone who loves me.*

They kissed and there was silence in the carriage for a very long time.

As the conveyance passed the Bull Ring and made a turn onto the street that housed Chernov Drapers, Lydia and Chase helped each other smooth their clothes and put their hats back on.

"It may be vindictive of me, but I wish Irina truly knew that she gave her wish to us, though I suppose there is no way to convince her."

"No. I think not. Besides, she is out of your life for good, I hope."

"I expect so. I cannot imagine Grandmama will still consider a business merger with Mr. Allerton after the way Irina lost the coin. But when Grandmama dies, Irina will inherit the shop and the dye recipe. Until then, I do not need to see her ever again."

"Good. We have no need of her ill will. Nor does your grandmama need her temper tantrums."

"Chase, that wish she made." Lydia faced him fully as the carriage drew up in front of the shop. "To use her words, what do you think we deserve?"

He kissed her lips, her eyes, her cheeks and pulled her into his arms. Home. Right here, right now, he saw the start of the first true family he had ever known. "What do we deserve, Lydia? Why, to live happily ever after, of course."

EPILOGUE

———◆———

The fisherman threw the line in the water again. Mr. Arbuthnot was tired and hungry, but this was the first dry day in a week and he hated fishing in the rain.

He pulled the line across the bottom of the river and came up with a nail and a coin. But not the coin he was fishing for.

His charge was clear: to care for the coin, to share its magic. It was a charge he took seriously. Mr. Arbuthnot put the nail and the coin on the pile of items his magnetized "hook" had caught that day and was about to toss out the line again when a man came by.

He was well dressed. A successful business owner of some kind, Arbuthnot guessed. Not inclined to believe in magic. But he could be wrong.

"You know, my good man, there are no fish worth catching this time of year."

"Yes, but then I am not trying to catch a fish."

The man gave him the kind of look that implied he was crazy, and Mr. Arbuthnot took pity on him. "I lost something very important and I am hoping that the magnet at the end of this line will bring it home to me."

"Huh," the man said. "How do you know where you lost it?

The river is running high right now. It is playing havoc with the waterwheel at the mill I own."

"I can see it flash every now and again," Arbuthnot explained as he congratulated himself on the accuracy of his identification of this man.

The mill owner stared at the river and then took a step closer to the edge. "There, right there!" He pointed to a place not two feet offshore. "I saw something flash."

Arbuthnot trailed the line over the spot and, sure enough, he caught something. Afraid to breathe, he pulled the line in and slowly, slowly dragged the catch to within reach.

Sure enough, it was the coin. The very coin that had been minted in 1808 and sent to India, only to sink with the ship just off the coast of England. He took the coin, sparkling gold, and dried it with a handkerchief.

The man stood beside him, smiling and nodding as though he had saved the day.

"Sir, I thank you. I thank you and give you this coin if you will listen and believe what I say."

"No, it's your coin." The man stumbled back and made to leave.

"It's yours now. If you will accept that it's a magic coin and will grant one wish. The trick is the coin will only grant the wish it feels is right. You will know it is the right wish when it glows bright and feels hot, just as it is at this moment."

Arbuthnot held out his hand. Indeed the coin glowed and felt warm, as much a sign to Arbuthnot that he was doing the right thing as it was to the man.

"Sir, bear in my mind, the wish is yours alone to make. Once you have made one, you can pass it on."

The man, who did not need more money, reached out and then hesitated. "I don't know what to wish for."

"The coin knows," Arbuthnot repeated.

The man nodded and took it. "I'm not sure I believe you, but even if it's a joke I will still take it. My nephew collects foreign coins and this will be a fine addition to his collection."

"Aha, but do wish on it first before you give it to your nephew, and then pass it on, please. It is not meant to be in a collection. If you will not share it, I must keep it."

The mill owner was obviously used to bargaining. "I'll tell you what. If I do win what I wish for, I will pass it on. If not, it will go into my nephew's collection."

"Very well." Arbuthnot nodded. "But bear in mind that the coin may interpret your wish in a way different from what you construe."

"All right," the man said and smiled. "I will be careful what I wish for."

Arbuthnot decided he had to be satisfied with that. Gathering his other finds and his fishing rod, he prepared to leave.

"Good night, sir, and thank you," the man called out to him.

"No, thank you," Mr. Arbuthnot called back. "You have made my task much easier."

Mr. Allerton shrugged his shoulders and walked back to find his nephew, who was skipping rocks along the bank farther down the path.

AUTHOR'S NOTE

———◆———

Stories with continuing characters have always been a favorite theme of mine both as a writer and a reader. I had no idea when I wrote "Poppy's Coin" in our first anthology, *Bump in the Night*, that the coin would be the element that continues in each novella.

If you go to my website, MaryBlayney.com, you will find a chronology of the coin in each of the novellas in which it has appeared.

The coin I call "Poppy's coin" does exist, though I have never seen it do its magic. The *Admiral Gardner*, a ship bound for India, left England in 1809 carrying a load of freshly minted coins. The ship sank just off the Goodwin Sands. Between 1984 and 1985, an authorized treasure-hunting diving syndicate recovered the cargo. My good friend, writer Lavinia Kent, gave me one of them, and it inspired "Poppy's Coin."

There are still some stories untold. What did Martha Stepp wish for? She is the maid who is fired in the second novella, "Amy and the Earl's Amazing Adventure" in *Dead of Night*, and Martha appears again as the baby's nurse in "The Other Side of the Coin."

At the end of "The Other Side of the Coin" in *The Other Side*, Miss Lucy Bright is left with the coin and knows exactly what she will wish for, but so far she has not told me what that is. I'm not sure how Alexei Chernov worded his wish, but it's the reason he never came back from his trip abroad.

I do know what Mr. Allerton wishes for: that someone will love him for himself and not for his money. His wish is granted when his selfish, feckless wife, Irina, eventually bears a son, and later a daughter. The two children love their father dearly and care for him all his life.

The coin interprets the wish as it sees fit. So, yes, be careful what you wish for.

Finally, a little history of purple dye. Before the chemistry of dyeing was perfected, purple dye came from mollusks. Discovered around 1600 B.C. on the Levantine coast, the process required twelve thousand shellfish to recover 1.5 grams of dye, making it the most expensive color to produce, and thus, the color of royalty. Who knows how the Chernovs developed their mollusk recipe, but it was, even in 1816, a very valuable commodity.

Yes, people used magnets in the early nineteenth century, though the relationship between magnetism and electricity had yet to be demonstrated. And yes, there were women who owned and managed shops then, mostly widows, just as Lydia pretended to be.

If you have any other questions, please let me know. My email address is MaryBlayney@gmail.com.

DEAR ONE

PATRICIA GAFFNEY

To everybody. Thanks for everything.

ONE

———◆———

"Hm?" Charlie Worth said the first two times his grandson, Oliver, asked him about the credit card bill. If he feigned deafness indefinitely, Oliver might give up and leave him alone. Although such a thing had never happened before.

"Grandfather."

A chair scraped on the kitchen floor. Charlie kept his binoculars focused on the insipid view, three floors below, of a flock of geese and an old lady pushing a walker around one of the bean-shaped lakes at The Lakes at Cartamack, Vibrant Living for Active Seniors.

"Grandfather," Oliver said at his elbow.

Charlie gave up. *"What?"*

"What's this?"

He squinted. Maybe he could feign blindness.

"Here." Oliver tapped a line on the bill. "I'm sure it's a mistake. It says you spent over four hours on the phone this month to a 900 number, something called 'M. Romanescu.' For a total of $780.39."

Stalling, Charlie pulled back his lips, trying to mimic his grandson's amused, incredulous smile. "M. Romanescu. M. Romanescu." He said that a few more times, then fell back on "Hm."

Gradually Oliver stopped smiling. At the moment his eyes went wide with shock, Charlie realized what Oliver was thinking.

"It's not phone sex!"

"Of course not. Of course not." Oliver actually blushed—Charlie hadn't seen that happen in twenty years. It diverted him until Oliver said, "What is it, then?"

Charlie opened and closed his mouth. This wasn't going to go over well. He got that cornered-kindergartner feeling Oliver was so good at provoking. "Hey, you're the one always telling me to get out more, do this, do that, mingle with the peeps." The best defense was a good offense. "And look what happens when I do—the third degree!" He retreated to the kitchen.

"Grandfather," Oliver said, following. Who called his grandfather "Grandfather"? Nobody but Oliver. "This is one 900 number. One peep. What, or who, is M. Romanescu?"

"You hungry? I got doughnuts."

"Who is M—"

"Romy, her name's Romy, and she's a friend of mine, okay?" He started rummaging in the pantry. "Chocolate, I got glazed, I got sprinkles. . . ."

"Romy?"

"Madame Romanescu to you. We could split a cruller." He heard a thump—Oliver falling back against the counter.

"A psychic. My God. A telephone psychic."

"What? I can't have a friend? We talk, that's all. She tells me things."

"I bet she does."

"Real things. Stuff she couldn't know!"

Oliver made the pained face that always made Charlie, who was seventy-seven, feel like seven. "We talked about this, Grandfather. We agreed. You said you'd stick to the new budget—no more shopping channel, no catalogs, no online poker."

"This is different. I'm being *sociable*."

"You're being—" Oliver pinched the bridge of his nose, making a big show of summoning patience. "I know it's been rough on you the last couple of years. Losing Nana, moving here—"

"Shoulda stayed where I was. Perfectly good house, should never've listened to you. Should never've . . ." He trailed off, didn't say "given you my goddamn power of attorney." He'd lose that argument, but only because Oliver didn't play fair. He liked to bring up things that ought to be water under the dam, couple of unfortunate little financial incidents, could happen to anybody. Water under the dam.

"You haven't given this place a chance," Oliver was saying in his tolerant voice. "All the activities—"

"I hate activities."

"—and golf, you haven't even tried your new clubs."

"I hate golf."

"You don't. You used to love golf."

"Used to. Now I hate it." He stuffed a doughnut hole in his mouth.

"Look," Oliver said, glancing at his expensive wristwatch. Always with the schedule. He started cleaning up the bills, the Medicare and Social Security forms, all the stuff he brought over once a month for Charlie to sign. Or explain. "I have to go, Grandfather, I'm sorry. I've got a thing this evening, but before—"

"A party!" Charlie pounced. "Some job *you* got. Wish *I* had that job." That always got to him. Oliver was some kind of big-deal energy lobbyist on Capitol Hill, but all he did was go to cocktail parties—or so Charlie liked to needle him.

"But before I go, I want you to promise me you'll quit calling this psychic. I mean it, Grandfather, this has to stop. You know better."

"What? What do I know better?"

"That it's bogus! A scam. These people prey on the elderly, the—well, frankly, the gullible. It's what they do."

"Romy's not like that."

"Promise me."

"Or what, you'll cut off my allowance?" He would, too; he'd done it before. "You don't take after me," Charlie said testily. "I don't know who you take after. Nobody in the family I can think of. I think it's very likely you were adopted."

Oliver just looked at him.

"All right. All right! Christ almighty, what a wet blanket. Talk about a killjoy."

"Sticks and stones," Oliver said, smiling again. He got his suit coat off the back of the chair, where he'd put it so it wouldn't wrinkle. The fact that he was wearing a suit hadn't tipped Charlie off that he had somewhere else to go this afternoon because Oliver *always* wore a suit. He probably took a shower in his suit. He put all the papers in his snazzy briefcase, put the briefcase under his arm, and threw his other arm across Charlie's shoulders, presumably to show there were no hard feelings. "You know," he said, oh so casually as they walked to the front door, "they've got a full-time staff person here at Cartamack—I saw it in the newsletter. Somebody, counselor type, you could talk to. If, you know, you wanted to."

A *shrink*? Oliver wanted him to go see a *shrink*? Charlie said, "Hm?" pretending not to hear, and Oliver didn't follow up. Hard to say which of them was gladder to drop the subject. Worth men didn't go to shrinks.

Although, come to think of it, Oliver might've gone to one after the accident, for all Charlie knew. How many years ago was that, five, six? Change that, then: Worth men didn't go to shrinks and *talk* about it.

Oliver paused, as he usually did, to look at Charlie's collection of Western bronzes on the glass shelves by the front door. He picked up his favorite, the biggest, heaviest one: five mustangs in full gallop. Charlie picked up his own favorite, a cowboy whipping his muscle-bound horse with his hat, hair blowing back in a realistic headwind. Thirty years ago, he and Oliver used to roll around on the living room rug in Charlie's house, making up games about posses and ambushes, cattle drives and gold rushes. Love of a mythical Old West was the main thing they'd had in common in those days. Probably still was.

Even now, just holding the heavy bronze horses had the effect of putting them back in favor with each other. "Got any shirts for the cleaners?" Oliver asked, and Charlie said no, not this week, thanks. They talked about Charlie's 401(k), whether he ought to renew his AARP membership. They exchanged their traditional manly, one-armed hug, and Charlie thought it went on a second or two longer than usual.

Then Oliver ruined everything by saying, "So we're clear about this psychic, right, Grandfather? No more of that. I'm holding you to your promise."

"Oh, hold this," Charlie said, and closed the door on him.

TWO

———◄———

Hold this?

Charlie must be going senile. A *psychic*. What next, wiring money to a Nigerian bank account? Oliver didn't like the look in his eye either when Grandfather had shut the door in his face. Shifty, that's what it was. Shifty and untrustworthy.

If you gave Charlie an inch, he'd take a mile—Oliver knew that from experience. So it was no good saying, *Fine, call Madame Romanescu anytime you want, and if it breaks the bank, no problem, I'll step in and save you.* Which he could easily do, but that wasn't the point. Charlie needed to live within his means for his own good, his own self-respect. If Charlie was tired of being treated like a child, Oliver was tired of acting like the heavy.

"Madame Romanescu." What a laugh. He'd seen their ads on late-night cable, the lady fortune-tellers. Such *obvious* fakes. How could Charlie fall for such a rip-off? Stopped at a light on Connecticut Avenue, Oliver rummaged in his briefcase till he found his grandfather's credit card statement, and at the next light he punched in Madame Romanescu's 900 number on his cell phone.

"Hello," said a soft, smoky voice in some kind of an accent. "It is Madame Romanescu. What is troubling you today, dear

one? What is the problem you cannot solve? Perhaps it's difficulty with a loved one. Someone you love who doesn't love
you back. Or is it your career? Money problems? Your child;
a beloved pet? Maybe a dream, or the memory of one of your
past lives. I have helped others, and I can help you. The cost
of the call is $2.99 a minute, and I accept all major credit and
debit cards. *And*"—the low-pitched, sympathetic voice rose a
note with genuine-sounding goodwill—"today is your lucky
day, dear one, a special offer—ten minutes for only $19.95.
What an opportunity for us, yes? So call me, and we will talk.
For now, I wish you light, life, and love."

Then the operator's voice, completely different, clipped and
no-nonsense. "Please enter your credit card number *now*."

Right, thought Oliver, and clicked off.

———

Cocktail parties were work, not play—Charlie's opinion
notwithstanding—and if you were smart, you didn't eat or drink
much at them. Otherwise you couldn't do your job, not to mention that in a year or two you'd be an obese alcoholic. The
drawback to all that moderation was that you came home empty
but not really hungry, and only buzzed enough to feel sleepy.

Oliver poured a glass of milk and carried it into the den.
Nine o'clock. A useless time of night, too early to go to bed,
too late to get any work done. He phoned Sharon, one of his
partners at Cullen Pratt McGrath, and told her the evening had
been a bust: The senator he was supposed to schmooze never
showed up. He'd had a good conversation with a couple of guys
working on a geothermal startup in Colorado, but he didn't
bother to tell her that. If work wasn't directly billable to a client,
Sharon wasn't interested.

He checked his e-mail. Turned on the TV and flipped
through the channels. Nothing but C-SPAN, and he wasn't in
the mood. A movie? He pulled *Tombstone* from his enormous
Western collection and stuck it in the DVR. He knew the film
almost by heart, though, and by the time Val Kilmer told
Johnny Ringo he was his huckleberry, Oliver was up and pacing
the room, restless. Something nagged at him. Something felt
unfinished.

Charlie had given his promise, but he might weaken. He

had before. He'd been known to go off the deep end. It was no more than a responsible grandson's duty to assess this new danger firsthand.

"Hello. It is Madame Romanescu." The exotic, honey-dipped voice sounded so familiar, he realized he'd been hearing it in the back of his mind all night. He listened to her spiel, happy to hear it was still his lucky day, and when the operator told him to, he punched in his Amex number.

A series of rings; a pause; another series of rings.

"Hello?"

How could anyone get so much . . . not sex, exactly . . . so much *tenderness* into one word? "Hello," Oliver said briskly. "Madame Romanescu?"

"Yes, it is I. How are you?"

"I'm— My name is Oliver Worth, and I'm calling about my grandfather."

"Oh dear. A problem with your grandfather. Yes, I can hear that you are worried, tense—"

"Yeah, you could say I'm worried. He racked up an eight-hundred-dollar phone bill last month talking to you."

Silence; he imagined it full of alarm and guilt.

"Ah," she said at last. "Is he . . . I can't divulge a caller's name. Is he . . ."

"Charlie, his name's Charlie. He's an old man on a fixed income."

"Charlie. Of course. A lovely gentleman. He lives in a retirement community."

"That's right. I've asked him to stop phoning, but I can't be sure he will, so I'm asking you to stop taking his calls."

"But, Oliver—I may call you Oliver?"

"Sure, whatever."

"Oliver—if he *wishes* to call, if it's a *help* to him, because there is no one else to whom he can say certain things—"

"Look, I don't mean to be rude, but if my grandfather needs to talk to someone, I'll get him a qualified therapist. He lives alone, and he's vulnerable. The highlight of his day is reading the obituaries and the foreclosures. So I'm asking you, if you've got any . . ."

"Decency?"

"Any . . ."

"Integrity?"

The rueful smile in her voice threw him off. "Look," he said again, "Madame Romanescu. What you're doing isn't illegal, I *assume*, but in this case it borders, in my opinion, on the unethical. I don't know what he's told you, but Charlie doesn't have that kind of money to throw around. He lives on his savings and his Social Security. That's it."

"Oh dear."

"*Limited* savings. *Limited* Social Security."

"Yes, I see. Very well, then."

"Not only that, he's got a history of not always— What?"

"I said yes, all right. If you insist. I didn't understand— naturally I don't want to make trouble for Charlie. It's just that . . . I'm afraid it will be sad for him. Because he is lonely."

"Oh, is he?" Oliver wavered between annoyance and embarrassment. She was probably right, but it was pretty damned presumptuous of her to point it out. "Everybody's lonely," he said in a careless tone he immediately regretted.

"That's true," she said gently. "Yes, that is very true," and for some reason he felt absolved. No wonder Charlie was in thrall to this woman. "Perhaps you could talk to him, Oliver? A bit more? Spend a little more time with him?"

"Sure. Of course. Although . . ."

"No," she agreed. He and Charlie weren't all that close.

"And I'm a . . ."

"I know," she said. Busy man.

"But I could . . ."

"Yes," she said. Try harder.

"Would you stop doing that?"

"Doing what, Oliver?"

He heard the smile in her voice again. Extraordinary voice. Not so much sexy as sensual, and so caring, it was practically maternal. "What, uh, if I may ask, what is your accent? I can't quite place it."

"Does it matter?"

"No, of course not, I just—"

"It's only that I prefer to keep the focus on my clients, not myself."

"I can see that. Then again, I'm not a client."

"That's true," she said consideringly. "Well, I grew up in

many places, Oliver, mostly around Budapest. But many places."

Budapesht, she pronounced it. "A Hungarian Gypsy," he said with a laugh he couldn't help. He cut it off quickly. Could any of that be true?

"No, not I. My mother, my grandmother, they were Gypsies."

"But you inherited the gift."

"The gift?"

"Of fortune-telling."

She made a low, humming sound, full of amusement and sly accusation. "With my deep clairvoyant powers, I detect a tiny trace of skepticism, Oliver."

"Tell me something about myself," he challenged on a whim. "My sign, my favorite color. My shoe size."

"Ah, you want to play games."

"No, seriously." He almost was serious. This almost mattered. "Tell me something you couldn't know. Something you could only intuit."

A long silence.

"You there?" he prompted.

"I am thinking, dear one. I am receiving."

He grinned and put his feet up on the coffee table, getting comfortable. This was how the dollars added up so fast. And yet he felt nothing but relaxed and patient, anticipatory. Not much like a chump at all.

"Something keeps you from contentment. Something is blocking you. Something stands between you and happiness."

His smile faded. "Isn't that a home run for just about everybody? 'Something.' I don't suppose you could be more specific."

Another thoughtful pause, after which she said, "Guilt?" so softly he barely heard. "Guilt for no reason."

He stood up, knocking over a stack of magazines. He controlled his temper by gripping the phone and squeezing. *Beep.* He must've hit a number—

"Oliver? Hello?"

"How do you do it when you don't have an inside source? Keep it vague, I guess, stick with 'something.'"

"An inside— Do you mean Charlie? He's told me nothing. Oliver, I'm sorry if I've upset you."

"Just stay away from my grandfather. Do we agree on that?"

"Yes, I've told you—"

"Because he can't afford you." He hung up quickly, before he could add, "Neither can I."

THREE

———◆———

"You're having a bad day."

"Oh, hi, Aunt Kit. Hang on a sec." Molly McDougal stuck her cell phone under her chin and shifted a stack of books and notebooks to one arm so she could reach across with the other to retrieve the ticket on her windshield. It said her student parking permit had expired. "How did you know?"

"I didn't divine it. Must've been something about the way you took my head off with 'Hello.'"

"Sorry. I'm fine, really." Especially now that, after a minimum of coughing and gasping, the Pontiac had fired up. Molly pulled out onto Nebraska Avenue and headed for home. "It's just a medium-bad day. How are you? What's new in Hoboken?"

"Everything's peachy, now back to you. What's wrong?"

Molly believed in empathy, not psychic power, and certainly not in mind-reading, but sometimes her great-aunt could be scarily acute. *Don't think about the foreclosure notice in the paper this morning,* Molly told herself—which was like a camper telling herself, *Don't think about that bear snuffling around the sleeping bag.* She thought instead of the *second* worst thing that had happened to her in the last two days. "I just lost my favorite caller."

"Who? Not Charlie. Oh no! Did he—"

"No, no, he didn't die."

"Thank goodness. I *love* that guy."

"But I'm not allowed to talk to him anymore." She told Aunt Kit about the call from Oliver Worth, how she'd agreed not to take his grandfather's calls anymore.

"I think you should anyway."

"No, I can't—apparently he's broke. And we were going to *meet*—I didn't tell you this—Charlie wanted a private reading, and I said yes, even though—but he's such a nice old guy, and after I told him my incredibly psychic great-aunt just sent me her old crystal ball—"

"Did it get there in one piece?"

"It's fine."

"Well, I miss it, but you'll get a lot more use out of it than I will, now that I'm retired."

"Anyway—after I told him about it, he really wanted a face-to-face reading." For which he'd have paid her a hundred dollars. *A hundred dollars.*

"This Oliver guy sounds like a prize stiff," Aunt Kit decided.

"Charlie calls him a stuffed shirt. But fondly," Molly added in fairness. "He always speaks of him with affection. I think he works for the energy lobby."

"Perfect. But this is terrible—you *love* Charlie."

"He was one of my first callers. I'm really going to miss him."

"And I liked hearing about him. But there will be plenty of others, dear. It's slow in the beginning," Aunt Kit advised, as if she'd been in the phone psychic business for years. "But it'll pick up when word gets around."

"What word is that?" Molly asked, making a left on Connecticut.

"Word of mouth, about the amazing Madame Romanescu. People will tell their friends, and they'll tell their friends, and the phone will start ringing off the hook. You'll have to hire employees."

"I'd be happy just to recoup my losses." Oh, she wished she hadn't said that—going into the phone psychic business had been Aunt Kit's brainstorm. But she'd had no idea how big an investment it took to get started.

"What losses? You mean the calling service?"

"Right, they charge for the setup." Eight hundred dollars, plus a fifty-dollar-a-month "maintenance fee." On top of that, Molly only got $1.69 of the $2.99 people paid for a minute. So far, her new part-time job was a serious net loss.

"Guess what," she said to change the subject. "I got an A minus on my Advanced Adolescent Psych exam."

"Yay!" Sounds of applause from Aunt Kit. "Go you! You'll have that master's soon, and then nothing but good times. You'll be back doing what you're *supposed* to do. I *feel* it."

"Two and a half more semesters. I wish I could go faster." But she could only afford nine credits a term, even after adding phone psychic to her other two jobs: dog walker and house sitter.

"You work too hard," Aunt Kit said—reading her mind. "After exams are over, you come up here and see me. I miss you."

"I miss you, too, but I don't think I'll be able to visit anytime soon."

"Think about it. Hoboken in springtime."

"So tempting. Heck, I've got another call—"

"Go. And if it's Charlie, *talk* to him. Don't let that stuffed shirt boss you around."

But it wasn't Charlie. It was a man from the loss mitigation department at the bank, calling to say his boss wouldn't go for her pro bono lawyer's proposal for paying down her mortgage. So the sale of her house was still on.

FOUR

And she loved her house. Her haven, her sanctuary, her pride and joy—but most of all, the brick-and-mortar *proof* she'd needed, after the divorce, that she wasn't anybody's helpless dependent. A 1940s bungalow with only two bedrooms, it had beautiful floors, small but perfect proportions, and a dream of a front porch. She'd bought it during the boom, and paid too much—easy to see that now. But she'd fallen in love, and they'd given her such a *great deal*.

Until the interest rate went up and, practically the next day, she'd lost her assistant counselor job due to budget cuts at Stone Creek Private Academy for Girls.

"This is an opportunity," Aunt Kit had tried to convince her from Hoboken, but for Molly (a *positive* person—"obnoxiously optimistic," her ex used to call her), it was hard to see the progression of her life lately as anything but a slow slide backward. Underwater.

"It's only a house," she told Merlin, her cat, settling beside him on the porch swing with her *Evolution of Human Behavior* textbook. "Just bricks and wood and glass." And she was only thirty, she could start over—she'd done it before. And for now, at least, she could still watch the world go by on sleepy Palmer Street, behind pansy-filled planters, on a beautiful late April afternoon. Really, life was what you made it. She used to say that to the girls at Stone Creek, so . . . so it might or might not be true.

Her psychic line rang.

"Romy, honey," Charlie said, his customary greeting, and immediately she dropped her accent. She'd dispensed with it long ago with Charlie, although neither of them could remember quite when or under what circumstances. It had just happened naturally.

"Charlie, hi, how are you?"

"You tell me." He always said that, too, and it was her cue to say something clairvoyant.

"Hmm . . . I think you're a little tired today."

"That's *right*."

"And you're not in such a great mood."

"Bingo!" Her perspicacity always amazed him.

"But nothing terrible has happened, and you're going to feel better soon. Very soon." While they were still talking, if history was a predictor.

But he was calling too often—she could hardly believe how much money he'd spent talking to Madame Romanescu last month, at least according to his grandson. "Charlie," she said reluctantly, "I think we might have to—"

"So listen, I had this dream. I'm in the store, but it's the first one I had, the one on Cordell Avenue, and I'm *young*." For forty years, before he retired, Charlie had owned Worth's Fine Men's Wear. "And who walks in but Dottie." His wife, dead for two years. "And she says to me, 'I could use a new hat,' and she *winks*. So I'm thinking she doesn't mean *hat*, but what does she mean? I don't want to make a mistake, see, leap to conclusions, because even though it's Dottie, in the dream we don't know each other yet. So I say, 'I got a whole new shipment of *hats* in,' but I can't tell if that's the right answer because just then, *bam*, the lights go out, and that's it, I wake up. So whaddaya think?"

"Um, I think you still miss her a lot. And I think right up to the end she kept you guessing."

"She was a helluva gal. I didn't tell her that often enough."

Molly knew where this was leading. "We all take our loved ones for granted, it's just human na—"

"So what time do you want to come over Tuesday?"

"Well, about that, Charlie, I'm going to have to—"

"I made us a Bundt cake. Dottie's old recipe, so I tried it. It came out! You like sour cream icing? I got this special tea to go with it. If it's nice, we can sit out on the balcony and look at the blue-hairs. So what time's good? Don't forget your crystal ball. Four?"

Molly made two fast decisions. "Four is perfect, and Charlie?"

"Yeah?"

"There's something I've been meaning to tell you. About my phone rates."

"Uh-oh. Is this bad news? Because to tell you the truth, there's something I'm supposed to tell you, too."

"What a coincidence. I'll go first. I have a new rate, a special fee for special customers."

"How much?"

"Nothing. It's free."

When he could speak, Charlie said, "Get outta town!"

"What I do is, I give you my regular phone number, not the 900 one, and you call me at certain times we agree on."

"I *love* this deal."

"And, of course, you never abuse it."

"Never!"

"No, I know."

"Right. But *how* do you know?"

"Oh, Charlie. I'm psychic."

FIVE

Not very psychic, though. Otherwise, she'd have realized Oliver Worth was a big fat liar.

Charlie wasn't poor at all! He lived on the third floor of a new, attractive high-rise overlooking the seventh hole green *and* a lake at The Lakes at Cartamack (or "Heart Attack," as he insisted on calling it). A uniformed guard in a gate-house consulted a list before letting Molly drive in, and the green awning in front of Charlie's building reminded her of a fancy hotel's. *Limited* savings and *limited* Social Security, her foot.

"More cake? More tea?" Charlie pushed the plate and the teapot toward her, and she took some more of both to please him, refilling his cup while she was at it. It wasn't only his apartment; *Charlie* didn't look like what she'd been expecting either. She'd thought he'd be small, a little sprite of a guy, probably bald, with a perpetual sideways smirk to go with his sense of humor. But he was handsome! Not tall, but upright and wiry, with silver hair still thick and wavy, and eyes as blue as his natty cardigan sweater. He even smelled good, and Molly was touched to think he'd not only cooked and cleaned but also dressed up for her.

She'd dressed up for him, in a way. Red skirt, frilly, low-cut blouse, and big hoop earrings; and she'd let her hair, unruly at the best of times, go completely wild. Going for the Gypsy look, to make him laugh. It worked: When he'd opened the door and seen her, he'd guffawed.

"You know what? I thought you'd be older," he confided, devouring a cream-filled cookie in one bite. "Not as old as me, but getting up there."

"How come?"

"The way you talk. You sound wise."

"That's just the accent."

"Also, I thought you'd be sorta fat, frankly."

"Fat!"

"Not sure why. And not fat, exactly. You know what *zaftig* means?"

Molly glanced down at her medium-sized chest. "But instead—"

"You're gorgeous! Also, I never thought for two seconds you'd have red hair and be Irish."

"Well, I never thought you'd look like Cary Grant, so there you go."

He made scoffing sounds and hid half his face behind his napkin, but she could see his cheeks turn pink. He was delighted. "Oliver's the good-looking one in the family. Speaking of, don't ever tell him we did this, he'd have a cow."

"Why would I ever tell *Oliver* anything?" She hadn't even told Charlie about Oliver's phone call, afraid it might embarrass him. Or get Oliver in trouble for going behind Charlie's back. Not that she cared.

"I know, I'm just saying. This here is private. Just us."

"Of course."

"Okay, then. Shall we get this show on the road?" He got up and went into the living room. "This a good place?" He indicated the coffee table. "You on one side, me on the other, ball in the middle. Holy Christ, is that it?"

She'd brought it in the same bowling bag Aunt Kit had shipped it to her in, and she liked to imagine her aunt schlepping the bag to bridge and mah-jongg parties or, better yet, *bowling alleys*, then whipping the ball out to amaze her friends. "It's pretty, isn't it? Like a giant glass paperweight."

"*Giant* glass paperweight," Charlie agreed, taking his seat, pushing up his sleeves. "So how much practice have you had on this thing?"

"Um, some. Not that much. Charlie?"

"Yeah?"

"Nothing, let's get started."

Which would be kinder to him, to pretend she was psychic or confess that she wasn't? She could never decide, so she just kept going along. Like a doctor, hoping to do no harm.

"Okay, now." She cleared her throat. "As I said, we have to be partners in this. I need your mental power and energy at *least* as much as mine, or probably nothing will happen. It helps if we hold hands." They reached across the table and clasped hands; his were dry and cool and scratchy. "Close your eyes. Concentrate."

"What am I concentrating on?"

"Dottie. Right? You said you—"

"Right, right. I want to contact her." He shut his eyes tight and screwed up his face.

Molly followed suit, then realized she had nothing to concentrate on. "A picture, Charlie, I need a photo or something."

"Gotcha." He disappeared, and came back with a gold-framed photograph, eight by ten, of himself and Dottie about twenty years ago, posing on the gangplank of an ocean liner. "On our way to Europe. Isn't she a beaut?"

She assumed he meant his wife, not the ship, and agreed. "*Both* of you, so handsome. And she looks like she adores you." Dottie was tiny, birdlike, with pixie-cut hair tinted strawberry blonde. They were holding hands, and she had her cheek on Charlie's arm, grinning up at him with a kind of mischievous trust. Molly envied them.

She and Charlie went back to holding hands and concentrating. She thought of all he'd told her about Dottie, how funny she was—not always intentionally—and how sweet. Her aversion to cats; her lifelong hypochondria. How much she loved music. The time she missed the brake and drove their brand-new Chevy through the back of the garage. The way she could put people at ease. How, on her deathbed, she told him her only regret in life was never having gone to college—*complete* news to Charlie. Mostly Molly concentrated on the photograph: that expression on Dottie's face, gazing up at her sharp-dressed husband, of irreverent, clear-eyed devotion.

"She misses you." Molly felt sure of that.

Charlie's hands tightened on hers. "You can see her?"

"She misses you, but she's all right. She wants you to know that." Molly shifted her attention from the photo to the crystal ball. The dense glass had textures, reflections, opacities; it was almost always possible to make out *something* in its shifting surfaces. A face—sure, she might see one. Or not. But maybe. And whether or not it was Dottie's face, and whether or not she was trying to tell Charlie she missed him—it did no harm to say so.

"Tell her—" Charlie's eyes moistened. "Tell her *I'm* all right."

"You can tell her."

He swallowed. Mouthed the words. "Tell her—I'll tell her—I'm sorry for not being a better husband."

"She disagrees. She thinks you were . . ." Molly was going to say "great," but changed it to "swell." Just a feeling.

"Aw. Tell her I'm sorry about Cancún."

"She forgives you."

"Some vacation. All we did was fight."

"Half of it was her fault."

"She said that? Tell her I'm sorry for—"

"Wait, Charlie. She's saying . . ."

"What?"

"She says quit with the apologizing. She can't even remember that stuff. A couple of bad notes, she says, in a . . . in a long, beautiful symphony."

Charlie's face looked young, almost; transformed. It erased any guilt Molly might have felt for telling him things he wanted to hear. "Tell her I love her," he said softly.

"She knows. Now she's saying . . . to live your life. Say *yes* more."

"Say *yes* more," Charlie repeated thoughtfully.

Molly released his hands and leaned in, peering more closely into the ball. If she'd seen anything before, it was beginning to fade. "I think that's it, Charlie. No . . . wait. She's saying something. . . ."

"What? What?"

Now this was weird. "I think she said somebody's thinking about you. Right now."

"Who? Somebody, who? Is it Oliver?"

So strange—the form, the essence of Dottie, if there was such a thing, the smoky outline that might be a face, who knew, but in any case the *thing* Molly had been staring at so hard—it changed. She couldn't have said how. But "Dottie" departed and something, or someone, replaced her. Maybe.

"Not Oliver. It's a woman."

Charlie sat back. "A *woman*. Is thinking about me?" He blinked repeatedly. "Really?"

"And she's nearby. Relatively. She's not, you know . . ." Dead.

"Well, who the hell is she?"

"I don't *know*, I can't *see*. She's . . . she's got gray hair. I think." She looked up helplessly. "Oh, Charlie, it's gone, there's nothing. I'm sorry. I think she had gray hair."

"Christ, Molly, everybody *around* here has gray hair." He stood up, looking pleased, annoyed, agitated. "'Scuse me, I gotta use the bathroom."

What was that? Molly fell back against her chair. She was feeling a little dizzy. "What just happened?" she asked out loud. Had she really seen a gray-haired woman in a crystal ball? Dottie she'd been making up—she was pretty sure—but that second woman had seemed so *real*. Aunt Kit was always telling her to be patient, if she wasn't psychic yet she soon would be, McDougals were late bloomers, the gift hadn't come to Kit herself till she was almost forty—to all of which Molly would say "mm hm" and privately roll her eyes. *I'm just sensitive,* she'd think; nothing magical about it. Well, she'd better be sensitive: She was studying for what she hoped would be a long, serious career in counseling young people. If she didn't have a little *natural intuition*, she might as well pack it in.

Somebody knocked at the door. Molly stood up, uncertain. "Charlie?"

"What?" from the bathroom.

"Somebody's at the door."

"Could you get it? I'm . . ." Inaudible; something about "goddamn prostate."

She went to the door and opened it.

"Hi."

"Hi."

After that, she couldn't think of anything to say. Neither could he—the man on the other side of the threshold. She registered tallness, good health, dark hair. Intense blue eyes and a serious mouth. A mouth that slowly, slowly began to smile. Molly stopped breathing. It was like watching the gradual revelation of a gift she'd wanted all her life, inside the most beautifully wrapped box. *Oh, it's you,* a voice—her own voice—said from a deep place inside. *Well, finally.*

"Um," she got out. So much easier to smile back at him than to put words together. Why be coherent when you could just stare? She felt a flooding self-consciousness, and at the same time, extreme excitement. "Have you come to see Charlie?" she asked eventually.

"I have," he said, as if just remembering. "Hello."

"Hello."

"I'm Oliver." He put out his hand—the tenderest gesture. She almost took it, she was so looking forward to touching him, when she heard what he'd said.

"You are? *You're* Oliver?" She backed up, backed away. "Oh. Come in. Hi. I'm, um . . ." She thought she'd been inarticulate *before*. "Charlie's just, um . . ."

Coming out of the bathroom, looking distracted. When he saw his grandson, he stopped dead, virtually froze where he stood. Molly had never seen such a vivid illustration of guilt. "Ha!" he exclaimed; a greeting. "What are you doing here?"

Oliver said something about taxes, a form to sign. He looked at Molly. He looked at Charlie.

"Did you meet?" Charlie said, moving again. "This is, this is . . ."

Molly said, "I'm, um, I'm . . ."

"Crystal," Charlie said. "This is Crystal."

"With a K," Molly decided for some reason.

"Oh," Charlie said, surprised. Then he said, "Smith," at the same moment she said, "Jones."

"Krystal Smith-Jones," they announced in unison.

After that, it got worse.

"Krystal's a Jehovah's Witness."

"No, I'm not! Oh, Charlie. He's such a kidder." Just then she remembered the crystal ball, in plain sight on the coffee table. She sidled around Charlie, pretended to look for something in her purse, which lay on the sofa.

"Yeah, just kidding," Charlie said, moving sideways to put himself between her and Oliver. "She sells time shares."

"Ha-ha! No, I don't." She got the crystal ball in the bowling bag and zipped it up so fast, she broke a nail. If Charlie had been the picture of guilt, the *zzzzzzt* of the bag closing was the sound of it. But at least it gave her an idea. "I'm a therapist," she turned around to say. "Physical. Physical therapist. Charlie didn't want you to know, Mr. Worth, but he . . ." She blanked.

"I have . . ." Charlie prodded.

"He has . . ."

By now Oliver had folded his arms. She barely recognized him. All the warmth was gone, along with that strange, uncanny look of—recognition. Nothing in his face now but growing consternation. "Charlie has what? I wonder," he said coolly.

"He has a strain in the C7 lumbar vertebra."

"The old C7," Charlie said mournfully, rubbing the back of his neck.

Time to go, Molly decided.

"Nice meeting you," she told Oliver, who didn't answer. So she didn't hold out her hand to shake, but she thought of how much she'd wanted to—when? Three minutes ago? A lifetime.

Charlie followed her to the door. "Thanks for the treatment. That's quite a . . . device," he said, indicating the bowling bag she was trying to hide under her arm. "I feel a lot better, Krystal. Not cured, though—probably need at least one more adjustment. There's a thing here next Saturday—maybe you'd like to come?"

"A thing," she repeated. Oliver, who was leaning against the wall beside a shelf full of horse statues, a collection of some sort, didn't even pretend not to listen.

"Yeah, Heart Attack Day or some damn thing. Picnic, entertainment. Last year they had a ukulele quartet, nobody in it under eighty. You wanna come?"

"Oh, gosh, I don't think I . . ." Moving to put himself between her and Oliver, Charlie made an urgent face by bulging his eyes and opening his mouth so wide she could see his fillings. "Ahhh," she changed her answer, "let me check my calendar. I'll get back to you."

"Sounds like fun. Can I come, too?"

Charlie looked surprised, but not nearly as confounded by this from Oliver—whose innocent-looking interest *had* to be manufactured—as Molly thought he should. "Sure," Charlie said, "the more the merrier. So I'll call you," he turned back to Molly to say, raising and lowering his eyebrows meaningfully. But what was the meaning? She felt confused, embarrassed, and depressed.

"Well, 'bye," she said, braving a last glance at Oliver. She took in details she'd missed before, the way his straight shoulders filled out the jacket of his dark suit, his sexy five-o'clock shadow. Tall men were her weakness.

That's all it was, she assured herself on the way down the hall to the elevator. Physical attraction, and already she was over it. Good thing she hadn't met her soul mate or anything. Because Oliver Worth couldn't stand her.

SIX

———◄►———

"Please enter your credit card number *now*."

Oliver obeyed, trying not to think too much about what he was doing. Which wasn't like him. But if he thought about it, he'd hang up, turn off the TV—muted on *The Virginian*, the 1929 version with Gary Cooper—and try to get some work done. Instead he crossed his bare feet on top of the leather ottoman that matched his Eames chair and waited for the voice.

"Hello. This is Madame Romanescu."

"Hey," he said in a dusty Western drawl he hadn't planned on using—it just came out. "How're you this pretty evenin', ma'am?" On the TV screen, The Virginian was riding the range with Shorty, one of his scruffy ranch hands. "Name's Shorty," Oliver said, unimaginatively. "Just thought I'd call up and say how-do."

Madame Romanescu had a friendly smile in her voice when she said, "Hello, Shorty. I am so glad you called. How are you?"

"I'm pretty peaceful. Don't know what it's like where you are, but out here, seems like there's more stars than sky."

"It sounds beautiful. You are somewhere out West, I'm thinking."

"Wyoming, ma'am, just outside Medicine Bend. How 'bout

you? If you don't mind me inquirin'," he added, recalling that she didn't like to talk about her personal life.

She hesitated before saying, "New Jersey. Just outside Hoboken."

Now, that had to be true. What kind of psychic, especially one with a Gypsy accent like hers, would say she came from *Hoboken* unless she did? "Well, I'm damned," Oliver said. "What's it like in Hoboken tonight?"

"Oh . . ." Her voice went away, as if she were craning her neck, looking out a window or a door. "I can't see any stars. The lights from the city, they turn the sky orange."

Lights from New York, she must mean. "Now, that's a shame."

"What is it like where you are?"

"Hot, ma'am. Hotter'n a whorehouse on nickel night."

"And what do you do out there in Wyoming, Shorty?"

He gave a low, lazy laugh. A Gary Cooper laugh. "Hey now, you're the psychic, ma'am, you tell me."

"Mmm . . . I'm thinking you work outdoors quite a lot."

"Now, that's amazing."

"With . . . animals? Is that right? I'm seeing animals."

"Say, this is incredible. 'Cause I work on a cattle ranch."

"Yes. And . . . you are the boss? Perhaps not the big boss, but there are men who work for you. Respect you."

"I like to think they do. I'm the foreman at the Double K. Aw, heck, I shoulda tried to make you guess that."

She laughed, an earthy rumble deep in her throat. Marlene Dietrich, but without the man-eating vibe. "I am no mind reader, Shorty. I can only read the messages you send me."

"Yeah, but send you with my *mind*."

"Tell me what is on your mind tonight, dear one. Something is troubling you, I think. Is it anything I can help you with?"

She was getting right to the point. He could've talked about the weather in Medicine Bend and Hoboken indefinitely—big bucks for Madame Romanescu. Maybe she wanted to go to bed.

"I doubt it," he told her, taking a sip from his cup of decaf. "Just wanted to hear a voice, tell you the truth. Gets powerful lonesome out here on the range, just me and the dogies."

"The dogies?"

"Cattle, ma'am. Longhorns. We're herdin' about two hundred head out to plains pasture for the summer."

"But you like this work, I think. It's hard, but it suits you."

"Most o' the time." Most of the time he enjoyed his job at Cullen Pratt McGrath. "Yeah, I reckon it suits me. Only . . ."

"Only . . ."

"Oh, it's a big ol' ranch, the Double K. Fact, it's a corporation, and lately there's been talk of movin' me up to superintendent."

"Goodness. That sounds like it would be quite different."

"Quite different, yes, ma'am. Lot more . . . administration."

"And how do you feel about that?"

"I got what you call mixed feelings. Course, it's nice they think I'd be good enough and all—"

"A feather in your cap."

"Yep, but then again . . ."

"So much more responsibility. It worries you."

"Nope. No, that's not it."

"No, it's not the responsibility," she amended quickly, "that doesn't bother you. It's more that . . ."

"More that . . ."

"That . . ."

"I always thought someday I might . . ."

"Go out on your own," she guessed.

"There you go."

"Have a little ranch of your own."

"Yeah. Well, not too little."

"No, not too little. Just right."

"That's it. You hit 'er square on the head, ma'am." After a little leading from him. But that was all right. He felt uncommonly tranquil, for some reason. It was that voice of hers.

"I can see it's a dilemma for you, Shorty."

"Well, I reckon it's time to shoot or give up the gun."

"But it's a good dilemma, yes? Two ways you can go, and neither one is bad. Or . . . ?"

"Wellll . . ." He thought about leaving Cullen Pratt, which would come out of the blue to most of his colleagues. "I'd hate to let the boys down, that's for sure. But then again, there's a few things about the way they're runnin' the place that don't set right with me anymore."

"You feel that you could do a better job."

"Well, different. More modernlike. There's big changes comin,' and the Double K's not, uh, not always ahead o' the curve, you could say."

"Cattle-raising is changing?"

"Oh, heck yeah. All kinds o' new techniques and . . . energy-saving measures and what-have-you. Long overdue. So, ma'am, what do you think I should do?"

A long pause this time. In the background, he thought he could hear a cat meow. Or a baby cry? "It's difficult," she said at length. "I'm sensing a great deal of ambivalence. Feelings of duty, loyalty, but also of restlessness and discontent. It's as if a chapter of your life is drawing to a close, but you are reluctant to end it just yet. It's easier for you to be passive, let others shape your destiny for you. But in the end, it is you who must take the action."

"Yeah, but what action?"

"Oh, dear one. I think you already know the answer to that."

She was either very good or he'd just been hornswoggled. Or both.

"If you like," she said, "I can read the cards for you."

"The cards?"

"Tarot cards."

"Do they tell the future?"

"I'm afraid not. They're only a guide, a vehicle, to help clarify the choice you must make."

"I guess not, not tonight. Prob'ly gettin' late for you."

"What time is it there?"

He calculated Mountain Standard Time. Or was it Pacific? "Almost nine," he hazarded. "Maybe if I call you again sometime, we can do the cards."

"I would like that."

"I could tell you all about my love life."

"Oh, a very *long* call," she teased.

He'd been joking, but now the thought of talking to Madame Romanescu or anyone else about his so-called love life brought him down. "Nope. Shorter than . . . than me."

"You do not have good luck with women?"

"More like they don't have good luck with me."

"Oh, I don't think so. No. No, that does not feel right to me, Shorty."

"It's true, ma'am. Either that or they're gold diggers. You shoulda seen the one I met today—just for instance. Meaning no disrespect to women, this one could give all o' you a bad name."

"Or perhaps you were too quick to judge?"

He thought of Krystal with a K and her "bowling bag." For about two minutes, she'd reduced him to speechless staring, and he didn't even know why. Attractive, sure, but she wasn't exactly a beauty queen. Still, something about her . . . But soon enough, luckily, he'd gotten her number, and if she was a physical therapist, he was Wyatt Earp.

"Don't think so," he told Madame Romanescu, "but I'll be keepin' my eye on her, so . . ."

"The truth will out."

"There you go."

A rather long moment passed while neither of them spoke. The soft in-and-out of her breathing sounded gentle and patient—and not just so the minutes could tick by. He was beginning to take a shine to Madame Romanescu.

"Well, ma'am," he said at length.

"Shorty?"

"Ma'am?"

"If you do call back, I hope you will call me Romy. It would make me feel . . ." She gave a light laugh. "A little younger."

"Oh. All right." How old was she? Middle-aged, he reckoned. But well-preserved.

"And," she added, sounding tentative now, almost shy, "it's what my friends call me."

"Well, then. I sure will do that."

They hung up, Oliver with a definite reluctance. He didn't understand himself at all lately. It took a while, but he finally figured out the source of some kind of pride or one-upmanship or . . . almost a *gotcha* feeling, all related to Charlie. It went beyond childish, but what it boiled down to was, *Look, Grandfather: I get to call her Romy, too.*

SEVEN

———◆———

Molly's final exam in Attachment and Affect Regulation was on Monday, and she wasn't ready. She had dogs to walk, plants to water, houses to watch. These days Charlie wasn't even paying her for her psychic expertise anymore, so why was she wasting a whole precious Saturday afternoon and evening at his place, first telling him his fortune, then going with him to Cartamack Day at his retirement community?

She liked him, that was why. That was the *only* reason. She'd come *in spite* of the imminent arrival of his obnoxious grandson, certainly not *because* of it. What an idea.

"I'm seeing the same thing, Charlie," she said, back in her old seat at his coffee table. "She has gray hair, and . . ." Molly squinted. Sometimes she really did see something, and sometimes it really did look like a face. "No, that's all. It's just too vague. She's got you on her mind, that's all I know. And she's important. Significant." She'd probably talked herself into that, but it still felt right.

"And she's nearby?" He sat beside her, leaning forward sometimes to gaze into the crystal ball himself.

"That's how it feels."

"So she could be *here*, for Heart Attack Day."

"Would you *stop*? I'm going to say that to somebody accidentally, I just know it."

He had a mischievous cackle that always charmed her. "So that's it? That's all you got?"

"Sorry. I told you, it's just so shadowy—"

"Okay, then, let's go." He jumped up, rubbing his hands together. "Let's get out there so you can find her."

"Oh, that's my job now?"

"You'll be able to sense it," he said with certainty, helping her put the ball back in the case. "After that, I'll take over."

"You're amazing," she said in his small foyer while she put on her jacket. "Hey, what happened to the horses?" The biggest piece was missing, leaving its shiny outline on the slightly dusty glass shelf.

"The mustangs? Sent 'em out to get appraised. I want Oliver to know what they're worth when I give 'em to him for his birthday."

In the elevator, their side-by-side reflections in the shiny doors made her smile. "You're looking especially handsome today," she told Charlie truthfully, admiring his cherry red sweater and pressed khakis. "Which makes it a lot harder for *me*, you know."

"How's that?" He smiled back paternally.

"Every woman here is probably thinking about you, Charlie. You're a *catch*."

"True, but I'm only interested in the one in the ball."

She tsked, elbowing him. "Your modesty's irresistible, too. Speaking of Oliver," and they had been, "where is he?" she asked casually.

"Said he'd be late, some meeting or other. Kid's a workaholic."

Cartamack Day was huge, a sort of street fair/open house spread out over the retirement community's sprawling campus. The main action was on the enormous stone terrace between the community center and the eighteenth green of the golf course, where tables and chairs, a buffet, a stage, and numerous booths vied for space under strings of unlit Japanese lanterns. Charlie took Molly on a tour of the nearest attractions—the lake, the main restaurant, the library, fitness center, bowling alley, concert hall, woodworking shop, hair salon. By the time he showed her the billiard room, she wanted to know when she could move in.

"Gotta be old and decrepit," he grumped, hands shoved in his pockets. "Believe me, you don't wanna move in a second before you have to."

"I don't know about that. I think I could be very happy here." She was only half joking. And Charlie, she could tell, was secretly pleased with her reaction. He stood a little straighter, sounded a little more proprietary, less mocking, when he told her about the bridge club and the lecture series and the drama club. It was a perfect day, dreamy white clouds high up in a blue sky, sun at a gentle slant behind massive trees edging the golf green. They sat on a stone ledge and sipped lemonade, people-watching. The current entertainment was a barbershop quartet that was, according to Charlie, "better than the ukuleles." Between songs, a woman emcee announced winning numbers in a raffle to benefit the Alzheimer's Association. Once in a while Charlie waved to an acquaintance, usually a lone man, but no one ever stopped to talk, and he never introduced her to anyone. It gradually dawned on Molly that Charlie didn't have many friends.

"So, you getting any vibes yet?" he asked for the second time in ten minutes.

She shook her head. "It's really hard to concentrate here."

"Okay, we'll shut up. You concentrate."

She looked around, studying the women nearby. Some were spry and attractive, some frail and disabled, most in between. They outnumbered the men about three to one.

"Sorry," she had to say after a few minutes of "concentration"— really just observing body language. "I'm not feeling anything."

"Guess she's not here. Maybe she's a gardener," Charlie said hopefully. "Wanna go look at the community gardens?"

"You even have gardens?"

"Vegetables *and* flowers."

"Charlie, this place is paradise. Seriously, when can I move in?"

"Not quite yet, I'm afraid."

She jumped. Oliver Worth stood behind them on the other side of the wall. The blue eyes she'd gotten lost in a few days ago were staring at her in disbelief. Distaste. She felt a hot flush rise to her hairline.

"About time," Charlie said, standing, reaching over the wall
to give his grandson a rough pat on the arm. "Bribe enough
congressmen for one day? You remember, uh, Krystal."

"Vividly."

"Oliver," Molly said, standing, too, and deliberately extended a businesslike hand for him to shake. She would *not*
fall under his stupid *spell* again—and then his hand enveloped
hers and she melted. *Oh, stop it,* she thought. *This is crazy.* He
and Charlie talked about the size of the crowd, the adorable a
cappella children's chorus singing "Doe, a Deer," the wisdom
of getting in the buffet line now or waiting, but Molly was
practically in a fugue state, able only to nod and smile. She
heard an actual buzzing in her ears. It didn't go away until Oliver did, to get them more lemonade.

"Still nothing?" Charlie asked.

"What?"

"The woman, the woman."

"Oh. Charlie, I'm just—" She put her hand to her forehead,
trying to think. She turned her back on him. Women everywhere. Did any of them give off a vibe? A woman in pale blue
velour, sitting with two friends at a table near the stage, was
staring. At Charlie? Yes. With an avid expression, practically
breathless. She had gray hair. She was pretty. "I think—
maybe—it could be—"

"Who? Who?"

"By the stage, the second table. Don't look!" She described
the woman, then shifted so Charlie could get a discreet gander
over her shoulder.

"Hm," he said, narrow-eyed.

"Go say hi to her."

"Me?"

"No, the invisible man I'm also talking to."

"What'll I say?"

"Say, 'Hello, my name is Charlie. What's yours?' "

"I can't do that."

"And then ask her to dance." A swing band called Sawyer
Bones and the Skeletons was tuning up. "Go. Just do it. You *can.*"

Oliver came back. Charlie took the glass he handed him
and downed it in two gulps. " 'Scuse me, I got business." He
pivoted and marched away.

Molly wanted to watch his progress with the lady in blue, but it was hard enough communicating with Oliver when she had all her senses trained on him. She couldn't afford to divert any of them elsewhere.

"Nice day," he opened.

"Lovely."

"They have this every year. Apparently."

"So I understand."

"There will be fireworks at nine."

"I have to leave before then."

"So do I."

They stood side by side, watching the band, the dancers, anything but each other.

"Charlie tells me you're a lobbyist. For the energy industry."

"Yes, I blow up scenic mountaintops for coal removal."

A joke? She stole a glance at him to see—and then it was hard to look away from his clean, sharp, perfect profile. Charlie said he always wore suits, but today he had on slacks and a red polo shirt. Loafers. She came up to his jaw. The setting sun picked out glints of gold in his dark hair, which was cut perfectly.

The first time they'd spoken—when he'd called her on the psychic line to tell her to stay away from Charlie—she'd gotten the strangest feeling about him, that he was suffering, that something from his past had a hold he couldn't break. But nothing like that was coming from him now, and all she felt was chilliness and discomfort.

"Do you live nearby?" he asked.

"Yes, quite near. That was—" She broke off, pretending she had to cough. She'd almost blown it there; she'd been about to say, "That was a surprise, finding out Charlie and I live so close to each other." *I'm Krystal,* she reminded herself, *not Romy.* She wished Oliver would stop asking questions.

He was looking at her strangely. "So you live in the neighborhood?" he pursued.

"Almost. I have a little house in Kensington." Did that sound wistful? She'd been trying not to think about her house.

"And how long have you been a—"

"Would you like to dance? I love this song." What song was it? Who cared? Anything was better than telling Oliver Worth about her career in physical therapy.

EIGHT

She smelled like strawberries. Must be something she put in her hair, which was tickling his chin. Thick hair, between short and long, the color of ripe peaches. "It had to be you," crooned the woman singer in the swing band. No, it didn't, and Oliver resisted pulling Krystal Smith-Jones's firm, warm body any closer. He had a lot of questions he wanted to ask her, but it was better when they didn't talk. When they talked, they had to pull back and look at each other, and then he'd become fixated on her mouth. Her full, sensitive lips, the prettiest part of her face. Except for her eyes, gray-green, not large but oddly luminous and steady. . . .

"How"—he cleared his throat—"how long have you known my grandfather?"

"Not long. Have you always lived in the Washington area?"

"Yes. No—I went to grad school in California, and stayed out there for a few years afterward." As he expanded on that, he realized she did it on purpose—turned the conversation back to him. Clearly she was hiding something.

"How about you?" he asked, this time without looking at her. "Where did you go to school?"

She began to answer, something about American University, but he forgot to listen as the absurd idea crossed his mind that her husky contralto sounded a bit like Madame Romanescu's. Just then the song ended and the Skeletons jumped into a dizzy cover of "In the Mood." Ms. Smith-Jones's raised brows and cheeky grin were a definite challenge, and he could never resist a dare. She took his outstretched hand and he launched them, more or less simultaneously, into the jitterbug.

When it was over, they were laughing and out of breath, and around them people were clapping—for *them*. "That was so much fun," Krystal said, pressing her palm to her chest. "But now I'm *dying*."

"Don't worry, the place is lousy with defibrillators." He was joking, of course, but with his usual straight face. Something in the combination set her off—she fell apart laughing. And he felt loose and silly, and more at ease with her than he'd have thought possible. She'd lost a barrette while they were dancing; he found it for her under a table, then had the pleasure of watching her put it back in, bright hair pulled up in both hands, her laughing eyes still on his.

Then Charlie came over and separated them. Physically. Unapologetically *moved her away*, so he could speak to her in private. Oliver stared in disbelief, then stalked off to watch a bunch of old men play bocce ball on the grass.

What the hell was going on? Who *was* this woman? Krystal Smith-Jones—he could barely say her name without an incredulous sneer. *What* was she, a physical therapist, or an old man's paid last fling? The latter, every instinct assured him she was the latter, and yet—

Nothing. Just because she didn't look the part today didn't mean anything. She'd certainly looked it the day they'd met. Like a streetwalker, practically, in a plunging halter top and garish jewelry, hair teased out to here. She'd dressed down for Cartamack Day, that was all. She wasn't stupid.

For the rest of the afternoon, they ricocheted off each other. When it was time to eat, he, she, and Charlie shared a table with an elderly couple and their visiting son, so the conversation stayed correct and impersonal. Krystal charmed them with a way she had of asking questions that required thoughtful answers, not just yes or no, and Oliver was as beguiled as any of them. But then Charlie, who kept craning his neck at something or someone behind them, would hijack her attention by moving in till he and Krystal were almost nose-to-nose, then speak to her in urgent whispers, sometimes *covering his mouth with his hand.* It was beyond rude; it was ridiculous.

Worst was having to watch them dance with each other. Unlike Oliver, Charlie didn't just shuffle around when he slow-danced; he was old-school, he *knew* how to fox-trot to "My Blue Heaven" and "Sentimental Journey." And Krystal followed him perfectly, thanks to the masterful arm he pressed her whole body to his with. "Fred and Ginger," one of their tablemates said admiringly, and Oliver thought sourly, *Yeah, if Ginger had been a half century younger than Fred.*

I'm jealous of my grandfather.

The realization was so humiliating, he decided to leave. How satisfying to just abandon them, leave them on the dance floor wondering what had become of him. But then he reminded himself he wasn't in middle school anymore. "Have to go," he told them during a break in their Arthur Murray performance. "I brought your quarterly tax statements, Grandfather. Just sign them, put them in the stamped envelope, and mail them."

"Got it."

Oliver turned to Krystal. "Nice to see you again," was all he could come up with.

"Yes," was the best she could do.

"Well," he said after another awkward minute. "'Bye."

The tax papers were still in his car. He retrieved them, jogged the short distance to Charlie's condo building, let himself in the apartment, and dropped the papers on the hall table. That was when he noticed the missing horses. *Five Mustangs Running*—Charlie's showpiece.

Krystal.

By the time he got back to the community center, she was gone. Charlie was sitting by himself on the stone ledge, staring out across the darkening golf course. He looked so forlorn, Oliver changed what he was going to say—some version of "Where is she? That thief!"—to a simple inquiry. "I noticed the big bronze isn't in its spot, Grandfather. Any idea where it went?"

"Hm?"

He repeated himself.

"Hm?"

A sure sign of evasion. Were Charlie and Krystal in this *together*?

"Oh, the mustangs," Charlie said eventually, eyes darting from side to side. "Guy in the building, he admired it, so I lent it to 'im."

"Lent it to him?"

"Yeah. Guy in the building, horse nut."

"You lent it to a guy in the building because he likes horses."

"That's it."

He was covering for her. Had to be. Oliver let it go, because he had no choice. But Charlie hadn't heard the last of this. Neither had Krystal.

Speak of the devil—he almost backed into her in the parking lot when she passed behind him in some boatlike American car with a sputtering muffler. She didn't see him. At the main exit from The Lakes at Cartamack, she turned left on Georgia Avenue. He was going that way himself. He didn't set out to follow her; it just happened.

She veered right onto Connecticut Avenue at Aspen Hill, but then she sailed right through Kensington, where she supposedly lived. Another lie. Twenty minutes later, they were in the District. He almost lost her at Dupont Circle. She took a sudden right on P Street, then zigzagged around O and Twenty-first until she found a parking place on a block-long side street near the park. Snazzy neighborhood. Sixty feet away, Oliver double-parked and turned his lights out.

He'd liked watching her legs when she'd danced with Charlie. Now he liked watching them slide out of the car, knees together, ankles trim above her high-heeled sandals. Beautiful rear end, too; he enjoyed watching it poke out the backseat door while she leaned in to get something. The bowling bag? No, a white plastic bag, not especially heavy-looking, so not the horses.

While she was locking her car, her cell phone must've rung. She fumbled it out of her purse, and talked into it as she crossed the street to the far sidewalk, went down a ways, and turned in at the brick walk of a handsome, three-story town house, white with black shutters. What would a place like that cost? In this neighborhood, well over a million. Not bad for a physical therapist.

Juggling phone, purse, and plastic bag, she found the house key and unlocked the front door. High-pitched barking began before she got it open halfway. She sidled in crabwise, presumably to keep the dog from rushing out. Beveled sidelights lit up.

Oliver got out of his car, closing the door gently, and walked to where Krystal had parked hers. Glancing around to make sure no one was watching, he bent down and peered in first the front, then the rear windows. There—on the floor behind the driver's side: the bowling bag. It had taken on an inimical unwholesomeness in his mind, a repository for something unsavory, either his grandfather's horses or the tricks, so to speak, of Krystal's "physical therapist" trade. Either way, the bag was evil.

Or it might contain a bowling ball. Anything was possible.

What to do? Nothing. *He* wasn't a thief, even if she was. (And he could see the headline: Prominent Capitol Hill Lobbyist Caught Breaking into Call Girl's Car, Stealing Sex Toys.) At least now he knew what he knew.

But he had to revise that on the five-minute drive to his house in Georgetown. Now he knew what he *didn't* know.

NINE

———◆———

"What? Wait, Charlie, I can't hear you, the dog's barking. Hold on."

Molly put down everything but the phone, dropped to her knees, and let ecstatic Harpo jump up and lick her on the face. "Sweet boy, was I gone *that long*? No, the dog. The Nathansons' poodle, Charlie, I told you I'm house-sitting— Hang on two more seconds, okay?" She got Harpo under one arm, carried him down the hall past the gated-off living room, the gated-off dining room, and into the kitchen.

"Good *boy*!" No messes, and he hadn't even chewed the rug or knocked over his bowl. "No, Charlie, the dog. Okay, tell me again—what was the matter with her?"

Charlie was in high indignation mode, but under his bluster Molly thought she heard true disappointment. "Well, for one thing, she wasn't even *looking* at me, never mind—"

"Yes, she *was*," Molly had to interrupt, "I saw her. She was *staring*, she was definitely—"

"She's got macular degeneration!"

"What?"

"Not that there's anything wrong with that."

"What is it?"

"It blocks your central vision, you can only see what you're looking at on the side."

"Oh. So you mean—"

"She was looking at the band!"

"Oh. Well, but after you introduced yourself and started talking—"

"Oh, that was fine, fine, like talking to my sister. There was nothing *wrong* with her, but hell, Molly, I thought—I thought—"

"I know. Gosh, I'm sorry, Charlie, it's my fault. I could've *sworn* I saw something."

"Yeah, well. So it's all—do you think maybe you're just . . . no offense, Moll, but—"

"*No.* No. I would tell you if I thought that, but honestly, I think she's out there, this special person who's—it's not just that she's got you on her mind, it's that she's *right* for you. I *feel* it." She did. Amazing.

"Okay, I believe you," Charlie said, as if that settled it. "So you'll keep looking in the ball?"

"I will if you want me to." Her psychic line rang. "Charlie, I've got—"

"And I'll call you tomorrow, okay?"

"Okay." Her one full day to study for Monday's exam. "But I have to go now, I've got a—"

"Go! Uh . . ."

"What?"

"Thanks for coming tonight."

"You're welcome. Thank you for inviting me."

"Did you have a nice time?"

"Oh yes." Her psychic line stopped ringing. "Except . . ."

"What?"

"Nothing." She wanted *him* to bring up Oliver first. That seemed important for some reason.

"No, what?"

"No, really. Nothing." Her psychic line started ringing again. "Gotta go, Charlie—"

"Go. G'bye."

It rang steadily for the next two hours, backed-up calls from people who'd phoned earlier and gotten Madame Romanescu's message that she would be unavailable from three until eight—

most unusual for her on a Saturday, her biggest call day. Luckily she could walk Harpo in this safe, quiet neighborhood and talk at the same time. She couldn't play Harpo's favorite game, though: soccer in the downstairs hall, her kicking the ball, him making "goals" by head-butting it into the front door. He got too excited and barked, and then callers would ask, "Is that a *dog*?" offended by the thought that Madame Romanescu wasn't focusing one hundred percent on their problems. So she sat in the Nathansons' lush living room with a cup of tea, Harpo at her feet, and gave her whole mind over to whether Tina should have it out with her mother-in-law, if Carla should get her eyebrows tattooed, if Venus in retrograde meant Walter should ask for a raise now or next month.

Usually she loved these questions, or if not them, at least the people who asked them. The concept of a "trivial" problem didn't exist, not if one person, just one, desperately cared about it. Molly had decided a long time ago that her singular talent was simply putting herself in the other person's place. Empathy. That's all it took. Oh, and a little common sense, so she could feel confident about giving advice that didn't put anybody in danger. That's why the answer to "Should I light my husband on fire while he's sleeping?" was almost always "No."

Tonight she was distracted, though; not sufficiently involved. Other people's earth-shattering dilemmas seemed almost . . . frivolous. Almost. She wanted to tell Donette, the lady who called every other night to ask if her husband was cheating, which he obviously was, to stop wasting time and throw the bum out. She didn't; she repeated her marriage counseling mantra, but it was a close call.

"I'm just in a bad mood," she told Harpo, who followed her from room to room as she watered the hanging plants, the ficus tree. Sadie Nathanson was one of the girls she'd counseled at Stone Creek Academy a year ago, and now she was feeding Sadie's turtle while the Nanthansons were seeing plays in New York. "How the mighty have fallen."

That wasn't it, though—she enjoyed house-sitting, and she'd never been mighty. It was everything else. Everything was piling up on her, exams, papers, debts, all her part-time jobs. Not to mention losing her house.

And something else, a brand-new burden, was weighing her

down tonight. "That jerk Oliver," she muttered to Harpo, un-wrapping the new tug-of-war toy she'd brought him. "Who does he think he is? You should've seen him—he never stopped glaring."

Except when he did, and then she'd felt a flip in her stomach, as if she'd been upside down and Oliver had righted her. So stupid. Cheap physical attraction, the most untrustworthy emotion in the book. "At least I'll probably never see him again, so that's good." And yet, the thought didn't cheer her up.

The Nathansons' guest room was as tasteful and comfortable as the rest of the house, but she still missed her own room, missed being at home. Missed Merlin, whom the neighbor was feeding. Free of charge—to pay somebody to house-sit her house while she house-sat somebody else's would've been too silly, even for her. And she'd done some pretty silly things to make a little money. Telephone psychic came to mind. . . .

Only for fifteen more minutes tonight, though: At 10:30, Madame Romanescu was off the clock. A woman called while she was brushing her teeth. Two women, and then it turned out they were girls, not women; teenagers on Daddy's credit card. She got rid of them quickly. She wasn't so hard up yet that she took advantage of children.

Harpo had his own bed, but he would only sleep in it if it was next to hers. Fine with Molly; she liked the company. She got her covers just so, aimed the reading lamp just right. As soon as she opened her class notebook, the phone rang. Of *course*. It had been that kind of a day. Why *wouldn't* the phone ring at 10:28?

"Evenin', ma'am."

"Oh, it's you," she said, no hesitation. She'd know that lazy Western drawl anywhere. Everything relaxed; everything went slack. "I am so glad you called, Shorty."

"Sure? It's not too late for you?"

"Not at all. Not at all." She felt as if she'd strained a lot of muscles today and she was about to get a massage. "How are you?"

"Better now," he said, which made her smile in sympathy. "It's been a day."

"It certainly has. Fortunately, it's almost over."

"Amen to that."

"Are you out on the range? With the dogies?"

"No, ma'am, we finished that drive. I'm here in the bunk-house, sippin' a cuppa Arbuckles'."

"A cup of . . ."

"Cowboy talk for coffee."

She pictured a big room full of bunks and sprawling cow-boys, stuffed buffalo heads on the walls, everything made of pine. He'd be at a big round table with his feet up, drinking Arbuckles' and playing poker. With his boots on.

"Doing some paperwork in my office," he said, and she amended the picture. He was a modern cowboy; he probably had a computer, knew how to do spreadsheets. But he still had his boots on.

"I didn't call for any special reason," he said.

A lot of her callers started out saying that. "I remember, when last we spoke, you were thinking about perhaps changing jobs."

"Still workin' that over in my mind."

"Good. I don't think there is any hurry, and you want to be sure."

"I'm with you there."

"Something else I remember," she said after a moment. "You were going to tell me all about your love life."

She liked his laugh, low and sleepy. "Yes, ma'am. I also said that wouldn't be a very *long* conversation."

Shorter than me, was the way he'd put it. She wondered if they called him Shorty because he was short or because he was tall. . . .

"Okay. There's this woman."

"I am not surprised."

"And she's . . . somethin' else. Damned if I know what, though. She gets to me, I won't lie, but here's the thing—I don't even like her. Can you feature that?"

"Yes. Yes, I can."

"It's crazy."

"I know. You feel—ridiculous."

"I feel like a sheep north o' the ears, and there's nothin' dumber than a sheep. When I'm with her, she takes up . . . she just sorta completely . . . Hell, it's hard to describe."

"When you're with her, you can't think of anyone but her. She blots out your good judgment."

"Bingo."

"Much of it is physical."

"All of it's physical. No, not all."

"Not all. There is something . . . something strange, a feeling of helplessness, because you are afraid. . . ."

"Yeah. Afraid . . ."

"Afraid that it is . . ."

"That it's . . ."

"Meant to be," Molly said, dejected.

"Oh Christ, that's it. Meant to be."

They shared a moment of mutual horror.

"But I don't *like* her," Shorty repeated. "I wanna just—tell you the truth, ma'am—I just wanna shack up one time and be done with her."

"Ah, but you wouldn't do that."

"I mighta, but now— You know what? I think she might be a thief to boot."

"A *thief.*"

"Maybe. I'm not a hundred percent sure. She's some kinda chiseler, though, and I don't trust her."

"Trust is everything. But if you're wrong," Molly said, thinking out loud, "if you have misjudged, then . . . it is too bad, yes?"

"Yyyeah . . ."

"Yes. It is very painful to be the one who has been found unworthy. Without cause."

"So you're sayin' . . . What are you sayin'?"

She wasn't sure. "Only that when we are in the grip of these strong emotions, it's important to use our heads, Shorty. Not only our hearts."

"With you there."

"I would only suggest that you be sure. Sure that this woman is so very bad. You are drawn to her for a reason—I believe that. And the reason isn't simply to torture yourself. So you must find out who she really is."

"Okay. How do I do that?"

"Ask her?"

"Ask her?"

"Could you do that?"

"Well, not in so many words. Not like, 'Okay, level with me—did you steal those horses?'"

"She stole *horses*?"

"She mighta."

"Isn't that—a hanging offense?"

Shorty chuckled, such a warming sound, and Molly slid lower in bed, stretching her legs. "Prob'ly not anymore," he allowed. "But if she did steal 'em, I might string her up myself."

"Oh, I don't think so. No. I think you are . . . quite a gentle person."

"You do, huh."

"I do."

"What if I told you . . . Nah, forget it."

"What?"

"What if I told you I did something real bad. Once."

"I would say, welcome to the world. The human race."

"I'm not talking about a mistake," he said, and the sudden harsh anger in his voice made her sit up. "I'm talking about somebody dying. You hear that? Because of me. *My fault.*"

She kept her own voice calm and steady. "In what way was it your fault?"

"Aw, hell."

"In what way, Shorty?"

"It was—bulls. A rodeo. Everybody liquored up. My—best buddy, somebody I cared a lot about, but I was drunk, and— hell, I'm not getting into this."

"That's all right." She could easily imagine foolishness and drunkenness, a reckless dare, a calamity. An accident. "You were young, yes?"

"No. Twenty-eight."

"Oh, Shorty."

"Bullshit. Young, that's—sixteen. I was a goddamn grown-up."

"All right. All right."

"Look, I'm sorry, I don't know what got me started on that."

"It's on your mind."

"Not really."

"Always. Just under the surface."

A pause. Then, "Yeah, okay. Whatever you say." He tried to snarl the words, but there was so much pain, Molly's heart felt pierced.

"I say it's time. I don't know how long ago this happened to you, but it's time. It's mean of you to hold on to it this long."

"It's *what*?"

"It's unkind. If this awful thing had happened the other way around, you'd have forgiven your friend by now. Long ago, in fact."

Silence.

"Wouldn't you? Admit it."

"That's sorta beside the point."

"It's exactly the point. Why are you being so cruel? This is not like you. You are going against your own nature. You are not a hard, unforgiving person. You're *not*. Shorty? Talk to me."

"Where're you gettin' all this?"

"I don't know," she answered honestly.

"You don't know me from—Adam." *From shit*, he'd been going to say, but he wasn't angry anymore. If nothing else, she'd talked him down from that. She wanted to do more than that, though. But how? Did she even know what she was talking about? No, but she knew a good man when she met one. Psychic-schmychic, as Charlie would say. She knew a good man when she met him.

"It's such a waste of your spirit, this self-hate. This bitterness inside. It stunts you. How can you forgive anyone else, of anything, until you forgive yourself?"

No answer, but he was listening.

"It's a kind of pride, isn't it? Not to accept that you can make mistakes? That you can be just like everyone else?"

"I can make mistakes. Oh, believe me. I got no trouble accepting that."

"You just can't forgive yourself for them."

"Forgive and forget, no. I can't do it."

"I didn't say anything about forgetting. That's easy. How much harder to forgive and remember."

The quiet between them was easier this time. She listened to his slow exhalations of breath, moved by them somehow, and wished she knew better words.

"Dear one," she said very quietly. "Listen. This is important. Have mercy on yourself."

Shorty made some sound.

"Please don't take this the wrong way. I know it's impudent, but important also. Listen." She had to whisper past the lump in her throat. "I forgive you."

Utter silence. Not even breathing. She'd gone too far.

Then he said, "So you're a priest now?" with a shaky laugh, and the tension broke.

She laughed with him. "A priest, a Gypsy. Whatever you please." She risked being earnest one last time. "Mostly I hope I am your friend."

"That you are," he answered in the same light tone. "So tell me, ma'am."

"Romy."

"Romy. How's *your* love life?"

A pretty obvious change of subject. Timely, too; she'd trespassed far enough into his personal territory. "Ah, Shorty," she said, laying her Romy voice on thick. It made it easier to talk about herself, something she rarely did with callers. With Shorty, though, it felt natural. And like the least she could do. "Ah, Shorty, I am very unlucky in love."

"Ever been married?" he asked.

"Yes, but I was quite young." Twenty-one—not that young. "You?"

"Nope."

"No one special?"

"Not really. Nobody to ride the river with."

"Ride the river with. I like that cowboy expression."

They sighed in unison, then laughed a little. They seemed so in sync now, it prompted her to say, "I have a man in my head these days, but he is no good for me. In fact, he makes me crazy."

"Whaddaya like about him?"

"Nothing! He is nothing except good-looking. He is not even nice to me."

"Dry gulch him. You don't need a sidewinder like that."

"I won't be seeing him again. But it's not so easy to forget someone who has crept inside you, is it? Your bad woman, your horse thief, she's not so easy to—dry gulch, am I right?"

"You're always right."

"That is true, Shorty. That is so very true."

"Except when—"

"No need to qualify."

She could hear him smiling. A long, comfortable silence passed. "Late for you," he said at the end of it. "Reckon I oughta let you go."

"Yes." But she was sorry.

"I'll call you up again."

"I hope so."

She waited for him to say good-bye. Instead he said, "Thanks. I, uh . . ." Long pause. "I'll think about what you said."

A cowboy, a manly man, leader of others—she could only imagine what it cost him to say that. "Just be kind to yourself," she said softly. "Dear one."

TEN

———

"I was *just thinking* about you."

"That's what you always say." Molly got a Coke from the fridge and carried it out to the front porch, Merlin in her wake. "You can't be thinking about me *all* the time, Aunt Kit."

"I'm always thinking about you right before you call, because I always know it's you."

"Plus I always call on Sunday."

"What are you insinuating?"

"Nothing!" They both laughed. "So how are you? How's your arthritis?"

"You know, I don't appreciate that."

"What?"

"The first thing you think of when you think of me is 'old lady with arthritis.' It's only my big toe."

"That's *not* the first thing I think."

"Shaquille O'Neal has arthritis in his big toe."

"You know what you don't do enough of, Aunt Kit?"

"What?"

"Complain." She thought of all the little inconveniences her aunt only mentioned in passing, if at all. Like the virtual abandonment of the second floor of her tiny house, for instance, because the steps were too much for that arthritic big toe. All the little indignities, the gradual scaling back of a once-full life.

"Complaining's for losers," Aunt Kit said. "How was Cardiac Day?"

"Heart Attack Day. It was fine."

"What went wrong?"

Molly sighed. "Don't do that. Don't read my mind."

"I'm not, I just thought you sounded . . . discontent."

Discontent. The very word. "No, I'm fine, and Heart Attack Day was fine, everything's fine."

"Well, if that's your story, you're entitled to stick to it. When you're ready, feel free to tell me what's wrong."

"Thanks, but what makes you think— Oh, never mind."

"Molly, I *know* something's wrong. Has been for weeks."

She tried not to think about her house. *Don't think about the house. Don't think about the house.* "Oh, it's this Oliver guy," she blurted out, purely to throw Aunt Kit off. "Charlie's grandson."

"The stuffed shirt?"

"He thinks I'm . . . It's complicated, but he doesn't have a good opinion of me, and I know it shouldn't matter, since he's a *jerk*, but it does."

"You're in love with him. Oh, honey."

"What? No! Are you crazy? No, no, no, no, no, no, no."

"But if he doesn't have a good opinion of you, he *is* a jerk, so get over him."

"It's not *altogether* his fault. It's partly Charlie's fault—but I *am* over him, I was never—*on* him. In love with Oliver? Ha-ha-ha! Don't make me laugh."

"That was the phoniest laugh I ever heard."

"Because you're not funny."

"Have it your way. What are you doing today?"

"Don't you *know*?"

"You're studying for tomorrow's final. You took a break to call your oldest living relative, but now you really have to get back to work."

"How does she do it?"

"So I will graciously let you go. Next time you call, though, we'll read the cards, see where this thing with Oliver's going."

"I'm graciously letting you go right now," Molly said, and hung up.

———

Monday afternoon, after her Attachment and Affect exam, she checked her voice mail on both phone lines. Three people had called Madame Romanescu, including Donette, the lady whose husband was a dog; she left a long, rambling message and asked for a card-reading tonight. Poor woman—but she *was* money in the bank. On Molly's regular line, two people had left messages: Mrs. Nathanson, saying thanks for house-sitting, and Oliver Worth, saying:

"Hello, this is Oliver Worth," in his stuffed-shirt voice. "I got this number from my grandfather—I hope it's Krystal Smith-Jones there. Uh . . . ah . . ." Throat-clearing. "I was wondering if we might meet for coffee or something. I'd like to speak with you about Charlie. I'm sure you can understand that it would set my mind at ease to know we *both* have his best interests at heart."

Coughing. Paper rattling. A calendar? No, he'd have that on a BlackBerry.

"I happen to have a free hour tomorrow afternoon. Do you know the coffee shop in Dupont Circle called Bardot's? If that's all right, let's say four o'clock. Call and let me know if you can make it, please." He rattled off three numbers, home, office, and cell, and hung up.

———

Molly called the cell and got *his* voice mail. "Oliver, this is Krystal. Number one, I'm busy tomorrow, and number two, even if I weren't, getting downtown at that hour would be incredibly inconvenient for me. I live in *Kensington*, you recall. So—the answer's no, I just can't take the time to set your mind at ease. Sorry."

———

"I've got a bone to pick with you."

"Hm? Who's this?"

"It's Molly," as if he didn't know. "Charlie, why did you give Oliver my number?"

"Hm?"

"I said, why did you—what if he'd—what if my voice mail message gave my *name*, not just my number? What if I'd said, 'Hi, you've reached Molly McDougal'? The jig would be up!"

"Hah. Never thought of that."

"Why did you give him my number anyway?"

"Why not? What happened?"

"Nothing, he . . . nothing. He wants to talk to me. Wants to have coffee."

"Well, that'll be nice."

"No, it won't—I told him no."

"How come?"

"Charlie! Oliver doesn't like me. He thinks I'm . . . he thinks I'm . . ."

"What? What?"

"He thinks—I'm your paramour!"

Startled silence. Then a laughter explosion that went on so long, it turned into a coughing fit. "Whooo," Charlie ended on a high note.

"Are you finished?"

"If only it was true," he wheezed. "If only it was true. The mystery would be solved."

"What mystery?"

"It'd be *you* who's been thinking about me."

Molly blew air through her lips. *Pbbbb.* Hopeless. "What am I going to do with you?"

"So what's wrong with having a cuppa coffee with my grandson?"

"We don't *like* each other."

"You don't like Oliver? Why not?"

"He's mean."

"He is not. You think so? No. He got beat up, still recovering. Taking a helluva long time, if you ask me."

"Recovering from what?"

Charlie took several deep, sighing breaths. "I'm not allowed to talk about it."

Frustrated curiosity had her practically dancing in place. It took every fiber of will to say, "Never mind, then. Of course I wouldn't want you to betray a confidence."

"Happened five or six years ago, maybe more. He was going

out with this gal in California. Not sure how serious it was *then*, but o' course it's a huge deal *now*."

"I don't know what you mean."

"They went to a party, and at the end, she was soberer than he was, so she got to be the designated driver."

"Oh no. . . ."

"Yeah, some *other* drunk plowed into the driver's side, killed this girl instantly. Oliver thinks it shoulda been him. That's it, that's all—he was sitting in the wrong seat—but he can't let it go."

"Oh, Charlie, how awful." She'd known something old and dark was holding him back, she'd *sensed* it in that first phone call. Guilt—what a useless emotion. She thought of Shorty's guilt over the death of his buddy at the rodeo. What made it so hard for some people to let go of guilt, even when it was misplaced and undeserved? So far, nothing she'd read in her psychology books explained that.

"Don't tell him I told you."

"Of course I won't."

"And trust me, Molly—he's a nice boy."

"So you say."

"Have coffee with him! You'll see."

———

"Oliver? Krystal again. I find that a tiny window has opened in my busy schedule. I can meet you tomorrow, but not downtown and not at four o'clock. At five thirty, I'll be walking a large brown dog in Boyds Park, which is a little park in Aspen Hill. A long way for you, but that's where I'll be. So . . . maybe I'll see you. Or not."

ELEVEN

After only five minutes of catching, occasionally even returning, the tennis ball Molly threw for him, Pancho was a wet,
muddy mess. It wasn't raining now, but it had for most of the
day, and the clouds still looked low enough to touch. Boyds
Park, except for a few slouchy, cigarette-smoking teenagers,
was deserted.

So it wasn't hard to guess whose purring, low-slung sports
car glided into the gravel parking lot at 5:35 and parked under
the dripping trees right next to Molly's car. How did he know
the Pontiac was hers? She pretended not to see him, kept heaving the soggy tennis ball for Pancho, but after a few seconds
of intense self-consciousness, she gave up the act and began to
walk in Oliver's direction.

She'd resisted the impulse to dress up for him, a choice she
now regretted. Bitterly. He looked like . . . not a model; too
real-looking. Like a model's friend, maybe. The one you liked
better because he *wasn't* perfect, but still pretty damn good.
Muscular, not muscle-bound; fit, not trained. He wore light-
colored slacks, an impossibly soft-looking white sweater, and
loafers, undoubtedly Italian. And she had on rolled-up jeans,
a T-shirt that said, "Ask me about my vow of silence," and
flip-flops. Life wasn't fair.

Pancho, the dog she was currently walking for a client, had designs on that white sweater, she realized almost too late. "Pancho! No!" She made a run at him, grabbing his collar a second before he could plant his feet for one of his ecstatic vertical greetings. "*Down*. Hi. *Down!*"

"Hi." Oliver looked more amused than annoyed, and that was her undoing. His face when he smiled—God, it disoriented her. Why was it, again, that she didn't like him? He was looking at her with a strange, intense expression, almost as if he didn't recognize her, or he'd been expecting someone else. Pancho found the tennis ball and headed for him, snout at perfect crotch height, but Oliver foiled him with a deft twist of the hips and a lightning-fast grab. Empty-mouthed, empty-headed, Pancho panted up at him, waiting. Oliver drew back and heaved the ball about six miles farther than Molly ever had and, after a stunned second, Pancho vanished in a blur.

"Hi," she started again. "I didn't think you'd come."

"Why not?"

"Oh . . ."

"Too many cocktail parties? Too many congressmen to bribe?"

She was about to take offense when she realized he was teasing. "Don't confuse me with Charlie," she said, grinning. "I don't believe *everything* he tells me."

"Good thing."

Now that she'd introduced the subject, she expected him to launch into the reason he'd wanted to meet—to make sure they both had Charlie's "best interests at heart." (Code for "Get lost, gold digger.") She was ready to bristle again, and was surprised when he only said, "Shall we go for a stroll?"

They began to walk around the empty ball field, past deserted playground equipment and soggy picnic tables. "You're sensitive about your work," she noted, for something to say.

"Am I?"

"You make fun of it before anyone else can. 'Blowing up scenic mountaintops,' you called it."

"Lobbying's a misunderstood occupation. Add 'energy industry,' and people assume I melt the polar ice cap for a living."

"It's true," she realized, abashed. "Well, what *do* you do?"

Hands in his pockets, he stared down at the path his expensive shoes were cutting through the wet turf. "Talk, mostly. Try to get somebody's point of view across to somebody else."

"For lots and lots of money."

He slanted her a look.

"I'm sorry, that was incredibly rude. Money's a—sore subject these days. Sorry."

"Forget it."

"So you're a professional persuader."

"There you go."

She stopped in her tracks.

He noticed; stopped, too. "What?"

"Nothing." He'd sounded so much like Shorty! *There you go.* It was uncanny.

They resumed their walk. Talked about the weather for a while, the likelihood of more rain, the imminence of summer. "How old is your dog?" Oliver asked.

Pancho had abandoned the tennis ball to chase after the low-flying barn swallows crisscrossing the field. "Two, I think. He's not mine, I'm just walking him for . . . somebody."

"Who?"

"Oh . . . somebody." She blanked. Physical therapists probably didn't do part-time dog-sitting. Oliver was scowling at her. "A friend," she said shortly. "Who do you think?"

"I really have no idea."

"No, you don't."

Were they fighting? What about?

Next he asked, "So you live around here," but in such a flat way, every word in the question implied disbelief.

"Yes, I've told you. I have a house in Kensington."

"Mm hm. How come you're not in the phone book?"

"I am." Oops. "I mean, I *was*." Krystal Smith-Jones was definitely not in the phone book. "I—now I'm unlisted, that's all. I just—decided to be."

"Mm hm."

"What is *wrong* with you?" They'd completed their circuit of the ball field and were back at the parking lot. "I don't see how you persuade anybody to do anything when you go around with an attitude like that."

"Like what?"

"What is it exactly that you dislike about me, Oliver? I would really like to know."

"I don't know what you mean."

"I think you do."

"Maybe we got off on the wrong foot."

"It's more than that. You said you wanted to talk about Charlie—okay, what about him?"

It started to rain.

"All right." Oliver wiped a drop of water off his nose and took an offensive stance. "For one thing, there's nothing the matter with his spine. Lumbar *or* cervical."

She blushed. Couldn't think of a response. Her hair was getting wet.

"For another, he's an old man, he's lonely. He lost his wife two years ago—"

"I know all that."

"He's trusting, vulnerable. And let's face it, not exactly rock-steady in his judgment sometimes. I'm not accusing you of anything—"

"Aren't you?" The soaked dog sidled over and leaned against her thigh.

"I'm just saying it would be easy to take advantage of him."

"I'm *not* taking advantage of Charlie."

The heavens opened up. Oliver swore out loud, Molly to herself. "In the car," he ordered, and started for the Pontiac, Pancho trotting behind him.

"What's wrong with yours?" A joke, and it worked—Oliver's look of horror made her laugh. They all climbed into her car, where Pancho immediately gave a vigorous full-body shake. Muddy water everywhere.

High humidity, smell of dog, and relative quiet, just the drum of rain on the roof. Within seconds, the windows steamed up.

"Here," Molly said, leaning over to pull tissues from the glove compartment. She and Oliver dried their faces. His clothes were stuck to him, hers to her. The situation was anything but romantic, but—she was steaming up, too. She could feel her body changing. The physical pull was so strong, she was almost trembling. What was this? She didn't like Oliver—she wanted to touch him everywhere. "Chilly," she mumbled, to mask the cause of the shivering. And then she blurted out,

"Okay, all right. I'm not exactly a physical therapist." Lust, apparently, was like truth serum.

"Except in a very broad sense." Oliver's sensuous lips sneered a little, but she didn't think his heart was in the insult. The look in his eyes made her feel completely naked. Completely willing. "What exactly are you?"

"None of your business," she decided. Charlie would kill her if she told him the truth.

Oliver's hungry stare didn't waver.

"Okay, I'm a student." What the hell.

"Of human behavior."

"Yes, as a matter of fact."

"Human needs and wants."

"You could say that."

They had a staring contest.

She gave in at the moment he reached for her, so technically it was a mutual kiss. But rough, an artless coming together that felt inevitable and overdue. Teeth clashed, hands grabbed. They made rash, automatic adjustments to get closer, feel more skin. She loved his open mouth on her neck, but it made her want more. She found his bare back under his clothes and pressed, stroked. Groans of pleasure and frustration, his, hers, were like music, but they couldn't say each other's name. Hers was fake anyway. "Let's . . ." "Can't we . . ." "God, you're . . ." The longer it went on, the more unbearable it became. She felt wound up tight, unable to think of anything but one thing. "How can we . . ." came out unintelligible, mashed against the heat of his delicious mouth. Oliver pulled away to look around, look behind them, find a way. "Is there a—thing, a—lever, we could . . ." He went still.

She thought it was Pancho, sprawled out and making juicy sounds as he licked mud from his paws, that cooled Oliver's passion. *Had to happen,* she thought, shaking again—with regret; this was crazy, plus the logistics were never going to work. But he wasn't looking at the dog.

He was looking at her bowling bag, lodged in the crack between the door and the seat. His face, before her eyes, changed from intense and aroused to hard and suspicious.

"So," he said in a winded voice, as if he'd been doing sprints. "You're a bowler."

She was too dazed to respond.

"That's funny, so am I. What kind of ball do you use?"

"What? What?"

"Tenpin or duckpin?" He reached over the seat back and grabbed the bag. "Duckpin," he guessed, hefting it in one hand. "Let's see."

"Give me that," she snapped, breathless, but he pulled the bag out of her reach.

"Can't I see your bowling ball?"

"No!"

"Come on," and before she could react, he had the bag unzipped, the vinyl sides pulled apart.

Even in the gray aquatic light, the crystal ball sparkled. Oliver stared at it in unblinking astonishment. Whatever he'd been expecting, this wasn't it.

"Give me that," she said, snatching the bag from his limp grip. "You know what your problem is? You're insane."

"What is it?"

"It's a bowling ball! A—a joke gift, from girlfriends. You wouldn't understand." She had an uncharacteristic urge to burst into tears. "Would you please get out of my car?"

"I—I—"

"Out, out, out, out—"

"Listen, I'm sorry, I thought, I mean—"

But whatever he thought he meant, he couldn't put it into words, and his inarticulateness enraged her so much she wanted to punch him. But she couldn't put her fury into words either, so she reached across him and shoved open the door on his side. "Out!"

He got out.

"Go blow up another oil rig in the Gulf!" were her parting words.

For once the Pontiac started up on the first try. It was a small, mean pleasure to see that Oliver was completely soaked again before he could get into his stupid car. Hers sent gravel flying as she peeled out of the parking lot.

TWELVE

—◆—

"You look terrible."

"Thanks, Grandfather. I was expecting 'happy birthday.' May I come in?"

"Oh yeah. Happy birthday." Charlie stepped back and opened the door wide. "Seriously, you don't look so good."

The first thing Oliver noticed was that the mustangs were still missing from their place on the shelf in the foyer. The second thing he noticed was the napkin tucked into Charlie's shirt collar. They went into the living room, where the TV was tuned, full blast, to *Entertainment Tonight*. "I'm sorry—you're still eating. I thought you said you were finished." That's what Charlie had told him when Oliver had phoned from the car, asking if he could come over.

"I'm finished. I never eat the cooked apples."

He looked more closely at Charlie's tray, congealing on the flat arm of his easy chair. "A TV dinner? This is what you eat? Grandfather—"

"Sometimes. So what? Siddown, I got something for you. Thought I'd have to wait till the weekend to give it to you." He disappeared into the bedroom, but kept talking. "How come you didn't go to that party thing at the office? If I'd known you were coming over, I'da baked you a cake." He came back into the living room. "Ha-ha, okay, not baked, bought, but I'da put candles on it. Not every day a guy turns thirty-five."

"It wasn't a party, just some friends from work. We were going to meet up at a club and have a few drinks. Nothing special."

"Yeah?" Charlie set a large, rectangular package on the coffee table, then collapsed on the couch. "So what happened?"

"Nothing, I just . . . We weren't in the mood for it after . . ."

"Hah?" He cupped his ear. "Siddown, siddown. And speak up, I can't hear you."

Oliver found the remote and clicked off the TV. He sat down in deference to his grandfather, but he wasn't in the mood for this either. He wasn't in the mood for much of anything. Hadn't been for days.

"I said, nobody felt like partying very much after I told Sharon I was quitting."

"Quitting? Did you say quitting?"

"I gave them two months' notice."

"Well, I'll be damned." Charlie slapped his knee. "Congratulations! That's great!"

"Why is it great?"

His delighted look faltered. "Aren't you glad?"

"Sure." Glad? He supposed. After all the fretting, soul-searching, and list-making he'd done to make the decision, he ought to feel elated, if only to have it over with. Something was dulling his emotions lately. What he mostly felt was numb.

"So what're you gonna do now?" Charlie asked. "Something big, I bet."

"Start my own firm—try to. Small, much smaller than Cullen Pratt. I'll focus on alternative energies—"

"Windmills," Charlie guessed. "I always liked windmills."

"Wind, solar, hydropower, geothermal, biofuels. It's what I've been doing, but I think I can do it better on my own. I hope."

"Oh, you will," Charlie said with confidence.

"Or I could lose my shirt."

"Nah, you'll do great."

"You think so?" A wave of affection welled up unexpectedly.

"Sure, absolutely. Anything you really wanna do, you're gonna be good at it. That's the way you are."

"Thanks, Grandfather."

"Don't mention it. Open your present."

"I wasn't miserable at Cullen Pratt, you know. It's a good firm, good people, but if I'm ever going to accomplish something on my own—"

"Right. You're not getting any younger."

"You put it so gently."

Charlie nudged the package closer. "Open your present."

"You didn't have to get me anything." The serious weight of the box surprised him; he had to get a better grip just to lift it. A hazy inkling awoke. He tore off the festive ribbon and paper with a curious, rising anxiety.

Inside the oblong box was exactly what he'd hoped for. Or feared. "The mustangs."

Charlie was rubbing his hands together with excitement. "I got that before you were born, y'know, a little store in New York, I was up there on a buying trip, paid diddly, and guess what it's worth now. Guess. Two thousand bucks! I know, I shouldn't say, it's a gift, but I wanted you to know, I'm not just unloading some old crap on your birthday."

"I always liked it," Oliver managed.

"I know! That's why I picked it, it was your fave. This appraiser guy—there's a card in there, explains everything—he says it's 'museum quality.' Eighteen hundreds, limited edition. Hundred percent bronze, special casting process. Who knew? I'm gonna get more horses appraised—I could have a gold mine here! So, you really like it?"

"I love it. Thank you, Grandfather, it means a lot. But I don't want to break up your collection—"

"Collection, schmolection, take it home, put it someplace you'll see it. I want you to have it."

Oliver leaned over and gave Charlie a wordless hug that left both of them a little misty-eyed. Charlie said this called for a drink and poured them brandies from a bottle he found at the back of a kitchen cabinet. Maybe that was what gave Oliver the courage to finally say what was on his mind.

"You and, uh, Ms. Smith-Jones . . ."

"Who?"

"Krystal."

"Who?"

"Your physical therapist, Grandfather. Except she isn't, is she?"

"Hm?" Charlie stuck his nose in his brandy glass.

"Don't you think it's time to level with me?"

"About what?"

"Krystal! I'd like to know exactly what your relationship to her is."

"Why?"

Oliver pressed all his fingers against his forehead. "I want to know. I just would like to know. Is it a secret?"

If he wasn't mistaken, Charlie was trying not to laugh. "Okay, okay, okay. What she is, is she's my advisor."

"Your advisor."

"Spiritual advisor, you could say. In a way. Spiritual and emotional. Also social."

"Social?"

"You're a direct kinda guy—so'm I. I'll sum Krystal up in one word for you, Oliver. She's my friend."

———

Maybe, maybe not. One thing Oliver now knew she wasn't: a horse thief. If he'd been wrong about that, what else had he been wrong about?

Only one way to find out.

"Krystal? It's Oliver Worth. I need to speak to you. Would you call me when you get this message?" He thought of adding something softer, something placating. *Hope you're well*, or *Sorry about our last meeting*. Or *Boy, was I a jerk*. But, no; he didn't really know anything for certain. This was an exploratory call, not an apology. Yet.

He shouldn't have been surprised, then, when she didn't call back.

THIRTEEN

◆

Nine hundred and twenty, twenty-five, twenty-six, twenty-seven, twenty-eight. Nine hundred and twenty-eight dollars and . . . a lot of change.

Was that good? It didn't seem like that much. Molly surveyed the odds and ends left over from her yard sale in the dwindling light of late afternoon. There was hardly anything left, which was good—less to donate or throw away—but if she'd known the detritus of her whole life was going to sell so quickly, she might've raised her prices.

Nobody had bought the crystal ball, she saw as she hauled the scanty leftovers onto the front porch; not even for a measly five bucks. She'd give it back to Aunt Kit, except Aunt Kit was so mad at her she probably wouldn't take it. ("Why didn't you *tell* me you were losing your house? *Why?*" Excessive embarrassment didn't seem like a good enough reason, so Molly had no answer.) She guessed she'd keep it, then, find room for it somewhere in the tiny efficiency on Colesville Road she'd be moving into tomorrow. Right after the sheriff auctioned off her house.

Oh, her sweet little house. Almost bare now, between the yard sale and Craigslist, and yet it still felt like home to her. Walking through the echoing rooms to the kitchen, she vowed not to cry—she'd done some of that, not much, yesterday, and it hadn't helped. "Bricks and wood and glass"—it was practically a chant now. It didn't help either.

The phone in her pocket rang. The psychic line—good; someone else she could deliver the news to personally.

"Hi," said Donette, the woman with the cheating husband. She had a new story of suspicion and treachery; Molly listened to it with the phone propped to her ear with her shoulder while she heated a piece of pizza in the oven and drank milk from the carton—she'd packed all the glasses.

"Donette," she said at the end of the familiar monologue and her own customary advice (leave him), "I am glad you called this evening, because it gives me the chance to tell you—I will not be able to speak to you again."

"Excuse me?"

She had different stories depending on the client. Some people wanted to hear she was going on to bigger and better things, some people wanted to hear just the opposite. She used her intuition. For Donette, she said, "I am starting a brand-new life. Scary, yes, but also quite exciting, I think. Freeing. But I will miss you—you are one of the ones I will truly miss." Strange, but true.

"But you *can't* quit. Madame Romanescu—what'll I do without you?"

"You will listen to the words I have said," so many, many times, "and you will put them into action, dear one. Bravely. You will lose all your fear. I see it so clearly: Like me, you are going on an adventure."

"I am?"

"Do you have a green dress?"

"A—? No, I don't think—"

"A green blouse? A green T-shirt?"

"Um, I've got a T-shirt that says 'Everybody loves an Irish girl.'"

"Yes, yes, I *knew* it. With shamrocks on it."

"Wow! Yeah!"

"This is what you will be wearing when you tell Bob it is time for him to go. Oh, I see it, it is so very, very clear."

Molly hardly ever gave advice this specific—too dangerous, not to mention *arrogant*—but she'd heard enough about

smarmy, lying, despicable Bob to have not a single qualm in
Donette's case. They went over the scene, what she would say,
all the possible arguments Bob might use, until Donette said,
"Okay, I got it," and Molly thought this time she really might.
"But can't I call you up after? Just one last time, to tell you
what happens?"

"Alas, dear one, I will not be here." As of midnight tonight,
the psychic line would be kaput. "But don't worry, all will be
well. I had a vision of a small bird, a sweet little bird, darting
out of her cage and taking flight. Flying high, free and happy.
At last, enjoying the life she was meant to live!"

Maybe it would work. Donette sounded hopeful by the end
of the call, and steady enough to thank Molly for "all your help,
all these weeks. I'd've been lost without you." Maybe she'd do
better on her own, no sympathetic Gypsy ear on the other end
of the line, constantly soothing, constantly reassuring. Tough
love. She'd certainly be *richer*.

Charlie called while Molly was loading the contents of her
bathroom cabinet into a cardboard box. "Oliver's trying to get
ahold of you."

"Oh?"

"You avoiding him or something? I think he's depressed."

"Charlie, I'm *so busy* right now, can I call you back? In a
few days?"

"A few *days*?"

She hadn't told him about the move, the fate of her house.
Not for any particular reason. Except that she found the whole
subject nauseating. "I know, I'm sorry, it's just that it's such a
busy time for me right now."

"Sure, sure. You got a life."

"Oh, Charlie."

"What? I get it—you're young, gorgeous, you got better
things to do. It's not a problem."

"Would you stop that? I'm moving."

"Moving! Where to?"

"A smaller place—easier to take care of. Also, I'm giving
up the psychic line. Tonight, in fact."

"How come?"

"But you can still call me, of course. How come? Oh, Charlie, I need a real job. A full-time job that pays, you know, real

money. So I'm taking the summer off from school and starting on Monday. It's a job in phone sales."

"That's crazy. Although you got the voice for it."

"Listen, Charlie. I tried to tell you this once before, but you didn't hear me. The thing is—I don't think I'm actually psychic."

"Oh, pshaw."

"No, truly. It runs in the family, but I don't think it runs in me."

"So you mean . . ." She could hear him processing the news. "You mean . . . *nobody's thinking about me?*"

"See, here's where it's confusing. I feel very strongly that someone *is* thinking of you. A meaningful woman, someone who could change your whole life."

"Oh. Whew. Okay, then."

"But I don't know where it's coming from! Because, God knows, if I *were* psychic, I'd've done something about my *own* life before . . . well, anyway."

"Before what?"

She laughed. "Nothing, I'm not in too great a mood tonight, that's all."

"Okay, you listen to me. Are we pals?"

"Of course. Of course we are."

"Then it goes two ways. Sometimes you help me, sometimes I help you."

"Oh, Charlie." She was so touched. "You are . . . so dear to me."

"Likewise. So what can I do to help?"

"Not a thing. Honestly. Except what you're already doing— being my friend."

"No problemo. Okay, here's what you can do for me."

"What?"

"Take my obnoxious grandson's call."

————

After that, every time the phone rang and it *wasn't* Oliver, she felt let down. Not that she would've spoken to him anyway, but it had given her a small lift—very small on this, the lousiest day of her life—to be the one not talking. And now he wouldn't even call her so she could not answer.

She'd have called her aunt, who always cheered her up with something sweet or funny or weird, but Aunt Kit was furious with her for not confiding in her about the foreclosure. "You know, Moll," she'd said at the end of their last conversation, "this wouldn't be happening if you'd taken my advice years ago and gotten some cash out of that worthless ex."

"So, you told me so?"

"Look at him now, raking it in, and who put him in a position to rake it? You. You threw away your career for his, and now where are you? He set you back *years*."

Exactly the sort of thing Molly didn't care to hear tonight, so she didn't call.

FOURTEEN

Her voice was like your favorite music, familiar and thrilling at the same time. "Hello. It is Madame Romanescu," she said, and the words went straight to your heart. Brought you back, in case you'd been missing.

"Howdy," Oliver said. "It's Shorty." Stupid name; he wished he'd called himself "Slim" or "Lefty."

But she repeated it with such gladness and relief—"Ah, Shorty"—it didn't matter. He settled deeper into the chair on his small deck overlooking Q Street, thinking the world would be a better place if everybody had somebody to call them "dear one."

"I am so happy you called, Shorty."

"Reckon you say that to all of us."

"No, oh no. Believe me."

He did. And that was another part of her magic. "How're you doin'? You sound a mite down."

"It has not been a good day."

"Tell me about it."

"You, too?"

"Yeah, but nothin' dire. I just called to hear your voice."

"I'm so glad. Are you drinking a cup of Arbuckles'?"

"No, ma'am. Glass o' whiskey tonight." Wine, actually. "We

cowboys got a saying: Never drink unless you're alone or with somebody."

Where did he come *up* with this stuff? But she laughed her low, throaty laugh, so it was worth it. "I love cowboy sayings," she said. "Tell me another one."

He thought. "Don't squat with your spurs on."

This time her laugh was higher, freer. Familiar . . .

"You like that one?"

"Shorty, you cheer me up. But I have something to tell you."

"I got something to tell you, too. You go first."

"No, you. Please. Tell me your news."

"Yeah? Well, okay. I just wanted you to know, I quit my job at the Double K."

"Oh *my*. Are you happy?"

"I'm . . . Yeah. I reckon I am, now that it's done. Feels right."

"Yes. I think so, too."

"Not sure what was holdin' me back."

"Caution. Your natural prudence."

"That, and maybe thinkin' . . . maybe I didn't quite deserve to get exactly what I wanted."

"Ah," she said lightly. "But that's gone now?"

"More or less."

"Good riddance. And now you will—what?"

"Well, I got my eye on a . . . a piece o' land not too far from here. I got enough saved up to buy it and start a little herd o' my own."

"And raise the dogies in new, modern ways."

"Did you know cattle-raisin' causes more greenhouse gases than cars do? If we changed their diets—the dogies, I'm talkin' about—we could reduce methane emissions, fix global warming, fix acid rain. . . . Okay, I'll shut up."

"I'm so proud of you, Shorty."

"You are, huh?"

"You're a good man. And you will be a great success, I know it."

"What about you? How come you're havin' such a low-down day, Miss Romy?"

"Oh, my friend. Where to begin."

"How 'bout the beginning?"

She heaved a sigh. "Not enough time."

Funny thing to say, he thought, for a woman who got paid by the minute. "The middle, then. Anywhere you want."

Another sigh. "It's nothing. I have fallen on hard times," she said with a laugh, mocking herself.

"Is it that sidewinder?"

"That—? Oh, him. No. Well, not only him."

"Because that's a varmint that oughta be shot."

"Did you take my advice, Shorty? Did you ask the lady you don't even like if she stole your horses?"

"Didn't get the chance. She's not talkin' to me anymore."

"Uh-oh."

"No big deal."

Silence from Romy.

"Okay, it's a big deal, but danged if I know why."

"I understand."

"I figure you do. How come?"

"The same thing has happened to me. The man—he is gone, and that's good, and yet it feels as if I have lost something quite . . . valuable."

"Yeah."

"Perhaps . . . irreplaceable."

"Yeah."

They shared a gloomy silence. He wished he knew a way to cheer her up but, too bad, he was all out of cowboy sayings.

"What's it like in Hoboken tonight?" he asked.

"There is a full moon. Are you outside?"

"Yep. I'm . . . sittin' up on a butte, lookin' out across the prairie."

"How beautiful it must be."

"You ever been out West?"

She said no, she never had, and he said she oughta come out sometime, he'd show her the sights. They talked about this and that, unimportant things, like old friends, and he wondered how he could feel so comfortable and connected with a woman he'd never seen and didn't know. A woman who made her living talking to strangers.

"Hang on a sec," he said, "I got another call comin' in." He checked the number. "It's my grampaw," he told Romy. "Kinda late for him to call."

"Do you need to—"

"Nah, he's okay, I'll catch him later."

"Shorty, I must go soon. But first I have something to tell you."

"Oh hell—you said that, and I plumb forgot. Sorry."

"Never mind. I didn't want to say it anyway."

"Now you got me worried."

"This is the last time I can speak to you."

"Say what?"

"I am resigning. As Madame Romanescu. This night is my last night. That's why I was so glad when you called, so I could tell you—"

"*Shoot*. Hang on two secs—" Charlie *again*. "Okay, I'm back. Now, what's this you're tellin' me? You're *resigning*?"

"It's part of having fallen on hard times," she said with another rueful laugh. "I have to get serious about my life. Oh, Shorty—I've said good-bye to so many people tonight. Why are you the hardest?"

"Well, wait now, maybe we can—" He heard a buzz on her end of the line. "What's that?"

"My doorbell," she said in a wondering voice. "Who could it be? It's almost midnight."

"I'll hang on while you—Well, *shit*." Charlie again! "I think I better call him—"

"Yes, you must—"

"But I'll hang on while you see who's—"

"I'm looking through the . . . Oh my God."

"What?"

"It's my aunt!"

"Oh. Well, uh . . ."

"I have to go. I'm so sorry. Good-bye, good-bye, dear one—"

"Aw, Romy."

"Have a happy life, my dear friend."

"I'll miss you."

"I will miss you!"

His phone beeped again. There was nothing else he could do—he hung up on Romy.

————

"What?" he said in a loud, not at all respectful voice to his grandfather, who answered before the first ring finished.

"Romy's getting foreclosed," said Charlie.

"What?"

"Romy's getting foreclosed!"

"What does that *mean*?"

"I'm *telling* you. Says right here." Sounds of newspaper rattling. "Can't believe I was about to throw this out. It's last week's."

"What?"

" 'Trustee's Sale of valuable fee simple property improved by premises known as 622 Palmer Street.' That's Romy."

"No, Grandfather, Romy lives in Hoboken."

"No, no, she lives here. Blah blah, terms of sale, yackity yack . . . 'for sale at public auction at the front of the Court-house for the County of Montgomery, on June 11 at 11:18 a.m.'—that's tomorrow."

"Grandfather—"

"You gotta do something!"

"Hang up. I'll call her."

"Hah?"

"Hang up!"

But when he dialed Romy's 900 number, he got a message saying it was no longer in service.

It was one minute after midnight.

FIFTEEN

"I still think this is a horrible idea," Molly said, holding the car door for her aunt. The older lady got out gingerly—arthritis in her toe—ignoring the hand Molly held out to help. "I don't need to see this, Aunt Kit, I don't need closure or—"

"Who said anything about closure?" Aunt Kit straightened to her full height—five feet eight—and brushed down imaginary wrinkles in her straight, slim skirt. She'd arrived last night wearing her silvery hair in a new style, short and snazzy. "I'm telling you, something's going to happen."

"Yeah," Molly muttered, stuffing quarters into the parking meter. "The bank's going to buy my house back. And you want me to *watch*. It's inhumane. I'm just not—"

Her aunt's arm around her waist cut her off. "Hush. I've got a *good* feeling about this. When did you turn into such a gloomy Gloria?"

She'd have answered—*Two months ago, when I got a letter called Notice of Intent to Foreclose*—but Aunt Kit gave her such a bracing *squeeze* just then, she didn't have the breath. "*You're* certainly not grumpy," she accused as they waited for the Walk light at the corner. "You're practically glowing."

"I am?" Aunt Kit widened her bright blue eyes, laughed her big laugh. Her fair Irish skin was etched with delicate lines that deepened when she smiled, which was often. At seventy-five, she looked—Molly studied her in the harsh morning sun—ten years younger. At least. *Hope I got those genes,* she thought, far from the first time.

Why did they hold foreclosure auctions outside? What if it rained? What if it snowed? She'd always thought "on the courthouse steps" was just a saying, a metaphor, a verbal holdover from the Middle Ages—but look, there they were, about thirty people milling around in a sort of courtyard area under the portico of the extremely ugly gray stone county courthouse. "Still have that *good* feeling?" she thought of asking Aunt Kit, but anything out of her mouth for the next twenty minutes or so was going to be snarky and mean. She vowed to shut up. *Just get through this, then you can go home.*

Except she couldn't.

Somebody's house was up for sale right now. A man in shirtsleeves and a tie was auctioning it off like a—a rug at an estate sale. "Three ninety, three ninety, do I hear three ninety-one, ninety-one, ninety-one, do I hear ninety-one?" Long pause. "*Sold* for three hundred ninety thousand dollars." *Barbaric,* thought Molly, looking around for the poor owner. Nobody was weeping, nobody looked heartbroken. Well, they wouldn't *come,* of course; they wouldn't have a crazy great-aunt who dragged them here to be eyewitnesses to the death of their dreams. They wouldn't have a sadistic . . .

Oh God!

She let go of Aunt Kit's arm to dodge behind the nearest column, pressing her back flat against it to stay upright. "*Oh my God, oh my God, oh my God.*"

"What, honey?" her aunt asked mildly, looking around. "He just announced your house. I think it's starting."

"This can't be, it can't be. This is a bad dream." Except for her ex-husband, there was no one in the world Molly less wanted to meet at this moment than Oliver Worth. And *still* her stupid heart skipped that stupid beat, just to see him. She peeped around the column, helpless not to look. He was wearing a suit and carrying a briefcase. Charlie was with him! Did they have a foreclosed house? Surely not. Were they *buying* a foreclosed house? Not Charlie—but she wouldn't put it past

Oliver. He'd probably *enjoy* profiting from someone else's misfortune. The next best thing to scenic mountaintop removal.

Aunt Kit was gazing about, trying to see what Molly was seeing. All at once, everything about her went still. Her face froze. Her mouth dropped.

"Stop, don't look!" Molly hissed. "They'll see us!"

"Who?"

"Oliver! Oliver Worth. And Charlie. I can't believe they're here! *God*, this is my absolute worst nightmare."

"That's Charlie?" And she started walking toward him.

"What are you *doing*? Don't go over there! Aunt Kit—" Molly made a grab for her shoulder, but her aunt shrugged her off like an annoying child and marched straight over to Charlie.

Molly looked up at the sooty concrete ceiling, thinking, *I'll kill her.* And then, *Well, this is as low as it's ever going to go,* which was a kind of comfort, and followed.

"Charlie," she heard her aunt say, but in the strangest voice, low and wondering. Charlie turned toward her and said— nothing; he seemed struck dumb. He just stared until Aunt Kit said, "I'm Kit." And then he echoed it, "Kit," like "Lord" or "Messiah." "I'm Charlie," he said. Then they just looked at each other.

Oliver, who had been attending to the auction, saw Molly and did an actual double take. She was grateful for the half-minute's warning she'd had; otherwise her face would look like his: gob-smacked.

"What are you doing here?" she said, taking the offensive.

"What are *you* doing here?"

"Did you come to gloat? You probably didn't think I had the guts, but I came to see it to the end." With a little arm-twisting from her aunt.

His struck-by-lightning look didn't waver. "What?"

"Bid!" Charlie poked him on the arm, and Oliver held up his hand.

"Hey!" Molly said. "What do you think you're doing?"

Aunt Kit said, "Hello."

"Hello," Oliver said, distracted. "Who are you?"

"This is Kit," Charlie said reverently.

Introductions seemed to be called for. "Katherine McDougal—my great-aunt—this is Oliver Worth." But Aunt Kit and Charlie were staring at each other again. "Have you two met before?"

"Seriously," said Oliver, "what are you doing here?"

"Why are you trying to buy my house?"

"I'm not trying to buy your house. I'm bidding on the—" He looked down at the folded newspaper in his hand. "On the—" He looked at it again. "McDougal house." He looked at Aunt Kit. "Oh, it's *your* house."

"Bid!" Charlie said, and Oliver held up his hand again.

"It's not my house," said Aunt Kit. "It's Molly's."

"Who?" said Oliver.

"It's my house," Molly said, taking the newspaper from him. "It says right here, Molly McDougal."

"Ha! So you're not Krystal Smith-Jones?" His beautiful lips twisted sarcastically. "What a surprise." He turned to his grandfather. "Why did you tell me it was Romy's house?"

"It is Romy's house."

"You're right," Molly said, "I'm not Krystal Smith-Jones. I'm Molly McDougal." If nothing else, it was a relief to finally be rid of *that* silliness.

"Also," Charlie said helpfully, "Madame Romanescu."

"No, she's not." Oliver looked as if he'd been insulted. "Don't be ridiculous."

"This man is awfully rude," Aunt Kit noted. "And yet I do believe you're going to be stuck with him, dear."

"Ah, but I am," Molly said to Oliver in her Romy voice. "Do you remember me now, dear one? We spoke on the phone once, weeks ago. You told me to leave your grandfather alone." She turned to Aunt Kit. "Yes, he is rude—I *told* you."

Oliver had turned into a statue. "Bid," Charlie said, nudging him again.

"Romy?" he finally managed between numb-looking lips. "You're Romy?" He tore his gaze from her to look at Charlie. "Why did you tell me she was Krystal?"

"Who's Krystal?" said Aunt Kit.

"Long story," said Charlie. "Your turn to *bid*, Oliver. Say," he said to Aunt Kit, "do you play golf?"

"Yes," Molly said, "I am Romy," still in her Gypsy voice.

"Romy." Oliver's face looked like Charlie's—reverent and wondering. "It's me," he said. "Shorty."

She laughed, a slightly hysterical sound. "No, you're not. Now *you're* being ridiculous."

"Yes, ma'am, I am," he said in that low, slow drawl she loved. "You gave me a lotta good advice when I was out there herdin' the dogies. I gave you some, too."

"You . . . did?"

"Yes, ma'am. I told you not to squat with your spurs on."

"Bid," Charlie commanded, and Oliver held up his hand.

"Shorty?" Molly's voice quavered. She pressed clasped hands to her heart. Could it be? "Shorty?"

"Romy."

"Sold!" said the auctioneer.

"What just happened?"

"Oliver bought your house," said Charlie, patting her on the shoulder. "Who's Shorty?"

"Who's Krystal?" said Aunt Kit again.

"You bought my house?"

"I thought it was Romy's." Oliver took Molly's hands. "Oh, Romy, look at you. You're so . . . *young.*"

"Oh, Shorty. You're so . . . *tall.*"

They moved closer, until their lips were almost touching. She ran her thumbs along his cheekbones, the line of his jaw. "Are you my landlord now?"

"I'll sell it back to you," he said tenderly. "Cheap. No money down."

Aunt Kit pressed her hands to her temples. "I'm not getting any clarity on this at all."

Oliver looked like a boy when he grinned. Molly fell in love with him when he spread his arms wide, as if to embrace them all, and said, "Let's go get a cuppa Arbuckles', straighten this whole thing out."

"Don't you have to pay them or something?" Charlie remembered.

"Whoa, Nellie." He patted his breast pocket. "Be right back."

"I'll go with you," Molly said, not ready to let go of him yet. Not when she'd just found him.

"Okay, but hang on. Something I gotta do first."

She hoped it was what she thought it was.

It was.

————

Charlie glanced at Kit—what a sexy name—who was exactly his height in her flat-heeled shoes. Crazy, but watching Oliver and Molly kiss, especially like *that*, was making him blush.

Kit didn't blush; she just looked interested. "When did this happen?" she asked, gesturing. "I thought they didn't like each other."

"Oh, I always knew they liked each other. Ha-ha—maybe I'm psychic!"

"Maybe you are." She lifted his right hand and peered into his palm. "Oh, *look*. Your fate line's like Route 66."

"Yeah?"

"Coast to coast."

"Not surprised. I always thought I was the sensitive type."

"And see this?" She ran a soft finger—he liked her French manicure—down to the base of his wrist, while his smile turned dreamy. "Here's where you meet the second great love of your life."

"Where?"

"Right here." They looked up at the same time, into each other's eyes. "And you live," Kit said seriously, "for freaking ever."

"What about you?"

"Same thing. My life line practically wraps around my wrist." She showed him.

"Amazing. Freaking fantastic." He looked forward to talking like someone from New Jersey. "Means we've got a long, long time, Kit. Okay if I call you Kit?"

They strolled away, arms entwined, leaving Molly and Oliver where they were. They could catch up later—they had even longer.

THE UNFORGIVEN

RUTH RYAN LANGAN

For Tom, whose heart will always be my home.

ONE

"There it is, missus." Duncan Logan, the burly, white-haired driver of the vintage Rolls, pointed at the stone manor house in the distance. "There's Ravenswood."

Brianna Kerr, who had alternated between anger and despair during her flight to Scotland, stopped fiddling with the strap of her purse and strained for her first glimpse of her late husband's family estate. Though she'd seen pictures of it, they had been taken years ago, when it had been beautifully maintained as one of the premier properties in the Scottish Highlands. She had to swallow back her disappointment. Now, after years of neglect, the hedges along the curving ribbon of road were sadly in need of a trim, the sloping lawns and gardens were overgrown, the statuary was faded and even toppled and broken.

Like me, she thought. *Like my life, my dreams. Broken.*

When the car came to a halt, the old man hurried around to hold open the passenger door. "You go ahead, missus. I'll deliver your bags to the gatekeeper's cottage and lay in some firewood as you requested. That is, if you're sure that's where you really plan on staying. As I've warned you, 'tis in sad shape indeed. I'm sure you'd be much more comfortable in the village where there are shops and . . ."

"I'm sure. Thank you, Duncan." Her credit card was already maxed. Besides, the last thing she wanted was laughing, chattering shoppers around her. She craved quiet. Peace. Time alone. To brood. To heal.

Would she ever heal?

As she climbed the wide stone steps, she saw the flutter of curtains at the window moments before the front door was thrown wide.

She forced a smile on her lips. "Mrs. Logan?"

Duncan's wife filled the doorway with her bulk. As wide as she was tall, with a simple white apron tied around her enormous middle, and her salt-and-pepper hair tied back in a severe bun, she looked more like an actor in a play than the flesh-and-blood housekeeper of an ancient Scottish manor house.

"Gwynn Logan. That I am." The older woman looked her up and down, as though taking her measure. "And you'd be Mrs. Kerr."

"Please call me Bree." Brianna offered a handshake.

There was a moment's hesitation before the older woman offered her hand. "Well, I'll try. Though things were more formal when her ladyship was alive. I suppose"—the older woman's tone was wistful—"with her ladyship gone, nothing's as it was in the day."

Nor will it ever be again.

The thought sent a sudden shaft of pain through Bree's already shattered heart. It was a struggle for her to remain composed.

She was grateful that the housekeeper took that moment to look toward the driver just stepping back into the car.

"Now, where is Duncan going? What about your things?"

"I asked him to put them in the gatekeeper's cottage."

"The gatekeeper's . . ." The older woman shot her a startled look. "As the widow of Barclay Kerr, and the only surviving heir to Ravenswood, this is now your home. The cottage is in shambles. It wouldn't be right for you to stay anywhere but here. Despite its sad condition, 'tis heaps better than the cottage."

Bree tried to put her at ease. "My husband once told me the cottage was a cozy place that had always charmed visitors."

"Master Barclay may have stretched the truth a bit. Besides, you're family, and it doesn't seem right for you to stay there when you have all this." When she realized that she was babbling, Mrs. Logan stepped aside. "There wasn't time to give it a proper cleaning, but I hope once you've had a tour of the manor house, you'll change your mind and perhaps spend the night here."

Bree put a hand on the older woman's arm. "I'm sorry about giving you so little notice of my arrival."

"Not to worry. I think it's grand that you've come at all." She stood aside to allow Bree to enter. "Welcome to Ravenswood, Mrs. Kerr."

"Thank you." Bree noted the formal title and smiled to herself. She'd just been given a not-too-subtle hint that the old ways would not be easily changed. "Just a brief tour, if you don't mind, so I can get my bearings. The flight was turbulent." *Like my life, these days.* "I'll take a more careful look after I've had a chance to rest."

As Bree followed the older woman up the stairs, she forced herself to look beyond the faded floors and walls to appreciate the beautiful woodwork, the fine old plaster, the exquisite crystal chandeliers cloaked under layers of dust.

The housekeeper paused at the doorway of a huge suite of rooms. "This belonged to her ladyship."

Despite the neglect, Bree could see what it must have looked like when the gilt bed was dressed, the chairs and settee devoid of their dust cloths, the closets filled with fashionable clothes and accessories.

Spying a family portrait, she crossed the room to study the figures of the handsome man, the beautiful woman, the boy with blue eyes and wheat-colored hair. All of them looking so happy, so carefree. Those were the innocent times. The times before . . .

"Master Barclay was the light of his mother's eyes." The old woman's tone was wistful. "There was nothing she wouldn't do for the lad. Nothing she wouldn't give him." She sighed. "She'd have given him the moon, had he but asked."

Had he asked? Bree wondered. Had he, in fact, demanded? Was that when he'd begun to feel entitled to the moon and stars and to all the pleasures of the world spread out before him?

She turned away, feeling a sudden need to escape.

"'Twould be no trouble for me to make up these rooms for you tonight, Mrs. Kerr. This is where you belong. In her ladyship's big, beautiful bed."

At the housekeeper's words, Bree gave a firm shake of her head. "No, but I do thank you, Gwynn."

Rebuffed, Mrs. Logan turned away. "Let me show you the upper floor, then."

Though it was an effort, Bree trailed the older woman up the stairs and peered into room after room, while the housekeeper relayed story upon story about each.

"This was where young Master Barclay used to play with his tin soldiers when the weather turned and he couldn't ride his pony. You can see the stables from this window. Such a fine equestrian he was."

In another room, "These had originally been used by Master Barclay's nanny. When she was no longer needed, her ladyship had this suite painted a lovely shade of blue, Master Barclay's favorite color, to celebrate his return from university. She wanted to give him some privacy, while keeping him close enough that she could enjoy his company. She'd hoped, of course, that he would be so content he would never want to leave."

In a third suite the housekeeper gave an expansive sigh. "When her ladyship learned that her son had wed, she ordered this entire section of rooms outfitted for him and his bride. No expense was to be spared. New beds, new sofas and chairs, new rugs for the floors." The older woman clapped a hand to her mouth. "I'm sorry. What was I thinking? You were that bride. And her ladyship had high hopes that she could entice you and her son to live here with her, as she had lived with her husband's family, as had all the generations before her. And here I am, running on and on, and haven't even taken the time to offer you my condolences. I'm so sorry for your loss. Such a handsome young man, with his whole life ahead of him and all that bright promise of a grand future, and now he's gone much too soon. I know how your poor heart must be breaking. I'm sure it's been a horrid year for you, Mrs. Kerr."

Bree could feel a vicious headache beginning at the base of her skull and radiating up to her temples. It was a struggle to keep her composure. "Thank you for your kind words, Gwynn. And for the tour. I believe I've seen enough for today."

"Of course." The older woman preceded her down the stairs before leading the way to a formal parlor, where a fire blazed on the hearth. Above the mantel, an ancient, brooding Highlander peered down from his lofty perch.

"You must be weary from your travels, Mrs. Kerr. Sit by the fire and I'll fetch some tea and sandwiches."

"Thank you. That would be lovely."

When she was alone, Bree sank down into an overstuffed chair. She'd thought she was prepared to meet people who'd known Barclay. But had they really known him? Just walking the halls of the home where Barclay had spent his childhood had a hundred questions flooding her mind. Every room, every wall, seemed to mock her.

Had he truly been happy here as a child? If so, why had he refused to return, even after their marriage? She'd all but begged to meet his mother, and to see the place where he'd spent his childhood, but Barclay had adamantly refused, saying he wasn't ready yet. But someday, he'd promised. There was plenty of time for a visit. All the time in the world.

How young and foolish she'd been. How trusting.

"Here we are now, Mrs. Kerr."

"Bree," she said gently as the housekeeper set a silver tray on the table beside her and began pouring tea.

Accepting a linen napkin, she nibbled a chicken sandwich. "Oh, this is heavenly."

"Thank you, ma'am."

Bree smiled and sipped her tea. "Will you join me, Gwynn?"

"'Twouldn't be proper. I'll take my tea later, with Duncan."

"At least sit a moment with me."

After a brief hesitation, the older woman settled herself in the opposite chair, though it was obvious that she wasn't comfortable breaking with tradition. She perched nervously on the edge of her seat, watching her young guest with a look of speculation.

After a brief silence, she took a breath. "I must warn you, ma'am, about staying in the cottage."

"Warn me?"

"There are . . . things that could alarm you."

"Such as . . . ?"

"The power is apt to go on or off at strange times. Dishes fall from shelves. Doors open and close."

When Bree held her silence, the old woman went on. "Nobody's ever managed to stay the night at the cottage."

"You mean I'll be the first?"

Gwynn Logan gave a sigh. "I mean that all who've tried have been driven away before morning."

"Driven away? By what?"

"Not what, ma'am. Who. He's a . . ." The older woman glanced toward the fireplace, then away. It was obvious that she was struggling to choose her words carefully. "Those who've seen him swear he's a fierce, vengeful creature bent on destroying anyone who dares to cross his threshold."

"Are you talking about a ghost?"

The old woman swallowed. "I am. A very angry ghost, by all accounts."

Bree took a moment to ponder this bit of news before nodding. "Very well. If such a creature exists—and I don't for a moment believe it does—then he shall have to deal with having a houseguest, won't he?"

"It's not something to be dismissed lightly. You could spare yourself the trouble by staying here, Mrs. Kerr."

Bree touched the napkin to her lips. The food and hot tea had restored, if not her energy, at least her determination.

She had come to this place for a number of reasons, the most important of which was to set her own rules and follow her own agenda, no matter what others thought.

"Thank you, Gwynn, for the lovely food, and for your concern. I believe I'll just rest here a few minutes and then I'll walk over to the cottage, before the light fades."

"As you wish." The housekeeper picked up the tray and glanced at the leaded window. "There's a storm brewing."

"I'll be on my way soon. I arranged to have an architect meet me here later. When he arrives, you can direct him to the cottage."

"Of course." At the doorway, Mrs. Logan paused to glance back at her young visitor.

Bree's head had fallen back against the cushion of the chair. Despite the fact that her eyes were closed, the lines of lingering tension were clearly visible.

———

Bree jerked awake, wondering how long she'd slept. It felt as though only minutes had passed.

Mrs. Logan was peering nervously out the window.

"Thank you again, Gwynn. I believe I'll head over to the gatekeeper's cottage."

As she made her way to the front door, the housekeeper trailed behind, unable to hide her disapproval. "'Tis little more than a hovel now."

"I don't mind."

"Duncan went ahead to lay a fire to chase the chill." She glanced out the window. "You're apt to get wet."

Bree was determined to put the old woman's mind at ease. "Please don't concern yourself. I'm really quite self-sufficient. I've brought a few supplies, so you won't need to bother fixing anything in the morning. Duncan told me that you and he have been living in the village, and only came back here to lend a hand during my stay. For that, I'm most grateful. But please don't feel the need to hurry back early in the morning. I asked Duncan to leave me a complete set of keys to the rooms of the manor house." She opened the door and stepped out onto the wide portico. "If you have the time to drive up from the village, I'd be grateful for your company tomorrow. And please, keep an eye out for the architect. Good night, Gwynn."

The housekeeper remained in the doorway as Bree descended the steps and started along the pathway toward the cottage. Bree heard the old woman give a gasp of surprise as the wind caught the door from her grasp and slammed it shut. She found herself smiling, imagining Mrs. Logan huddling behind the draperies, watching and waiting to hear the wail of banshees or the glint of fairy lights.

Let her watch, Bree thought. Let the whole world watch and wait.

What could ghosts do that hadn't already been done to her? There was no room in her life for fear. No time to indulge in self-pity or recriminations. There was enough anger in her to fuel whatever work lay ahead. From now on, it was full steam ahead, regardless of the consequences.

TWO

———◆———

Angry storm clouds roiled across the sky—a sky punctuated by quick, jagged flashes of lightning. The wind had picked up, sending the branches of trees into a frenzy.

The pathway leading to the stone cottage was overgrown with brush. Ivy, wild and tangled, covered nearly every inch of the exterior of the building, giving it a mad-fairy-tale look.

Bree pulled open the heavy front door and stepped inside. Shivering in the damp cold, she hurried across the room and dropped to her knees before the hearth. Why hadn't Duncan started a fire?

She sat back on her heels.

It would seem that he had. The wood was charred and wisps of smoke still lingered.

She carefully checked to see that the flue was open before holding a match to fresh kindling. When the fire was blazing, she closed the fire screen and noted with satisfaction the generous supply of firewood neatly stacked beside the hearth.

She stared around at the white sheets that covered the furniture.

"Like shrouds," she muttered.

Despite her weariness, she circled the room, pulling them

off, folding them, and setting them in a neat pile in a corner. Then she turned on every lamp to chase away the gloom.

"That's better." She looked around to admire the furnishings.

Though the sofa and chairs were old and worn, they appeared comfortable enough. There was a padded rocker pulled up before the fireplace, with a footstool and a lovely old ornate table alongside it, just right for a cup of tea.

Feeling her spirits begin to lift, she made her way to the bedroom, where Duncan had left her suitcases resting beside the empty closet. Crossing to the second fireplace, she found the fire had gone out there as well. After checking to ensure that the flue was open, she added fresh kindling and restarted the fire. Then she began the task of emptying her luggage and hanging her things.

She'd barely begun when there was a puff of smoke. She looked up to find that the fire had gone out again.

She felt the quick shiver of a breeze and checked the windows. All were latched. Puzzled, she held a match to more kindling until the fire was blazing. Then she made her way to the parlor, only to find that the fire there had gone out as well.

Again she felt the breeze against her cheek, and hurriedly checked the windows and front door. They were securely latched.

Annoyed at the waste of her precious time, she repeated the process of restarting the fire, using more kindling. When the flame was strong and steady, she returned to the bedroom, where she continued unpacking.

When she turned away to hang a blouse, she heard a rustling sound, as though a sudden windstorm had stirred up a pile of autumn leaves. Turning back to the suitcase, she found her things scattered about the floor.

She must be more tired than she'd realized. Annoyed, she retrieved everything and hung the clothing quickly before stowing the empty suitcases on the floor of the closet.

Just as she finished, the storm began in earnest. Wind and rain pelted the roof and rattled the windows as she closed the closet door and turned.

A man was standing across the room, scowling at her. He was tall, at least six feet, with dark hair that brushed the collar of a saffron shirt. His legs were bare beneath a length of plaid. Muscular legs, Bree noted. He looked every inch like those contestants she'd seen in the airline's magazine article about the Highland Games.

Startled, she shrank back against the closet door. "Who are you?" The words were out of her mouth before she even had time to think.

"I would ask you the same, madam." The voice, deep and rich, was thick with Scottish burr.

"I am Brianna Kerr. Now you will tell me your name and why you are here."

"I am Laird James Kerr. Jamie, to those who know me. This is my land. It has been in my family for more than five hundred years, madam. And I do not recall inviting you to share it with me." He crossed his arms over his chest and glowered. "You will leave this place. Now."

Bree's gaze swept the room, looking for something with which to defend herself. Was this the man who terrorized guests in the night? Ghost indeed. He was nothing more than an actor. And not a very good one at that. There was nothing otherworldly about him. He didn't shimmer or glow. Nor did he weave and float about the room. He was flesh and blood, firmly anchored to that spot, and giving every impression of a man about to do battle.

"I was told that I am the last remaining heir to the Kerr line."

"Then you were told an untruth, woman. I am here, and here I remain, to make a lie of whatever you may say."

She drew herself up firmly. "Duncan will be here any minute with the rest of my supplies. I'll have you deal with him."

A smile tugged at the corners of the man's mouth. "I'll give you this. You're quick-witted. But not a very good liar, madam. The old servant has been here and gone."

She bristled at his archaic term. "There are no servants here. Only good people who earn an honest day's wages for an honest day's work."

His smile widened. "Those good people of whom you speak are terrified to come near this place after dark."

"Then I suggest you leave before I call the authorities." While she spoke, Bree dug into her pocket for her cell phone.

"'Twill do you no good." He shot a quick glance at her pocket and the phone seemed to leap from her hand to the floor.

"How did you do . . . ?" She visibly paled. "What sort of trick was that?"

"I need no magician's parlor tricks." He pointed. "That thing you were clutching is useless here. Didn't the old woman, Gwynn, tell you? She refers to this place as a dead zone." That had him smirking. "An interesting choice of words, don't you agree?"

Bree blinked. "I don't believe any of this." She bent to retrieve her cell phone. "You're an actor, and an insulting one at that. And since you're intruding on my privacy, I'm ordering you to leave at once."

His smile was wiped away in an instant. His voice lowered with passion. His distinctive burr thickened. "Nobody orders Jamie Kerr from his home. Nobody. Least of all a bloody, trembling female. Now leave, before I show you just how much power I possess."

Bloody, trembling female indeed. She felt her temper flare, and with it, her courage. "In case you weren't listening, my name is Brianna Kerr. I am the widow of Barclay Kerr, and the legal owner of this land and all the buildings on it. If anyone is going to leave, it's you." She pointed to the open bedroom door. "If you leave now, I won't press charges. If you refuse, I'll have no choice but to alert the authorities."

"They won't bother coming here. They know better. I'm surprised the old biddy in the main house didn't warn you about me."

"She told me there was a presence in the cottage that enjoyed tormenting guests who attempt to stay here. I told Mrs. Logan that I don't believe in such things."

"Then you're a fool. And I'll not tolerate fools in my presence."

"Nor will I." Taking a calculated risk, Bree snatched her jacket from the closet and turned her back on him to stride from the room. Over her shoulder she called, "I'm going to walk back to the main house and get a signal for this useless phone, and then I'm going to alert the authorities. I suggest that you leave as quickly as you came, or you'll be spending your night in the local jail."

When she stepped into the parlor, she was startled to see him standing in front of her.

"How did you . . . ?" Before she could finish her sentence, he vanished.

From the bedroom came the sound of breaking glass. She rushed back in time to see the man picking up an expensive antique vase, poised to toss it on the floor alongside the shattered remnants of another.

"Don't you dare! That's probably worth a fortune." She raced across the room and snatched the vase from his hand.

He forcibly took it back. "And that's all this means to you? The money 'twill fetch?"

"Since it obviously means nothing to you, I won't have you smashing it to bits."

"'Tis precious to me. I personally chose it on a journey to Edinburgh." He glanced at the broken shards at his feet. "I brought the pair of them here to adorn my hearth. And if I now choose to break it, it's nobody's business but mine."

Bree made another grab for it. When their fingers brushed, she experienced a sudden rush of heat followed by the sweet smell of heather, as though she'd stepped into a lovely Highland meadow on a warm spring morning.

She took a quick step back and wrapped her arms around the vase, hugging it to her chest.

At the look of astonishment on her face, he regarded her with interest. "So. You felt it, too. Interesting. Not all do. Most are immune to my touch. You must be more sensitive than others. Tell me again, Mistress Kerr." At the mention of her name, his eyes narrowed slightly, as though the mere words annoyed him. "Did you say you don't believe?"

"I . . ." She swallowed. "I don't know who or what you are. A very good actor, or"—she forced herself to speak the word—"maybe you really are a ghost."

He exploded with fury. "I despise that word."

Before she could ask why, he held up his hand to silence her.

"I prefer the term *restless spirit*. I am here, as I've been since the year of our Lord 1611. And here I must stay, until I find my way out."

"You . . . aren't here by choice?"

He gave a sound that could have been a laugh or a sneer. "Do you think any sane man would choose to live alone for hundreds of years, forced to watch all that is familiar pass away, to be replaced by"—he gave a contemptuous glance at the light switch on the wall—"what your contemporaries call *modern conveniences*?"

At once the lights flickered on and off, on and off, sending sparks of electricity in an arc across the ceiling like lightning, until he shifted his attention back to her.

At once she felt the heat of that furious gaze.

He pointed. "And that damnable thing in your pocket."

She placed the vase back on a shelf and reached for her cell phone. "Why don't you like this?"

He arched a brow. "I would ask why you do. You think, by talking to people far across the land, that you're somehow close to them? How do you know your connection with them isn't all a lie? What makes you think they give a care about what you have to say while they're busy with their own lives?"

His words had her remembering her last phone call to Barclay. Oh, the words he'd spoken. Words that she'd been so eager to embrace, like some lovesick teen. Later, when she'd learned the truth, all those sweet words had mocked her. And in truth, mocked her still.

She felt a knife pierce her heart.

Seeing the stricken look in her eyes, he crossed his arms over his chest and gave a knowing look. "I see. Ye've been lied to a time or two, have you, lass?"

When she remained silent, he nodded. "Aye. 'Tis true. In all the eons I've been here, while all around me everything external has changed, within the hearts of people nothing has changed. Nothing." He spat the word before turning away. "So take your gadgets and your annoying self from my home and leave me to my own private hell."

She brought her hands to her hips. "You haven't been listening to me. I have no intention of leaving. There's nothing you can do that will drive me away. This is all I have left in the world. I'm not about to forfeit it for the likes of you. As for hell, I'm well acquainted with it."

At the vehemence of her tone, he turned and studied her for a long, silent moment.

"You only think you know hell," he muttered. "Beware, Mistress Kerr. You're no match for the likes of me."

As she watched, he began to shimmer and fade. And then he was gone, as quickly as he'd appeared.

She stood perfectly still, waiting for her heartbeat to settle.

For all her brave words, she'd been absolutely terrified of this angry creature. And was, still.

She hadn't simply imagined him. Though Gwynn Logan may have planted the seed, this wasn't hysteria brought on as a result of an overactive imagination. Nor could it be blamed on jet lag. Bree had no doubt that the spirit of someone, some ancient, unhappy ancestor, still haunted this place. She didn't have enough energy left to question the why or the how of it. There would be time enough for that in the days to come.

Numbly she tossed aside her jacket and crossed to the bed, quickly making it up with the fresh linens Duncan had left folded atop the bare mattress. While she worked, she had to fight to hold her tears at bay. These weren't tears of pity, she told herself. She was simply sick and tired of being sick and tired. Of feeling overwhelmed by things beyond her control.

There would be no more of that. Hadn't she come here to start over? To take control of her life?

The betrayal she'd experienced at the hands of Barclay, the pity she'd felt from friends when they discovered the truth, had to be put away, once and for all.

As for this ghost, this . . . creature, who seemed determined to be the latest obstacle in her life, she would deal with him as firmly as the rest of her baggage.

But not now. Not tonight.

For now, she needed to rest, to gather her strength for whatever ordeal lay ahead. If it was a battle of wills this restless spirit wanted, she would stand toe-to-toe and fight him with all her might. No man, neither flesh-and-blood nor ghostly specter, would impose his will on her ever again.

Never, she thought with such vehemence her teeth clenched. Never again. She settled herself into bed.

As the storm raged beyond the snug walls of the cottage, it was her last coherent thought before she gave in to utter exhaustion and sleep overtook her.

THREE

Strong arms enfolded Bree in a welcoming embrace. Oh, she'd missed this. Missed this feeling of being cherished. This knowledge that she was loved above all others. It was worth all the sacrifices she'd made. The loss of her hard-won independence. Walking away from the rewards of a satisfying career. Disappointing her coworkers who had cheered her talent, her discipline, her drive to be at the top of her game. She may have caused more than a few eyebrows to lift when she'd given up all of that. But hadn't she always known that love, true love, was worth any price?

She curled into the warmth beside her and felt his lips nibbling hers, his hands moving slowly over her. He had always known just how to gently, painstakingly arouse her without fully waking her. In that breathless moment between sleeping and waking, he would take her up and over, so that she would be vibrantly aware and fully engaged the instant she awoke.

She felt that hard, muscled body imprinting itself on hers. Felt his mouth begin the slow journey down the column of her throat to nestle in the little hollow between her neck and shoulder. Absorbed the delicious tingles as he trailed his mouth lower, his tongue circling her breast.

Her breath was coming faster now. Harder. Her body arched up to his.

With a slumberous smile, she opened her eyes.

And froze.

Not Barclay.

The stranger. The spirit. Murmuring words she couldn't quite comprehend, though she knew instinctively they were words of love.

When she stiffened and pushed away, his head came up sharply, and in that instant she saw the same slumberous sensuality in his eyes that she'd felt moments before, followed by the same sense of shock and surprise.

"You monster! How dare you!" She shrank back against the mound of pillows.

"How dare I? I'll remind you that you initiated this. And were enjoying it every bit as much as I, woman." His features twisted, from the handsome man who'd been seducing her to a look that ranged between fury and frustration.

Bree tossed aside the covers and slid out of bed before shooting him a look of contempt. "You have the morals of an alley cat."

"I'd say the same for you, madam. Not that I'm surprised. All women, it would seem, know how to use their wiles to get what they want. If you think to drive me from my home in this manner, ye'd best think again. I've nowhere else to go."

"Nor do I. And now that I know just how low you're willing to sink, I'll be better prepared to fight you."

Without a backward glance, she flounced from the room, slamming the door behind her with such force it rattled the windows.

In the parlor she paced, arms crossed, mind awhirl. How was she to remain here, knowing she would have to face this evil creature both day and night? How was she to find any peace if she had to continue to deal with him while dealing with her own survival?

She dropped wearily into a chair positioned in front of the fireplace and let her head fall back, deep in thought.

Had he seduced her? Or had she, as he'd accused, been the seducer? In truth, she could vaguely recall in sleep sensing a warm body beside hers. Could remember turning into that warmth and running her hands over his chest, thrilling to a sense of power when he'd responded. She'd snuggled closer then, wanting desperately to feel him, heartbeat to heartbeat. In such a state, what man could refuse?

But he wasn't a man. He was a spirit. One who'd come unbidden to her bed.

Weren't such creatures above worldly desires?

Perhaps he wasn't just a spirit, but an evil one, sent here to destroy her.

Whatever he was, this devil was not to be trusted. Nor, she decided, could she trust herself while asleep.

As the midnight hours ticked by, her racing heartbeat began to slow and her troublesome thoughts faded. Lulled by the patter of rain against the windowpanes, she fell into a deep, dreamless sleep.

———

Bree awoke to a shrill whistling that had her eyes going wide. It took her a moment to get her bearings. Then it all came into focus. The cottage in the Highlands. The scene in the bed she'd shared with Jamie Kerr, and later, this solitary chair where she'd obviously spent the rest of the night.

The angry stranger was here, standing directly in front of her, arms crossed over his chest, scowling, and looking not in the least sorry for what had transpired in the night. If she'd thought him contrite, she'd been very wrong.

She lifted her head, determined to hide any trace of her own shame in the matter. "I would have thought you'd be gone by now, after the things you did."

"I could say the same for you. Have you no pride, woman?"

"More pride than you have shame."

"Oh aye. So much pride, you cried out in your sleep like an infant, hoping to touch my heart." He gave a sigh of disgust. "I've never been able to deny a weeping female."

"I'll see that it doesn't happen again." She pushed herself from the chair to escape his gaze and to put some space between them.

Sunlight slanted through the ivy-covered windows. A fire blazed on the hearth. And the whistling sound that had awakened her was a kettle on the stove.

She hurried across the room and lifted it aside.

In the sudden silence she turned to see Jamie standing beside her.

"What is it that troubles you, Mistress Kerr?"

"If you're a spirit as you claim, why don't you just read my mind?"

Her snappish attitude had him smiling. "Wake with a bit of a temper, do you?"

"More than a bit. Now, if you don't mind, I'd like to be alone."

"As would I. But it seems we both want to be alone in the same place. And since I was here first, Mistress Kerr, by hundreds of years, I suggest you pack up and find something more suitable."

"I prefer this cottage."

"I've already claimed it for my own. What's wrong with living in the manor house?"

"I can't afford to."

"Can't afford? The lady of the manor must do without?" He gave a mock sigh. "What's this world come to?"

"The cost of maintaining the mansion and grounds for the benefit of just one person is unthinkable. There are far too many things in need of repair. Besides, it's not my style." She lifted the kettle to fill a teapot and set it on the table, along with a little basket of biscuits and a pot of jam she'd bought at the airport the previous day.

She looked over at him. "Would you care to join me?"

His frown became more pronounced. "Unfortunately, I've no need of food."

"I should think that would please you. No need to shop. Nothing to store or prepare."

"I used to enjoy a hearty meal." He stared broodingly into the flames. The tone of his voice had gone from angry to sad.

"Then why did you put the kettle on?"

"I thought you'd want something when you woke."

Bree was unexpectedly touched. "You did it for me?" She paused a moment, completely taken aback. "Thank you."

He brushed aside her gratitude. " 'Twasn't a kindness on my part. I just wanted you awake and gone. I thought the whistling of a teakettle more effective than breaking another vase. And heaven knows I wasn't about to touch you again." He waved a hand distractedly before taking the seat across from her at the table. "Since you don't want to live in the manor house, why are you here?"

"This land and these buildings are all I have left."

"Left of what?"

"Of my marriage to Barclay Kerr."

"Was it a happy marriage?"

She fell silent.

He studied her more closely. "I suppose that's an answer of sorts. And now that you're here, what do you intend to do with all this?" His eyes narrowed in sudden understanding. "I see. You've come to sell Ravenswood?"

"Not sell it. Use it to earn a living."

"And how would you do that?"

"I thought I'd restore it to its former glory and turn it into an upscale inn."

"An inn? What rubbish." He pounded a fist on the table and stormed across the room, flitting from doorway to window to hearth like an errant flash of lightning. "You'd bring strangers here to trample the gardens and fish in the lochs? Foreigners who'd filch the silver and mock the hallowed grounds where brave Highlanders shed their blood in battle?"

Before she could reply, his fist slammed again. "Never! By heaven, I'll burn every inch of it to the ground and, for good measure, plunge my dagger through their black hearts before I'll let that happen."

Bree could see that he was working himself up into a terrible, blinding rage.

Brooding, he crossed his arms over his chest. "But then, why should I expect anything different from the likes of you? How could you possibly love this place the way one would who'd been born to it?"

Instead of flinching, she glowered at him. After a few hours of sleep, she was more than ready to take up a fight with this man.

"That's right. I don't love it as you do. But I need what it can give me: a way to earn a living. As you suggested, I intend to invite strangers here to fish, to ride, and to enjoy the gardens. Foreigners who will be introduced to a way of life that is gone for good and will never be seen again, except for these few castles and manor houses that are left standing. In case you aren't aware of it, travelers will spend a great deal of money to see how people lived in earlier times. At least, I hope they will."

"What makes you think you'd be a good innkeeper?"

"It's what I was trained to do." She broke open a biscuit, slathered it with jam, and took a bite. "I was very good at my job."

"Then why aren't you still doing it?"

"I . . . gave it up."

He studied her more closely. "For a man, I'll wager."

She looked away. "It's none of your business."

She didn't see him move, and yet in the blink of an eye he was beside her, lifting her face, forcing her to meet his steady gaze.

"Aye. For a man. And from the look of you, one who obviously wasn't worth the sacrifice."

She slapped his hand away and was startled to feel nothing but air.

He was already across the room with his back to the fire as he stared daggers at her.

She picked up her cup and headed toward the bedroom. "I'll remind you to respect my privacy while I bathe and dress."

When he made no reply, she closed the door. Then for good measure she turned the lock. And missed the sudden smile that tugged at the corners of his lips.

————

Wrapped in a towel, Bree emerged from the bathroom to find Jamie lying on the bed, his hands folded comfortably beneath his head.

He looked her up and down before smiling. "Did you really think a locked door would keep me out?"

"I'd hoped you were gentleman enough to respect my privacy."

"If you insist upon invading my privacy, why should I treat you any better? Besides," he added with a grin, "I'm very much enjoying the view. As I did when you showered."

"You're insufferable." She huffed out a breath and picked up her clothes.

As she headed back toward the bathroom he called, "What makes you think I won't follow you in there again?"

"Stay away from me." For emphasis she slammed the door.

In the bathroom, she dressed with as much haste as she could manage, all the while glancing around to see if he'd made good on his threat.

When she emerged a second time, Jamie was nowhere in sight. She didn't know whether to be relieved or dismayed. Maybe he'd decided, since she refused to be afraid of him, to simply go away and do his haunting elsewhere. Or, she thought, he could be gathering his strength to torment her even more.

Armed with a camera and her laptop, Bree stepped out of the cottage, ready for a day in the manor house, exploring the rooms with an eye toward developing the mansion and its property into a moneymaking proposition.

She glanced at her watch, hoping to get in a few hours before Gwynn and Duncan Logan arrived.

As she made her way along the path, she kept looking over her shoulder, half expecting Jamie to fall into step beside her. Did ghosts avoid sunlight, preferring the night?

That thought had her pausing in midstride. Yesterday she'd denied the existence of ghosts. Here she was, scant hours later, not only believing that her visitor was a spirit, but conversing with him.

Jamie Kerr's powerful presence made it impossible to deny him.

Good heavens. She was beginning to sound like Gwynn Logan.

Before she could turn the key in the lock, the door was thrown open by the housekeeper.

Bree's eyes went wide. "Did you stay the night?"

"We did. Both Duncan and I were too worried to leave you alone. We slept in our old rooms beyond the pantry. I told Duncan you'd surely be here sometime in the night. I can't believe you lasted until morning." She studied Bree's eyes. "Did you see him?"

"Yes. He tried to scare me off. I told him I wouldn't budge." She saw the incredulous look on the older woman's face and couldn't help smiling. "After that, he left me alone."

"He left you . . ." Mrs. Logan swallowed. "After an encounter with the likes of him, I'm surprised that you were able to sleep at all."

"I slept like a baby." Not quite the truth, but Bree decided there was no point in admitting how she'd spent the latter part of the night in a chair.

"He didn't try to harm you?"

Bree shrugged. "He stormed around the room threatening, and managed to break a vase."

"But he didn't do you any physical harm?"

"No." Bree took in a deep breath, determined to change the subject. "I'm guessing that the architect never made it here last night. Did he call to explain why?"

"Not a word."

Bree sighed. "Then I'm ready to take another tour of the house." She pulled her camera from its case. "A nice long tour, if you don't mind, Gwynn."

The housekeeper gave a curt nod of her head. "Where would you like to begin?"

"I believe I'd like to see the kitchen and dining rooms first."

She followed the housekeeper along a hallway beyond the sitting and living rooms, and was pleasantly surprised to discover a fairly modern facility.

Bree used her camera to record the spacious cook's pantry, the oversized stove and oven and wide, empty counter space that could accommodate quite a number of people working side by side.

"Oh, this is so much more than I'd expected." She set aside her camera to admire glass-fronted cupboards filled with the finest china and crystal. Several drawers revealed chests of gleaming silver tableware.

Bree looked over at the housekeeper. "It looks as though you have enough here to serve several dozen guests."

The housekeeper nodded. "In earlier days, her ladyship often entertained on a lavish scale. Why, I remember one grand holiday when there were so many titled guests, we had to hire more than a dozen young girls from the village to help with the serving. Duncan was sent to Edinburgh to fetch additional crystal and silver her ladyship ordered for the occasion."

As they moved on to the elegant dining room, Bree took pictures of the floor-to-ceiling fireplace, with its spectacular marble surround, and a half dozen round tables with matching upholstered chairs. Though the upholstery was faded and the tables covered with a layer of dust, she could see the potential.

The housekeeper stood watching her. "Are you planning on entertaining, Mrs. Kerr?"

"In a manner of speaking." Bree pointed to a set of double doors. "What's beyond there?"

"It's the rooms Duncan and I occupied for forty years, and where we stayed last night." Mrs. Logan led the way and stood aside to allow Bree to precede her.

Duncan looked up from the table where he was drinking his tea and reading a newspaper.

"Oh, I'm sorry to bother you, Duncan." Bree stepped back, but the older man gave a quick shake of his head.

"Please, missus. Gwynn told me you'd be touring the premises today. Come in," he said affably.

Seeing the tall, leaded windows looking out over rolling hills covered with heather, Bree put a hand to her throat. "Oh, what a beautiful view. You must have been so happy here."

Glancing at her husband for confirmation, the older woman's face radiated warmth and pleasure. "Duncan and I were saying just this morning that we've never forgotten how much we loved this place. The rooms we're renting in the village are comfortable, and we've done our best to make them feel like home. But after a lifetime at Ravenswood, our hearts are still here."

"Then you and Duncan might be willing to consider coming back to work here?"

Gwynn Logan's eyes filled. "It would be the answer to our prayers, Mrs. Kerr." She ducked her head, ashamed of her tears. "Ever since we received your letter saying that you were coming to Scotland, we've been afraid that you were planning on selling off the antiques, and then the estate, before returning to America."

"I may still be forced to do so. But I think I have a solution that could spare me the pain of selling this beautiful place." Bree took a deep breath, thinking of the furious reaction from Jamie Kerr, and wondering if her next words would have the same effect on these two. "I'm thinking of turning Ravenswood into an inn."

FOUR

—◄►—

"Why the smile, lass?" Jamie fell into step beside Bree as she followed the path from the manor house to the cottage.

"It's no thanks to you." She shot him a sideways glance.

"You didn't care for my jokes while you whiled away your time in the big house?"

"Whiled away? I was working. Which is more than I can say for you."

"Aye. I was playing. And having a grand time of it, I might add."

Playing. The very thought had her smile fading, just as Jamie's image faded from view yet again.

She'd spent hours touring the house and taking dozens of photographs of the rooms, which she hoped to share later with a local firm she'd contacted about making the changes needed to transform Ravenswood from a private dwelling to a charming inn.

Afterward, over a lovely lunch with Gwynn and Duncan in their quarters, she'd talked about her plans for the inn, and was buoyed by their enthusiasm. Having the two of them on board with this transition meant the world to her. After all, these two old people knew this place better than anyone, and loved it. They knew its history, its pride, its sorrows. If they could share her vision for its future, she felt one step closer to making her dream a reality.

She'd felt comfortable enough to share her concerns that the initial cost would be great, both in labor and material. Each suite of rooms would have to be brought up to local code, and to have modern amenities while keeping the original flavor of the ancient manor house. When the two old people realized that she wasn't the wealthy heiress they'd expected, but rather burdened with debt, they became genuinely concerned. It was Duncan who had proposed hiring unemployed workmen in the village to help with the remodel, while Gwynn volunteered to locate as many ambitious young women as were needed to help scrub everything to a high shine.

There had been one terrible moment over lunch, when Bree had seen Jamie standing between the two, scowling at her. She'd lost her train of thought, glancing from Gwynn to Duncan, until she realized that neither of them could see what she was seeing.

How did Jamie do that?

She'd had to put him out of her mind and concentrate on the task at hand. But it hadn't been easy. Throughout the long day she'd seen him at the windows, standing by the hearth, even reclining on one of the upstairs beds, and each time looking smug, knowing that he was playing havoc with her senses.

"Stop that," she'd muttered at one point.

The housekeeper paused to glance over at her. "I beg your pardon? Did you say, 'Top hat'?"

Bree flushed and pointed, grateful for the chance to cover that little slip of the tongue. "There in the closet."

"Oh. That." The older woman smiled. "Her ladyship insisted upon formal attire for her garden parties. That belonged to Master Barclay."

"Did he attend many garden parties?"

"One or two during his university days." As Gwynn was closing the closet door, Bree saw Jamie smash the top hat between his hands before glowering at her.

Fortunately, the housekeeper saw none of it.

Bree was sorry that the things she was planning on doing to Jamie's ancestral home would cause him pain, but she didn't see that she had any choice. She needed to move ahead, or she would surely be beaten down by the shambles of her life. The creditors were snapping at her heels. Creditors she hadn't even known about until she'd been left alone to deal with them.

Jamie's presence had come very close to ruining her day. Despite his disapproval of her plans, he had no right to torment her this way, showing up when she least expected it, throwing her off stride when she was trying so hard to get on with her future.

Bree was determined to put aside her concerns about Jamie. Instead, she allowed her mind to work overtime, considering how much she could possibly earn by selling off some of the crystal and silver, since it would be more practical to have less expensive tableware in an inn. She just might have an appraiser look at some of the other pieces as well, to see if they might bring in additional revenue to cover the start-up costs. Surely there were vases, lamps, and furniture that was too old, too fragile to be used by the public, yet would fetch a good price from collectors. It was sad to consider letting priceless family treasures go to strangers. But desperate times called for desperate measures. She'd been left with no alternative.

She wouldn't think about that now. She would concentrate, instead, on the future. It had to be brighter than her recent past.

She was attempting a smile as she opened the door to the cottage.

Her smile faded at the sight of Jamie standing by the window, arms crossed over his chest, his usual scowl darkening all his features.

She pulled the door shut and dropped her camera and computer on a nearby table. "How can you be miserable on such a lovely day as this?"

"What's lovely about it? As far as I can see, 'tis just another day spent trapped in this hellish place. And now you actually plan on bringing strangers here. Tradesmen, village wenches. Busybodies. And all of them crowding my space."

"They're necessary to help with the work. If you're worried about feeling crowded, there are plenty of places you can go to escape. There's always a walk in the hills, or a swim in the lake."

"If only I could. Alas, I'm confined to these four walls and that"—he pointed toward the manor house—"hellish site of my betrayal."

Betrayal. The word brought her up short. Perhaps someday he would tell her how he'd been betrayed, and by whom.

For now, she pushed aside the thought, hoping to distract him and his famous temper.

"What would happen if you tried to hike the hills or swim in the lake?"

"Do you think I haven't tried? Each time, I've come up against an impenetrable wall. The few times I was desperate enough to try bullying my way through, I was so weak I had to take to my bed with utter exhaustion that went on for years."

"Years?"

"Well, 'tis true that I have no concept of time anymore. Years are like minutes, really. And minutes like years. At any rate, I've no desire to pit my will against the wall again. It completely drained me. And so I'm here. Just here, until such time as I've earned my freedom."

Though she hadn't expected to, Bree felt a wave of sympathy for this being. What would it be like, she wondered, to spend eternity trapped between two worlds, unable to move forward or back?

She walked to the bedroom and hung her jacket in the closet. When she turned, she realized that Jamie had followed her.

"You spent a great deal of time up there." His tone was accusing.

She arched a brow and tried for a light touch. "Did you miss me?"

His scowl deepened. "Now, why should I miss an annoying intruder?"

"Why indeed? Especially since I saw you there, hovering, eavesdropping everywhere."

"And why not? 'Tis my home you're about to rearrange to suit your whims."

"I'm sorry for that, but I have no choice."

"We all have choices."

"Mine have narrowed considerably." She studied him carefully. "How is it that I could see you, and Gwynn and Duncan couldn't?"

He shot her a wicked grin. "'Tis a trick I've learned through the ages. I can appear and disappear at will, allowing some to see me while remaining invisible to others."

"That little trick would come in handy if I wanted to spy on someone who was bent on deceiving me."

His smile fled. "Aye. 'Twould've served me well in life. Alas, I've only mastered it in the past hundred years or so."

She walked to the kitchen and set the kettle on the stove before removing the foil from a dish that Gwynn had sent.

Jamie peered over her shoulder. "Is that a potpie?"

Bree nodded. "Chicken. Gwynn made it while Duncan and I toured the house, and insisted that I bring it home for my supper."

He closed his eyes and breathed in the wonderful aroma.

Bree took her time setting out a place mat, arranging her dishes and flatware, before cutting into the pastry and filling her plate. While she ate, Jamie's eyes took on a wolfish look as he stared at her from across the table.

With each bite, his gaze narrowed, and she could swear he was actually tasting the food, chewing, swallowing, right along with her. Though it was unnerving, it was also extremely intimate, and she found herself chewing slower, taking the time to really savor the delicate flavor of the chicken and vegetables swimming in broth.

"Is it as good as it smells?"

"It is." She nodded, before a sudden thought struck. "If you can smell, why can't you taste?"

"I believe I can. I think I can actually taste it, or else I have a memory of the way potpie tastes."

"Would you like to try a bite?"

He shook his head. "I'm beyond human pleasures."

"Now, why do you say that?"

He shrugged. "It is the way of it."

"If that's so, how do you explain your anger? Isn't that a purely human emotion?"

"What an odd question." He arched a brow, as though he'd experienced a sudden epiphany. "Are you saying that, though I'm a spirit, I'm also still human?"

"Are you sure you aren't? If you can smell, you ought to be able to taste." She pinned him with a look. "If you can feel anger, then surely you can feel joy."

"'Tis true. I can feel." He spoke the words with a sense of awe.

"It would seem so."

They both fell silent, remembering the almost unbearable arousal they'd shared under cover of darkness. The feelings, at least for Bree, had been deeply intense. From the look on Jamie's face, she had an idea that he'd experienced something similar.

He stood and began to pace, hands linked behind his back, deep in thought, wearing the familiar scowl.

Uncomfortable with the silence, Bree felt the need to say something. "After your reaction to my plans for an inn, I wasn't looking forward to sharing them with Gwynn and Duncan." She sat back, sipping her tea. "But they couldn't have been more excited."

He stopped his pacing to stare at her. "Aye. I saw how eager they are to be of help to you. You must be very persuasive to bring those two old harpies around."

"They're good people. They've missed this place since moving to the village. They spent the night in their old apartments, in case . . ." She paused, realizing what she'd been about to say, and amended quickly, "In case I needed them."

"You mean, in case the evil spirit of the cottage drove you away screaming into the night."

Bree smiled. "I told them that you and I had met, and had come to an understanding."

"And what would that be?" His scowl deepened.

"Since neither of us is willing to turn this place over to the other, we'll simply have to find a way to coexist here."

"Coexist." He spat out the word.

"Tolerate, then. I'm afraid you'll have to tolerate my presence here, since I have no intention of leaving."

"Not even when the inn is ready for guests?"

She shook her head. "Now that I have their word that Gwynn and Duncan are eager to be a part of this, I'd prefer to live here and let them take over their old apartment in the inn." She looked around, as though assessing her surroundings. "Once the contractors are finished in the manor house, maybe I'll have them make a few improvements here as well."

"I should have known." He threw up his hands and stormed out of the room. Over his shoulder he shouted, "Leave it to a female to think of a score of ways to add to my torment and make my life as miserable as possible. Workmen," he shouted. "Here. Underfoot all the day. Woman, I'll not be lulled into . . . *coexisting* with the likes of you."

Bree sat very still, listening to the sound of doors being slammed while the lights flickered on and off. She could hear the breaking of glass as he took out his anger on the few remaining vases left in the bedroom.

Instead of fear, she felt only disgust. He was going to have to learn to curb that nasty temper, or he'd feel the sting of hers.

As she set about clearing the table and washing her dishes, she realized that even Jamie's latest temper tantrum couldn't completely dampen her spirits. After a day with Gwynn and Duncan, she was feeling more positive than she had in months.

Opening an inn here was no longer just a sweet dream. Though it would mean a great deal of hard work and sacrifice on her part, now more than ever she was convinced that she could make it happen. And not just because she was alone and desperate, without any other choices, but also because she could see the potential here to succeed.

Ravenswood was set in spectacular rolling hills, surrounded by clear, sparkling lakes. Once restored, the gardens could become world-class. The village below was a lovely little jewel, with shops that would appeal to tourists. A successful inn would mean that the villagers would see their lives improved as well.

She wasn't about to permit Jamie's negative attitude to color her decision to move forward on this. She dried her hands on a towel and bit her lip. But she couldn't help wishing that she could change his mind. Not just for the sake of a little peace here in the cottage, but also because they were running out of vases.

Gwynn had called him violent. A monster.

Bree had certainly seen that side of him. She could only hope that he was never inclined to direct that same violence against her personally.

If she should find herself in the fight of her life against a raging spirit, how much strength could she hope to summon?

She prayed she never needed to find the answer to that. In the meantime, she would remain vigilant. And fully prepared for anything.

FIVE

Bree stoked the fire before pulling the chair close to its warmth. A steaming cup of tea rested on the little table beside her.

After Jamie's latest tirade, the silence that settled over the cottage was a welcome relief. Considering the day she'd put in, she ought to be ready for bed. But in fact she was reluctant to go into the bedroom and face the carnage. At least that was the reason she gave for remaining by the fire. It was not, she told herself firmly, because of that little scene in bed the previous night. Whatever had happened between them had been completely unintentional. She'd been simply caught up in a dream. Now she would see to it that it never happened again. Even if it meant sleeping here in the chair for the foreseeable future.

"Sorry." Jamie appeared, holding a wastebasket brimming with shards of iridescent glass.

"Oh no. Not that lovely bowl on the side table." Bree eyed the pieces as he dumped them unceremoniously into the kitchen trash bin.

"I'll have you know that it gave me a great deal of satisfaction to smash it to bits. I never liked that bowl, or the female who bought it."

"Your wife?"

"A great-great-granddaughter. A self-centered wench, like those who spawned her."

"So much anger."

"You think I'm angry now?" He gave a dry laugh. "You should have seen me in my prime."

He dropped to the footstool and stared into the flames. "I spent the first hundred years or so after my death in a blaze of fury."

"You mean you're capable of more fury than I've witnessed?"

He shrugged. "You've only seen a few broken vases. I did that to get your attention. If I were truly angry, I'd have destroyed windows, doors, furniture. Once I even set fire to the cottage. Unfortunately, a rainstorm put it out before it could do damage. Old Duncan summoned the authorities, who told him it had probably been ignited by lightning."

"I'm sure that only annoyed you more. You were probably hoping to add to your reputation as a fierce, angry spirit."

He surprised her by throwing back his head and roaring with laughter. "Aye. That I was. But there were plenty of other times I managed to create enough havoc to have the villagers whispering and the authorities cowering in their boots. To this day they refuse to come out here to the gatekeeper's cottage alone, and especially after dark."

"And that makes you happy?"

"Why not? What's the harm? There's little enough to amuse me here." He went silent for so long, she thought he might be ready to pull one of his disappearing acts. But then he surprised her by drifting from the ottoman to settle into an overstuffed, high-backed chair, his feet reclining on a footstool, his arms folded imperiously over his chest, looking for all the world like the lord of the manor. "Time moves as though in a dream. At times quick as the blink of an eye. At other times so slowly it feels as though 'twill never end. At first I found it so confusing. Was I dead or alive? Awake or dreaming? How could this be happening to me? That's when I began slamming about, breaking things. It helped pass the time, and proved to me that I wasn't dreaming. This . . . this existence is real, and I must endure it even though I loathe it." He crossed his legs and leaned back, warming to his subject. "The first hundred years

were the worst. After that the hard edge of fury seemed to dull
a bit, and I spent another hundred years or so just frightening
visitors away so I could have some peace."

"Did you find it?"

He shook his head. "Peace eludes me. There's something . . .
something just out of reach that I can't seem to grasp. I've
begun to sense that it's something I need to do, or something
I need to know. Whatever it is, there is some impossible task
that binds me to this place. When I discover it, I'll have the key
to leaving this earth forever."

"Maybe it has something to do with how you died." She
hesitated, wondering if she were overstepping her bounds. "Is
that a subject you're willing to talk about?"

He waved a hand. "Ah, but you see, I haven't died. Not
completely. But to put your mind at ease, I died by the sword.
For a Highland warrior, 'tis the only honorable way to go."

"You were in a battle?"

"Of sorts. Our history is rife with them. Barbarians determined to take what we have." His brows drew together in a
fierce frown, and she could see that he'd gone somewhere in
his mind. Somewhere she couldn't follow.

He turned to peer into the flames of the fire. In profile, Bree
thought he could have been chiseled from stone. The proud,
high brow. The strong jaw. The shock of dark hair falling rak-
ishly over his forehead. He was a handsome devil. The thought
caused her to shiver as she was reminded again about her sudden, stunning arousal while in that dreamlike state.

"I should"—she got to her feet—"get some sleep."

He turned toward her and arched a brow. His smile was
quick and disarming. "Aye. I've a mind to do the same."

She hesitated, alert to the teasing tone of his voice. "If you'd
like the bed, I'll sleep here in the chair."

He got to his feet and faced her. "I wouldn't want to deprive
you of your comfort."

"Look." She sighed, weary of his badgering. "Only one of
us can sleep in there." She nodded toward the bedroom. "Since
you were here first, I'm willing to concede it to you."

"Not at all." He swept a hand in a courtly gesture. "I'll not
be outdone in generosity. The bed is yours."

She eyed him suspiciously. "You're sure?"

"I am."

"All right. If you insist."

"I do."

"You promise you won't sneak in there after I'm asleep?"

"I make you no promises." He paused dramatically. "But so long as you wish it, I'll not intrude. If, however, you have need of me, I'll be more than happy to comply."

She studied his face, but could see no trace of his usual sly humor.

"Thank you. Good night then, Jamie."

"Good night." He shimmered and began to fade before disappearing completely.

Alone, she made her way to the bedroom. A short time later she fell thankfully into bed and was asleep almost at once.

———

Bree heard the ringing of a phone and felt a sudden sense of dread that had all her muscles clenching. Phone calls in the night were never a good thing. She picked up the receiver and listened to the voice at the other end.

"No!" She wanted to silence the words but they continued on, recounting something so hurtful, she couldn't bear to listen. "No. Please. Stop."

She tossed aside the covers and leaped to her feet as she began to shake, then to weep. Great wrenching sobs that were torn from her heart, wracking her body.

Without warning, strong hands took the phone and tossed it aside, ending the connection. But not the pain. The pain continued in waves.

Arms came around her, holding her while she wept bitter tears, and her poor heart shattered into millions of tiny pieces until her throat was raw and her eyes swollen.

At last, drained by such intense emotions, she gave a shuddering sigh and pushed free of the comforting embrace. She accepted a handkerchief and wiped her tears before looking up.

She gave a gasp of surprise. She'd thought, for just a moment . . .

"Jamie."

"I know that I promised to give you your privacy tonight. But I heard you cry out, and wanted to help."

"Thank you." She crushed the handkerchief against her mouth to keep her lips from trembling.

She dropped to the edge of the mattress and glanced around in sudden knowledge. "There's no telephone by the bed."

"Nay."

"It was all a dream?" The truth dawned. A horrible, hateful dream. So real, she could still feel the pain of it.

Jamie dropped to his knees before her, his eyes steady on hers. In the faint light cast by the glowing coals of the fire, he could read her anguish.

"I can't believe how real it all seemed." She took in a breath and shook her head, as though unable to accept the truth. "A . . . dream."

"A bad one, from the looks of you. How can I help?"

"You can't." She looked away, ashamed of such a display of emotion in the presence of this stranger. "Nobody can."

"I'd like to try." He took her hands in his. "You're cold."

"I'm fine."

He crossed to the fireplace and stirred the coals before adding a fresh log and kindling. Within minutes a fire blazed.

He returned to sit beside her on the edge of the bed. "Is that better?"

She nodded. "Much. Thank you."

"Would you like to talk?"

She shook her head. "I'm not ready to talk about it."

"I understand." He wrapped an arm around her shoulders, lending her his warmth as well as his support.

As they sat in companionable silence, Bree thought how comforting it was to have him here. A mortal would have expected some sort of explanation. Jamie was quite content to allow her to deal with her grief in her own way, in her own time.

Time.

"You told me that time often passed in the blink of an eye, though at other times it seemed to slow to the pace of a snail."

"It's true. I only knew time was passing by watching the wee ones who were born, and then grew old and died, while I remained here in this place."

"How I wish I could stop time, and even reverse it. If only I could go back to those glorious days when all the possibilities had seemed endless. The entire world had been mine. I'd felt so alive. So filled with joy and hope and love."

When Jamie remained silent, she gave a short laugh. "Listen to me. *Love*. The very word mocks me now."

She sighed and Jamie's arm tightened. Without thinking, she leaned into him and turned her face against his throat. "Oh, what a fool I've been."

He gathered her close and pressed his mouth to a tangle of hair at her temple. "As I recall, 'tis the way of mortals."

"Maybe. But I'm the biggest fool of all." One wet tear slipped from the corner of her eye.

Jamie framed her face with his hands and, frowning, kissed the tear away. "No more tears, lass. No man is worth them."

She glanced up at him and shivered at the intensity of his look. "I know. I'm afraid you'll have to allow me my weakness. I've tried so hard to be strong, but this storm has been building for such a long time."

"A storm. Aye. I'd know a thing or two about them. A storm has been building inside me as well."

For the longest moment he merely stared at her with a look she couldn't fathom.

Then, ever so slowly, he lowered his face to hers and covered her mouth in a kiss that sent heat rushing through her veins.

He lingered over her lips, teasing, tasting, as though learning some long-forgotten pleasure.

When at last he lifted his head, he saw the look of surprise in her eyes. And something more. The warmth of desire his kiss had awakened.

"Ye can tell me to leave now." His voice was thick with passion. "Or ye can let me know that ye want this, lass, as much as I."

"What does it matter? It isn't possible." She sucked in a breath. "Is it?"

"I've no idea." He captured her mouth again and kissed her, long and slow and deep. "For I've never before had the desire to explore such a possibility. But here, with you, I'm more than willing to find out."

When he again lifted his head, she could feel his searching gaze, as though assessing whether she welcomed what he was offering.

In answer, she wrapped her arms around his waist and nestled her cheek to his. "It's been so long since I was held like this. Kissed like this. I've missed it."

"Aye." That single word was a long-drawn-out sigh. "Oh aye, lass. I've missed this, too. The warmth of a woman's touch. The thrill of a lover's kiss."

And then by mutual consent they came together in a kiss so hot, so hungry, it threatened to consume them.

The arms holding Bree were strong; the lips on hers warm and firm. The pulse that pounded against her palm was as wild as hers, and just as unsteady.

This was no formless spirit, teasing her, tempting her. Here was flesh and blood. Heat and need. And hers for the taking. All hers.

Without a thought to the consequences, she took with a need that bordered on madness, returning his kisses with a hunger that matched his.

He pressed her down against the pillows. His mouth moved down her body, igniting fires everywhere. With sighs of pleasure, she opened to him, welcoming the passion.

"My beautiful, wonderful Brianna." He breathed her name against her throat, causing a sob to rise up in her.

"Oh, Jamie. Hold me."

"I'll not let you go, love."

Love.

The endearment had tears stinging the backs of her eyes. But there was no time to weep. No time to think as he moved over her, his kisses, his intimate touches, lifting her higher, then higher still, until her breath was burning her lungs and her heartbeat was racing out of control.

She thought he would take her quickly and end this terrible need. Instead, he continued to lead her higher and higher, keeping release just out of reach, as he touched her now at will, until her body begged for release.

His voice was a low command. "Look at me, Brianna. I need to see you."

Her lids snapped open and she found his gaze, hot and fierce, fixed on her with such intensity, as though he was seeing into her soul.

She knew in that instant that he could do so. With but a look he could read her very heart and know her most intimate secrets.

"I've waited so very long for this. For you. For someone as beautiful, both inside and out, as you, my beloved Brianna. Do you not see? 'Tis no accident that you're here. We were destined through time, through eternity, to meet. To love."

His words touched her heart in a way that nothing else ever had.

"Jamie. Jamie." Her sultry plea was torn from her lips as he entered her.

At once she experienced the most unbelievable pleasure. Pleasure so deep, so intense, it bordered on pain.

They came together in a firestorm of passion, blood throbbing, pulses thundering, as they took each other on a heart-stopping ride to the heavens.

High they soared, and higher still, until they felt themselves flying among the stars.

For the space of a heartbeat they paused on the very edge of the universe, nearly blinded by a blaze of white-hot passion that consumed them. They were fire and ice. They were one with the moon and stars.

Their climax was shocking in intensity as they felt themselves hurtling weightlessly through space before shattering into millions of glittering fragments.

It was the most incredible journey of their lives.

SIX

Bree lay very still, waiting for her heartbeat to slow and her world to settle. Jamie's face was nestled in the hollow between her neck and shoulder. His breath feathered her damp flesh, sending delicious curls of pleasure along her spine.

She touched a hand to the strand of dark hair that tickled her throat. The hair was real. The body pressed to hers was flesh and blood. As if to prove the fact, she moved her hand along the flat planes of his taut stomach, up and over the corded muscles of his chest and arms. Real. All of him.

The lovemaking they'd shared had left her spent and sated. In her life, she'd never felt so thoroughly loved.

How could this be?

She had no rational answer. But this much she knew: She wasn't dreaming. She was wide-awake, and this man, who claimed to have died hundreds of years ago, was warm and real and here in her arms. And though she knew that none of this seemed possible, she no longer cared. After all that she'd been through. After all the pain and anguish of the past year, it was enough to be here, feeling safe in his arms, steeped in a warm glow like nothing she'd ever known before.

He stirred and touched a finger to the corner of her eye. "Tears, love?"

She sniffed, unaware until that moment that she'd been weeping. She wiped the back of her hand over her eye. "Crazy, I know. But I'm feeling . . . a little overwhelmed." She looked away, ashamed to meet his eyes. "I like to think of myself as a sophisticated woman. I certainly don't want to read too much into this. I know that lovemaking is different for a man, but this felt . . . special."

He leaned up so that he could stare directly into her eyes. She felt a tiny thrill course along her spine as he touched his hand to her cheek in an achingly sweet gesture. "It was more than special to me, Brianna. In all the years I've remained here in this twilight world, this was the only time I've been driven to such madness. This wasn't just about my needs, but rather my need for you alone. You're like a potent drug. One I haven't the strength to resist."

He rolled to one side and drew her into the circle of his arms before gathering her close and kissing her long and slow and deep, until she sighed and returned his kisses with a need that bordered on desperation.

"My bonny, bonny Brianna." Something about those whispered, sultry words alerted her moments before he took her down, down with him into a steamy, darker side of love. A side she'd never tasted before.

With Jamie's clever hands and mouth and tongue leading the way, she followed eagerly on a fast, furious ride to paradise.

The sky was still dark outside. Rain splashed the windowpanes and pattered on the roof. Inside, a log burned on the hearth, casting a warm glow over the figures in the bed.

"Warm enough?" Jamie drew a blanket over Bree's shoulder.

"I'm roasting. You're like a furnace."

"The heat you feel is a reflection of you. Most humans who encounter me feel only a cool dampness."

"Why is it different with me?"

He shrugged. "I've asked myself that question since you first came here. Why are you different from all the others? My only thought is that you are part of some grand design."

She sat up, hair tumbling around her shoulders. "What's that supposed to mean?"

Again that indifferent shrug. "I know not, lass. I know only that from the first, you've been unlike any other. You refused to be frightened away. You chose, instead, to stand and fight." He shot her one of those heart-melting smiles. "There's nothing I admire more than that."

"You have an odd way of showing it. Why didn't you tell me?"

"I was too busy resenting you. And trying to fight this damnable attraction." He drew her down into his arms. "But now, lass, it's not fighting I have in mind."

She sighed. "I'm glad of that."

He ran slow, easy kisses over her face, brushing her eyebrow, her cheek, the curve of her jaw. "You make me forget my anger, lass."

She relaxed in his arms, trusting him to take the lead.

"You make me forget everything except this. Just this."

His mouth, his hands, began to weave their magic.

This time their lovemaking was as slow and easy as that of old lovers who had all the time in the world.

————

Sunlight trickled through the damp panes, burning off the last of the morning mist. The fire had long ago burned to embers.

Brianna stirred, feeling something heavy across her body. Jamie's leg lay over hers, his arm thrown across her torso.

If he were truly a spirit, wouldn't he be weightless?

As gently as possible she rolled aside, intent on slipping from bed without waking him. The minute she sat up, his hand closed around her wrist, holding her when she tried to stand.

"Sorry. I didn't mean to wake you."

"I wasn't asleep. I never sleep." He shot her one of those heart-stopping grins. "Where are you going?"

"Up to the manor house. Gwynn needs me."

"Not as much as I do." He moved aside the covers and patted the mattress. "Come back to bed, love."

"You know where that will lead."

His smile was quick. "I didn't hear you complaining through the night."

She pressed a kiss to his cheek, and felt the rush of heat all the way to her toes. "I loved every minute of it. But now I have to get ready to work."

"Work. What about me?"

"I'm sure you'll find a way to amuse yourself. Maybe you can walk up with me and try to frighten poor Gwynn and Duncan."

"I'm not in the mood."

"Not in the mood to scare people?" With a laugh she touched a hand to his forehead. "Is it possible for you to have a fever?"

He surprised her by pulling her down on top of him.

"Woman," he growled against her throat, "I've had one since you got here. You're a raging fever in my blood. And I fear there's no cure for it."

All thought of resisting fled as she laughingly wrapped her arms around his waist and returned his kisses.

"I suppose I can spare a few . . ." The rest of what she'd been about to say died in her throat as he brought his clever mouth down her body, igniting little fires everywhere.

———

"You're looking very smug." Bree emerged from the shower to find Jamie lying in bed, hands under his head, his eyes watching her every move as she stepped into her dress.

"And you're looking very tasty. Why don't you come here and let me help you with that zipper."

"Because I know where that will lead. And this time I intend to get to work."

"Work." He frowned. "Why would you want to work when we could spend the entire day at play?"

"One of us has to be sensible."

"Just my luck to be stranded between heaven and earth with a beautiful, sensible mortal."

She waved from the doorway, knowing that if she got too close, she might be tempted to remain for yet another round of lovemaking.

———

The manor house was teeming with people. As Gwynn had promised, at least a dozen women from the village were already hard at work cleaning, polishing, and stripping away years of dirt and dust that had settled over everything.

While one team of women removed the heavy draperies from the windows, another climbed ladders to polish the glass to a high shine, allowing sunlight to stream in, casting aside the shadows. Rugs were rolled up and carried into the fresh air while dull wood and marble floors were brought back to their original luster.

Bree moved through the rooms and was reminded of a hive of busy bees, and all of them taking orders from their queen, Gwynn, who proved to be a harsh taskmaster.

"You there, Claire. Lend a hand washing that crystal. And you, Sarah. No time for woolgathering. The silver needs polishing."

Bree climbed the stairs to the second floor and watched as closets were emptied of whatever clothing and bed linens remained, each of them carefully marked before being carted away by brawny lads who cheerfully tipped their caps as they passed her.

When Bree started up the stairs to the top floor, Gwynn stepped away from a group of villagers and followed.

Bree found herself in a narrow, open gallery. As she peered over the balcony railing, she could see down the ornate staircase past the second story to the main floor far below.

"Such a pretty place, Gwynn. What purpose did this serve?"

"It was once a spot reserved for the laird of the manor to observe his guests from above." She pointed to the ornate frames that hung in an orderly fashion. "Now it is a gallery that holds the portraits of the Kerr ancestors."

Bree moved from portrait to portrait, studying the faces of Barclay's ancestors, from bare-chested warriors in the fifteen hundreds to the most recent formally clad lords and dukes in ruffled shirts and kilts. And all of them handsome enough to take her breath away.

When she suddenly let out an exclamation of surprise, Gwynn paused beside her.

Bree pointed to the portrait she had first seen hanging in the parlor. "Why was this moved?"

"One of the housemaids just returned it to this spot." Gwynn sighed. "Not that it will remain here for very long."

Bree turned to her. "What do you mean?"

"This is a portrait of Laird James Kerr. Each time we hang it here where it belongs, it mysteriously disappears and is found hanging over the mantel in the parlor." She frowned. "Our old staff refused to come near it. But the young lasses from the village are new to such things. In time, I suppose they'll learn to let him be."

Bree studied the portrait. "Tell me about him."

"As far as I know, he was a once-noble warrior who was called Jamie the Fearless." The housekeeper pointed to the dates listed in the little brass plaque beneath the ornate frame. "He died in 1611. From that time on, his name was changed to Jamie the Ruthless. Cast out by the clan for killing his poor wife and causing their wee orphaned bairn to be raised by kinsmen." Her voice lowered. "What's more, he did that terrible, evil deed from the grave."

"What do you mean?"

"Word came to the household of his death in battle, sending his young wife, Flora, into labor. The servants assisting her heard his voice, like a roar of thunder, causing her to cry out just as she delivered a son. Moments later they heard his voice cursing her. Some said he lifted the wee bairn into the air, while others claimed he merely lifted the wee lad's hand, as though linking his fingers with that of his son as he passed from this world. Within minutes of the birth, Flora was dead. Those who witnessed her death swore they saw Jamie hovering over the bed, as though to assure himself that his curse was carried out. What's more, they found his best friend and man-at-arms, Ewen, lying dead in a field of battle with Jamie's dirk through his heart."

Bree swallowed before saying softly, "He's the one."

Mrs. Logan shot her a startled look. "You mean the one haunting the gatekeeper's cottage, causing so much destruction all these years?"

Bree nodded, afraid to trust her voice.

"You're certain?"

She swallowed. "I am."

"I've suspected as much. You mustn't stay there alone another night, Mrs. Kerr." The housekeeper drew close to mutter, "I'll have Duncan prepare her ladyship's rooms for you."

"No, Gwynn." Bree stood a little taller, thinking about the passion she and Jamie had shared throughout the long night. In the light of day it seemed to be nothing more than some impossible figment of her imagination. And certainly nothing she could relate to this dear woman. But it was too real to dismiss lightly.

"If he intended to hurt me, he'd have done so by now. I truly believe that as long as his curse wasn't directed toward me, I'm safe."

The old woman huffed out a breath. "And what if you're wrong?"

Throughout the day, that question continued to play through Bree's mind. What sort of mysterious, dangerous creature had captured her heart?

She'd felt so happy and carefree again while in his arms. And wildly in love. But surely she was old enough, and wise enough, to know that such feelings can blind a person to the truth.

Had she been bewitched last night? Had Jamie Kerr planted that image in her mind, just so he could take advantage of her grief and insinuate himself into her life?

But what could he possibly hope to gain by it?

He'd cursed his wife into the grave. A wife who had just given birth to his son. Could there be a greater betrayal than that?

She would certainly know a thing or two about cruel betrayals.

As she followed Gwynn down the stairs, all the joy drained from her heart. And as she went through the motions of helping the women who worked and chatted happily, she felt weary and foolish beyond consolation.

What had she done?

How could she have been so careless, so love-starved, that she would once again put her trust in a charming man who was, in fact, heartless? A man who could use that trust to betray her yet again?

Would she never learn? Was she doomed to repeat the same mistake over and over?

SEVEN

"You're awfully quiet, Mrs. Kerr." Gwynn studied Bree's pale face. "You've been working too hard. Why don't you take some time for yourself now?"

Though it galled her to admit defeat, Bree nodded. "Thank you, Gwynn. It's been a long day." She glanced down at the dust that stained her work clothes. "Maybe I'll go back to the cottage and change."

The housekeeper hurried away and returned minutes later with a brown paper bag. "I baked a loaf of my special bread."

Bree inhaled the wonderful fragrance of citrus. "Mm, that smells wonderful."

"Orange and walnut. Have a bit of it with some tea, Mrs. Kerr. It will revive your energy. My mum used to say 'tis as restorative as a nap."

"Thank you, Gwynn." Bree turned away and let herself out.

By the time she arrived back at the cottage, she'd worked herself into a frenzy of self-doubt and self-loathing. Jamie would expect her to fall into his arms and welcome the passion he would offer. She had no way of knowing how he would react when he discovered that she'd learned about his past and wanted nothing more to do with him.

As she opened the front door, she steeled herself for the coming confrontation.

A deceptively cozy fire burned on the hearth. From the small kitchen came the wonderful aroma of something simmering on the stove.

Bree crossed the room and lifted the lid on an ancient cast-iron pot to reveal a hearty beef-vegetable soup, like the one Gwynn had been preparing in the manor house for the workers. Hadn't the older woman remarked that she suspected someone of helping themselves to the soup? Apparently that someone had been Jamie. But why? He didn't eat.

Or had that been a lie as well?

"Here you are." He appeared beside her and dropped a hand on her shoulder. "I saw the way you were working, and knew you'd be hungry."

"You stole Gwynn's soup."

His eyes danced with mischief. "In a manner of speaking, though it's actually my property, since I'm laird of the manor." He glanced at the loaf in her hand. "The old biddy's orange walnut bread?" He put a hand to his heart. "She only bakes it for special occasions. Is today your birthday?"

Bree forced herself to meet his steady look. "Not really. But you could call it my growing-up day."

"And what's that supposed to mean?" As he spoke he steered her toward the table. "Sit and talk to me while I feed you."

"I can feed myself."

"Humor me."

He turned away and ladled soup into a bowl before opening the bag and cutting several thick slices of bread. He carried it to the table and set it in front of Bree.

Her hunger got the best of her, and though she'd intended to confront him immediately, she decided to wait until she was well fortified with food.

She couldn't help sighing over the wonderful taste of it. This simple meal of soup and bread was finer than some of the meals she'd enjoyed in five-star restaurants.

Jamie sat across from her and watched, as always, with an intensity that was unsettling.

She set aside her spoon. "Why don't you have some?"

He shrugged. "I've told you."

"You said that you can't enjoy the things of this world. What would you call the things we shared last night?"

His smile was quick and charming. "I'd call it heavenly. What would you call it, my beautiful Brianna?"

"A lie." She shoved aside the rest of her meal, feeling strong enough now to face the coming storm. "It was all a lovely lie, just so you could indulge your own selfish needs."

His expression never changed. And yet, she saw something flicker in his eyes. Not anger so much as sadness. "You're afraid, are you? And feeling betrayed?"

"Do I have a right to?"

He shook his head. "I will never betray you, Brianna."

She looked away. "Don't. I've heard it all before."

"But not from me."

"Why should you be any different? All men are the same. Promise whatever you need to in order to get what you want." Before he could respond, she held up a hand to stop him. "Don't try filling my head with your lies. I saw your portrait. And heard why you're now called Jamie the Ruthless."

For long moments there was no sound in the cottage except for the hiss and snap of the log on the fire. Bree watched as Jamie disappeared from view, only to reappear across the room. His figure shimmered and faded, then grew stronger before drifting around the cottage, landing by the fire, then sailing toward the bedroom, then returning to stand before her. It was a sure sign that he was highly agitated.

"I've never spoken of this before to any mortal. You must bear with me as I recall it as precisely as possible, for it's been a while since the actual deed."

She nodded, afraid of what she was about to hear, but determined that she had to know the truth, now that she'd forced his hand.

"I was the son of a laird. The grandson of a laird. And great-grandson of a laird." His voice rang with passion. "I was proud of my trusted position with my good people. From the time I was very young I'd been trained in the art of battle, and could handle broadsword, dirk, and longbow with ease. And from childhood on, my dearest friends were young Flora, who later became my wife, and Ewen, who became my man-at-arms. I trusted Flora with my heart, and Ewen with my life."

He fell silent, and Bree waited, knowing there was much more to his story.

"My men and I were often gone for weeks, even months, as we drove off the barbarians who tried, without success, to steal our flocks or our women and children. And always, Ewen was beside me, and Flora was awaiting my return to our stronghold. It was the way of things until Ewen was gravely wounded in battle. Together Flora and I nursed him back to health. When next I left to fight the barbarians, I ordered him to remain behind so that his wounds could better heal. In return, I asked him to see to the safety of my wife and the other women of the village. When I returned weeks later, he was once again strong and hale and ready to resume his position as my man-at-arms. As if that news weren't enough to flood my heart with happiness, Flora told me that she was expecting our first child. It was a time of great rejoicing."

Bree wondered at the way her heart skipped at his news. She fought the conflicting feelings of both excitement and dread at what he would reveal.

"As the time drew near for Flora to deliver our child, Ewen reported that barbarians had been spotted in the hills. Though I was reluctant to leave my beloved, Ewen suggested that he and I ride ahead and scout their numbers, then return to the stronghold and permit him to lead the rest of our warriors to drive them off, while I remained by Flora's side. I agreed. When we reached the high meadow, we saw the signs of invasion everywhere. Paths in the tall grass, made by horses that were not ours. Bits of coarse cloth and animal hide clinging to the bushes that seemed strange to the eye, and obviously worn by barbarians.

"While I was looking toward the ground, studying the tracks in the heather, I felt a sharp blow from behind and was knocked from my steed. I landed with such force it snapped my arm like a twig. I looked up in surprise. Ewen was standing over me with his broadsword lifted. He admitted that these were old tracks that he'd discovered while I was off doing battle across the river. He'd tricked me into coming to this place alone in order to kill me."

Bree sucked in a breath. "But why?"

"I asked if he wanted to be laird. He told me that he would take that honor, if the others thrust it upon him, but what he really wanted was Flora. Ewen said calmly that they had become lovers while he lay recovering in my chambers, and that even now she carried his child. I couldn't believe that Flora, my sweet bride, would betray me. At first I was merely incredulous, but as he brought his sword down again, barely missing me, I knew that he must be speaking the truth. Why else would my dearest friend wish me dead? I knew, too, that I was in for the fight of my life. With one arm useless, and my judgment blinded by fury, I was no match for Ewen, who had spent weeks preparing himself for this day. I felt his sword pierce my chest, and as I lay in the heather I felt my life blood slowly spilling away, draining all my strength. Ewen took a weapon from his tunic, which he'd retrieved from an earlier battle with the barbarians, and dropped it beside me, leaving me there in a pool of my own blood. The weapon, he told me, would be proof that I died at the hands of an intruder to our land. And as I took what I feared was my last breath, his parting words to me were that, since the child about to be born was not mine, there would be no one left to carry my name. Clan Kerr would die with me. His words were seared into my brain and branded on my heart, fueling the last bit of energy I needed to toss my dirk, which was tucked at my waist. It found his heart. But even that small revenge was not enough for me. Though the angel of death hovered, waiting to claim me, I resisted, determined to remain on this earth long enough to see the child born of this damnable betrayal."

"Oh, Jamie." Feeling his pain, Bree reached a hand to him but he stepped back.

"Nay. Ye must hear it all." He took in a deep breath, as though each word exhausted him. "I watched my bairn being born. A maid washed him and laid him in Flora's arms. At once Flora began weeping, and she begged the maid not to show him to Ewen when he returned from the field of battle, believing as she did that her lover was still alive."

"But why would she choose to hide the child from its father?"

Jamie's eyes narrowed. "Flora had lied to Ewen. The child

was actually mine. She said as much to her maid. Hearing her confession, I cursed Flora so loudly, the house shook with my fury. The maids were so terrified, they all fled. And Flora, who recognized my voice, was filled with such fear and remorse, she died on the spot. Her heart simply stopped beating."

"And all these hundreds of years, people have believed that you killed her in a rage."

"It matters not what others believe, Brianna. I care only that you know the truth. And the truth is this." His voice lowered to a mere whisper. "My rage was so great, my fury so all-consuming, it became a roiling cloud, a mass of energy that refused to be extinguished. I found myself caught up in it, tossed about helplessly like debris in a raging inferno. And when it had burned to cinders, and the dust of it finally settled, I realized that I was still here, locked inside my own misery. And so it has been, for all these years."

Bree couldn't keep from asking. "But, Jamie, if Flora was willing to lie to you once, how do you know she didn't lie again? How can you be certain the baby was yours?"

"I saw him." Jamie sighed, and a strange light came into his eyes, for the moment his misery forgotten. "A strong, bonny lad. Aye, so bonny. Though Flora had thought him to be not mine, and perhaps she had hoped he was not, she knew the truth once she saw what I saw. He bore the same birthmark that has stained all the Kerr men from the beginning of time."

He stuck out his hand and on the back of it, between thumb and index finger, Bree saw the small, port wine–colored mark that resembled a half-moon. "'Tis our heraldic badge since the earliest of times, when the first of our kin was born with it. It has marked each of us since then. Even some who do not bear the name, because their mothers married outside the clan, wear the mark."

Bree nodded. "I never got to see my husband's birthmark. He showed me where it had been, before he'd had it removed by a plastic surgeon."

"Removed?" Jamie frowned. "Why would a man have his birthright removed?"

"Vanity. Obviously, his birthright meant little to him. Barclay saw it as a flaw."

"A flaw." Jamie shook his head from side to side while muttering under his breath. He turned to fix Bree with a look. "I knew Barclay Kerr as a spoiled, willful lad when he resided here, though I chose to keep my distance from both the lad and his parents, who never came near this poor cottage, considering it beneath their station. What sort of man did this descendant of mine grow up to be?"

She sat back, willing herself to breathe. His question unsettled her. "Even now, I can't stand to speak of him."

"If you loved him, I should think it would soothe. If you didn't love him, I should think speaking of him would drain some of the bitter poison that remains."

Poison. It was the perfect term for what simmered deep inside, tainting everything with its toxin.

She took a long time before answering, and he thought at first that she would resist.

"I suppose, since you've shared your story, it's only fair that I share mine. It's a tired old story, and one that has been repeated through the centuries, it seems. But each time it happens, it's new. And horrid. And as you well know, a knife in the heart of the one who has been the object of such betrayal."

Jamie waited as she seemed to draw inward.

Her tone went flat. "When I met Barclay Kerr, I was managing a posh hotel in Cannes. It was a long climb from my first job—cleaning rooms in my parents' motel in our poor little town—to assuming the top post in one of the world's most successful hotel chains. In all those years, I never had a real home."

Jamie looked startled. "No home? I thought everyone had roots and history and a . . . forever home."

"A forever home." Bree could have wept at his choice of words. "That sounds so lovely. Instead, I lived in motels, hotels, and inns, doing the most menial of jobs, while spending every spare moment studying and learning and moving on. Along the way I'd met my share of sleek, sophisticated men who were also shallow and empty. I prided myself on being able to read a man's character. Barclay was different. Or so I thought. Funny and charming and adventurous. When his friends grew bored and moved on to other playgrounds on their yachts or in their private jets, he remained behind to court me." She gave a dry laugh. "*Court me*. Such an archaic term. But it suited him at the time. He was so attentive, so steady, so very persuasive. I admit that I was flattered by his lavish gifts. I loved seeing the reactions of my coworkers, who were in awe of the parade of flowers, the clever little surprises, and later the jewels and expensive trinkets that would arrive on my desk each morning to greet me. Barclay took me to dinner in lovely, out-of-the-way places. Seaside resorts and lovely villas. He showed me a way of life that I'd provided for my clients but had never personally experienced. I suppose he saw me as a challenge. One he simply had to win over. And slowly, gradually, he wore down my resistance. He asked me to give up my career and travel the world with him." She looked down at her hands, clenching and unclenching in her lap. "I thought about the years I'd spent working to achieve my goals. And then I thought about the grand, once-in-a-lifetime opportunity to be with a man who loved me above all else. A man who promised me a home. A man who yearned to start a family with me. How could I weigh my career against my most precious dreams?"

Jamie had gone very quiet, choosing to stand beside the fireplace, one arm resting atop the mantel, his gaze steady on her. His voice was unusually quiet. "And he betrayed your trust."

She swallowed and nodded. "He promised that we would start a family as soon as we were settled into our dream house. But he couldn't seem to settle. Nothing ever suited his taste. We tried New York, London, Paris. Soon, he would say. Soon. But not yet."

She drew in a breath. "He was out of town. Business in Palm Springs, I'd been told. I was in a cramped little apartment in San Francisco. We talked every day." She winced as she touched a hand to the cell phone in her pocket. What had Jamie said when she'd first arrived? Did she really believe that a brief phone conversation was the same as intimacy?

She let go of her phone and clenched her hands together tightly, barely holding on to the rising tide of anger. "He told me how much he missed me. How eager he was to get back to me. Just hours after we spoke, I was awakened from sleep by a call from the authorities. Barclay had been in a fatal accident on a highway heading out of Las Vegas. He'd died instantly."

She swallowed before going on. "He wasn't alone. A young woman had been killed along with him. An autopsy found that she was"—Bree sucked in a breath—"she was carrying his child. Her friends claimed that he'd promised to marry her, but that he would first have to take care of a little business." Anger blazed, white-hot, and she welcomed it rather than the tears that threatened. "I guess I was that 'little business' he needed to take care of."

Jamie watched the way her eyes narrowed. Her fury was palpable, like a dark cloud gathering overhead, filling the little room with an amazing, fiery energy.

"The news just kept getting darker and more horrifying. I started getting phone calls from creditors. It turned out that Barclay had squandered all our money. No wonder he'd refused to give me a home. All that I'd saved from my years in the hotel business, and all his inheritance, had gone for his gambling debts and his lavish lifestyle. When I learned that before his death he'd contacted an investor about selling this estate, I decided to see it for myself. And on the flight here, it occurred to me that Ravenswood might be my salvation. I need to work, and what better way than by doing what I've been trained to do?"

"Have you no other means of supporting yourself?"

She shook her head. "I've run out of options. Barclay left enormous debts, and his creditors are demanding payment. Unless I can find a way to keep them at bay, they could be tempted to try to gain control of this property to satisfy that debt."

Jamie could see that she was dangerously close to tears.

"Aren't we a pair of fools?" He crossed the room, caught her hands in his and helped her to her feet before drawing her into the circle of his arms.

Even in the warmth of his embrace, Bree held herself stiffly. They stayed that way for the longest time while Bree struggled to control her raging emotions. Despite her will to resist, the strong arms holding her, Jamie's quiet, steady heartbeat, his calm demeanor in the eye of such a storm, were like a soothing balm to her ravaged system. Gradually he felt her relax against him.

Finally he stepped back and caught her hand.

She arched a brow. "What are you . . . ?"

"Shhh." He put a finger to her lips to still any questions.

Still holding her hand, he led her toward the bedroom.

Once there he gathered her close and kissed her with a reverence that had her sighing, as, for the moment, the last of her anger slipped away.

Without a word they offered each other comfort in the only way they could.

EIGHT

From her position in bed, Bree watched as Jamie walked to the window of the bedroom to stare out at the vista of Highlands and heather. Since their lovemaking, he'd fallen into a pensive mood.

She was in a strange mood herself. She was beginning to question her sanity. How was it possible that she trusted the spirit of a long-dead Highland warrior more than she could bring herself to place her trust in any flesh-and-blood man?

But there it was. The truth of the matter was that she would probably never trust another man. Whatever hope she'd had of finding true and lasting love had died in the fiery wreckage of Barclay's car.

At least she would have her work to fill her days, and a ghostly lover to fill her nights.

She glanced at her watch and realized that it was time to get back to the manor house.

After a quick shower, she dressed and ran a brush through her hair.

Jamie tore himself away from the window to walk with her to the door of the cottage.

She stood on tiptoe to kiss him. "You're in a strange mood."

"Aye."

"If you'd like some company, you could walk with me to the manor house."

He shook his head. "I've some heavy thinking to do."

"About what?"

He stared down into her eyes, and once again she had the feeling that he could see into her soul.

"About the meaning of life."

She touched a hand to his cheek. Just a touch, but she felt a sudden chill. "Jamie . . ."

He caught her hand and lifted it to his lips. "Go. You've your work to see to, and I have mine."

She turned away. When she glanced back, he was gone.

When she arrived at the manor house, she was startled to see Jamie standing in the parlor, staring at his own portrait.

She walked up beside him. "When I left here, that was hanging in the upper gallery. Are you playing games with me?"

"I wish it were a game, love."

At the seriousness of his tone, her smile faded. "What's wrong?"

"Something is happening. For all the time I've been here, except for those times when I tried to walk away, my energy has always been supernaturally high. Now I can feel it beginning to fail me. It took all my strength to will the portrait here where it belongs."

While he spoke she saw the way his image faded in and out. She touched a hand to his shoulder, then drew it back when she encountered a rush of damp coolness. "You're growing cold."

"Aye." Jamie took her hands and held them tightly. "There are things I must tell you now, before I fade away forever."

"Forever? Jamie, you can't . . ."

"Hush, love. Listen. For what I have to say is of utmost importance." He caught a breath. "When I heard your story, and felt the depth of your pain, I realized for the first time that I was trapped here, between heaven and earth, by my own selfish choices, and that you were becoming trapped as well. You vowed to never open your heart again, because of your betrayal."

"Why should I open my heart to more pain?"

"Because in order to love, we must first trust. Once that trust has been destroyed, it becomes more difficult to trust again. I was consumed with anger for those who had wronged me. It's what kept me here. And I sensed that same anger in you. Like a poison infecting every facet of our lives. But here's the amazing truth. I realized after telling you of my betrayal, and hearing about yours, that I'd suddenly been filled with a strange sense of peace. Did you feel it, too?"

Bree wanted to deny it, but she found herself nodding.

"You see? I believe it's a signal that the time for me to leave this world is at hand."

"No. Please, Jamie. I don't want you to go. I've only just found someone I can trust. Someone who shares my most intimate secrets. Don't you see? You're the only one who really knows how I feel, because you suffered the same pain and humiliation."

"Aye, love. 'Twas the same for me when I told you of my life and my betrayal. But for me, it was the final step in my healing, while for you, 'twas the first step."

When she opened her mouth to protest, he touched a finger to her lips. "I've had hundreds of years to ponder. Now, suddenly, it's all clear. This, then, is what I know to be true. Some people are weak. They make unwise choices. Cruel choices. Choices that hurt others, even those whom they truly love. I now realize that my Flora did love me in her own way, even though she carelessly gave her heart to my best friend as well. That was her failure. And mine was in refusing, for all these many years, to recognize that weakness in her and to forgive."

Bree was shaking her head in denial. "If you're suggesting that I should forgive Barclay for what he did, you ask too much of me. I'll never forgive him."

"You must, Brianna. You must accept that he was a flawed man, who loved you in his own way, but he wasn't capable of exclusive love."

"Don't you understand? My pain is too deep. How can you ask me to forgive him?" Her voice shook with passion. "I simply can't."

"Hush now, love. I speak the truth. Those of us who are harmed by such selfish actions must be stronger, better, kinder. The world is what it is. Good and evil. Harsh and kind. And in order to spend eternity in peace, we must learn to forgive. Others. Ourselves. Their weaknesses and our own. This was the lesson I needed to learn. And only now, finding you, my soul mate, have I been able to forgive the wife and friend who betrayed me in this life. And it must be the same for you, Brianna my love. Do you not see? You deserve to love and be loved. Not by one who selfishly asks you to choose between career and love, but by one who understands that true love is a partnership. A real sharing and blending of two lives. But only when you forgive the one who was weak and selfish will you be open to all the love that can be yours in this world and the next."

"What about our love? Yours and mine? Was this just a passing . . . lesson?" She spoke the word with a harshness that revealed the depth of her pain.

He lifted his big hands to frame her face and stare deeply into her eyes. "The love we share is deep and real and everlasting. Our love will never die."

She shivered from the coolness of his touch. "And in the same breath you tell me you're leaving me."

"I have no choice in this, Brianna. But you must believe me when I tell you that I shall love you not just now, but for all time."

Tears filled her eyes. "What good is your love if you can't be with me?"

"I will always be with you, my love. Now, today, tomorrow. Forever. This I vow."

Even as he spoke the words, she could see him fading.

While she watched, his image began to shimmer and dance, until it resembled the sunbeams that flitted across the wall.

Tears streamed down her cheeks. "Jamie, please don't leave. I swear I will never love anyone the way I love you."

For a moment the portrait was bathed in light, and Bree saw the warrior's gaze bearing a mischievous light as it fixed on her, his lips curved into a teasing smile.

She blinked away her tears. When she looked again, the portrait was as it had been before. There was no smile. The look of him was once again stern and unseeing.

She dropped into a chair in front of the fire and buried her face in her hands, allowing the tears to fall. Harder and harder they fell, her body wracked with shuddering sobs, until there were no tears left.

Jamie's last words were etched into her soul. Forgiveness. Was it possible? Until this very moment, she would have scoffed at the idea. She had not only endured the pain of her betrayal, she had nurtured it, allowing it to fester and grow in her heart and soul.

Now she felt a new, uneasy feeling stirring within. Perhaps it was the beginning of forgiveness. Perhaps it was sheer exhaustion.

Drained, her head dropped back against the cushions of the chair and she fell into a deep sleep.

"Mrs. Kerr."

At the sound of the housekeeper's voice, Bree woke with a start. For long minutes she stared around, trying to get her bearings.

She was in the parlor of Ravenswood. There was no sign of the village lasses, or the work they'd done. The furnishings, which had earlier been removed by workmen, now stood once again covered in their faded dust cloths. The dust of accumulated years layered everything.

Had it all been a dream?

A log burned on the hearth.

Mrs. Logan was standing beside her chair.

"A gentleman is here to see you. He says you instructed him to meet you at the cottage, but when he went there he found it empty."

"Thank you, Gwynn." Bree struggled to her feet, trying to focus. She stared down at herself, surprised that she was dressed as she'd been when she first arrived. "What day is this?"

"What day?" Startled, the housekeeper bit back a smile. "'Tis Monday, Mrs. Kerr. Duncan delivered you to the door. We toured the house a bit, and then you had tea and sandwiches and fell asleep. You were just about to head up to the cottage before dark. Unless, of course, I could persuade you to stay the night here."

"No. I'd prefer the cottage." Feeling dazed and disoriented, Bree turned to the handsome man in the doorway, dressed in casual denims and a corduroy jacket, his dark hair wind-tossed, his eyes cool and assessing. Though she'd never before met him, there was something oddly familiar about him.

"You're the architect."

"I am. James Keith." He crossed the room and offered a firm handshake.

"Brianna Kerr. I was told that you specialize in reconstructing ancient manor homes into functioning, modern facilities."

He nodded. "And you told my assistant that you hope to turn this into an inn."

Out of the corner of her eye Bree saw the housekeeper listening with keen interest, as though she'd had no idea. "That's right. But what is equally important to me is that we do so while respecting the home's historic background." She thought of Jamie's anger when he'd learned of her plans for the place. "After all, many noble Highlanders shed their blood on this land."

"I pride myself on honoring that fact, Mrs. Kerr."

She smiled. "I hope, after you've had a chance to study Ravenswood, you'll come up with some acceptable sketches for me to consider."

"As a matter of fact, I'm already familiar with Ravenswood. My grandmother was a Kerr, distantly related, and I spent many happy holidays here when I was a lad." He indicated the portfolio in his hand.

As he did, Bree caught sight of the birthmark between his thumb and index finger. It was a bloodred image of a half-moon.

She caught her breath as he added, "I've brought you some preliminary sketches to look at." He paused. "Since it's nearing dusk, why don't I walk with you to the cottage, and you can study the sketches after you've had time to settle in?"

Mrs. Logan indicated a basket of food. "I've made a hearty vegetable soup and a chicken potpie. There's more than enough for two, if you've a mind to stay awhile," she added to the man.

Moments ago Bree's head had been spinning, her thoughts in turmoil. Whether she'd been dreaming or had actually lived the events that were now vividly etched in her mind, it was of no consequence. Now a strange sense of calm, of perfect peace, stole over her, and she knew, without question, that being here in this place was all part of some grand plan.

With a warm smile she accepted the basket from the old

woman's hands. "Thank you, Gwynn. Would you care to join me, Mr. Keith?"

He gave a nod toward the housekeeper. "I believe I can already taste your excellent soup and potpie, Mrs. Logan."

When he opened the front door, Bree stepped out into the fading light and moved along beside him.

Up ahead, a dark plume rose from the cottage chimney, filling the air with the wonderful scent of wood smoke.

"Will you be staying here at Ravenswood, Mrs. Kerr?"

The voice beside her was deep and rich with Scottish burr. She absorbed a delicious shiver of warmth.

"I don't think I could bear to leave it. I've decided that Ravenswood will be my home, Mr. Keith."

"I'm glad. And please, my friends call me Jamie."

She wondered that her heart didn't burst clear through her chest. "Jamie, my name is Bree. Short for Brianna."

"I believe I prefer Brianna. The elegant name suits you." He steadied a hand beneath her elbow as she made her way along the rough path. Glancing skyward, he added, "It's begun to rain."

Bree turned to him with a radiant smile. "I've always loved the sound of rain on the roof."

"So have I." He gave her a smile that was reminiscent of another's as he reached around her and opened the door to the cottage. "Welcome to your forever home, Brianna Kerr."

For the space of a heartbeat she was thunderstruck. And then she knew, without a doubt, that her own dear Jamie was letting her know, in his own way, that he had kept his word to her. His choice of words gave her a sense of utter peace and contentment.

Here was, she realized, all that she'd waited a lifetime to share.

HIS BROTHER'S KEEPER

MARY KAY MCCOMAS

For my brothers:
Bill Perry, Greg Perry, and Jim Perry.
I love you guys!

ONE

"Are you feeling any better, honey?"

"I am. Yes. A little, I think." A tiny fib to prevent another worry wrinkle in her mother's face was never a bad thing to Ivy. She and her brother had given her plenty to worry about in the past. She deserved her peace. "The quiet here is nice, but if I listen to the sound of the waves for very long, I get sleepy."

And jerk alert again, afraid to dream. The same dreams that had been plaguing her for months. Dreams that made her restless . . . even after she woke up. Restless in a way that affected her work—the writing and illustrating of the Patty Ann Pettigrew series of children's books that were, to her wondrous astonishment, quickly becoming very popular. And rather lucrative.

Getting away from it all had been her mother's idea. A good one, initially. She'd even arranged for Ivy to stay in the summer home of a friend who was spending the season in Europe instead. It was supposedly their "little cabin at the lake," but it was five times larger than Ivy's two-bedroom town house in the city, with a vaulted ceiling in the living room and enough glass to display panoramic views of forest and mountains to the east and the broad expanse of Lake Lackey from atop its high cliffs to the west.

"Have you seen this . . . cabin?"

Her mother laughed. "One man's cabin is another man's—"

"Castle?"

"I was going to say palace."

"Close enough. And what's with the lap pool? The lake isn't long enough?"

"The cliffs, dear. The Rossinis are seriously fitness oriented and they love to swim, but with no beach there on the cliffs, they have to get in the car and drive to one to swim in the lake. As it is, they have to drive to the marina to use their boat, since there's no place to put a private dock. Which reminds me . . . Grace said they store their boat in the winter, but if you'd like to use it, all you have to do is talk to anyone at the marina and they'll put it, in the Rossinis' . . . um . . ."

"Slip?"

"Yes, that's it. There's a sailboat, too, but I said I didn't think you knew anything about sailing."

"I don't know anything about rowing a boat, much less sailing one. I think I'll leave them both in storage. Besides, I have a book to write, and I'm going to finish at least the first draft before I leave here." She pushed open the heavy sliding glass door and her eyelids slid slowly over brown-hazel eyes as a gentle breeze brushed across her cheeks, barely disturbing the wisps of golden brown hair that curled close to her face. The air was a pleasant mix of water and rich earth, lush vegetation and . . . whatever the cleaning crew used to prepare the house for her. Watching the late-afternoon sunlight sparkle and dance across the surface of the water and listening to the rhythmic lapping of the waves against the cliffs about forty yards away, she attempted to force open a can of *relaxation*—and failed. "Even if it kills me, I'll finish it."

"Try to get some rest, honey. You've been so tense lately that it's no wonder your imagination's stifled. Take the next couple of days off. Put ten drops of the California poppy extract I sent in water and drink it three times a day to help you relax. Drink as much as you can of the valerian root tea during the day—it takes a while to build up in your system, but the calming effects are fabulous. Then, before bed, make a nice cup of chamomile tea with just a few drops of the hops extract—be sure to keep that in the fridge, now, because heat and light will destroy it. Sip that in a nice warm bath with the lavender and almond bath oil. That should do it. *But* if it doesn't, then take one of the 450mg passionflower capsules and *that* will. Get some good sleep. Soak up a little sun and you'll be your old self in no time. Just wait and see."

Sleep again. What wouldn't she give for one whole night of dreamless sleep?

"I'll try . . . And, Mom?"

"Yes?"

"Thank you for setting—" Ivy broke off at the sound of a knock on the front door.

"What is it?" Her mother went to DEFCON 1.

Ivy chuckled. "Nothing. Who needs to relax here, you or me? It's just someone at the door."

"Peek to see who it is . . . *before* you open the door."

This time she laughed. "You mean through the long glass panels in the door? The ones whoever-it-is can see me coming all the way from the kitchen through? Press my nose up against one of those and peek . . . *before* I open the door? Way to make a great first impression on the neighborhood, Mom."

"Don't be flip, young lady. I'm serious."

"Yes, ma'am," she said, her tone indulgent as she frowned at the empty panels of etched glass in the oversized door. A child standing between the panels, maybe? A wood sprite from the forest beyond, perhaps? A severely emaciated serial killer standing sideways preparing to pounce, she guessed, peeking, looking, searching through the glass as far as she could in both directions. "Huh."

"What? Who is it?"

"No one." She turned the dead bolt and stepped out cautiously. "There isn't anyone here. I thought I heard someone knock. I guess I was wrong."

The long, chipped-rock drive that curved uphill through a sparse woods to the house was empty—well, except for her secondhand Volvo that stuck out like a prune in a bowl of raspberries in front of the elegant house.

Then she saw it . . . or not. Smoke . . . or fingers of fog . . . or a trick of evening light and shadow. The figure of a man, a tall boy . . .

No. Nothing. There was nothing there—despite the certainty in her mind of what she'd seen.

She used her middle finger to firmly push the crease between her brows away and shook her head as she stepped back into the house, once again feeling the . . . unquiet inside herself that had been plaguing her for months. "Don't you ever get tired of being right?"

"No, dear," she said without hesitation. "What am I right about this time?"

"I need this. Getting away. Getting some rest. Taking time to clear my head. Thank you for setting this up for me. It was a great idea."

"Let's hope it works, huh?"

They talked for a few more minutes, and her mother ended the conversation with, "Don't forget to check in once in a while. I'll be thinking of you."

Ivy smiled as she broke the connection and slid her cell phone into the back pocket of her jeans. Her mother always requested a check-in, but it was never necessary. She'd call again in a few hours when the sun had set to make sure all the doors and windows were locked and again in the morning to be certain her only daughter hadn't been throttled during the night. She was a worrier.

Stepping barefoot out onto the warm gray flagstone patio, Ivy sighed and curled up on a chaise to peruse her temporary domain. *Beautiful* was an understatement. So was *magnificent*. A wordsmith by profession, and still she found some things simply defied language.

A half width of the large terrace ran the length of the house and surrounded the Rossinis' lap pool and convenient hot tub, which was quartered off on the near end, situated next to a fire pit and a stand-alone bar that was empty at present—she'd checked. Beyond, all the way to the cliffs, was a neatly manicured but mundane lawn . . . made spectacular by large asymmetrical chunks and blocks of pale granite strewn across the grass like so many pieces to a giant's puzzle. Some stood alone while others were a backdrop for blooming bushes and flowers. Here and there, trees seemed to have pushed straight up through the rock.

Wild and raw, then artfully domesticated . . . inevitably awe inspiring.

To think of the thousands of tons of granite extracted from

the hillside in just such slabs and hunks to create the precipice just a few yards away was mind-boggling. At least 100 feet of the total 380 feet of the old quarry jutted jagged and coarse above the water on this end of the great lake created by the Mumford Dam—named after the quarry and the small mining town that were flooded out of existence when they stemmed the Lackey River for hydroelectric power and, more important, to prevent spring floods in the lowlands.

Ivy stood again, feeling fidgety. After a daylong drive, maybe stretching her muscles and exploring the terrain would help. First things first, she decided, wandering out across the cool, soft grass toward the cliffs.

As nice as the house was and as striking as the scenery could be, perhaps water wasn't the best milieu in which to find the peace she was looking for—not that this beggar could afford to be choosy. In fact, she couldn't afford much of anything now that she'd taken the leap and quit her day job to write full-time.

The wind picked up as she neared the high rim of the lake, grabbing at her hair and flapping the sleeves of her cotton shirt. It carried an early spring chill that hadn't been evident back at the house. It was nice. Clean, fresh. And she had to admit there was something . . . consoling in the endless splashing and lapping of the water against the cliff's face. A few more yards and she could see the mesh of grass, weeds, and loose gravel along the edge.

Her stomach turned and her eyes played wavy tricks with her eyesight—but only long enough to make her stop in her tracks. Still a good thirty feet from the edge, she knew she wasn't as afraid of the height as she was of the strange sense of familiarity that washed over her, overwhelming . . . and frightening.

Goose bumps zipped across her shoulders and down her arms. Her fingers turned to fists. The blood draining from her face pooled in the veins of her neck and made her throat tight; air was hard to get. Worst of all was the confusion—a lot of strange vibes with no cause and no understanding of what was happening to her.

Her muscles were stiff, sluggish, as she forced them to turn her around toward the house, yet the moment she saw the man they went limp and spastic. She staggered and her scream echoed out over the lake and down the river valley.

The man looked horrified and pushed out his arms, fingertips up, to make her stop, but he didn't move to come closer. He stood halfway between her and the house. Looking right and then left at the trees that made the house covert, she wondered which direction to run for safety—bare feet forgotten.

"Wait! Wait. I'm sorry." He took a step back. He looked inclined to run as well. "I thought you heard me coming, I'm sorry. I didn't mean to frighten you." Then, like the proverbial light bulb flashing on, he announced, "I'm a neighbor!"—like that made all the difference in the world.

Actually, it did make a slight difference, but only in as much as her vision stopped careening around for an escape route and for the first time truly focused on him. An average-looking man . . . maybe slightly better than average when the artist in her took in the fine symmetrical bone structure of his face. Tall and built on the large side, he looked athletic—or at least fit. His dark hair was clipped short and he was clean shaven. But frankly, she was an eye girl who believed that everything she needed to know about a person could be detected by the life in their eyes. He was wearing aviator shades.

"You're Ivy Bonner, right? I'm guessing everyone on this end of the lake has been asked to watch out for you, but I live closest so I thought I'd come over and introduce myself." Despite the fact that a dozen feet separated them, he stretched out his hand in friendship. "I'm Craig Tennet?" He asked like maybe she'd heard of him—but she hadn't. He took a step forward. "Next house . . . about a mile that way." He used his friendly hand to point north. "I've known the Rossinis"—he shook his head—"all my life, I guess. Gracie's my godmother," he said, like that ought to do it. When it obviously didn't, he grew frustrated and whipped off his sunglasses. "Look, I just came over to introduce myself and to tell you that I'll be here most of the summer, and if you need anything, just give me a call." He patted the back and front pockets of his khaki slacks and finally pulled a business card from the pocket of his white oxford shirt. "My numbers."

Holding the card between two fingers, he stretched out his arm like a ten-foot pole and started inching forward, his eyes sharp and quick, concerned and wary. By the time she could tell they were a lovely moss green color, she'd decided to meet him halfway and plucked the card from his grasp. He gave her a small, tentative smile even as he started backing away again.

"So. Okay. If you have any questions, need to borrow some sugar, anything . . . I'm right next door. If you can't get through on my cell, call the house. Someone will always answer." She nodded and he sighed—mission accomplished. "Great. All right then, I'll probably see you around. And sorry about before . . . startling you. Next time I'll . . . wear a bell or something."

That made her smile, but he missed it when he turned to leave.

"Mr. . . . ah . . ." She looked at the card.

He stopped and turned back to her. "Craig."

His voice was soft and deep like the purr of a really big cat—she liked it.

"Did you knock a few minutes ago? At the front door?"

"I rang the doorbell. When no one answered . . . well, I saw your car so I assumed you were here somewhere and took a chance you'd be swimming or reading or something back here. I shouldn't have intruded. I'm sorry."

She shook her head—that no longer mattered. "But you didn't knock?"

"I rang the bell." He was defensive. "Twice, in case you didn't hear it the first time. When you didn't answer, I decided to take a chance—"

"I understand." She gave the card a little wave. "And I appreciate your neighborly . . . um . . . ness. I'm so sorry I screamed at you."

He relaxed and smiled. "Well, if it's any consolation, you scared the hell out of me, too."

She couldn't stop the chuckle. "Sorry."

"We'll call it even. Fair enough?"

"Fair enough."

"Good." He turned again to leave, then shouted back over his shoulder. "Call if you need anything."

"I will. Thank you."

He waved without a backward glance. She watched him stride across the lawn and around the pool. Taking one last, long baffled look at her, he disappeared along the side of the house—and she abruptly, out of the blue, was fighting an urge to run after him, through the house, to stop him in the driveway.

She felt very alone all of a sudden. Not alone-alone like she usually was, but *very* alone . . . like desert-island alone, with no mother or brother or friends on the other end of her cell phone, no neighbors or police to come to her rescue. And it wasn't the being alone that bothered her—often she needed to be alone just to think. It was the desert-island part that was getting to her, she realized. She glanced back at the cliff. There was something very unsettling about this place. She was beginning to wish she'd stayed home.

———

She woke up falling. Again. Panic replaced the oxygen in her blood, it made her heart race as she gasped for air. Skin clammy, muscles quaking, she thrashed in the sheets until she could sit up and hang her legs over the side of the bed. She was desperate to feel the floor under her feet. She wanted to cry but her gratitude, just to be awake, wouldn't allow it.

So now she knew for sure. She couldn't outrun the dream. It had followed her to Lake Lackey clearer and more detailed than ever before. Now she wasn't simply walking on a sidewalk or down a street or along a garden path and then suddenly falling, falling, falling until she fought and clawed her way back to consciousness. Tonight she'd been walking along the cliffs . . . in the rain. The wind blew droplets of water against her face—it stung and made it hard to see where she was going. She stopped. Peering over the edge at the waves crashing and pounding against the craggy rock made her woozy. She turned away, intent on walking back to safety. Lightning struck, twice, in rapid progression along the slope of land still several yards away but directly in front of her. Jerking back in surprise, she felt her foot slip in the soggy grass-mud-gravel mix at the rim of the overhang, felt her arms flailing to keep her balance, the instant awareness that nothing could save her . . . and falling . . . falling . . . falling.

She buried her face in her hands until her breath came easy and her heart returned to her chest from her throat. She fell back on the bed and let her arms fall wide. Staring at a new ceiling, she went over the same old questions. Why was she having the same sort of dreams over and over? Did they mean something? If so, what? And how could she make them go away?

TWO

She discovered it by accident on her fourth day at the lake—having spent the three preceding days bored to death but safe in the sanctuary of the Rossinis' summer home.

The dreams aside, there had been no more sudden, unaccountable attacks of fear or panic, no more puzzling noises or illusive light tricks. Eventually she came to the conclusion that she'd been overtired that first day and it was foolish, not to mention a giant waste of gorgeous scenery . . . and warm summer sunshine . . . and clean fresh air, to hide and cower from her own imagination.

She controlled her state of mind, not the other way around.

Directly after an early breakfast that morning, she strapped on her backpack and marched out to the cliffs—mostly just to prove she could.

Again the wind picked up once she left the shelter of the trees that protected the house from all but a pleasant pine-scented breeze. And because she wasn't careless or stupid, she stood well away from the edge but close enough to note the discrepancy between the rhythmic pattern of the waves and their erratic intensity, causing the surf to first swell and break against the great stone wall as if testing its strength before it rose up and came crashing back—angry and unmerciful. Exhilarating and intimidating at once.

Taking the path of least resistance, Ivy turned south, away from the crest of the old quarry. And then, for no reason she could identify, she changed her mind and went north along a clear-cut, well-traveled path. It wasn't a steep hike but it did require more effort than a downhill jaunt. Still, with the wind in her face and the spirit of the lake speaking to hers, she topped the summit in no time.

And there, to her great delight, set back a hundred or so feet from the cliff, was a gazebo. An ornately carved octagon with a high-pitched roof and open sides—of the old Victorian Stick Style, the likes of which one didn't see often enough in her opinion. Stunning. She imagined it had once been white but was now a seasoned silver-gray . . . and completely irresistible.

Secreted away in a hollow below the primary grounds of what she assumed was the Tennet family summer home, it looked sadly neglected. Lovely, but in dire need of a broom, maybe a paintbrush . . . and a hammer and some nails, she noted as the floorboards slid loose and worn below her feet.

Yet, what struck her hardest was the calm, the sense of relief she felt moments after stepping inside. The quiet, the peace, the protection were . . . spiritual, she decided—as nurturing as one would wish any church to be. For several minutes she stood with her hands on the straps of her pack, eyes closed, simply breathing, deeply, in and out, as if she were home again. At last.

"Ho there!" a male voice, deep and throaty like the growl of a bear echoed in the clearing. "Yer trespassin'."

Odd. Rather than the surprise or alarm she would normally feel in this situation, his tenor resonated with something familiar inside her. Calm and . . . expectant, as if he should recognize her, she turned to face a short burly man in stretched-out denim and soft flannel. His face was bushy and his hair was gray, but his movements were sure and determined as he approached her, double-barreled shotgun in hand.

Odder. She knew it wasn't loaded. She knew she was in no danger. She knew he was sweeter than he looked.

Oddest . . . she was delighted to see him.

"Hi!"

"'Ello. Yer on private property."

She nodded. "The Tennets'. Yes, I figured that."

"Mumford Manor, miss. You oughta be leavin' now."

"I'm Ivy Bonner." She met him on the back side of the canopy and held out a hand. "I'm staying at the Rossinis' this summer."

A moment of confused speculation crossed his face before he glanced at her hand, shifted the rifle from his right to his left, and stepped forward to take hers.

"Mr. Craig mentioned ya. Gus. I keep an eye on things here."

"This"—she held her arms out to indicate the gazebo—"is lovely. The scrollwork is amazing. It must have been spectacular once."

He took a good look and gave one firm nod. "Gone to ruin of late. Rotting. Could be dangerous."

"Mm. The floorboards, I saw those."

"A couple ties in the roof ain't as strong as they oughta be neither."

"What a shame Mr. Tennet doesn't care enough to keep it up."

The old man looked as if she'd slapped him—he was annoyed.

"He cares, miss. Best you go now."

"I didn't mean anything by that. I was . . . It was just an observation." She spoke hastily. She didn't want to leave. But even before the last word left her lips he was pointing south with his shotgun, toward the woods and the Rossinis' property beyond. "Fine. But I was heading the other way . . . to the top."

"Private property."

"What—the whole cliff top? I don't think so."

"Think what you like, but it's true. Too many cracks and gaps in the rock to have folks wandering up and down the cliffs, killin' 'emselves fer pictures. The park put in a lookout a few miles up the road. You can have a look-see from there."

"But . . ."

"Come along now," he said, patient but determined, as he moved to meet her at the south-side entrance.

Reluctantly, she took the first and then the second step

down, looking back over her shoulder, pondering the strange
pull she felt toward the little ramshackle structure that even its
owner didn't seem to have much use for.

"It's been here a long time but . . . it was originally built for
something else, wasn't it?" She didn't want to know how or
why she knew this—especially in light of the fact that it looked
perfect in its current location.

"Yes, miss." He led the way to a gap in the woods and
an obvious path to the other side. "Miss Ruth's wedding
canopy."

"Miss Ruth. Mr. Craig's . . . sister?"

"His mother, God keep her. Last Mumford, she was."

"Mumford? Like the dam?"

"And the mine and the town I was born in." He stopped
where the path started. "Good to meet you, Miss Bonner."

"Ivy."

He nodded. "Miss Ivy, then. You find you need somethin'
just give a call to the house and I'll come a-runnin'.'"

"Thank you, Gus. Enjoy the rest of your day."

"Will do. You do the same." He tipped his head at her,
turned, and walked away.

She watched him lumber off, but then her gaze gravitated
back to the gazebo.

In general, Ivy was not an impulsive person in spite of the
180-degree bend in her nature to be expressive and artistic. She
was logical and cautious and a bit of a perfectionist in most
everything she did—and very aware when she was, well, out
of sync with herself. So resisting the urge to return to the gazebo once Gus was out of sight was . . . jarring. As was the
driven compulsion to remove sketch pad and pencils from her
pack as soon she got home and the feverish style of her strokes
as she made first a rough draft, then quickly sharpened and
polished it until she was satisfied she had a true image of the
wedding canopy—draped in gossamer white silk with a bum-
per crop of pendulous purple wisteria flowering from thick
vines in the eaves.

It was stunning . . . literally, in every sense of the word.
Beautiful and shocking.

She tossed the pad away from her as if it had burst into
flames. *Silk and wisteria?* How could she have possibly known

that? Her imagination . . . ? Then why not radiant white satin
and bold red roses with just as much certainty?

Her eyes stung with tears of frustration and anxiety. She
closed them and lay back in the chaise to breathe deep and
search for calm.

What was happening to her? The nightmares . . . hallucinations . . . and now this insane obsession with a gazebo. *Was* she
insane? She thought about it—would a crazy woman question
her sanity? She chose *no*. Otherwise she'd have to call and
explain everything to her mother, listen to the litany of roots
and powders and extracts to ingest or rub or soak in, and then
drive herself to the nearest asylum.

After a few more minutes she was able to convince herself
that it was all stress. Yeah, stress! It had to be. Her eyes popped
open and she groaned over how foolish she'd been. She picked
up her sketch pad, smiled at the drawing of the gazebo, and
went inside to make valerian root tea . . . a lot of it.

That night the nightmare started in the gazebo. She was happy;
more content than she'd been in a long, long time—looking
forward to the future. Dark clouds rolled in from across the
lake. Lightning sparked and thunder rumbled. Fat drops of rain
made hard-hitting noises on the ground first and then on the
roof above. A clean, fresh summer storm. Gradually she noticed that night, too, was coming. The land around her safe
haven was turning to a thick, sloppy mud . . . but she didn't
care. Slipping her hands into the front pockets of her jeans, she
stepped down into the rain. The wind blew in gusts and water
streamed down her face as she walked toward the cliffs. She
hesitated, and then peered over the edge at the waves crashing
and pounding against the craggy rock. A jolt of panic coursed
through her and she turned quickly . . . toward home. Lightning
crashed, twice, in rapid progression along the slope of land in
front of her. It startled her. She jerked back. Her foot slipped
in the mud. She pulled her hands from her pockets, waved them
through the air to keep her balance, and then suddenly she was
falling . . . falling . . . falling.

"Hello?"

"Craig?" Holding her cell phone in one hand, she used his business card to scratch at the bug bite on her knee with the other. "It's Ivy Bonner. Am I disturbing you?"

"No. How are you doing?" He had the nicest voice—mellow and friendly.

"Good, thanks. I'm calling to ask . . . well, Gus probably told you about our meeting yesterday."

"Gus?"

"Your caretaker? Scruffy-looking older gentleman? Built like a big shoe box? Carries an empty shotgun around?"

He chuckled. "I know who Gus is. He just didn't mention meeting you."

"Oh. Good." Pretending to be shamefaced, she confessed, "I was trespassing."

"I see." Though his voice was serious, she could hear the smile in it. "And now you've called to apologize?"

"Not really . . . but I will if you give me permission to trespass some more."

"Of course. Feel free to roam around all you like. In fact, please drop in when you do, anytime. I'm always looking for a nice distraction."

"From what?"

"Work. I travel quite a bit so when the opportunity presents itself I try to work from home. This is the first time in almost two years I've had any real time off, so this summer is a bit of a working vacation for me. So you see, you'd be doing me a huge favor if you stop by once in a while to get me out of my office."

"Well, put like that, it seems like the least I could do."

"Good. Now I have something to look forward to."

So did she. And it wasn't an unwelcome realization.

"You'll tell Gus not to shoot me on sight, then?"

"I will."

"Thank you."

"See you soon."

They said good-bye, but two seconds after she ended the call on her cell, the house phone rang.

"You know Gus is harmless, right? You can trust him."

"I guessed that." She'd been certain of it.

"Okay. See you later."

" 'Bye."

Packing a notebook and sketch pad and pencils along with a bottle of water, an apple, and an energy bar in her pack, she became aware of the smile that lingered on her lips . . . and a definite sense of anticipation that wasn't entirely about the gazebo.

So okay, she could admit it, she got a little lonely sometimes. And there was no doubt that it was nice to have something to take her mind off the weirdness happening around her.

She took the cliff trail back to the gazebo, spread out a yoga mat she'd snatched from the Rossinis' stash of athletic equipment, and spent the afternoon sketching the views of every angle from the tranquility within—the lake, the woods, the steep slope covered in scrub vegetation and wildflowers just beginning to bloom.

Granted, it wasn't the sketching she was supposed to be doing, the kind that paid the rent, but it came easily and flowed from her fingers like it hadn't in months—she'd take it and be grateful that her mental block was beginning to crumble.

The next day she slept late into the morning, having spent the better part of the night tossing and turning, eager to sleep but reluctant to dream. Close to midnight, in a fit of desperation, she swam to exhaustion in the Rossinis' endless lap pool. Then she slept . . . she dreamt . . . and she was falling, falling, falling.

Weary, impatient for the tranquility she'd quickly come to expect inside the gazebo, she took the cliffside path in a hurry. Right away she noticed something different and hurried over to the canopy to get a closer look.

Furniture. A chair, footstool, and small table, all of the Adirondack style, were set smack in the middle of the floor— where three new unfinished planks of wood were set snug and tight, replacing those that had rotted and warped. Even the struts holding up the roof had been reinforced with several metal brackets.

Now it was perfect, she deemed, unloading her supplies. Beautiful, safe, and comfortable—perfect.

She settled back in the chair, feet up on the stool, with her notebook and pencil in hand. She drew a line down the middle of the page and divided it into eight rectangles. Rough-draft storyboards were her basic outline for the story she wanted to write and the even more coarse sketches to go with it . . . when they presented themselves. Which they weren't, at the moment.

She inhaled the fresh air, leaned her head back, and closed her eyes to concentrate. She heard the water beat against the granite wall . . . and woke up shortly before sunset.

THREE

———▸———

"A psychotic break? Seriously?" She put her mother on speaker so she could look up the term on her BlackBerry. "You came up with that one pretty quickly. It isn't from one of your TV shows, is it? There was no screaming or blood involved. I fell asleep and when I woke up, my storyboard was finished—all *five pages* of storyboard. *Patty Ann Pettigrew Meets a Ghost.* That's the title someone gave it. A ghost, for Pete's sake . . . and there isn't even a Halloween theme to it." She read, *An acute psychotic episode lasts longer than one day but less than one month*—her nap had lasted about four hours. "It says here the patient will have at least one of the following: delusions, hallucinations, markedly disorganized speech, or markedly disorganized or catatonic behavior. There's nothing about working in your sleep, Mom."

"Have you hit your head lately? Maybe you just forgot you finished the storyboard and then . . . you were *unconscious*, not sleeping."

"Like amnesia?"

"Yes!"

"Umm . . . no. I think I'd remember having had amnesia, wouldn't I? Besides, I haven't hit my head on anything. Not that I haven't wanted to," she added under her breath.

"Hitting your head isn't the only way to have amnesia. Stress can—"

"I'm not that stressed." Or, she hadn't been until now. "I swear."

"Ivy, honey, would you like me to drive up? I can bring you some fresh rosemary. We'll fill the house with the scent of it, put it in our food. Oh! And I'll bring this marvelous new tea I've been working with . . . and with a dash of tincture of ginkgo biloba and a few drops of concentrated Ashwagandha root and a little ginseng you'll . . . well, if we're not careful with the Ashwagandha root, you'll be jumping every man in the vicinity," she laughed at the thought. "But at least you'll remember doing it." She laughed again despite being entirely serious about her herbs.

And while the child in Ivy was sure she'd feel better with her mother nearby, the greater part of her was already gagging on the tea and suffocating from the constant fussing that was her mother's . . . specialty, to put it lovingly.

"You're the best mom I've ever had, you know that?"

"I'm the only mom you've ever had. So I'm guessing that's a no."

"It's a no, thank you, and I appreciate the offer, but I'll figure it out. In fact, I wonder . . . If I fell asleep with a copy of *The South Beach Diet*, would I wake up with Cameron Diaz's body?"

"There you go, my upside-to-everything girl." She tried to sound cheerful but her voice was still thick with concern. "If that works, you won't be able to keep me away."

"You'll be the first to know."

"I want to be the first to know *everything*, understood?"

"Yes, ma'am."

"I'm serious."

"I know."

They ended the call—and there and then Ivy resolved to stop relating her worries and woes to her mother. She was anxious enough by nature—her coronary two years ago was proof of that—and aside from her teas and tinctures, there wasn't a lot she could do to help.

Leafing through the pages of the finished storyboard, it became more and more confusing. Not only was it not the sort of story she generally wrote, it wasn't a good story. It was the ghost trying to tell Patty Ann Pettigrew, in several different ways, not to be afraid of him. Clearly inspired by the gazebo, it was in a very similar structure that Patty Ann and the ghost, Oliver, felt most at ease together.

She growled and ripped the pages from her pad, wadded them up tight, and tossed them to the far corner of the room. She didn't know what was happening to her, but she knew she had to get control of it. Ignoring it and moving on with her life was her best bet, as there wasn't anything else she could think of to do. How did one battle nightmares and, well, sleep in general now?

Though, looking back on it for the first time, she hadn't jolted awake from her nap, caught in the sensation of falling. Her eyes had opened on a satisfied sigh. A gentle breeze tickled her cheek with wisps of her hair. She'd stretched her muscles out like a lazy cat. Too soon, she'd glanced down at her sketches. . . .

Opening a fresh bottle of pinot noir—high in antioxidants and resveratrol, according to her mother—she poured twice her usual dose into a large wine glass. She practiced her own form of pharmacology.

Curling up on one end of the couch, she strained her brain trying to recall what she'd dreamt that afternoon. Nothing? There was a vague impression of a woman . . . with red hair . . . that deep, rich hue of mahogany . . . maybe. The harder she tried to get a clearer image, the fuzzier it got—and that had nothing to do with her second glass of wine. In fact, she was so clear thinking that when the house phone rang, it barely scorched her nervous system.

"Hello?"

"I woke you up." That wonderful voice . . .

"You did?"

"I didn't?"

"Didn't what?"

"Wake you up."

"When?"

"Just now, with the telephone?"

"Oh! No." She rolled her eyes at her stupidity. "I'm awake."

"Are you drunk?"

"Maybe. Yeah, I might be. A little tipsy, I think."

"Special occasion?" She heard amusement in his voice. He wasn't going to judge her.

"Not really. No. Truth is, I lost my mind this afternoon and I was just sitting here trying to decide if I could get along without it altogether or if I should go looking for it."

"What'd you decide?"

"I haven't yet."

"Would you like a second opinion?"

She chuckled. "You'll have to bring your own bottle of pinot. Mine's almost gone."

"No problem. I'll be there in five minutes."

It was closer to twenty minutes—not that it bothered her. As a matter of fact, when he rang the bell, she didn't even bother herself to get up, simply bellowed out for him to come in.

"Ivy?" he called, walking slowing down the wide hall that opened into the big family kitchen at the back of the house.

She'd chosen the library as her sanctuary. The furniture was big and soft and cushy, and so many of the books she loved stood sentry along the walls protecting her. "Here."

He stopped in the doorway—filled it for the most part. He had a presence, that's for sure. Not the sort of man to go . . . unnoticed.

He smiled a hello and then shook his head.

"Is this how Dr. Seuss wrote his children's books?"

"It would explain a lot if he did . . . couldn't it, shouldn't it, wouldn't it?"

He laughed and approached her, carrying another bottle of pinot noir and a large brown paper bag.

"You shopped?"

"No." He looked in the bag, then back at her. Hands down, his eyes were his best asset. Ivy sighed, staring. "Wanda and I raided the fridge. I didn't know if you'd eaten or if you were drinking your dinner tonight." He raised his brows in mock disapproval and gave her an eloquent look that made her giggle, and then he grinned. "Actually, I had the munchies so I brought enough for the both of us."

"You"—she pointed a finger in his general direction—"are an excellent neighbor." Her gaze caught on the wine bottle. "You need a glass."

She wasn't so blasted she couldn't get up. It was the furniture . . . so plush and comfy she thought she was going to have to turn around and back herself off the couch bottom first.

"Stay put." Craig chuckled. "I know where they are," he said, already walking away—with the bag of food! You couldn't just offer a dog a bone and then wander off with it. His excellent neighbor status was in serious jeopardy.

"So who's Wanda?" she hollered through the big house.

"My housekeeper," he yelled back. She could hear him opening and closing cupboards in the kitchen.

"Your housekeeper . . . and you being over here with me means you're not married, right?"

"Right. Divorced."

"Me, too." Then she muttered, "In case you were wondering."

"Wanda is the sister of your friend, Gus."

Her friend? "He fixed the gazebo up for me."

"Oh yeah?"

"He left me a chair and a table and everything."

"He's a good man, our Gus."

Minutes too late it occurred to her that Gus worked for *him*. "So, so are you," she said in a normal voice that wouldn't carry to the kitchen.

Unfortunately, he was standing in the doorway again. "What?"

Jeez. "I said, 'So are you.' "

"So am I what?"

"A good man." She watched him cross the room, his arms and hands filled with a bowl of fruit salad—grapes, strawberries, pineapple chunks, slices of banana, wedges of peaches and pears—a plastic container of bread, another of cheese, a box of Pop-Tarts, a Coke, a large bottle of Gatorade, a glass of water, a bottle of Tylenol, and a rocks-glass-capped decanter. "Ah, but not a wine man."

He shrugged. "It has its moments, but if I drink, I prefer Scotch."

"Munchies, huh? I was thinking pretzels and gummy bears. This looks more like a feast."

He set everything down on her end of the coffee table, then crossed his legs and lowered himself fluidly to the rug in front of her. He pointed to the Coke and the salad. "Fructose to help us metabolize the alcohol. Bread and cheese to help absorb it."

Patting the box of Pop-Tarts, he grinned and said, "Both. Every frat house in the world buys them in bulk." He opened the bottle of analgesic and dumped out four tablets, then gave two to her with the glass of water. "And for tomorrow's hangover, we have these for the headache"—he took the half glass of water from her when she'd finished and downed his, draining out every drop, then reached for the sports drink to fill it again—"and this to make us feel semi-human again."

"Wow. Should I be concerned with your obvious expertise in overimbibing, or is this just common knowledge that I've missed out on?"

"I've known a few . . . overimbibers in my time. You don't forget the tricks." Though his voice was still light and jovial, there was something in the tone that cautioned her.

Clearly, he had a sensitivity to alcohol abuse, and being in her present state of hammeredness was definitely a downer. She brightened her expression. "Wanna play Parcheesi? I found a board in—"

"No." He laughed. "I'd rather ply you with more wine so you'll tell me all your secrets."

"Good luck with that one." She sipped on the sports drink—a sweet-tart taste that made her tongue stick to the roof of her mouth . . . not that it stopped her from talking. "I don't have any."

He narrowed suspicious eyes at her. "You're not secretly afraid of your left hand or the number seventeen?"

"My left hand does make me nervous but, no, I'm not afraid of it . . . or seventeen."

"You don't snoop in other people's medicine cabinets or steal decorator soaps at parties?"

She laughed and reached for the fruit. "I wouldn't dream of it." But . . . "I did once skip school and lie to my mother. In high school, I left after lunch, took a bus downtown to a Stephen King book signing. The line was ridiculous, but it was so worth standing there all afternoon just to see him, in person, and get my book signed." She sighed dramatically. "He said, 'Hi. How ya doing?' And I said, 'Great.' He smiled at me." Another sigh. "Then, of course, I was late getting home from school. My poor mother was worried sick and I told her I'd been kept in detention for forgetting my gym shorts."

"Did anyone at school catch you for skipping?"

"I wasn't the sort of kid people missed if I didn't show up. I got off scot-free."

He considered her for a long moment. "That's it? That's not the worst thing you've ever done, is it?"

"Oh—oh no. The worst thing was in college. I dated two boys at the same time."

He chewed on a strawberry. "For how long?"

"Six hours, maybe?" He looked confused. "See, I'd been dating Tommy Payne for a few months. He even came to visit over the semester break to meet my mom and brother. We were deeply in lust, could barely breathe without each other. Two weeks later, Jack Bonner walked into my creative writing class. He was cute and funny and a really, *really* good writer. I was in awe. I would have given anything for half his talent. When he finally asked me out, I was still dating Tommy . . . but I said yes anyway. By the end of our date I was head over heels in love with Jack and broke up with Tommy the next day."

"You broke his heart."

She grinned. "Well, there was this hot blond math nerd he'd had his eye on for a while . . . he was relieved and we parted friends."

"And you married Jack Bonner."

"I did. The same summer we graduated from college . . . for almost five years."

"Mind if I ask what happened?"

"No. I . . . well, two writers can easily starve to death if one or both of them don't get a day job, for one thing. For another: There are as many methods of writing as there are writers. Jack is the kind who thinks of himself as a pure artist, who needs to feel inspired in order to write, who labors over each word like he's carving it in stone. And that's okay, it works for him. But then there's someone like me who thinks writing is as much plain old-fashioned hard work as it is talent and luck. One's no better than the other, but put one of each in the same house and it can get complicated."

"And did one or both of you get a day job?"

"We both did originally. He was . . . arty, not unrealistic. But he needed to write when he needed to write—there's no

controlling the Muses, you know—and they don't always co-
incide with a work schedule."

"So you kept your day job and he stayed home to write."
She nodded, put the fruit back on the table, and took a piece
of bread from the container. "You became resentful."

"I'd be lying if I said I didn't but"—she took another chunk
of bread and a slice of cheese—"I wasn't the only one."

"You fell in love with a coworker and he resented it."

"No," she scoffed. "Too simple."

"A coworker fell in love with you and he resented it."

She shook her head. "Too cliché."

He looked askance.

"I published first—also cliché, I suppose, if you consider
that one of us had to be first eventually." She leaned over to
pinch more bread and cheese. "In the beginning it was okay.
It was a *dumb kid's book*, after all . . . and probably a fluke, but
wasn't it great that I'd found an outlet for my little sketches at
the same time? The money would come in handy *and* until I
got serious about my writing and produced something worth-
while, it might be kind of fun."

He grimaced. "Ouch."

She laughed, though that last barb still made her angry. "He
was a good sport about *Patty Ann Pettigrew Learns to Swim*,
too. It was *Patty Ann Pettigrew's Tree House* and the contract
for three more Patty Ann stories that finally got to him." She
turned a vapid smile his way. "I was stifling his creative spirit
with my nonsense—he had to leave."

She very much liked the perceptive and sympathetic expression on Craig's face. Her words were blithe, her tone sarcastic,
but he could tell it was a tender subject for her even three years
later.

"I'm blathering . . . and you're not drinking. How am I
supposed to extract secrets from you if you don't drink
something?"

"Believe me," he said, reaching for the Coke and filling the
rocks glass from atop the decanter of Scotch. "I haven't got one
secret less risqué than both of yours put together."

She hooted out a laugh and then frowned as she replayed
his words—several times. "That means . . . all yours are
worse?"

He grinned. "You're not as drunk as I thought."

"No. Unfortunately." And to his quizzical look, she said, "Normally, I'd be sound asleep after this much wine."

"You're not sleeping well? You should have told me to stay home."

"The wine wasn't working and I wanted the company more." Abruptly she put her feet on the floor and pivoted her backside into the opposite corner of the couch. "Come on, get comfy and tell me all your juicy secrets."

He complied. "Where would you like me to start? Ask me a question."

"Okay. I'll start out easy: What do you do?"

"I run a mining company."

"Mumford Mining."

"That's the one. Formed by my great-grandfather, a British immigrant, a miner who came over and cut granite in the mines in Vermont before he and his nine partners formed the Lackey River Mining Company in 1872. Ten years later, he bought out five of them and the families of two more who'd died in the meantime and changed the name to Mumford Mining Company. Five years after that, he bought out the last two and became sole owner of—"

"Man. All that work and time just to have it flooded when they built the dam. Did the government buy him out so he could start over somewhere else, or did they do that public domain deal?"

He had bright, astute eyes anyway, but when they lit with humor, they could bowl a girl over.

"Well, according to my granddad, Charles Mumford wasn't a man to be messed with, and it was just luck that the Lackey River site was nearly tapped and ready for reclamation when Congress passed the Flood Control Act of 1934, otherwise they might have had a little war on their hands. As it was, when the Army Corps of Engineers came around in the early '40s, old Charley saw the need for the dam and was willing to forfeit a few more months on the mine—a year tops—for first pick on the waterfront property once the lake had formed. Hence our home on the crest of the cliffs."

"Very shrewd."

He nodded. "He was ninety-two by then and still the sharpest tool in the shed, they say. And that's just a small example of his business acumen. The Lackey River site was his first mine but not his only. Working only one mine is like . . . putting all your eggs in one basket, as the saying goes." He paused. "You know, in reality I don't think I've ever seen or heard of anyone collecting eggs in more than one basket, have you?"

"I haven't seen anyone collect eggs, period. Two baskets make a lot of sense considering the way eggs break, but I can't imagine anyone using two baskets if one would do the job."

Even though they'd been talking face-to-face all the while and even though they both had the direct manner of looking into someone's eyes when they spoke, in that moment their gazes bumped, locked, derailed, and simultaneously they realized they were no longer thinking about eggs . . . or mines, or careers, or exes or food or . . . breathing.

Craig inhaled first. He glanced at his watch. "I should probably get going."

"What? But what about old Charley? And all his eggs? Your secrets . . ."

He laughed and tipped his head to one side, appreciating her reluctance to end the evening. "Why don't you come out to dinner with me Friday night; let me tell you then. All of it. I'll bare my soul. And wake you gently when I'm finished, I promise." He chuckled because she did. "Please. The marina has a four-star restaurant, but it's only open on weekends this early in the season. It'll be a real treat for me not to have to eat alone."

"Me, too. I'd love to go."

His exodus was rather hurried with his quick clarification that the containers were disposable and the unopened Scotch belonged to Jerry Rossini—from his hidden stash. He grinned and ordered her to stay put; he'd lock her in when he let himself out. Then he was gone. And she started counting the minutes till Friday.

FOUR

Apparently the anticipation of having a dinner date with a handsome man wasn't enough to occupy her mind—more specifically her subconscious mind, which continued to have an active life of its own.

She decided not to go to the gazebo the next day. She wanted to, badly, and was annoyed and disappointed that she couldn't overcome her trepidation about the place but, well, one glance at the *Patty Ann Pettigrew Meets a Ghost* sketches rolled up in the corner and goose bumps ran amok. She was totally creeped out.

Still a little sluggish from the wine the night before, it took three large mugs of coffee to get her back on her feet and into a nice, safe mode of denial. She would exert more control on her mind to keep from losing it altogether. She locked the disturbing sketches in the trunk of her car, and armed with a new, uncontaminated pad, she settled on the patio in the comfort of the midmorning sun and started another storyboard.

And there she sat, paper as blank as her brain, until her rear end and right leg fell asleep from inactivity. Exasperated, she stomped feeling back into her foot, gathered her art supplies, and headed for the cliffs.

A few warm-up sketches—of anything—to get her creative

juices flowing was her intent. The lake and the mountains were the biggest and most obvious subjects, but for the detail girl inside her, most any *little* thing did her best. Bugs, blooms . . . or even banana peels if the angles caught her fancy.

Turning her back, literally and deliberately, on the Tennet property and the gazebo thereon, she walked south. When she came to the woods along the property line, she saw the trees were sparse enough near the cliffs for someone to have set an ornate wrought-iron bench among them to create a secluded retreat from which to watch the lake and its constantly changing view—and she smiled. She'd only met the Rossinis once, years ago, and didn't know them well. But anyone who took the time to enjoy the beauty around them had her heartfelt approval.

Too soon, however, the trees and rocks and underbrush crowded out all signs of the narrow path she'd been following. And for good reason, she quickly discovered. The rocks were an overgrown barricade against a three-foot fissure in the cliff face—a high, wire fence on the other side of it impeded any travelers going north.

She carefully retraced her steps off the rocks and returned to the bench a few yards away. Gus's warning was no lie. The cliffs were clearly treacherous to hikers, and the residents had gone to some lengths to discourage them.

She sank down on to the bench, downcast. There was no denying the lovely aspects of the lake and the mountains from this vantage, but she'd been hoping for something a little more . . . specific, more intricate. She glanced back at the barrier, at the burgeoning plants and vines coming back to life after a long winter's nap. Standing, she backed away from the bench, taking it into her perspective, capturing it in her mind's eye. The ironwork, the rocks, the foliage, the cliff, the sky, the trees—plenty there to throw her pencil into for a while. . . .

She drew.

———

The woman's husband called her his Ginger Cookie and bent low over her right shoulder to kiss her lips as she sat watching a young fair-haired boy—three or four years old—playing with metal trucks and cars at her feet. Her long curls were a light reddish brown; she had porcelain skin and bright, happy eyes the color of a summer sky.

Ivy recognized the wedding canopy . . . but just barely. In a mostly black-and-white dream, the white it was painted was nearly blinding; it seemed to sparkle as it reflected the sun and gave the illusion of being a special, magical place. Certainly the people inside thought so—*they* were colored with life, vibrant and real, as she approached them, unseen, from the cliff top. An indistinct house loomed in the near distance and she realized the gazebo was in its original position, where it belonged, instead of in the tree-lined alcove below.

Thick wisteria stems were supported independently on either side of both entrances—fragrant violet clusters of flowers hung in profusion.

The boy looked up, saw her, and smiled.

I've been waiting for you, he said, *with* a mature voice, *without* moving his lips—neither of which bothered her as much as knowing who he was: Patty Ann's ghost, Oliver.

"This is another nightmare, right?" A rhetorical question.

I'm Oliver.

"I know."

He was speaking to her but not at her, and his parents were unaware of her presence. The three of them continued to love and laugh and play as if she weren't there, as if nothing existed outside the gazebo.

You have to help me.

"Do what?"

You have to free me.

"From what?" Already she didn't like the direction this discourse was heading.

Please. Tell him.

"Who?" The three of them turned to look expectantly at the house. Oliver jumped up and ran to the top of the stairs to watch someone, an older boy, emerge from the thick fog that was the house. "Tell who what? Oliver?"

She was back on the cliff, in the dark, in the rain. The wind blew and lightning slashed the sky. She searched for the gazebo; caught sight of it, weathered and empty among the trees again.

Help me. Oliver's voice reverberated in her head as lightning crashed, once and then again, in rapid progression along the slope of land in front of her. She wobbled backward, slipped, started to fall . . . then simply leaned back into a sunny field of blue and white and pink wildflowers. *Help me.*

Her eyes drifted open slowly—warmth from the sun cooling on her cheeks, the scent of rich earth and sweet flowers still in her nostrils. It sure beat waking in panic from an endless fall into darkness but . . . what did it all mean? If dreams meant anything at all, that is.

She slipped her palms under her head and stared at the ceiling with tired eyes.

Maybe her subconscious was working out the kinks in the Patty Ann story. What if her ghost needed help with something? Patty Ann was an obliging sort of girl most of the time, but . . . what could he possibly need help with? Well, it wasn't like he was a real ghost, right? Another youngster in a ghost costume—perhaps his sheet is caught on something or his bag of Halloween candy is too heavy to carry. Nah. But he could be lost. He might have wandered too far from home and can't recall how to get back. That could work—lots of safety lessons to be taught there. . . .

Clearly the story had to have a Halloween theme. Why hadn't she noted as much on the storyboard and saved herself the confusion and needless anxiety? If she could ignore the fact that she'd drawn it in her sleep, of course.

Still, it was a start, she decided, rolling over and wiggling into a comfortable position with a sleepy but satisfied smile.

Finally, she slept, deep and dreamless.

FIVE

"I knew it. Once the valerian root kicked in and you started to relax, I knew your imagination would break through the block. Like a detox cleanse for your mind." She chuckled at her own cleverness. "A big brain flush."

Ivy glanced at the trash compacter where she'd tossed the herb tea when she suspected it of causing the sleep-working incident. Or what her mother was now calling her *short blackout*.

Four hours was not a short amount of time to be doing things she was unaware of—it wasn't. In four hours she could have driven into town, robbed a bank, and shot the security guard. In four hours she could have baked a cake, eaten the entire thing, and cleaned up the mess. However, in her four hours of unconsciousness she had completed a five-page storyboard—a task she couldn't have accomplished if she were conscious, not on the best of days.

Ivy believed most of her mother's herbs and concoctions were, in general, harmless. However, some could be as poisonous as others could be helpful. Her mother had been studying them for years and was fanatically cautious when it came to mixing and dosing with them. But mistakes are made. . . .

"Mm. Big brain flush. Good one, Mom. But maybe you

shouldn't recommend the valerian root to any of your friends until you've had a chance to do a more complete check into its potential side effects. I mean—"

"Oh my! A twofer. A brain *and* body cleanse. But that's—"

"Mom! It didn't give me diarrhea. Just don't give it to your friends. There's no way of telling who's going to be . . . ultra-sensitive to it, and I know you have lots of other things you can suggest for relaxation and sleep."

"Honey, it's been used for centuries. Hippocrates described its—"

"Mom?" She waited a beat for her mother's attention. "Please. Rip that page out of your book."

"No," she said after a moment. "But I will look into it further. I'm sorry it made you ill, sweetie. As you say, you might be ultrasensitive to it or allergic, or it might even have been cured improperly, there's no telling. Just toss it."

"Okay."

A few minutes later, her backpack dangled from her right hand as she took long-legged strides across the lawn toward the cliffs and the path that would take her to the gazebo. It had rained during the night but at present the sky was big and bright and empty, save for a few gulls that preferred the ledges—both natural and man-made—along the cliff face for their nests.

Though the grass was still damp, the pebbles and rocks on the cliff path were as dry as cornmeal and her steps were quick and sure.

Stepping off the path and around a few trees into the clearing, she stopped and marveled at the quiet, peaceful, home-again sensation that washed over her. What was it about this particular wedding canopy that attracted her so? In light of the strange happening during her last visit, she ought to be terrified, but she wasn't—only glad and lighthearted.

She worked well for the next two hours. The sketches shifted easily from her head to the paper, which for her was the hardest part. Not the effort of drawing itself but the telling of the story via pictures rather than with words. It could be tricky some-times, and it was important to her that a young person who hadn't yet learned to read could understand the tale as well as a slightly older person who had. Later, the details in the pictures and the expressions on the characters' faces would appeal to adults, making it "a book for children of all ages," as one re-viewer described *Patty Ann Pettigrew Picks a Peck of Peaches.*

And still another hour passed, and she was oblivious to everything but Patty Ann and Oliver—now in her mind as a towheaded scamp with gray eyes and freckles. She was con-templating making Oliver one of Patty Ann's permanent, recur-ring friends when the bushes behind her rustled and Craig emerged from the woods where the path connected the two properties—picnic basket in hand.

He smiled when he saw her, and the lurch in her abdomen was not unpleasant, she noted with interest . . . very not unpleasant.

"I'm sort of jumping the gun on Friday night, but Gus said you were down here working, so I thought I'd take a chance on it being time for a break. Are you hungry?"

"Famished." She closed up her sketch pad and set it aside. "Please don't tell me Gus was down here and I didn't see him. I get a little absorbed. My mom came over once, did my dishes, cooked me dinner, and left it under a cover on my counter. I thought I had elves."

He chuckled as he reached the bottom of the stairs, barely hesitated, and then stepped inside. "By the end of the summer you'll realize that even though you might not see him, Gus is everywhere, sees everything, and knows all. It's spine-chilling."

"He's been with you a long time." It wasn't a question.

"All my life. And if he wasn't ratting me out to my dad, he was secretly helping me out of one giant jam or another, so I guess you could say he helped raise me."

"And you love him," she said, leaning forward on the edge of the chair and pushing the stool out for him.

He looked put on the spot for a second, then nodded as he sat. "Yeah, I do."

Setting the basket on the floor between them near the little table, he swiveled his head from side to side, looking around, mixing memories with the sad reality of the condition of the canopy. His eyes gravitated back to her; he grinned and rubbed his palms together. "So, how's the story going?"

"Great. Finally. I love working here. Thank you for letting me."

He dropped his gaze to the picnic basket and shrugged. "No problem." He reached in and brought out two neatly wrapped sandwiches. "Turkey or tuna?"

"I like both, you choose."

He looked torn. "Me, too. Let's go fifty-fifty."

"Deal."

His expression was calculating. "Wanna eat dessert first?"

She gasped, shocked and delighted by the devil inside him. "What is it?"

"Wanda's tapioca pudding. Left over from dinner last night." Without waiting for an answer, he gave her a spoon, handle first, and then dove into the basket for the custard cups. "It's one of my favorites, so she makes it pretty often. It's the only reason I keep her around."

"Now, why don't I believe that?" She yanked off the plastic wrap.

"It's true. She's the bossiest woman I've ever met. And she always gets her way. Even my ex-wife couldn't stand up to her."

"Well"—she paused to get every molecule off her spoon before scooping up more—"you could put up with a lot for a dessert like this."

"Tell me about it."

They hummed and groaned and wiped the bowls clean with their index fingers, feeling no embarrassment because they both knew there was tapioca pudding and then there was *tapioca pudding*. He waited patiently for her to take her last lick, then gently took the cup from her fingers.

"Can I ask you a personal question?"

"After sharing your pudding with me? Of course."

"Do you have children?"

"No."

"Then why didn't you go back to your maiden name and just use Bonner as a pseudonym? I mean, would you have, if you hadn't started writing the Patty Ann stories as Ivy Bonner?"

"God, no. Changing my last name was always a huge incentive for marriage . . . to anyone." She chose water when he offered it or bottled sweet tea to drink.

"How bad was it?"

She took a sip of water. "When my dad's father came here

from Sweden, through Ellis Island, someone misread his surname Garde as Gardner. Being new and not wanting to rock the boat, he didn't say or do anything about it. Unfortunately, he gave his oldest son a very traditional Scandinavian name: Leif."

The corners of Craig's lips twitched. "Leif Gardner."

She nodded gravely. "Leif fell in love with my mother . . . Rose."

He put his elbow on his knee and his fist in front of his mouth before he muttered, "Rose Gardner."

"Mm. Now my mother doesn't believe in suffering in silence . . . or suffering alone. So when she had a daughter—me—she wanted to name me Daisy or Petunia or Orchid or Lily or—get this one—Mum."

He sucked air in between his teeth like something hurt, but his eyes were dancing with merriment.

"My dad talked her out of those and they compromised on Ivy, which is almost tolerable if you think of the alternatives."

"The other night you said you had a brother."

"Jay." He looked first confused, then disappointed. "That's the name he finally settled on . . . though his could have been much worse, too. Greene, Jersey—you know, for the state, the Garden State?—Spade, Tater—Tate for short—Sonny, Able, and, um . . . oh, or Bean." She shook her head at his silent chuckles. "Once again my father interceded, and his full legal name became Random J. Gardner. The J is just a J.

"We used to call him Randy until he hit puberty and the other kids were learning what they thought were dirty words . . . then he was a randy gardener and everyone would howl with laughter. So in college he went by RJ. He said the girls he dated spent most of their time trying to guess what the initials stood for, which was okay because he didn't really want to talk as much as he wanted to get in their pants. But by the time he graduated that was getting old, and he started wanting something a little more serious. So now he goes by Jay, and if anyone asks if he has a middle name, he says it's just J, and they don't think to ask if it's his *only* name."

"What does your mother think of that?"

"Oh, she did her damage. She doesn't really care how we

deal with it. And she was gracious when I decided to keep Bonner . . . though I did rely heavily on Patty Ann for my argument." Having cleared their palates with water and tea, Ivy picked up the turkey sandwich, took half, and handed the rest to Craig. "Tell me about this gazebo. I know it was your mother's wedding canopy. Why'd you move it down here?"

"I didn't." He considered her and collected his thoughts as he chewed, then answered. "Actually, Gus helped his father make this for my grandfather, who wanted it built in honor of his new baby daughter, Sophia. My mother. The idea was that she'd sun in it as an infant, learn to walk in it as a toddler, practice reading in it as she got older. I heard she was a bit of a tomboy, and when she had friends over, they used it as a fort against bad guys or a castle where she chased away dragons. Everyone used it, but it was hers, meant to be her wedding canopy when the big day came. Which it did, of course, and she and my father lived happily ever after for almost twenty-one years. She died when I was nineteen—pancreatic cancer. It . . . broke my dad. He just sort of checked out, emotionally." He sighed heavily and looked around. "He couldn't stand looking out the windows and seeing it, but he couldn't bring himself to destroy it either, so he made Gus move it down here, out of sight."

"I'm so sorry," she said, though it didn't seem enough. Nor was it sufficient to describe the ache in her heart or the certain knowledge of the pain he was feeling—as if it were her loss as well. "And I'm sorry I asked to use it. It didn't occur to me that it might be a special family place that strangers shouldn't—"

"No. Please. Come and use it every day if you want. I'm glad you love working here. It was built to be loved . . . for happy memories. My mother would be very pleased to know you're enjoying her canopy." He stood, kept his back to her as he inspected a support column and the railing beside it. "In fact, there was a time when I'd planned to have it restored and put back, up near the house, but . . ." After a moment he turned to her with a new, different, greater sorrow in his eyes that he tried to shrug off. "Time gets away from you, you know?"

"I do." She hurried to change the subject. "So did you want to go into the family business or did you do it because it was expected?"

"No, I wanted to. I couldn't wait to take over and do things my way." He shook his head at his youthful ignorance, bent his knee, and lowered himself to the railing, his back against the post. "I studied mining and geology in school. After I graduated I came back to work the mines while I got a Masters of Mining Engineering. Lots of paper on my walls but I still don't know as much as old Charley Mumford did when he came over here. Safer, more modern techniques of mining, certainly, but neither my granddad or my Dad or I got Charley's nose for great rock."

"You mean prospecting? Like for gold?"

"Well yeah, sort of, but you can find granite anywhere. Most of the North American continent is underlain with granite. There are deposits that are many miles long and wide and deep, and then there are smaller stocks like the original Mumford Mine." He tipped his head in the direction of the cliffs. "It's a very coarse-grained rock, so the prize is in the content of the rock, the minerals . . . mostly feldspar and quartz and some hornblende and mica. Then, depending on the combination and color of the minerals, you get a whole range of colors from white to yellow to gray and black; to pink and green and red and even blue. And because the minerals vary drastically, or not so drastically, from place to place, no two quarries produce the same color granite."

She listened attentively while he explained in simple terms all the uses for granite, aside from fine-looking countertops—sand, gravel, ready mix and asphalt concrete for highways, tunnels, dams, bridges . . . buildings, sidewalks, and patios . . . statues and tombstones. She'd already heard somewhere that granite was less porous than marble, which made it a harder stone and less susceptible to scratches and stains when used for countertops, but it interested her to learn that it was replacing marble as a building stone because it stands up better to acid rain and that some of the Egyptian pyramids were actually built of limestone and then covered in granite for its beauty and protection.

It wasn't until he got to the accessory minerals—apatite, magnetite, and zircon—that many of his words melted away, leaving only the deep rumbling sound of his voice rippling through her muscles—warm, relaxing, hypnotic.

". . . rare minerals deposited in the spaces in granite . . .

tourmaline and topaz . . ." and her hand slid from the arm of the chair and touched her drawing pad on the floor. While his rocks were seriously boring to her, his face was anything but. He was enjoying his topic, and his expressions were animated, his eyes lit from within.

"The feldspar in the granite contains some radioactive components. All natural rock material does." She glanced down to find her pad open to a clean sheet and a favorite 2B sketch pencil in her hand. "Granite is formed when cooled volcanic magma hardens over thousands and thousands of years, millions sometimes . . ."

Her gaze barely left his face as her hand guided the pencil down the page—over, across, and diagonally. She caught the strong lines of his chin and the softly squared symmetrical angles of his cheeks that had struck her that first day. But after that it got . . . well, it went all wrong.

". . . and as the granite breaks down over time the thorium, radium, and uranium release a colorless, odorless radioactive gas . . . you've heard of radon, right?"

"Sure. My mother has a detector in her house."

But her outline of his lips was a little askew and not full enough. Her hand slipped, not once but three times, as she attempted to capture the mold of his hair around his face and near his ear. She accidentally drafted a notch, a bump, on the bridge of his nose—she botched the rhinoplasty, and in the end even his eyes, his very best feature in her opinion, looked like someone else's.

". . . and in 2007 the Marble Institute of America announced the amount of radiation and radon released from granite countertops was inconsequential."

Ivy looked up when she became aware of the silence—their eyes met and he shrugged, saying, "Of course, there are those rare instances of young children growing buck teeth and rabbit ears, but like I said before, it beats fins and gills."

She stared at him as if she'd just woken up. "What?"

He laughed. "That's an interesting method of keeping your eyes from glazing over when you're bored. Do I get to see it?"

"Oh no. I wasn't bored I . . . No. It's not very good." Blood rushed to her face and burned in her cheeks. "I'm sorry. I like your face."

He grinned. "I like yours, too. Without remorse."

"No, I meant . . . I doodle. I draw a lot. All the time. Too much, probably. Even when I'm watching TV, but it doesn't mean I'm not paying attention."

"That's a relief. I'd hate to think I wasted all that hot air for nothing." She could tell he was still teasing her. He stood, took a step, and then held out his hand for her pad. "Mind if I look?"

"Yes. No. Not ordinarily, but this one didn't turn out . . . it doesn't even look like you. I'm better with still life. Faces are harder." And they were, but she had a real talent for drawing them . . . usually. "If you have the time, I'd love to try again. I can do better than this. Much better."

"Come on. How bad can it be? I promise not to laugh."

With care he pulled the pad from her grasp and turned it over. Embarrassed and dissatisfied, she waited with dread for his reaction. Here was a chance to impress him with her skill and talent and she hands him a . . . a stupid doodle!

She watched the animated face she'd been enjoying as he studied the sketch. The confusion in it she'd anticipated, but there was also a moment of recognition that not only surprised her but flattered her as well. She hadn't expected him to recognize anything of himself in the portrait. Yet, in the next second when he looked at her with raw pain and disappointment in his eyes, she began to panic. When his emotions finally settled on anger, she was stunned.

"I can do better." But she didn't want to try—clearly he was touchy about his looks.

"I think it's time for you to leave." He ground the words out as if speaking was the last thing he wanted to do—pinching her head off appeared to be at the top of his list. "If you're caught on my property again, I'll have you arrested."

"What?"

"You heard me. Pack up your junk and get out."

SIX

—→—

"Are you crazy?" she asked, even as she started gathering her supplies. "It was just a sketch. Not a very good one, I admit, but—"

"Look, lady, I don't know who you're working for or what you're up to, but it's over. And I'd start packing up over at the Rossinis', too, because once I tell them about your real purpose for being here, you'll be out on your ass."

"My . . . what real purpose? I write books for kids. I told you that." She zipped up her pack and stood. "What's wrong with you? I don't understand any of this."

"Like hell. . . . You used the Rossinis to get to me, wormed your way into my life, and then casually drew a picture of my brother to get my reaction for whatever story you're doing. I think your understanding is clear and very cunning." As an afterthought—and his most damning complaint—he added, "And cruel."

"You have a brother?" The veins in his neck engorged and his eyes went dead. "I didn't know. I didn't draw—"

"Right." He spit the word out like a curse and with such fury and hatred in his voice that she should have been terrified. Yet, as sure as she knew . . . well, anything, she knew he wouldn't touch her. "Get out."

"Fine. I will." Her ire rose to the occasion because she didn't want to cry. Confused, frustrated, and hurt more than she might have imagined, she stomped down the stairs and marched toward the cliff path, keeping her spine straight, refusing to look back at him.

She didn't get far before she heard him call out. "Where the hell do you think you're going?"

"Home, you idiot, like you told me."

"More games? Okay. I'll play if it'll make you disappear faster. You're cold. You're heading in the wrong direction. The path is back that way."

"I'm cold? Well, if I'm cold, you're . . . you're frozen," she hollered, slashing the air with her hands because she'd hoped for a better comeback. "And I know where the path is. Contrary to what you may want to think, I didn't fly over here on my broom, you know."

"Ivy? I'm serious. Knock it off. Turn around and leave."

"Make up your mind, Craig. Turn around or leave? Actually, you made your decision. You don't get to pick anymore. And I pick leave," she shouted, still heading for the cliff path. "I pick never seeing you again. I pick packing up and going home. I pick forgetting I ever met . . . you."

"Ivy! Stop!" His order came too late—she already had. "Ivy?"

She stood staring . . . at the rocks, the foliage, the cliff, the sky, the trees, and the ornate wrought-iron bench she'd drawn the day before. Her heated blood drained from her face, leaving it cold and tingling—her fingertips throbbed from a surge of raw adrenaline when she began to comprehend that there was no cliff path. There was only the dead-end alcove, though in her mind she could recall every step of every trip she'd taken along the well-worn trail . . . that didn't exist.

Her body was quaking as she turned, weak-kneed, back to the gazebo and Craig—to see if they really existed or if she'd made them up, too. There was no way she could make it back to them in time, to anchor herself, to keep herself from lifting off from the earth and into oblivion. She was alone, on the cliff, losing her mind. . . .

Craig moved. To the bottom of the steps. To thirty feet away and then fifteen—but he didn't seem to be walking, just flashing forward, toward her; it was taking forever. If only she could hang on till he reached her. *Hang on.* He was mad at her but he'd help her. He was . . . Craig. *Craig the Dependable. Craig of the Everthere.* The words echoed from a dark corner in her mind, over and over, attempting to soothe her.

Finally, he was there, taking a firm grip on her shoulders and shaking gently. "Ivy? What's wrong? Can you hear me? Talk. Speak to me. Tell me what's happening? Are you ill?"

Her head wobbled on her neck then settled on a nod.

"What's wrong? Talk to me, baby, tell me what I should do." He pulled her close, latched one hand to her waist, palmed her cheek with the other. She leaned back against his arm for support. He lowered his voice and spoke calmly. "What's happening?"

She glanced back to make sure the path was still missing— then let him pull her face back to his. She clung to his moss green gaze.

"The path is gone. I drew a whole story in my sleep. I hear things and see things, but nobody's there. I fall. All the time. In my sleep. I don't sleep. And I know things. I know things . . . like the silk and wisteria . . . like there weren't any bullets in the shotgun."

"What shotgun?"

"Gus's. And I knew him. He didn't recognize me, but I knew him. I did." His expression was becoming more and more confused. And alarmed. Worse, she could hear how completely nuts she sounded but she couldn't stop talking. "And the gazebo. I remembered it and it felt so . . . oh God, it was so peaceful and I felt so quiet . . . inside." She lifted a fist to her heart. "Like when I hear your voice."

His eyes broke contact then came back. "What about Oliver?"

Whoa. That came out of left field and pulled her up short. "Patty Ann's Oliver?"

"My brother Oliver."

"You have a brother named Oliver?"

"Had. He died. Two years ago."

"I didn't . . . I'm sorry."

I'm here! A voice whispered in her head. *I'm here.*

"I don't . . ."

Get it? You will.

Her knees finally gave out, and Craig followed her to the ground, breaking her fall. It felt as if she was entering a tunnel, backward—her vision growing darker and darker peripherally but focused on the light at the end. "He can't . . . he needs . . . he's a . . ." *Ghost.*

Good. Finally. Man, it took you long enough.

————

She came out of the tunnel facing the light, the foggy blackness receding at a crawl, her senses returning even slower.

Nausea and cold were the first signs of life she recognized. Voices, near and far, and then one particular intonation, low and soothing, that drew her like the moon pulled the tides.

"Yes, yes. Here she comes, Mr. Craig." A woman's voice. Ivy felt something cold and clammy pressed to her face, here, there. "She'll be dandy in a minute or two. She's only fainted, you see."

"Yeah?" The relief in his voice made her heart smile—he wasn't angry anymore. "Okay. So let's load'er up and get her to the hospital and—"

"No, no, no. She'll not thank you if she faints regular. Big fuss for nothing. Wait and see how she feels once she's full awake."

"You're sure?"

"Course."

"Here, give me the cloth. I can do that." A big sigh. "Go tell Gus to keep the motor running, will you?" A moment passed and she felt the clammy pressure on her face again. She reached up to push it away. "Ivy? Hi. Can you open your eyes for me?"

She did . . . and looked straight into his. They smiled and crinkled at the corners for her.

"I like your eyes."

"I come from a long line of miners, so I'm very attracted to the gold in yours."

He was—she could see it. His attraction, his passion, his desire to kiss her. A mighty temptation. Unfortunately, she was under the distinct impression she was falling in love with him, and what could be worse, more unfair, more unkind, more *unloving* than acting on it while in the process of losing her mind?

"What happened?"

He shook his head. "I don't know. You started talking crazy and passed out. I thought you were having a stroke or something, but Wanda said no. Do you faint often?"

"Never."

"Do you want to go to the hospital? Get checked out? We won't think brain tumor until we've ruled out everything else."

"No. No hospital."

Tell him, the voice in her head whispered. *Tell him I'm here.*

"Not yet. I have to tell you . . . Oliver—"

"Shhh. Don't. I'm sorry I accused you of lying. I should have believed you, trusted you. I'm sorry. Your sketch . . . there was a strong family resemblance between us. My brother and I . . . well, except for our hair. He had lighter, sort of reddish blond hair. And my mother's blue eyes. He was nine years younger but you could always tell we were brothers. I believe that you didn't know anything about him."

"Will you tell me about him?" She struggled up onto her elbows, and when he would have kept her prone, she smiled and shook her head as she pushed herself up and lowered her feet to the floor. "Was he a pain in the neck?"

Hey!

"Jay was, until we grew up. Still is, actually. Sometimes."

"Yeah, he had his moments." He laughed from his perch on a coffee table in front of the big soft leather couch she sat on. From the many mementos along the wall, she gathered they were in a family gathering place with a lot of oak and a deep, rich green and gold paper above the shelving, a huge fireplace, pictures and keepsakes everywhere. A comfortable room. "When he was little it was like having this really great pet you could teach to do tricks. Like sit up and walk and talk. Of course, after he mastered all that he was a pest. Following me everywhere, getting into my stuff . . . and he was so much younger he couldn't keep up. I constantly had to go back and get him, help him up, wait for him to catch up. And questions—he used to drive me crazy with questions." One corner of his mouth curved up. "I was pretty smart, though. I'd tell him to go ask Mom or Dad and off he'd go and then I'd hide from him. I was a horrible brother."

"At least you went back for him. I'd have left Jay in the dust if he hadn't been able to run faster than me. He's only fourteen months younger . . . and a *boy*, you know?"

"You like boys better now, though, right?" He grinned at her, playing hopeful.

"Some." She let her eyes tell him which one in particular, but then remembered the circumstances and lowered them away. "You and your brother became friends eventually?"

He leaned back physically—pulled back emotionally, reluctant to go on, but he did. "I don't know. I thought maybe . . . I hoped, but I don't know." He sighed heavily. "He was barely nine when our mother got sick. I was eighteen, ready for college. I wanted to stay home but my parents insisted that I go as planned, that they were going to lick the cancer. They didn't want me standing around like a ghoul waiting for her to die because it just wasn't going to happen. So I left. I drove home every other weekend to spend a few hours with her. She looked worse every time I saw her. It wasn't long before I was forcing myself to go home, using every good excuse I could think of not to but . . . I was there when it happened." He shook his head, laced his fingers together between his knees, and leaned on his forearms. "She warned me. She tried to tell me but . . . too much time went by before I realized . . . before I knew what she meant. I was too late."

"For what?"

"Oliver." He lowered his lids over the guilt and regret in his eyes, concealed his pain from her, kept it private and untouchable. "After . . . I stayed away as much as I could. I hated going home. It was like a museum—all these cold facts of the past, a lot of artifacts of what had once been a family but no sign of life. My dad was a hollow shell. He threw himself into the company. He started drinking. A lot. Oliver got kicked out of a new school every other month it seemed like. Dad finally put him in a military school." He stood suddenly, stepped to the front of the big empty fireplace and kept his back to her. "They damn near broke him completely. A school for delinquents was the last place he needed to be." His voice said he wanted to argue his point but there was no one there contradicting him.

"I stayed in school, nursed my sorrow in private, moved forward. Summers, and for four years after I graduated, while I worked on my thesis, I worked the mines. Most of them. Straight labor at first, then some of the heavy equipment. I drove a truck for a few months one winter in New Mexico. Just about the time I got good at something or started settling in, word would come down from on high that I was to go somewhere else, do something different. And that was okay." He shrugged. "It was part of the plan. He couldn't just turn the company over to some green kid fresh out of college. I needed to work my way up like my grandfather and my dad after him." He chuckled absently and half-turned to her. "Lucky for me I wasn't trying to marry the owner's daughter. Dad used to say his love was sorely tested."

"I bet." They shared a smile but all too soon his faded.

"Point is: Oliver was alone. I was older and still connected to Dad through the company, but Oliver was ten, eleven, twelve, then fifteen and sixteen, and without my dad or me, there was no one to support him or share his pain or show him how to go on without a mother . . . without a family, really. He tried shutting himself off like my dad did and running away like I had, and all it got him was a military school for 'last-chance kids'—that's straight from the brochure I found in my dad's desk after his funeral." A long moment passed before he spoke again, his voice strained with emotion. "He wasn't a last-chance kid." He cleared his throat and turned to her. "He also wasn't in that school anymore. I had to get special permission to check him out of court-ordered rehab so he could go to Dad's funeral. And I . . . I was like everyone else in his life who thought he was a spoiled little shit, a rotten rich kid who didn't care about anyone but himself."

She watched the battle in his expression as he tried to decide if he could reveal any more of his shame and sorrow—felt an urge to cry when his faith in her won out. He sat in the rich green and maroon striped high-backed chair beside the fireplace and crossed his legs, though he was anything but relaxed.

"It took his first suicide attempt to shake some sense into me. I stood at the end of his bed watching him after they pumped his stomach, waiting for the pills he took to wear off—waiting for him to come around and explain himself. I was mad . . . and so oblivious. For weeks he just sat in a chair in his room staring out the window, not talking to me or his therapist or the staff. Anyone. They had him on suicide watch because they suspected he'd try again first chance he got. One afternoon we were sitting there in the silence and I was racking my mind for answers, wondering what I should do with him next, wondering how my parents would have handled it, thinking how awful my mother would have felt if she'd known that her *sweet baby, Oliver*, had given up on the life she'd given him." He paused, took a deep breath, and let it out slow. "I must have said something out loud because he looked at me and said, 'How would I know? I can barely remember her.'

"I was so self-absorbed," he said, flashing his palms in failure. "All those years and I never once asked him what he was feeling or how he was handling . . . any of it. I didn't even think about it. I realized that what had started as a cry for a little attention had ended as a scream for help. Even if I had thought about it, I think I would have simply assumed Dad was handling it. My dad, the emotional zombie . . ."

"But you were young, too. You were learning to cope as best you could with your own life. Sorrow is . . . hard. It's personal, and everyone deals with it differently. You can't teach someone else how to grieve."

"No, but you can share it with them. You can be there and listen to them, pay attention and act like you care about them. My dad and I just wandered off and left him hanging. He was a kid. Dad . . ." He shook his head. "I should have been there for Oliver."

He was. Tell him he was . . . when it mattered most.

"Your dad's heart was broken." He nodded, looked away as if recalling. The voice in her head kept issuing orders, but she knew if she gave in to it she'd be lost. "Your parents must have loved each other very much."

A single chuckle bubbled loose in his chest and he smiled. "Embarrassingly so. My teen years were a nightmare. I couldn't go anywhere with them. I used to try to tell Oliver how awful they were . . . always holding hands and whispering to each other and laughing and sneaking kisses when they thought no one was looking. Mortifying. And he'd end up crying, from laughing so hard. And the more he laughed, the more I'd exaggerate . . . but not by much."

"Laughter's good. They say it's very healing."

He nodded, sobering. "I thought so, too. I did. And after that I hung around as much as I could. We moved out here permanently. He loved it here. We both did. We'd hang out. He went to AA meetings, stayed clean, and saw his therapist. He'd sit down there in the gazebo for hours writing in his journal, and every day I thought I could see him getting stronger and stronger. I thought he was getting better. I thought we were back on track . . . until he killed himself."

SEVEN

———◆———

No! No. Tell him!

"I'm sorry." She couldn't bear the distance between them, so she stood and went to kneel beside his chair. "I'm so sorry."

He took the hand she placed on his knee, held it with gratitude and relief. "People told me there was nothing I could have done differently, that I did the best I could, that he was clearly determined, but . . ."

"You feel like you missed something, like you could have done more."

He gave a slow nod as his gaze caressed her face.

Please. Help me. Now! Tell him.

His lips jerked into a crooked smile; their eyes met and his hand left hers to graze the back of his index finger down her cheek. "Would you like to hear something crazy?"

"Sure." It couldn't be crazier than the voice in her head.

"I dreamt about you."

That was crazy? "Not good dreams, I gather."

"Great dreams."

"Oh?" Even as heat rose to the top of her head, she was tempted to tell him that she'd trade his dreams for hers anytime.

A soft laugh rumbled in his chest. "Not quite that great . . .

at least not until after I met you. That dream's a more recent development. And I don't have to be asleep to have it." They grinned, unabashed, at each other. He leaned forward, using his left hand to curl over hers; the other slipped into her hair and cradled her face. "For months now I've been sleeping in as late as I possibly could, racing through my days and blowing off evening commitments just so I could go back to bed and back to sleep and back to dreaming of you."

For months? Well yeah, okay, that *was* crazy. She hadn't been here a whole month yet.

"I knew who you were the minute you turned around and screamed at me. I told you that you scared the hell out of me, too? You did. But it wasn't in the same way I startled you. I was really spooked. I couldn't get away from you fast enough." He chuckled. "First thing I did was go straight to bed for a nap. I never nap. Wanda and Gus were worried sick about me."

"But they're not worried anymore?"

"Because now you are?" He was amused but she was . . . Well, who was she to comment on his strange dreams?

"Not really. Not if you aren't, but . . ." She cocked her head. "Do you think they mean anything? I mean, do you think your dreams were trying to tell you something?"

"*Are* trying to tell me something . . . They haven't stopped. And yes, I do think they're trying to tell me something because it's always the same basic dream, over and over—more vivid now that I've met you, but they're basically the same. You save me. Seriously. You pull me out of the water into your boat. I'm down a well, I look up, see your face, and I know I'm saved. I'm hanging off the top of a tall building, you reach down and grab my arm, and I'm saved. The worst one . . . I'm in a sewer or a cave or a dungeon or something; it's dark and dank and it has rats. I hate rats, worse than snakes. They're lurking and scrambling closer to me. I call out. I know you're out there. I know you're looking for me. I know you'll save me. They're squeaking. Their teeth are three inches long, for Christ's sake. I yell . . ."

Screams! Like a girl!

". . . and then I'm outside in the sun, with you. I'm saved."

Tell him. Tell him! TELL HIM!

The voice grew so loud inside her head that she sucked in air at the sharp pain it caused behind her eyes. Automatically, she covered both ears in a futile attempt to muffle the sound.

"What is it? Ivy? What's wrong? What's happening?"

Testing, she lowered her hands and opened her eyes slowly. No voice, only Craig's anxious face. Her smile was feeble.

"Sorry. Aftershock, I guess. From the faint? It's gone now."

"You should lie down again." He stood and helped her to stand. "Come on, I'll take you upstairs. You can lie down, get some sleep. You'll feel better tomorrow. Or the hospital . . . let me take you to the hospital."

"No. I'm fine. Really."

"You're not. You're pale and—"

"Oh no." The words came as a soft whimper as she stood numbly staring at the wall opposite the fireplace, behind the couch, above a console table, at a portrait of a man and woman. "It's Ginger Cookie and . . ." She turned in Craig's loose embrace to face him. "She's your mother? Ginger Cookie? And the man's your father?"

He nodded, unmistakably baffled but without the distrust and resentment he'd had before. Now the confusion was mixed with deep concern. "Sophia. That's her name. How do you know he called her that?"

"I saw them. In the gazebo. In a dream. That's how I know that he wants me to set him free . . . except I think I'm going insane." Tears welled and slipped one at a time down her cheeks. "My mother's aunt, Betsy Marie, heard voices. And she talked back to them. She used to sit in corners and have long conversations with herself."

"Shhh. Here, let's sit."

"I haven't slept well in months . . . then when I did, in the gazebo, I finished an entire storyboard. In my sleep, Craig. In my sleep! And did I tell you I know things? Things I have no way of knowing?"

"Oh God, here we go again. Take deep breaths. Slow, in and out. I'll get Wanda—"

"No." She reached out and held his face with her hands. She sniffed and closed her eyes, squeezed the remaining tears out, and released him long enough to brush them away before making contact again—on either side of his neck below his ears.

The scruff of his beard was natural and grounding. "I'm fine. I promise. Physically, I'm fine. Mentally . . ." She took a moment to search his eyes with hers. They were patient, not scattered; curious, not critical; caring—and that's what she needed. "I don't know. I see it. I see that there's every outward indication that I'm certifiable, but I don't feel it. Inside, I don't feel it. Confused? Yes. Terrified? Yes. Delusional? Probably, but when I hear or see or know something I have no way of knowing, I'm as certain about it as I am of being here with you now." She paused. "That sounds like a textbook definition of delusional . . . and the cliff path is still a puzzle to me because I walked it, I did, half a dozen times or more, but it doesn't exist." She lowered her hands reluctantly from his neck to her lap and bowed her head. "I guess I am insane."

"No. We'll figure—"

Help me. Tell him.

"Oh, for crying out loud, tell him what?" she cried out to the ceiling, hands pleading. "I've told him everything I can think of." She glanced at Craig and assessed the shock in his face. It was amazingly mild. With a defeated sigh, she decided: in for a penny . . . "I also hear voices. Inside my head."

He didn't break eye contact with her. "Tell me about them. What do they say to you?"

"Not them. Him. He says, 'Help me, tell him, free me.' Sometimes he gets a little . . . snide with sarcastic remarks."

Who, me?

"He wants you to tell me something?"

"I guess. Or Gus. You're the only two 'hims' I've seen since he started talking."

"And this has all started since you got here? The seeing things and the voice?"

Tell him. Tell him about the dream.

"What is it?" he asked, noting the expression on her face—it begged forgiveness for what she was about to say.

"I told you about the dream of your parents, in the gazebo?" He nodded. "There was a little boy there with them—blond, freckles across his nose—it's him. The voice is his."

"Oliver." The name came on a whispered breath. She nodded, though she would have given anything to save him the pain.

"I'm so sorry."

He leaned back into the couch beside her and laced his fingers in his lap, pondering the possibilities. He wasn't yelling at her to leave or glowering with fury—she let hope take root.

After a few minutes, he said, "What are you supposed to tell me?"

"About the dream, I guess. That's all he's told–"

The other dream. The other dream.

"The falling one?"

"What?"

"I think he wants me to tell you about a different dream. I've been having it for months. Long before I got here."

"He's talking to you now? This moment?"

She gestured yes.

"Can he hear what we're saying?"

"I guess. He sounds annoyed that I'm not telling you what he wants you to know." She didn't hesitate to add, "It wouldn't kill him to be more specific."

She heard laughter and turned to Craig . . . who wasn't laughing, and in a sudden moment of pure horror realized what she'd said. "Oh God. I didn't mean kill him, kill him. I meant . . . I'm . . . Stop it. It isn't funny."

"He's laughing?"

"Jerk," she muttered.

Craig turned more completely toward her, eager to try something. "That last week while I was away he took my *pristine*, fully restored 1970 Chevelle LS6 454 big-block V8 hardtop Coupe out for a joyride. Where'd he put the damn keys?"

Backseat ashtray. Rider's side.

"He says they're in the ashtray in the backseat on the rider's side."

"Wait here." He hurried from the room and returned the same way—stood in the doorway panting and held up a set of two shiny keys. "I told you what would happen if you took it again."

"He says you're too late."

His body sagged with the weight of the truth. His steps were heavy as he crossed the room and stood looking down at her. He looked deep into her eyes, half-dreading what he might see in them. He smiled, seeing only Ivy.

"I'd forgotten how clever he was." He sat back down beside her and took her hand. "He was good at worming himself into people's heads. And if anyone could figure out how to do it from his grave, it would be him."

"You believe me?"

He held up the keys. "You're not crazy, Ivy. You're possessed."

"What? No."

The look on her face must have been something—he laughed, but not in an unkind way. "It's okay."

"No. I don't think it is. Last I heard it was not okay to be possessed. In fact, I think I'm leaving." She started to get up, but he held tight to her hand.

"Where are you going?"

"Home. If I'm turning into Linda Blair, I want my mother to be there." Standing, she muttered an afterthought. "I hope there's a tea for this."

"Please, Ivy, stay. We can talk about it. End it maybe, right here, right now."

She studied the conviction in his face and had nothing better to refute it with. Looking up at the man and his Ginger Cookie in the portrait and down again at the keys in Craig's hand, dream and reality swirled together as if her hard drive were frying. She felt herself begin to shut down, one system at a time—she needed to reboot. She was exhausted, physically and emotionally, beyond confused mentally, and if what he was saying was true, her spirit was not entirely her own.

"We can talk. But does it have to be now? I'm . . . I don't know how much more of this I can take. I need time to think this through. So much has happened. My head aches."

No. Free me. Tell him.

"And I'm so . . . loud inside." She spread her fingers and shook her hands, desperate and frustrated. "I need quiet. Peace. Real sleep. I need my head back . . . to be me again so I can sort this out." She used her last ounce of energy on a deep sigh. "Look, I'm sorry. I want to help him—"

"No." He stood quickly. "Don't apologize. I can't even imagine . . . You're amazing. I'm sorry I didn't see the toll this was taking on you. You can stay in the guest room. Sleep, whatever. Take all the time you need. We . . . What is it?"

"I'm going home. To the Rossinis'. I need to be alone. But more to the point, you're more distracting than Oliver."

He wanted to argue, to take care of her, to protect her, but he acquiesced with good nature. "That's pretty great, right? For me? To be more distracting than a ghost."

She smiled and used the hand he still held to squeeze his. "Actually, it's pretty great for me, too." On an impulse that was all her own, she went up on the balls of her feet to settle a quick good-bye kiss on his lips. "I'll call you tomor—um!"

His mouth took hers with an urgent passion that was so hot and wild it sent waves of shock and excitement and . . . well, more and more excitement like ever-increasing volts of electricity shooting down through her body to her toes and back up, then down to her toes again and back.

Aw, gawd!

Ivy snorted a giggle and pulled away, but he didn't let her get far. "What?"

"I think we grossed out Oliver."

"Tough." He tipped her chin up and kissed her again, soft and slow. "I've wanted to do that since that first dream, the first time you saved me."

"Since I wasn't there, I'm glad you waited."

"And aren't you glad we aren't being recorded right now? Anyone listening would have to wonder what we've been smoking."

They both had a nervous laugh for the strangeness of the reality they were living. They both knew there was no one else in the world they could share this particular experience with, and they both knew it as a good thing—a very good thing.

"At least let me drive you . . . or Gus can. For my sake. I want to make sure you get there in one piece." In jest, he shook a finger at her. "No more taking the cliff path, understand?"

She blinked at him twice, was aware he was teasing—as aware as she was that she'd taken the cliff path, that didn't exist, too often to simply brush it off as part of a dream.

"No. You're right. It's not funny yet." He gathered her in his arms and she leaned into him for comfort. "But it will be. I promise. Someday we'll look back at all this and we'll laugh. People will ask how we met and we'll say, 'In a dream.' Then we'll look at each other and we'll laugh. Trust me."

"Oh, see now, that's the drawback to the valerian root," her mother said a short while later. It was early evening, the sun was down, and darkness pressed against the many windows. "It works but there's such a letdown once you stop taking it. Actually, since it helps you calm down and relax, it's probably a let*up* when you stop taking it . . . but either way it's not this quick, generally. Although as we agreed this morning, everyone reacts differently, don't we?"

That was just this morning? It felt like a year ago to Ivy.

"No, I think it's still working, Mom. I can hardly keep my eyes open, I'm so sleepy."

"You're not taking too much, now, are you? Only take what I prescribed . . . just the way I told you to take it or—"

"No, Mom. I'm not. Everything's working. Just like you said it would."

Jeez. Harp much, Mom?

"Butt out."

"What did you say?" Her mother's voice had that pre-spanking tone of yore.

"I said . . . it's a shutout. You know, like in baseball when the pitcher is having a really good day, everything's working for him, he pitches a perfect game, and no one on the other team makes a run? Well, that's me. Everything is working great—me, my book, everything."

"Oh. I'm so glad, honey. I've been worried."

"I know. I'm sorry."

Nice save.

"Don't be sorry, sweetie, just be well. That's all I want."

"I know. And I am. I'm much better. Coming up here was exactly what I needed."

My idea.

"I'm so glad. It came to me out of the blue, and I just knew you'd love it up there."

"I do. And now I'm going to bed. I have something to take care of first, but I wanted to check in before it got too late."

"It's ten after eight."

"I know. I'm beat. I'll talk to you tomorrow."

"Sleep well, honey."

"Leave my mother alone. Stay out of her head," she told the air as she disconnected. "I'll do my best to help you, but leave her alone."

Free me.

"Tomorrow . . . if you let me sleep tonight."

EIGHT

---◆---

So, technically, she should have asked for a sleep without dreams—but who thinks of technicalities when they're dead on their feet?

Still, even in sleep she balked at the cliff path, turning away, running, running, searching for the path through the woods, fully aware the cliff path no longer existed . . . never existed . . . and that the overhang was far more dangerous than she'd realized.

The sounds of their laughter and low-pitched voices filtered through the trees and beckoned her like the scent of hot chocolate on a snowy afternoon. She emerged, not from the trees but from the house behind the gazebo. Mumford Manor, Gus had called it, a gorgeous Victorian Stick house—Craig's family's summer home. Then, abruptly, she was heading for the gazebo . . . from the cliff side as she always had before.

They were as before: Lit with life in a black-and-white picture—the rugged-looking, handsome man stood to one side of the woman's chair, the boy at her feet.

She could smell the wisteria as she got closer, which she did slowly, a sense of foreboding heavy in her chest.

The boy looked up, saw her, and smiled.

I've been waiting for you, he said, as he had before.

"I know."

She was a car length away but couldn't get closer.

I'm Oliver.

"I know."

He went back to his trucks and cars and his parents remained unaware of her presence, speaking softly in words she couldn't quite make out. The three of them were happy and content, impervious to everything outside the canopy.

Please help me.

"I'm *trying*. You have to tell me exactly what you want me to do. I've never done this before. Be specific. Tell me what to do."

Free me.

"Oh, for God's—"

All three of them turned to look expectantly at the house. Oliver jumped up and ran to the top of the stairs to watch an older boy, a young teen, leave the colorless house and cross the neat, dark lawn toward them—a fishing pole over his shoulder, tackle box in hand. The blatant adoration on the youngster's face was heart-cracking.

They all smiled down on the newcomer when he stopped a few feet away. He grinned and Ivy recognized him immediately, though his face was still midtransition to the man she knew. He spoke to his family, the sound of his words coming from such a distance that she could only grasp the intent—no plan to join them at the moment, he was going fishing.

That's when Oliver turned his head to look at her directly and fill her head with his voice.

Tell him.

Though his lips hadn't moved and the moment was brief, his brother caught his temporary distraction and followed his gaze to her.

"Ivy?" The young Craig knew her, was shocked and confused.

"Craig?"

After a moment's hesitation, he made the jerking gestures of several false starts: run to her, point her out to his parents, run to her, drop his gear, or return to the house. . . . Finally, he stood as he was, staring through the open sides of the gazebo at her. Helpless.

And as was the mystery and trickery of dreams, she would

have gone to him but remained annoyingly stationary. "Are you here? I mean, are you just part of my dream or . . . what's happening?"

"This is your dream?"

"I think so. Have you had this dream before?"

He looked at his family, the bright white gazebo, and shook his head.

"I have. This is the one I told you about. This is how I knew he called her Ginger Cookie because of the color of her hair. I can't make out most of what they're saying to one another but I knew that . . . like I knew the other stuff."

No, I knew the other stuff.

"You knew . . ." She looked back at Oliver, who seemed completely oblivious to her.

You feel as I feel. Know as I know.

"Yeah? Then maybe now's the time to ask how and why me?"

You let me. I let you.

"What? Is this what all dead people do? Talk in riddles? You're driving me crazy. Think maybe this is how ghosts got a bad reputation? Because I'm sick of it." Her attention was diverted back to the boy, the uncolored Craig, as he beat at the air with his pole and box at the bottom of the canopy steps. His parents and joyful younger brother continued to smile down on him, seeming not to notice his frantic attempt to join them.

"Craig." She spoke softly, with a calm she was far from feeling. The fear and anger and pain in the boy's face were unlike any she'd seen before. She longed to touch him, to ease his torment, but she didn't know how. In her heart she stretched out to embrace him, but it was Oliver she begged to help him.

Tell him was his reply.

"Craig. Look at me."

His thrashing slowed gradually, reluctantly, and eventually he gave up and looked her way. "Why won't they talk to me like they're talking to you? Why won't they let me in?"

"Only Oliver's talking to me . . . if you want to call it talking."

"Then tell him to let me in. Tell him I need to talk to him. Tell him it's important." He let loose a defeated sigh. "Tell him I'm sorry I let him down."

Tell him. Tell him!

"He can't let you in. It's not your time. You need to go ahead and go fishing. They're fine and they'll be waiting for you when it's time for you to join them." Wearily, she added, "And don't ask me how I know that because it's not what he said."

"What'd he say?"

" 'Tell him. Tell him.' " She crossed her legs and sank down onto the grass. Tiny pink and white flowers sprouted and bloomed everywhere. "So I told you."

"Why the hell doesn't he talk to me?"

She lay back in the grass. The sky was bright blue and the clouds were tall and billowy with flat bottoms—her favorite kind. "He tried, but you wouldn't listen to him." Stars twinkled beside a big full moon. "Which, frankly, I find amazing, since I don't seem to be able to ignore him at all. Do you think we'll remember talking to each other when we wake up?" A rainbow arched through the sky repeatedly like a neon sign. "Although, considering the dreams I've been having lately, this one is pretty tame."

She heard birds chirping in the woods and the sound of the waves from the bottom of the cliffs . . . but no Oliver . . . or Craig. Rolling her head slightly in the grass, she glanced at the gazebo. And there with her forearms flat on the railing and her chin on the back of her hands, Patty Ann Pettigrew stared back at her.

"Oh, hey. Hi." She was on her feet again. "What are you doing here?" She looked around for Craig. The canopy was empty—a drab gray sketch of the structure except for Patty Ann. "Where is everyone?"

"I need a dog. Or a goldfish." The little girl stood up straight and put her hands on her hips, determinedly. "All kids have pets."

"I didn't."

"You had Jay. I want an iguana."

"No lizards."

"What about a bang, bang, bang?"

"A what?"

"Wake up."

"What?"

"Answer the window."

Patty Ann, the gazebo, the stars, the tiny flowers, and the rainbows went to black and were replaced by the rapid-fire sounds of knuckles on glass.

"Ivy, wake up!"

With a groan and a grunt she threw off the covers and staggered to the curtains covering the sliding glass door that led to the flagstone patio at the back of the house. She didn't need to lift the curtain to know who it was, it was simply automatic while her other hand fumbled with the buttons on the security alarm.

"Finally! Open this." His face was in shadow by the motion lights as he rattled the door by its handle. She slipped the security bar and unlocked the door, and he was on her before she could open her mouth. "Judas priest, woman, you sleep like the dead." He scolded even as he held her so tight she could scarcely draw air. "I thought you were dead."

Her lips tangled in his T-shirt when she tried to speak. He slackened his grip but didn't let go. "Why? What's happened? What made you think I was dead?"

That's when she felt him trembling; his muscles tight as piano strings. It was too dark to see his face clearly, but his hands were shaking when she pried them from around her waist and pulled him over to the bed to sit down. He tossed his flashlight on the bed and let his knees—his whole body—go limp. Bending at the waist, she turned on the lamp on the bedside table and felt his head come to rest against her abdomen before she could right herself. He held her around the waist; she caressed his hair, then his face, and whispered, "Talk to me. What happened?"

His shoulders shuddered with a derisive chuckle and he shook his head. "A dream. A nightmare, but it was so real . . ." He looked up at her with beleaguered eyes. "Look, I know it's too soon. I know we barely know each other, but you need to know that it's important to me that nothing happens to you. That *you* are important to me."

"I know. And I'm fine. Nothing's happened to me."

"You went over the cliff. In the dream. Like Oliver."

In her mind she saw the furious bashing of the waves against the cliff wall and flinched. "That's how Oliver died?"

Falling, falling, falling . . .

"We were talking, in the dream. You were dressed in a long white dress and you were . . . You are so beautiful." She smiled, not pretending she didn't understand that he meant in the dream *and* at that moment—even in her way cool oversized T-shirt and mismatched baggy boxers. "My parents were there, and Oliver. Except for you, it was a typical scene from our past, I guess. We practically lived in that old gazebo when my mother was alive. She loved it. My dad was still young and happy. We all were and—"

"You were going fishing." It wasn't a question.

His eyes narrowed and he tipped his head to one side as he gave her a slow nod. "Oliver wouldn't talk to me. He hates me."

"He adores you."

"He only talked to you, and they wouldn't let me be with them. They shut me out."

"It isn't your time," she said, repeating it from her dream.

He pressed his lips together, looked away, and returned quickly to her eyes. "We had the same dream."

"Weird, huh?" In truth, she was getting accustomed to weird.

"Very."

"Does this mean we're both possessed, or is it still just me?"

"I don't know." He reached out and touched her from elbows to hands, holding tight, making certain she was real, sure she was there. He wore flip-flops and flannel sleep pants—he hadn't bothered with a jacket against the chilly mountain night—yet his palms were fire hot against her skin. "All I know is you were there and then you were gone and all I could see were the cliffs and . . . I knew. God forgive me, I wanted to follow you over. Go with you. I tried. I fought. They just stood there smiling down at me. I couldn't make it . . . you know, go. Move."

"You couldn't make the dream change, couldn't control it."

"Yes. I woke up in a cold sweat and, well, here I am. I just needed to make sure you're okay."

She let her smile reflect her well-being—waited for his to do the same, weak and tentative as it was. "Do you still think the dreams mean something? What do you think they were trying to tell you?"

"That I don't want to live without you."

She cradled his face with her hands; he reclamped his around her wrists, unwilling to break his connection to her.

They stared at each other, making wordless declarations and promises with their eyes, seeing truth in the soul of the other. Their eyes closed slowly as she bent to press her lips to his forehead. She kissed each cheek and pressed them in gently with her thumbs. The temptation his lips presented was sore and raw, but it suddenly felt too imperative to be out from under Oliver's influence before they went any further.

His eyes opened, dreamy, awash with passion and desire. Studying her expression, it was his lopsided smile that gave away his understanding and reluctant agreement. With a light touch, he pulled her hands from his face and held them in front of him. "Okay. So what else could the dream mean?"

"Beats me."

He was thoughtful for a moment. Reluctantly, he released her right hand when she moved to sit beside him on the bed. "Why isn't it my time, Ivy? Why won't Oliver talk to me, too?"

"Why won't he just tell me what he wants you to know? Why is he making it so complicated?"

"I don't know. All I do know . . . well, what I believe is that this happens more often than most people think. Being haunted, being possessed. Not always by demons or evil spirits and not always in this exact same way, but in similar enough ways to make it a real possibility.

"In the Bible, for instance, Jesus healed lots of demon-possessed people . . . Once He even sent a herd of demons from two men into *two thousand* pigs, they say. But over and over you read of people coming under the influence of the Holy Spirit, too. And they always make that sound like a good thing. For centuries Indian shamans and priests have been mediators between their people and the spirit world. Even in Islam they have angels and jinns.

"Oliver told me that for years after Mom died he'd feel her—touching his hair as he drifted off to sleep. Or sometimes, when he was looking for some way to get back at Dad for something, he'd feel her disapproval or disappointment and back off. He said he knew how weird it sounded but when he was younger, right after she died, when he cried, he could smell her perfume and feel her arms come around him and hold him. He said eventually she just went away, like everyone else, and he stopped caring—about anything."

He sighed. "I've had time to think about that, though, and I think it happened the other way around, you know? The older and angrier he got, the harder he tried not to care, and the easier it became to ignore any comfort she might have been able to give him."

"So you think he was possessed, too?"

"Maybe. I don't know." He gave her a gentle smile. "I don't know." He looked down at their hands, knotted together. "When we moved out here, after he left rehab, I worried about him spending so much time alone down in the gazebo. At first I just talked about moving it back where it belonged—keeping to myself that it would be easier to keep an eye on him if it was closer to the house. He was all for it. Eventually, I finally asked him why he enjoyed it so much. Was it all the memories or the view or whatever? He said it made him feel quiet inside." He looked at her. "That's what you said. Before you fainted, you said it made you feel quiet inside, like when you hear my voice."

"It does." She nodded. "You do."

Moved and pleased, he smiled. After a moment he looked away to retrieve his thoughts. "Oliver asked if I thought it was possible that Mom might be reaching out to him there. He said sometimes he had that feeling—not in a creepy, scary way, just sort of a caring, watching-over-him way—but trusting his own emotions wasn't something he was real good at yet, not with any certainty. Like I'd know anything about things like that," he said, glancing at her again. "But I'd vowed I'd never blow him off again, so I suggested we both look into it, together. It was . . ." He broke off, searching for the right word. "Great. On so many levels. We went together and talked to priests and rabbis and ministers, a Buddhist monk and a couple of philosophy professors. A psychic. Anyone we thought of, we talked to. But best of all, we talked to each other. All the time. And not just about this. Everything. Girls. Cars. The company. Going back to school eventually. Video games. You name it. I loved it. I—" He stopped abruptly and glanced away, frowning.

"What?"

"I thought I was getting to know him again. He was getting to know me. Trust me." He looked back at her. "I don't know what happened. I don't know what went wrong. And I know . . ."

I know I shouldn't wish this on someone I care about, but there's a part of me that hopes *you are* possessed, that it's Oliver, and . . ." He blew out a breath. "Why won't he talk to me? Why won't he let me in?"

She didn't know any more than he did. Not for sure. But this kettle of fish had been brewing on her front burner for a long time, and it was finally showing signs of a boil. . . .

"I think I might have a theory on that."

NINE

"What if . . ." She couldn't believe she was going to say it out loud; couldn't even look him in the eye as if she were serious. "What if the gazebo is their heaven?"

She held her breath, and when he didn't speak, she peeked at him—he was patiently waiting for more.

"What if those few minutes, there in the gazebo with a small Oliver and you at thirteen, on your way fishing, is their perfect, heavenlike moment, the one they wouldn't mind spending eternity in?" He was still listening. "What if they won't let you join them because it isn't your time, you're not dead yet? And Oliver can't talk to you directly because . . . well, it isn't part of that scene? I mean, he can talk to me because I'm not a part of it. I'm looking in from the other side." Now he was thinking about it and she got bolder. "What if you couldn't hear what Oliver was saying to me in the dream because you were on the wrong side of the gazebo? What if you were on my side with me?"

That was one step too far, he looked up frowning and confused—she'd lost him.

"I tried to get to you. I wanted to. But I couldn't even drop my fishing gear. I had no control."

"No, I know. In a dream you don't, you can't control it. Not in ordinary dreams."

"Ordinary dreams."

She nodded. "The kind we generate on our own, from our own subconscious, that neither one of us has had in several months." She watched dawn break in his eyes. "Oliver's been controlling our dreams. Mine certainly, and yours, too, I suspect, since you saw me before I even got here."

"Okay. So how do I get back into the dream on your side of their heaven?"

She looked at him, shook her head, and passed her free hand through her hair in disbelief. "I feel like we're already there, in the same bizarre dream I've been having for weeks. You were right before, about it being a good thing no one's recording us. We sound completely nuts."

"What's your point?" he asked, deadpan . . . and then they both laughed with as much relief as humor.

Taking a deep breath, she jumped in with both feet. "Let's go with it, then. Completely nuts, I think we should start our dream in the same place, together."

He looked askance, and her gaze drifted over his shoulder to the head of the bed, where one pillow lay indented, the other not. When her eyes came back to his, he was asking something else.

"Knock it off. First we help Oliver. Focus."

He made a minor production of it. "We sleep together. Literally. Then what?"

She shrugged. "We let Oliver take over." She stood and started padding toward the bathroom. "If it works, we get firm with him." She went through the doorway. "We're a united front. Okay? We finish this here and now and no more riddles or talking in circles. He tells us what he needs us to do to free him, tells you whatever it is he needs to tell you . . . and you say what you need to say, and then it's over. All right?"

Finished, she lingered in the doorway and turned out the bathroom light, though the lamp on the bedside table still shed plenty to reveal him lying on his side in her bed, head propped on one hand as he grinned and patted the bed next to him with the other.

Raising one deadly brow in jest and pointing an admonishing index finger at him, she reiterated in a mostly serious fashion, "All right?"

"All right. All right." He chuckled when he leaned back and stretched out his arm to turn out the lamp as she got to the bed. "I don't want my kid brother lurking around in your head the first time we make love any more than you do, so let's make this work. I'm getting jumpy."

"Jumpy, huh." She got into bed next to him—even though she was lying stiff as a board along the very edge of her side of the bed, she was aware of every breath he took. His long arms and legs took up a lot of room. It was a king-sized bed, and she felt like he was all over it. She could feel his body heat a foot away . . . and was a little jumpy herself.

"Mm, jumpy. Under my skin. All pins and needles like my body's been asleep for the past ten years. Tingly, you know? Jumpy." Yes! She got it. She knew. "And whether you're lying eighteen inches away or not it doesn't change anything. I feel this way just knowing you're in the neighborhood . . . in the northern hemisphere . . . on the planet, actually." The sheets rustled and pitched when he turned toward her. "So don't you think it'd be easier for Oliver if we were closer together?"

She rolled her head to face him—the shadow of his shoulders and torso loomed like a sloping mountain range. "How much closer?"

"Oh, say, share-a-pillow close." Those were the words he used but the low, rich rumble of his voice made it sound like in-my-arms, smell-your-hair, kiss-your-neck close.

"Anything to make it easier on Oliver." Sportingly, she began to scoot to the center of the bed, and next thing she knew, he had her tucked against his body—her back to his chest—one arm under the pillow supporting her head, the other wrapped tight around her middle. "Ah . . . are you . . . are you really, really, really happy to see me or did you bring a missile to bed?"

"A what?"

"A metal pipe maybe?"

After a bit of thrashing about, he started to laugh. "You're going to be so disappointed." A blinding beam of light shone on the far wall when he flipped on the flashlight that he'd retrieved near her ankles. "Sorry."

"Don't be. I'm faint with relief."

They laughed and settled in again; any tension they felt was dispelled and replaced with an intimate sense of sharing a common purpose. They took comfort in the other's presence. Ivy grew warm and effortlessly relaxed in Craig's arms.

She sat on the ornate bench overlooking the cliffs, waiting, spinning a daisy stem between her thumb and index finger. To pass the time she started plucking petals, slow and deliberate, one at a time, kissing the *loves me* and eating the *nots*.

She ate a rose the same way.

And just as a cluster of lilacs appeared on her lap, Craig—clutching a fistful of tulips—asked what the hell was she doing?

"Petal roulette, of course."

"Oh." Like that made perfect sense to him. "Try these."

His hand was empty when he held it out to her, but she was just as happy taking it as any flower he might offer. "What took you so long? I could have eaten a whole garden by now."

"I waited to make sure you fell asleep. I didn't want to come alone." They walked hand in hand between the trees. "I don't want to be alone. Ever again."

"Okay." She wrote that down in a memo pad.

They came upon the gazebo in the niche in the woods—faded, chipped, and unoccupied. Craig crumbled like a fragile house of cards. "It didn't work. He isn't here."

"Sure it worked. We're here. Together." She pulled him toward the canopy. "He's here somewhere."

They looked everywhere, leaping from one side of the clearing to the other, bouncing off trees like ninja warriors, until Ivy arrived cliffside to peer over the edge. She was reluctant at first—afraid of what she might see, knowing now how Oliver had taken his own life. But she was quick to squash her qualms—better she looked than Craig.

"Don't," he said from behind her. She could feel him, unsteady and fearful, all around her in a tight embrace. "Stand back. Stay away from the edge. I can't lose you, too."

Smiling, she turned in his arms and wrapped her arms around him. With her head on his chest she listened to the rapid tattoo of his heartbeat and felt the heavy heaving of his chest as he fought his terror. "You won't lose me. I promise. Try to remember we're dreaming. We're here together. We're safe and—"

Yo ho ho! echoed in the wind. *Ahoy, me maties. Arrrg.*

Thrilled, they both threw wide their arms as if to burst into song.

"Oliver!"

"He's a pirate?"

"No, he's a jerk," she said, marching to the rim to take a look. Craig couldn't make himself get closer or he, too, would have seen a near-grown man bobbing erratically on the waves in a wooden rubba-dub tub. "You know, if you were my brother, I'd push you off this cliff myself. Who do you think you are? Do you have any idea what you've put him through?"

You gotta love her.

She spun around to see the brothers picnicking on a black plaid blanket in the shade of the trees.

"I do." Craig patted the blanket next to him, and she was suddenly seated next to him—frowning malevolently at Oliver. "So maybe we should talk about what you've been putting *her* through. Apologize maybe?"

I tried to tell you, bro. I wanted to keep it between the two of us but you wouldn't listen to me. I couldn't get through all the guilt and anger and . . . His expression changed to a humble gracelessness that Ivy found extremely endearing. *And the pain, the sorrow. Thanks for that, man. Thanks for missing me.*

"Oliver." He became urgent, finally taking in who he was talking to—and how. It was an opportunity not likely to present itself again. "I love you. You're my brother. I'll always miss you. I'll always be sorry I wasn't there for you that night. I failed you. I'm sorry I—*ooph.*"

Oliver knocked him over, sat on his chest, and closed his mouth with his hand . . . and not too far away Ivy plucked a wildflower from the grass and popped it in her mouth—the taste was bright yellow.

No more sorrys! You got it? Don't you see that you saved me? You gave me a reason to live, man. You gave me hope. He lost a little steam. *I'm the one who should be sorry. I'm not,* he said after a brief search of his soul. *But I should be. I was so pissed off at everyone all the time. I let my anger rule my life for so long . . . I did a lot of stupid shit. I guess I can't blame you for just assuming I jumped. Which I didn't. But even*

*if I had, it wouldn't have been your fault. You did your best for
me. You know you did. You were great, in fact. Those last
couple of years with you, they were the best, man. I was happy.
But more important, remember that I have a will of my own.*
He paused to display their surroundings with the palm of his
hand. *I haven't always been able to do stuff like this, but I
always made my own choices. My life was mine. I was the
decider, not you. It's lame, man, and pretty damn conceited
to think you had that much control over me.*

With no effort at all, Craig reached up and peeled his brother's hand from his mouth—not that he needed it to state, "You
didn't jump."

No. He looked over at Ivy. He rolled off his brother and
leaned back in the grass on his elbows. *Which the flower-eating
dragon lady could have told you weeks ago if she was any good
at interpreting dreams. I couldn't have made it any plainer for
her.*

" 'It was a dark and stormy night; the rain fell in torrents,' "
she quoted Sir Edward George Earle Bulwer-Lytton, First
Baron of Lytton, with great élan around a mouthful of highly
addictive buttercups. " '—except at occasional intervals, when
it was checked by a violent gust of wind which swept up the' . . .
well, up the cliff in this case. And down the hillside and
through the trees. It was terrible. And the lightning and the
noise . . .' "

What happens?

"I slip in the mud and fall." Her eyes lifted to Oliver's steady
gray-blue gaze. "You slip. You fall." Her mind flashed on the
few quick glimpses she'd caught of his last moments, the panic
and horror; the desperate screaming desire to save himself, to
live . . . the raw realization and acceptance . . . Tears rivered
down her cheeks. "Oh, Oliver."

Aw, gawd.

Dashing the back of his hand over one eye, Craig wrapped
his other arm around her and gave a reassuring hug. "Girls,
huh? Remember how Mom could laugh so hard she cried?"

I remember everything now.

"Yeah? Including what I said about you taking my Chevelle
out?"

I was about to die, man.

"Now that I know you didn't know that . . ."

Ivy chuckled and cheered as Craig chased Oliver around and through the old gazebo in a brotherly ritual they'd performed a hundred times or more—laughing, stumbling, shouting grisly threats. This time, however, when the younger was caught, there was no noogie or dangling spit over his face. Craig clutched him in his arms, shook him, held him a few moments more, kissed his cheek, held him, and finally whispered something in his ear before reluctantly letting him go.

They stared at each other long and hard, saying things with their eyes that no words had been made for . . . until Ivy sniffed back her tears and broke the silence. She intended to call Jay first thing in the morning. Craig smiled and started toward her—Oliver beat him to her side.

Ask.

"Why me?"

I tried everyone in his near future and you were the only one who let me in.

"His near future?"

The Rossinis will be planning a Glad to Be Back party in the fall. Your mother would have brought you. I just rushed things along.

"So you can just pop in and out of my head . . . whenever?"

Nah. I've done what I needed to do. I'm leaving and I'll close the door on my way out.

"The door?"

Whatever it was that made you susceptible to me—I don't know, being unsuspecting, being creative and imaginative . . . open-minded? Maybe it was just destiny. But whatever it was, it isn't there anymore. You'll be wary now, and that closes doors on all sorts of possibilities. He nudged her gently with his elbow. *Lighten up. It's okay. In this case it's a good thing. I'm pretty sure my brother doesn't want his wife running around talking to dead people. Not to mention how horrible you are at it.*

"Bite me." Irrespective of her words, they grinned fondly at each other.

Thanks, Ivy.

It wasn't like she'd had a choice, but she nodded her

acknowledgment anyway. But as he turned to leave her, she stopped him.

"Wait a second." She stood, looked around for Craig, who was nowhere in sight, but still sidled up close before she spoke again. "You said 'wife.' Is that, you know, your idea or his? I mean, we were going to meet at the Rossinis' party anyway, right? How am I supposed to know if this is real love or if it's just, like, residual emotion from sharing this . . . Well, what is it? A haunt? A possession? How will I know?"

His grin was knowing and amiably evil. *Don't you need to have a little faith about things like that? You know, take a leap and all that?*

"Not if you know someone with surefire answers. So, how will I know?"

This feels like giving you the answers to the final exam but I guess I owe you a hint at least.

"At the very least."

He came closer and closer, clearly intent on whispering the answer in her ear, so close she closed her eyes to focus her hearing.

It's . . .

Her eyes popped open, her gaze darted. Ceiling, open bathroom door, plump, peach-colored comforter, big male body, Craig watching her wake up . . . She growled and battered the bedding until she came to a sitting position. "I hate your brother! If I ever get my hands on—" She glared at Craig. "What's so funny?"

He slipped his hands under his head and gave her the same knowing, amiably evil grin she'd seen in her dream. She narrowed her eyes at him.

"Did you hear the answer? Did you hear him?"

"Maybe."

"Maybe?" He wasn't her brother, but she knew what to do with a male who thought he had a secret—possibly the most important secret of her life. "Maybe?" She was on her knees and had him by the ribs before he could blink. "Maybe?" With his legs still trapped beneath the sheets she took full advantage—straddling his waist and grabbing his arms when he freed his hands from behind his head. "Maybe?" She pinned one forearm under her knee and held the other over his head leaving one entire set of ribs exposed to her. She never learned how to spell mercy. "Maybe?"

"Yes! Yes. All right. I heard."

"And you'll tell me?"

"Yes! Yes, I promise." She stopped but she didn't let up. Not that it mattered. With barely any effort at all—certainly a great deal less than poor Jay had had to muster during most of his formative years—he flipped her onto her back and under his body between heartbeats, clamping both wrists in one hand on the pillow and using the other to tenderly rearrange stray wisps of hair around her face. "However, first you have to tell me what you asked him."

She groaned her disinclination.

"Come on. Have a little faith. Leap. I won't let you down."

She eyed him suspiciously. "That's what he said. You heard my question, too."

"I didn't. I swear."

She could see in his eyes that he wasn't lying. But she didn't need to see or hear or taste or touch him to know that he not only knew the answer, he was the answer. She didn't need to ask anymore, but she was curious. "I asked him how we'd know if what we're feeling is real love."

He laughed softly and repeated Oliver's words. "It's in the kiss."

And it was . . . dreamy.